Also by Owen Mullen:

Old Friends and New Enemies

Before The Devil Knows You're Dead

For
Devon and Harrison, the Carney boys,
who always make me smile.

The footsteps came after him, racing as he raced; slapping the sand, crunching shingle, beating against rock. Grass beneath his bare feet meant he was almost home. Almost safe. Then the crunching became a heavy pad. Gaining. He ran faster.

His chest burned. Heavy legs refused to carry him; he couldn't go on. He fell, panting and terrified.

The footsteps stopped.

For a long time he lay, too afraid to move, expecting a hand to touch his shoulder.

But no hand came.

He gathered his courage and looked behind him.

There was no one there.

Ayr, 35 miles from Glasgow.

They walked along the beach and stopped not far from an old rowing boat with a hole in the bottom. Mark carried the folded push-chair and his daughter. The sun fell towards the horizon. It had been a great day, a scorcher, but the best of it was behind them. Noisy gulls scavenged, soaring and diving and calling to each other. Lily pressed her face against her father's chest, too tired to be interested in the birds.

'We ought to get back,' Mark said, 'Lily's tired. She should be in bed.'

Jennifer didn't reply. He knew what she was thinking.

'Surely not?'

'Last one? Five minutes?'

Mark glanced at his watch – ten past seven – and limited his concern to a sigh. The last thing he wanted was to spoil things with a quarrel; there had been enough of those. Red flags fluttered in the evening air. He pointed to them.

'Be careful, Jen. The waves are getting bigger. Don't go far.'

She dropped the bag with their towels and the baby's things at his feet.

'I will. In and out. Promise.'

The water was cold; colder than in the afternoon. When it was waist high she kicked her legs and headed out. Jennifer caught a glimpse of Mark and Lily standing on the sand: her whole universe. She loved them so much. That thought almost made her turn back. Instead she took a deep breath and dived.

It happened so fast. One minute she was swimming, the next the current was dragging her to the bottom. Seawater flooded her mouth. She fought, thrashed to the surface and tried to shout; a hoarse whisper was all that came. Her head went under and stayed under. Her lungs were on fire. With no warning it released her and she saw blue sky. Jennifer gulped shallow ragged breaths, shocked and scared, and started towards her family. She would never leave them again. But the decision was no longer hers. The force drew her back into a world without light or oxygen and this time it didn't let go. Her arm broke free in a desperate attempt to escape. Tongues of spray pulled it down and Jennifer knew she was going to drown.

She'd dreamed of watching her daughter grow into a woman. That would never be. And Mark, poor Mark. How unfair to leave him. Her body rolled beneath the waves. She stopped struggling, closed her eyes and disappeared from sight.

Seconds passed before Mark realised something wasn't right. 'Where's mummy? Where's your mummy?' The baby sucked her thumb. 'Where is she, Lily?'

At first he couldn't move. Cold fear consumed him. A hundred yards away a group of boys played football; apart from them the beach was deserted. He yelled. They didn't hear him. He threw the push-chair to the sand, yanked it open and sat Lily in it. His hands were shaking. The damned straps wouldn't fasten. He spoke to himself. 'Please god, no. Please god, no' and raced into the sea.

The water was freezing. What the hell had Jen been thinking? This was Scotland, for Christ sake. He swam to where he'd last seen her and went under. Mark was a good swimmer but it was dark. His frantic fingers searched until the pressure in his chest forced him to the surface. He took in as much air as he could and went back. Something bumped against him; he grabbed hold and dragged it up. Two boys ran into the water to help: the footballers. They hauled her body the last few yards and Mark fell to his knees. Jennifer wasn't breathing. People appeared on the beach, silent witnesses to the nightmare the day had become. Where had they been when he needed them? He shouted, half in anger half in desperation.

'Somebody call an ambulance!'

The crowd kept a respectful distance, believing what he believed, that he'd lost her. Jennifer's face was white. Mark covered her mouth with his and breathed into her. His hands pressed against her chest demanding she come back to him.

One of the boys took over with no better luck. Mark tried again, refusing to let her go. He pumped her heart, whimpering like a child, sobbing for himself as well as his wife. Jennifer's eyes fluttered; she retched and vomited water. Mark turned her on her side and rubbed her back, whispering reassurance, blinded by tears, aware his prayers had been answered. A siren sounded in the distance. It was going to be all right. She was safe. They would be together again.

The three of them.

He raised his head and saw ambulance-men racing towards him across the sand. Mark jumped to his feet. They must have drifted... except the boat was there. His voice rose from a cry to a scream.

'Lily. Lily!'

He spoke to the group who had offered nothing.

'I left a baby here, somebody must've seen her.'

They stared, no idea what he was talking about.

A new terror seized him. He ran a few steps up and down the beach, lost and afraid. The bag lay where Jennifer dropped it. But no push-chair. No sign his daughter had ever been there.

Lily was gone.

1

I opened the door and stepped into a cloud; the unmistakeable musk of marijuana and the sound of copulation.

The couple on the bed were naked, the girl straddling the boy, too absorbed to notice me. He held a mobile phone, recording a souvenir of the occasion while his partner performed, squeezing her breasts together and pushing them at the camera; rolling her head in a parody of ecstasy. Blue movie sex, and about as far from the real thing as it was possible to get.

Their bodies were lean and bone white. Though the rest of the country basked in the heatwave a suntan hadn't made it on to their list of priorities. Tidying up wasn't on it either: the floor looked like the bottom of a river; pizza boxes, crushed beer cans and empty cider bottles. Dirty sex had a new meaning.

On a fold-down table a used condom, slicked and crumpled, lay beside a pouch of Virginia Special Gold tobacco, a penknife, and what looked like an Oxo cube carelessly wrapped in silver paper. Two joints were already rolled from a production line I guessed had been going all weekend. As a Tracy Emin still life it would've been okay. As a love nest it fell short of the mark.

People can't keep secrets – they always tell somebody. Maryanne Mulholland was no different. Her confidante was a friend at school. It had taken seventy two hours and a ferry crossing to find her but I had. Shagging her brains out in a caravan in Dunoon.

The boy sensed rather than saw me, dropped the mobile and threw the girl aside. His jaw was slack and his eyes were glassy – it wasn't called dope for nothing.

He snarled. 'Who the fuck're you?'

In the circumstances, a fair question.

I answered with some snarling of my own.

'Get away from her.'

He turned his anger on the female. 'You told me your father didn't know where you were.'

She shook her head. 'He's not my father. I've never seen him before.'

All the encouragement he needed. He picked up a bottle by the neck and crashed it against the wall. It disintegrated. Blood dripped on the discoloured carpet; the cut would need stitches. He stared at his injured hand, dumb with surprise. I could have told him not to depend on that tough guy shit; it hardly ever worked. And he wasn't a boy, more like twenty eight or twenty nine.

Even by his standards his next move was stupid. He lifted the penknife and charged. Comic, made more ridiculous by his nudity. I didn't laugh too long because room to manoeuvre was limited. There was always a chance he'd get lucky and actually stick the stubby blade in someone. Maybe me.

He was fearless. Drugs do that to you.

And slow. They do that to you as well.

I grabbed his arm, pushed it behind his back and manhandled him through the door. His shoes and jeans followed. He lay on the ground, out of his head, screaming.

'Bastard! Fucking bastard! She's sixteen!'

Loser chat.

He wasn't getting it. I moved towards him pointing a threatening finger.

'Yeah, but you're not. Don't come near her again.'

Inside the caravan broken glass crackled under my feet. I lifted lover boy's phone and put it in my pocket. Maryanne Mulholland was on the bed hugging her legs; crying. Mascara, smudged in black circles, reminded me of a panda I'd seen on a visit to London Zoo.

'You can stop bubbling. It won't change anything.'

She drew a slender arm through tears and wiped lipstick from her chin. 'Did he send you?'

I wasn't in the mood to explain. 'Clean yourself up and meet me outside.'

It was over for her and she knew it, yet she had spirit. She said, 'I'm not going back to Glasgow. I'm not going back and you can't make me.'

I'd been hired to locate a runaway teenager. Just that. All I had to do was tell my client where his daughter was and send him my invoice. Forcing her to return with me wasn't what I'd signed on for. Four days earlier in my office Bill Mulholland set the tone of our relationship with an opening line that guaranteed we would never be friends.

'I wouldn't normally have anything to do with someone like you. No offence.'

This job wasn't for the thin-skinned, so none taken. Cheeky bastard.

I sat on the grass in front of the caravan listening to the gentle hiss of the shower and waited for the girl to appear. When she did her hair was wet and she was carrying a plastic rubbish bag and a grudge the size of Dumbarton Rock. She ignored me, dumped the bag by the door and went back in. Minutes later I heard the hum of a Hoover. Maryanne was cleaning up. Strange behaviour for a delinquent, and the first inkling I'd been misled. This was no wild child, more like a child acting wild. Certainly not the renegade her father had described. I'd decided long ago that kids were a responsibility I could live without.

Eventually she showed herself, surly and unrepentant. The way any sixteen-year-old at war with her parents should look. The shower had done her good: her eyes were clear. The smoky emptiness wasn't there anymore. And she was angry. I didn't blame her. I had chased her boyfriend and nipped a promising career on YouTube – where the video clip would surely have ended – in the bud. But I wasn't getting points for protecting her reputation. She stood, hands on hips, squinting into the sun, preparing to give me my character. An interesting role reversal, all things considered.

What she said reminded me of her old man; pompous and judgemental, overflowing with righteous indignation.

'People like you make me want to throw up.'

This young lady was her father's daughter all right. Short memory too.

'Nobody's perfect, Maryanne.'

No reaction. Teenagers don't do irony.

'Who gave you the right to hound me? I meant what I said. I'm not going back.'

'Your decision. I'll give you a lift to the city if it's any help. Or stay. I don't care.'

'So why are you still here?'

I changed the subject, away from me. 'That guy, your pal, he's a tosser, what you doing with him?'

'His name's Fraser and you can't say that. You don't know him.'

'Yes I do. He's using you.'

Colour rose in her cheeks. No make-up made her seem younger than sixteen; too young to have been doing what she'd been doing. She turned away and took a last defiant stab at maturity.

'Maybe I want to be used.'

'Yeah now, while you're mad at the world. Not tomorrow.'

She shook her head as if my naivety saddened her. 'You wouldn't understand.'

'Try me.'

It took a long time. By the end she was crying again. Somewhere in the middle she almost laughed. 'Fraser thought you were my father. He thought you were going to kill him.'

'If I was your father I would have.'

She gave me a look; a mixture of wonder and disbelief.

'Would you? Would you really?'

'Yes. I probably would.'

Later, on the ferry to McInroy's Point and Gourock, I bought coffee in the downstairs bar and brought it up top. The girl took the plastic cup without a word, walked to the rail and gazed across the glittering Clyde at the Cowal Peninsula fading into the distance behind us. She was tall, almost as tall as me. Her face turned away so I couldn't see. It was four o'clock in the afternoon and blistering hot. So much had happened. She needed to be alone to make some sense of it. Outside the caravan she'd sat beside me and let me in. And as she spoke, I realised we had something in common; we didn't get on with our fathers. Both of us had headed for the hills to escape them, though her exit was more dramatic than mine.

Inevitably, she remembered I was a private investigator working for the enemy and shut down. That was where it stood and it would take more than a watery Nescafe to change her mind.

Bill Mulholland had struck me as a severe individual. A man who ruled his domestic kingdom with an iron hand; the reason the household was a daughter short. He'd played the exasperated parent confronting teenage rebellion to a tee when he asked me to take the case.

Maryanne told a very different tale. I knew who I believed and gave her space.

Further along the deck a guy in a yellow t-shirt, engineer boots and denim jeans torn at the knees, was pounding out the Bob Dylan songbook on an old acoustic. Between verses he vamped the harmonica in a holder round his neck, adding reedy bursts to Maggie's Farm, Mr Tambourine Man and Like a Rolling Stone. Somebody requested Don't Think Twice and he played it for them. Not great, not even good, but he played it. His voice was raw, discordant at times, bang on for Dylan. At the end of the song he fiddled with the guitar strings and joked to the people nearest him.

'Was in tune when I bought it,' he said.

A sense of humour: given the nuclear arsenal anchored just miles away at the Holy Loch and the Ban the Bomb badge on his chest, he'd need it.

His hair was greasy. Above his mouth a wispy excuse for a moustache was having second thoughts about growing. Likely he didn't have a pot to piss in but the contrast with Mulholland's daughter couldn't have been more marked. This kid was happy.

Halfway to the mainland he kicked into In the Summertime and, from the opening line, the ferry came alive. A couple started dancing. Others joined them, mouthing the lyrics. Close to me a guy grabbed his girlfriend – his wife for all I knew – and tagged on to a conga line that had sprung from nowhere, making its way round the deck.

Argyll on acid. Surreal. Salvador Dali would've loved it.

Maryanne stayed where she'd been, facing out to sea, alone with her troubles, oblivious to what was going on behind her.

In the stern, beyond the conga dancers, a flash of red caught my eye; a dress, and a girl of eight or nine being twirled by an older man, ducking underneath his arm, with him smiling down at her. Perhaps she was smiling back – I couldn't say. It was the tousled blonde hair that did it. For a second my heart stopped. Everything good emptied out of me and, despite the burning sun, I felt cold.

slapping the sand, crunching shingle, beating against rock

The grey-haired man spun the child again and I saw her face.

A nice face. A laughing face. A stranger's face.

When would I learn? The answer it seemed was never. Months could go by – years even – enough to believe it was no more than the memory of a nightmare I couldn't shake off. In those times, thinking I was free and clear, I got on with my life, until like today, a fragment of the past rose from nowhere and took me down.

Guilt never leaves, it never lets go, not really, and it hadn't with me.

The singer finished to claps and cheers. He was pleased with himself and so he should be; he'd made his contribution. Without his music the scene returned to a pleasant sail on a Sunday afternoon. I searched the crowd for the man and the little girl, they were gone. My fingers wandered to my wallet and the photograph inside, faded and cracked and torn at the edges. A fragile thing. I took it out. Innocent eyes stared at me, bright and clear, no trace of reproach in them. No blame. None needed. I had that covered.

Maryanne Mulholland's bid for freedom had been reckless and foolish. And doomed, thanks to me. I dropped the boyfriend's mobile over the side and watched it disappear beneath the grey water; the least I could do for her.

The announcement for drivers to return to their vehicles brought us together. We got in the car and waited while the crew lined the boat up with the jetty. She didn't speak. If there's one thing kids do better than anybody it's freezing you out. I broke the silence with the obvious question. 'So where will you go?'

No response.

'Isn't there somebody?'

'No.'

'What, nobody at all?'

'Got an aunt in Manchester.'

'Call her.'

'Haven't got a phone. I'm not allowed.'

A sixteen-year-old without a mobile!

'Use mine. What's the number?'

She couldn't tell me. Directory Enquiries could.

I tried not to listen.

The journey from the coast to Glasgow takes an hour. Any other day we'd have time to spare, but it was Sunday. That and the weather meant the roads would be busy. The Manchester train left at 5.35. Missing it wasn't an option. I parked in Renfield Street. Central station booking office was inside the main entrance. Maryanne hesitated. 'I haven't any money.'

I emptied my wallet and handed the contents to her.

'You have now.'

At the barrier a woman in a uniform gave her ticket a cursory glance and waved her through. Maryanne said, 'We only met a couple of hours ago. I mean, I'm nothing to you. Why are you doing this?'

Why indeed?

'Because I do understand. More than you know.'

I doubted she believed me. She said, 'I'll pay you back. Honest.'

I wouldn't hold my breath.

'There is something you can do.'

Her face brightened, the first real smile of the afternoon. 'Name it.'

'You're running from your father. He'll survive. Your mother's the one who'll suffer. Call her. Let her know you're all right. She deserves that much.'

The next morning the sun was still shining but it sure as hell wasn't shining in my office. Storm clouds rolled in my direction from the man seated across the desk. The day before, I'd let the Manchester express pull away before I contacted Maryanne's father and asked him to meet me. Now he was here, whatever he'd expected it wasn't this. We had an agreement. I was breaking it.

And I'd lied to myself about how thick my skin actually was. Put to the test it turned out to be: not very.

Mulholland was probably in his late forties; a tightly wound individual with a clipped voice that would irritate no matter what he was saying. He listened then spoke with deliberate care, the way he might address a disobedient lackey already on a final warning.

'Let me be clear on this. You know where my daughter is but aren't prepared to tell me.'

A statement rather than a question. No answer required.

There was nothing to like about him so I didn't try. The girl had convinced me I wasn't on the side of the angels.

'We had an understanding. You were supposed to find Maryanne so we could bring her home.'

'She won't be coming home, at least not yet.'

Being defied wasn't something he ran up against very often. I tried not to enjoy myself too much.

'She doesn't want to.'

His jaw tightened against the strain of keeping himself in check.

'That isn't your decision, Mr Cameron.'

'It's Maryanne's decision.'

I expected him to lose it completely – part of me hoped he would – then I'd have the excuse I needed for hurting him. Any father worth his salt would have dragged me to my feet and beaten the information out of me. That wasn't going to happen. This guy was a petty tyrant and a coward. Besides, I was bigger than him.

He staked a claim for the moral high ground. 'Do you usually go back on your word?'

'Not usually, no. I'm making an exception.'

Mulholland had brought his wife with him. I didn't know her name; he hadn't bothered to introduce us. She took no part in the conversation. Her head stayed down while her husband did all the talking. Thin and nervy, she fiddled with her fingers like someone who had lost confidence in herself and was unlikely to rediscover it, unless she followed her daughter's lead and got well away from this man.

She broke her silence.

'Please, please. I just need to be sure she's safe.' Her voice trembled. 'She doesn't... she didn't...'

The dam broke, the tears came, and before my eyes she got smaller than all the years in the shadows had succeeded in making her. Watching her bowed under the pain of not knowing wasn't easy. Maryanne left in the middle of the night without saying goodbye – because of her father – before she became a sad defeated woman like her mother. The police couldn't help; running away isn't against the law, so Mulholland had come to my door with an attitude that grated from minute one and a yarn the length of Sauchiehall Street. The girl had never given him a moment's peace. He had recited a litany of trouble at home, trouble at school, none of it true. His daughter was no different from any teenager I'd ever met. He was the problem.

He blustered. 'This is outrageous. I'll be spreading the word about you.'

I wanted to remind him that children were precious, people not possessions. Instead I let him rant and spoke to the mother. 'Maryanne's safe but she doesn't want to come home. Sorry.'

'Can't you tell me where she is?'

I shook my head. 'I promised.'

Force of habit made Mulholland attempt to reassert his authority. 'You realise you won't be getting paid? Not a penny.'

He'd have to try harder than that to surprise me.

'God forbid, if anything happens to my girl I'll come after you.'

No he wouldn't. He'd take it out on his wife, same as always. I wanted to put my arm round Maryanne's mother and reassure her with as much of the truth as she could handle, but I stayed where I was and let the melancholy drama play. Mulholland stared ahead, ramrod straight, while his wife died a little. The feeling I got from him wasn't compassion, it was shame; he was embarrassed. He spoke in a rough whisper out of the side of his mouth, as if he was bringing a dog to heel. 'Jean. Jean! That's enough. Enough!'

His daughter had come to the same conclusion.

2

The heatwave was moving towards a second week. When I arrived outside New York Blue the atmosphere was like a Saturday in July, females in print dresses and men in t-shirts at every table; sunshades and laughter.

Jackie Mallon was standing inside the door, determined not to let the fine weather affect her mood. We were friends, except on days like today she was better at hiding it than me. I guessed the profiterole she was holding wasn't her first. Jackie was a feisty lady, slim and fit, blonde and attractive, able to spot a phoney at a hundred yards. Unless he was handsome. Then her instinct deserted her. WANKERS WELCOME tattooed on her forehead would've saved a lot of time. The aftermath of her failed romances wasn't easy to be around. The cakes were only the start of a journey into darkness. Her downers were famous, junkathons lasting until a new loser landed on the scene, bringing smiles and low fat yoghurt to our lives. Wherever the next one was I hoped he'd get a move on because she was in a foul temper and it wasn't even lunchtime.

Through a mouthful of choux pastry and cream she said, 'You missed a call.'

'Yeah, who from?'

'Didn't give a name. Says he'll get back to you. Your phone redirected it to the bar. Again.'

'Sorry, Jackie, my mistake, should've gone to my mobile.'

Her face scrunched up the way it always did when she was narked.

'Point is, Charlie, we're too busy to be involved in your Sherlock Holmes shit. Look outside if you don't believe me. It's chocka. Why can't you get an answering machine like everybody else?'

On the surface it sounded reasonable, I saw it differently.

'Because anybody who contacts me is probably worried out of their head. They need to be able to talk to somebody, not some pre-recorded voice message.'

She didn't pretend to be sympathetic; she was running on resentment and mad at the world.

'And by the by. Just so you know. I'm going to speak to Alex about the office. If anybody could use some space around here I could. I'm stuck in that cubbyhole underneath the stairs while you have a big room you hardly use.'

The office was an old bone. Alex would say what he'd said the last time she raised the subject, and the time before: that he owed me.

Jackie Mallon had a bad case of poor me, sorry for herself and lashing out.

'I've got an excuse. I have to be here, but you... you've got money. Don't get it, Charlie, never have.'

'Take it up with Alex,' I said, and walked inside.

Alex was Alex Gilby, the owner of New York Blue. Andrew Geddes introduced us. At the time Gilby was in partnership with a guy called Lawlor. Their relationship was breaking down, though I didn't know that until a couple of weeks later when Alex spoke to me. He was in trouble. Lawlor had withdrawn a lot of money from the business account and run off. Could I help? As it turned out, yes I could, the thick bastard didn't leave right away, giving me time to locate the hotel he was staying in and step between him and an Emirates flight to Dubai. Alex was delighted and offered me a percentage of what I had recovered or an empty room upstairs for as long as I wanted it. A city centre address was too good to turn down and I'd been here ever since. Thus far, Gilby had resisted Jackie's attempts to put me out on the street; it hadn't stopped her trying.

A copy of today's Herald lay unopened on the bar. I lifted it and took it to a table near the Rock-Ola. The newspaper's front page carried a story about a baby abducted from Ayr beach and a photograph of a man comforting a woman wearing a bathing costume, her shoulders covered by his jacket. She looked physically broken, as if he was all that kept her from falling to pieces on the sand. His pain was no less; his eyes held the bewilderment of someone who didn't comprehend what had happened. There was a time a news item like this would have had me reacting, but I'd learned. And accepted.

It had been over for three decades.

The picture showed a sad scene. I skipped the details, they wouldn't make my day.

On page five an item caught my attention. The Irish rocker, Paul Finnegan, had been found dead at his home in St John's Wood. His well known drug and alcohol problems hadn't stopped him from becoming a star. In spite of his chronic – and fatal – addiction, his band, Northwind, sold millions of records. At thirty-seven the front man joined Hendrix, Elvis, John Lennon and Michael Jackson; the latest addition to the super group in the sky. Lloyd Kennedy, the group's bass player and Finnegan's writing partner, wasn't available for comment.

I skimmed the rest of the newspaper and went upstairs to my office. No mail, no messages and a blank diary: the world had no use for me today. My work ethic was fragile at the best of times and this morning, I needed no encouragement.

Jackie realised she'd gone over the line, when I was leaving she spoke to me – about business, something she rarely did.

'Big River had a bust-up in the dressing room last night. Robbie walked out. Says that's it for him. The band played to the end. It was a struggle, Robbie's the main man.'

'No, Alan's the main man. He started Big River.'

'True, but he can't sing, and he's a drummer. They need Robbie. Guys with his talent are hard to find. It's taken a year and a half to build Sundays in the club. All that effort could crumble in a few weeks.' She made a face. 'A busy Sunday makes a difference. Hate to admit it, Charlie, but losing it would be a backward step for the whole operation.'

'Have you told Alex, yet?'

'He'll be in later.'

'What's Alan saying?'

'Already got a replacement in mind. Wants to audition downstairs on Wednesday.'

'That was quick. Who is it?'

'No idea. Seemed pretty relaxed about Robbie splitting. "Fucking hassle" was how he described it.'

'What was the problem with Robbie?'

'Demanded the band change the name.'

'You're joking. To what?'

'Robbie Ward and Big River.'

'Always a mistake to underestimate the people around you.'

'Tell me about it.'

The day burned through the afternoon. I sat in the garden letting the sun bathe me and considered what Jackie had said. Alan Sneddon had been around the Glasgow music scene forever. When I was a student I saw him gig at Strathclyde Uni. That wasn't yesterday. If losing Robbie Ward was no more than a "fucking hassle" he must have somebody very special in the wings. I looked forward to meeting him.

That night and the next morning the TV was full of the baby abduction. I switched to a smiling weather man, who assured me the heatwave wouldn't last much longer – rain was on the way – and telephoned Jackie to find out if anybody was waiting for me. Nobody was.

By mid-afternoon too much sun had soured my mood. A call from my mother didn't help. She launched into the interrogation that had become the mainstay of our chats: had I met a nice girl yet? When was I getting married? And was she ever going to be a grandmother? Finally I changed the subject, said 'How's dad?' and listened to her sigh four hundred miles away.

'To be honest, not great. You know what he's like around this time of the year. Very down. Sometimes he stays in London and I don't see him. Then I worry. This year he's promised he'll be home. I'm glad about that, of course. Not looking forward to it though. It'll be better after next Thursday.'

'Want me to come down?'

'No, no, we'll have a quiet dinner, get through it together.' She hurried past the suggestion and added a familiar admonishment. 'Although it would be helpful if you two could talk about it.'

I imagined her at the window in the lounge surrounded by Laura Ashley prints and Royal Doulton figurines, clutching the phone in her manicured fingers, willing me to say I was coming anyway, and that yes, I would have the conversation with my father we'd both avoided for three decades. The exchange, or something like it, passed between us often since I moved north.

'It wouldn't change anything. It's too late, mum.'

'You're wrong, Charles, he's always asking about you.'

Now she was lying.

'I'm up to my eyes at the moment.'

Now I was lying.

She cut through the drivel. 'God's sake, give the man a break.' Her voice trembled. 'You've got him all wrong.'

Reducing my mother to tears wasn't in the plan, I gave ground. 'I'll think about it, Mum.'

'Make an effort. It takes two, you know.'

'I said I'll try.'

'Do better than try. For me. He's next door, shall I put him on?'

Before I could say no I heard her shouting 'Archie! Archie! It's Charles. Come and say hello.'

The world had nothing but admiration for George Archibald Cameron. I was the exception. Archie was chairman of the Conservative Party. A lifetime's worth of political manoeuvring had earned him the job of Tory top dog; a place on the board of the whisky company my great grandfather started, where he had ruled as CEO for more than twenty years, was a move in the other direction. I never touched the stuff myself, an act of rebellion that went unnoticed and a moot point since the Japanese owned Cameron's now. He thought my life choices were flawed and inferior set against his own – law then into the family business – and would have preferred me to become another pin striped posh boy in Gray's Inn Road. Like father like son. It didn't bear thinking about.

We rarely spoke. Okay with me because, even on the odd occasion when he tried to be nice, he still managed to shoehorn a criticism in somewhere. "You're throwing it away" he'd tell me, making no secret he considered I'd let the side down; squandered my gifts, evaded my responsibilities and gone to live in a backwater he couldn't leave fast enough. Jackie had failed to pick up on an important detail: it was my father who had money, not me, and he had no intention of sharing it with his errant son.

But real though it was, the tension between us was a smokescreen. His disapproval had deeper roots. Our relationship difficulties went all the way back to Cramond.

He lifted the telephone, no doubt as reluctant as I was. 'Charlie, how are you?'

'Fine, you?'

He avoided answering. 'Your mother makes a fuss. You know how women are. So you're all right? How's business?'

'Busy.'

'What... case are you working on?'

'Got a couple right now.'

'Wherever evil raises its ugly head, that kind of thing?'

The mockery was impossible to miss; the man couldn't help himself. I felt my chest tighten. 'Yeah, that kind of thing.'

'Making money?'

'Enough.'

'No such thing, Charlie.' A line his well-heeled friends would find funny when Archie played to the gallery.

'There's more to life than that.'

'Is there?'

We had been down this road more often than I wanted to recall. I changed the subject.

'Six months to the election: the polls are predicting a close run thing.'

'We'll be ready for 'em. We're ready now.'

'So you're confident?'

'Mmmm, quietly. Still got to get the message across, of course. Could always use another good man if those SNP idiots haven't brainwashed you. Wouldn't survive five minutes on their own.'

Something else we disagreed about.

I said, 'No thanks, I'm happy where I am.'

'Playing silly buggers in Glasgow. Your mother would like you nearer to home.'

'I am home.'

A mirthless laugh came down the line. 'Well there's a place for you as soon as you come to your senses.'

I counted to ten. It was always the same, both of us primed for an argument. Under starters orders Patrick Logue would call it.

'How much longer do you intend to run up and down Buchanan Street with your arse hanging out?'

'That isn't what's happening, father.'

'Your mother and I have talked about it. We know exactly what you're doing.'

His voice rose, close to shouting, close to breaking down.

'And you're wasting your time, you won't find her. She's dead, Charlie, she's dead!'

'I'm not trying to find her, I... Put mum back on, will you?'

It had taken seconds, a record even for us.

My mother took over.

'Charles? That was my fault. I shouldn't have tried to get you two together. Not now.'

'I tried, mum, it's hopeless. He's hopeless.'

'He's concerned about you.'

'Got a queer way of showing it.'

'No he doesn't, he's sad. Your father's sad. We both are.'

For as far back as I could remember she had been the arbitrator in our family, the peacemaker, standing between the men she loved. Never giving up. Some things didn't change. I rang off as soon as she would let me, feeling like shit.

The weather man was right: the rain started late on Tuesday night and didn't stop. Next morning, NYB was deserted; the sun worshipers might have been a scene from a pleasant dream. Private investigation was often a juggling act. Nothing for weeks then I was swamped. I was in the nothing-for-weeks phase – why sitting in the garden had been possible. I ordered breakfast, coffee and a roll and sausage, and sat near the piano watching Jackie float around like queen of the fair. At eleven thirty she buzzed me. Her mood was better and I wondered why.

'Someone for you, Charlie. I'm sending him up.'

Someone was a thin man in his thirties. He seemed familiar. Like everyone in the city his face was tanned. That didn't disguise the dark pockets at the corners of his eyes, the lines and the shadow on his jaw. His shirt was grubby, trousers creased in a hundred places; a guy who had given up caring for himself just as sleep had given up on him. He held out his hand. 'Mark Hamilton. Thank you for meeting me at such short notice.'

The name meant nothing; our paths hadn't crossed, but I'd seen him: on a beach with his arm round a woman in a bathing suit. It was his expression I remembered, a mix of confusion and fear. He'd brought it with him.

'Take a seat, Mr Hamilton.'

He was bound to assume I knew about his trouble. Since Monday what had happened at the coast was everywhere; paper sellers shouted it from street corners, STV news opened with it and I'd even overheard snatches of conversations between customers in NYB. I had only a vague idea of the details and was happy to keep it that way.

'I saw your advert in Yellow Pages. It says you find people, although I expect your advice will be to speak to the police.'

'You don't have a choice; it's a police case. I'm sorry, Mark. I'd like to help but I can't get involved.'

His head went down, his shoulders heaved, and he cried. 'Please. Please, let me get it out at least. If I don't my head will explode.'

By some superhuman effort he drew himself together. 'You'll know about Lily,' he said.

'Only what I read in the press.'

'I haven't bought a newspaper. Seeing it in black and white would be too much. As it is we're out of our minds. My wife...'

'Start at the beginning. Take your time.'

Over the years many people had bared their souls to me. My job wasn't to judge. What he told me tested that premise. The quiet voice became a whisper.

'I know who took my daughter. I know who and I know why, and it's driving me insane.'

He covered his face with his hands and sobbed. 'It's my fault. All my fault.'

I shifted in my chair. 'The beginning,' I said again, 'go back to the beginning.'

Hamilton spoke without looking at me. 'We'd had a perfect day. Lily loved it, she'd never been to the seaside. We were a family. It was wonderful.'

He pulled two photographs from his pocket and handed one of them to me. A baby, pretty in pink, grinned a toothless grin. Against my better judgement I accepted it.

'It's strange, you can't see yourself as a parent, the responsibility, the sacrifice, and it's scary. Then a child comes along and life without them is unimaginable. Jennifer and I resisted the idea. Lily was an accident. The best accident.'

'So Sunday was great. What went wrong?'

'Jen was worried it would be too hot for the baby. Lily didn't seem to mind. We arrived in the afternoon – a whole day would've been pushing it – the beach was more crowded than I'd ever seen in Scotland. My wife hadn't been in the sea since our last holiday.

She went swimming. I stayed with Lily. We bought ice cream that melted and made a mess.'

His voice cracked. I was sure he was going to cry again.

'It was well after seven when we packed up. Most people had gone home. The last thing we did was walk along the sand.'

'How far?'

Hamilton thought for a moment. 'Hard to say. There was a rowing boat, near it. Jennifer fancied going in the water again. Lily was tired and the red flags were out. I should've stopped her.'

Guilt clawed at Mark Hamilton.

'Everything was fine at first. Jen waved to us; we waved back. Then I realised she wasn't waving, she was in trouble. It was late. There was nobody to help. With the baby I mean. I put her in the push-chair and ran into the sea. I didn't find my wife, she found me. I dragged her to the shore. She was pale and so still. I was certain she was dead. I'm not religious but I'll tell you I prayed on that beach. I was determined she wouldn't die. I kept breathing into her and pressing her chest. One of the ambulance men said I'd saved her life.'

'How long were you in the water?'

'Minutes. Four at the most.' His eyes closed. 'I thought it was over. It wasn't; it was just starting.'

'The baby.'

footsteps... racing

'Somebody had taken her. And that's why I'm here.'

He stroked the stubble on his cheek. Behind his story was a greater horror. His wife had almost drowned, his child had been abducted, and still there was more.

'I said we resisted having a family. The main reason was our relationship, Jennifer and I... we've been through some rough times. We almost ended the marriage. We didn't, instead I had an affair. More than one if you want the truth.'

'I'm not sure what you're telling me.'

'Donna Morton has Lily. You need to find her. Find her and get Lily back.'

He was asking the impossible. Hamilton handed me the second picture, the camera had caught him and an attractive brunette with their arms round each other.

'Mr Hamilton... Mark, you believe you know who has your child. All right. Go to the police. Let them deal with it.

'I knew you'd say that. I knew you wouldn't understand.'

'You're right, I don't. Why would she steal Lily?'

'To get back at me.'

'To get back at you for what?'

'Breaking her heart. We were drinking wine one night in her flat after making love.

Stupidly I promised I'd leave my wife. I didn't mean to say it, it just came out. The alcohol I suppose. Then Jennifer announced she was pregnant and I finished with Donna. She called me every name you've ever heard. Swore to get even.'

I wondered if Hamilton wasn't deluding himself, taking comfort in the unlikely belief that Donna Morton – someone he'd known – had stolen his daughter. A better option than a paedophile.

He bowed his head. 'They've taken Jen to the Royal Infirmary, she's in bad shape. Heavily sedated. The doctors are worried about her. If this came out it could put her over the edge. You see, she believes that when we made the baby we made the marriage right. Everything will be fine if we get Lily back. I realised on Monday it must be Donna. Who else could it be?'

'How long did the affair last?'

'The best part of a year.'

'Threats aren't proof.'

He wasn't convinced. 'I've spent two days trying to trace her. She's disappeared. Doesn't that tell you something? Her sister wouldn't even open the door. She despises me. I can't do this alone, it needs a professional. If Lily's been... Jen would never get over it and neither would I. You say bring in the police. Jennifer would have to be told. One way or another it means disaster.'

'Was there anything about Donna that makes you think she would harm the baby?'

'No. Never. But I let her down badly. She said she'd never forgive me.'

'Did she harass you, threaten you?'

'There was no contact. None at all. I assumed she was getting on with her life.'

'And she wasn't on the beach?'

Hamilton's mouth moved. No words came out.

'You didn't see her on the beach yet you're convinced she abducted your daughter. Does that really make sense?'

His face had the hollowed out look of a Halloween pumpkin. He didn't answer my question.

'You think I'm imagining it. My wife is clinging to her sanity because of me.'

'That's not what I think at all.'

'I'm not asking you to get involved in the official investigation. I want to hire you to locate a missing person. I want you to find Donna Morton. I'll tell Jennifer when she's better and Lily's safe. Help me.'

First the blonde kid on the ferry, now this. Forces too powerful to resist were gathered against me, taking me where I didn't want to go. I understood. I shouldn't touch this one, yet I felt the decision slipping away from me.

Hamilton hadn't shirked; he accepted his actions were the reason his family had been torn apart. Self-justification never entered into it. He had wronged not one but two women; blame for his daughter's disappearance was his alone. I could take the job on the basis that, if I was unsuccessful, he would come clean no matter what it cost him. At the start of the affair Donna Morton didn't realise her boyfriend was already married. When Hamilton told her it was too late: she was in love with him.

'I should've ended it, and I wish I had. It was selfish and wrong. I didn't. The night I told her it was over she cried and cried then she got angry, shouting and screaming all kinds of stuff about what she'd do. It was a mess.'

'The sister, did you ever meet her?'

'Lucy. Once. We had a drink together. She had her own problems.'

'Like what?'

'Just that. Drink.'

'Donna told you that?'

'Yes. Been in and out of AA for years.'

'You thought Donna and Lily might be with her?'

'It was all I could think of.'

'How did you meet Donna?'

'She did some secretarial work for us.'

'Us?'

'Templeton Warwick. I'm an accountant.'

'Have you got her mobile number?'

'No, I didn't keep it in my phone in case Jen found it. We had an arrangement, we didn't phone.'

I asked him about friends, workmates, anyone close enough to know where Donna could have gone. Why Lucy Morton despised him became clear; he was unable to add much, as if we were discussing a stranger, someone he'd known casually, not the woman he'd promised to leave his wife for. In spite of his tragedy I began to dislike him.

Over and over the voice in my head said turn him down, though at face value it was straightforward: find his former lover, stay clear of the abduction, and, however it went, don't let it get to me.

A fine line.

3

Andrew Geddes watched me guide my latest client to the door. When Hamilton left he tapped me on the shoulder. 'Charlie. Don't go there.'

He'd been sitting at his usual table talking to Pat Logue. The two men could hardly have been more different. Patrick, a Glasgow fly-man one step ahead of the law who worked for me when I needed him, and Andrew, a DS with Police Scotland CID, at war with a soon-to-be-ex-wife. Stocky and moody with an unshakeable concept of right and wrong, divorce had given him a singular view of the world he shared at every opportunity. Patrick was certain the detective had his eye on him and he wasn't wrong. The policeman in Andrew never slept. He could laugh at Patrick's jokes, even share a beer with him, without changing his opinion – that Pat Logue was just another small-time wide boy whose luck would eventually run out. When it did he'd be waiting. It was an uneasy relationship that left me in the middle. Yet they had more in common than they realised: both were generous, shrewd and completely committed to their side of the tracks. But they would never be friends.

'Go where, Andrew?'

'Whatever he was after, stay clear.'

'Have I done something I shouldn't?'

'I hope not. The man who just left is part of an ongoing investigation.'

'And?'

He bit his lip. 'I'm trying to help, Charlie.'

'What makes you think I need help?'

'You always need help, and you're not slow to ask for it as I recall.'

'Mark Hamilton's the victim. Or one of them at least.'

'It's not that simple and you know it.'

He glanced at Pat Logue. Patrick got the message. 'If you don't want to know the score,' he said, 'look away now' and went to the bar for a refill.

'So how do you know it's not simple?'

'Listen, reputations, careers even, are made on cases like this. Unless you want to be trampled by a herd of stampeding egos it's better to keep your distance.'

'I'm not on the Force. Why should I worry?'

'Don't be an idiot, I'm putting sugar on it. You know what I'm saying. No kids. We agreed. Leave it, man, leave it.'

'All right Andrew, thanks for the concern.'

Andrew Geddes was a good guy. A friend. A man worth listening to. So why wasn't I? And I did know what he was saying.

Pat Logue sidled back over. For a while he'd been heading for divorce too. His wife threatened to kick him out unless he made some changes, starting with his drinking. He realised Gail was serious and cut back, which still left him NYB's best customer and a fixture at the bar. Before, he drank heavily every day; now he just drank every day. Glasgow was full of characters like him, gifted with extraordinary insight into other people, blind to the chaos of their own lives. He was a couple of years older than me. His dark hair was peppered with grey: he wore a thin moustache and sometimes a goatee. An animated character who dressed as if he was on holiday, short sleeved shirts and sandals: the costume of an optimist. Between fights with his wife he spent his life in the pub doing deals. Gail Logue had hitched her star to a womaniser, a chancer who always had an angle, and a story, usually a funny one. No luck, Gail.

Patrick was a born under-achiever. None the less he had gifts. Well known around the city he could lay his hands on anything, anything at all – he knew a man who knew a man. A black marketeer par excellence. But he couldn't hold on to money: it slipped through his fingers; he was always skint. I used him because he could go where I never could. His street cred was unimpeachable. Compared with him I was a kid-on Celt. Pat Logue was the real McCoy. He dished out advice on life in sporting terms, emphasising the importance of keeping the ball on the ground, or playing to the whistle. I didn't understand half of it. Yet I liked him; it was impossible not to. He was the most tolerant person I'd ever known; kind, intelligent and generous. Behind the wide boy façade was a sharp mind. Some unnamed insecurity had held him back. He could have been anything. Instead he'd chosen to be nothing.

"If you don't want to know the score, look away now" was typical Patspeak. That one I got. He nodded towards Andrew. 'What was your man sayin'?'

'Just talking, Patrick.'

'Anythin' for me, Charlie?'

'Maybe. Don't know yet. '

'Make it quick will you? Funds are low.'

'Funds are always low with you. You're your own worst enemy.'

'Not while Gail's alive I'm not. I'm serious, whenever you're ready so am I.'

His timing was a mile off. Irritation crept into my voice. 'I hear you, Patrick.'

Alone in my office I unlocked the cabinet and took out the file. Every case I'd been involved in had a record with a label on the jacket: name, date, and outcome. Except one. Pamela's was the thinnest, inside there wasn't much: just a few newspaper clippings yellowed with age and a list of notes I'd added over time. Unlike the others there were no details on the front. No name. No date. No outcome. My eyes ran over the familiar headlines. It had been so long. Andrew's warning had got to me, and he had the right of it. The abduction wasn't for me. I needed no part of it.

Mark Hamilton's daughter had been taken in broad daylight. Three days later there was still no sign of her. The dilemma Hamilton faced was to tell his wife and the police he suspected a woman he'd had an affair with could be responsible. Then again, she may have nothing to do with it. Angry words and criminal actions weren't the same. If he confessed, the damage to his marriage would be irreparable. As it was the strain on the mother must be unbearable. On the other hand to keep knowledge of where the child might be secret could never be forgiven – why he'd come to my door. Hamilton had given me a straw, Donna's sister. It was a place to begin, and time to do what most of the city had already done: read about baby Lily.

There was no news, just a rehash of what had gone before; the police had opened a Baby Lily hotline and a television appeal by the parents was being considered. The Herald filled space with an article about child abduction in Scotland, apparently it was on the increase. I hoped somebody had the sense to make sure Lily's mother didn't see it.

The address Hamilton had given for Donna Morton was a grey sandstone tenement two floors up in Queens Park, south-facing which meant plenty of light, and there would be a fair old view from the bay window. As a place to stay, more than acceptable for a single woman. The flat was empty. Unoccupied. I looked through the letterbox and saw open doors and bare floorboards. A guy and a girl came up the stairs, whispering and giggling. His hair was long and dark – a wash wouldn't have gone wrong. Hers was blonde, cropped short like a man. They were so taken with each other they didn't notice me until I spoke. 'Excuse me. Did you know the woman who lived here?'

He shrugged. 'Not really, people keep themselves to themselves. Always a bit of coming and going. This hasn't had a tenant in a long time. Landlord's thinking of selling if you're interested.'

'I'm not.'

'Then sorry.'

I knocked on the door opposite. Nobody answered. Donna Morton left around the time Lily was born, realising she'd put her faith in a faithless man: Hamilton was never going to leave his wife. I tried to imagine her resentment, her sense of isolation and the pain of accepting what a fool she'd been.

When I got to NYB I nodded to Patrick to follow me to the office; I had something for him after all. Jackie was downright friendly, she said, 'Alan's here. Robbie's replacement is with him.'

'What's he like?'

'Different.'

'Should I prepare myself for a shock?'

'Might be an idea, Charlie.'

Patrick was keen to start earning. I didn't tell him who the client was, he didn't ask. We were looking for a woman called Donna Morton. His job was to check the local haunts; the shops, the video place, the pub; contact her landlord and see if there was a forwarding address or telephone number. 'Start with the neighbours.'

He got the information he needed and some of my money masquerading as expenses.

The amount didn't impress him.

'Do they always have to be missing, Charlie? Couldn't we take on some sleazy divorce stuff for a change. A quick half dozen, maybe, get the money up?'

I didn't reply. I had a crime scene to visit.

In Ayr, I parked in Pavilion Road, named after a post Victorian red sandstone relic with tall Italianate towers at each corner. A hundred years ago this lady would have been the toast of the coast, with variety shows packed to the rafters during the summer. Since then the old girl had been used and abused and gone downhill; a dance hall in the forties, a rock venue in the seventies; in the eighties and nineties a place a generation of teenagers, who had lied to their parents about where they were going, raved the night away to acid house and techno, high on E. Now it was home to Pirate Pete's kiddies indoor play area. And it was closed.

Beyond, closer to the shore, a car park and another play area gave way to the Low Green, a stretch of grass skirting the

Esplanade. Esplanades were a thing of the past; they didn't build them anymore or, if they did, they called them something else, but Lily Hamilton's abductor had been here. Watching. Waiting.

It wasn't difficult to imagine how it had been; people basking and burning in the afternoon sun and, later, with the heat going out of the day, the crowds drifting towards home, tired and happy, leaving the sands deserted until only the Hamiltons and the baby that had saved their marriage remained, oblivious to the drama about to befall them.

All I had to go on was a distraught Mark Hamilton's version of events. One thing Lily's father said jumped out at me: when I'd asked how long he'd been in the water he'd reckoned four minutes. Little time for something so bold. Not in character with the woman Hamilton had described. Was it really possible that Donna, so besotted she allowed herself to be used by a married man for sex, could morph into a calculating stalker prepared to risk capture to avenge herself on her former lover?

What kind of nerve did that take?

And assuming she was responsible, was it a spontaneous action driven by obsession or always the plan? From her vantage point high above the water, did Donna realise before anybody else that Jennifer Hamilton was drowning and see her chance? Then what? Donna didn't drive so unless she had an accomplice that ruled out an escape by car. I set my stopwatch and headed for the beach.

Beaches weren't my favourite places, even the tropical paradise kind, lapped by blue seas and edged with coconut palms. Ayr wasn't one of those; a cold wind was coming off the water and, on a blowy day with the tide out, no surprise it was deserted.

I stopped at the abandoned boat Mark Hamilton had mentioned and checked how long it had taken me to get here. A minute and a half, a three minute round trip. Tight.

A stone wall, built to keep the rough winter seas at bay, ran the length of the front. The nearest access to the shore was the way I had come, the next about the same distance further on; everything else was too far. The Hamiltons walked away from the town centre, away from the Pavilion; this was where Jennifer went swimming, where her husband and daughter waved to mummy seconds before the horror that would change their lives forever.

The timing said it, and the fact that Hamilton couldn't find anybody to look after the baby when his wife got into difficulties. Snatching the child hadn't been an instant decision, somebody was there, ready to move if a chance, even one as slender as this, presented itself. That much I could agree with and, though none of the possibilities called to me, they were all there was. I examined them in turn, beginning with what struck me as the least likely: that Donna Morton, a loner if her former lover was to be believed, hadn't acted by herself. The sequence of events played in my head: Donna on the Esplanade, keeping out of sight, while her accomplice, maybe her sister, drummed her fingers on the steering wheel and listened to the car's engine purr. When the moment came, running along the sand, lifting the baby and racing to the vehicle waiting for her, perhaps a small van with the back doors open.

Unbelievable.

I was mistaken about which scenario was least likely. Donna alone was even more implausible. No car meant pushing the baby through the streets to the bus or train station, yet there were no witnesses. Taxi firms would have been contacted and told to be on the look-out for a woman with a child; again nothing. The journey by train from the coast to the city takes approximately fifty minutes; the police had to have examined the CCTV footage at every stop and have officers waiting at Glasgow Central. That type of surveillance could have produced a result at the beach. Unfortunately "Safe Ayr", an initiative using portable cameras to reduce antisocial behaviour in and around the Esplanade, had ended in August so Donna Morton or anybody else couldn't have been filmed.

What did I make of all that? The abduction was opportunistic – nothing else made sense. Public transport was out; the clue was in the name. Someone with a car, then. Or a local, and I saw problems there, too. A baby wasn't an easy thing to conceal: for a start they cried, especially at night.

But as a suspect, Donna didn't feel right, unless she'd spent the time since her break up with Hamilton learning to drive. And useful though it would have been to speak to Andrew Geddes, that option was a non-starter. What I was doing wouldn't get his approval.

When I got back, Patrick was nursing a pint. 'Nada,' he said. 'Nothing to find. Could've spun it out. Thought you'd prefer me not to.'

'And?'

'Nada with the landlord too. Wasn't keen to answer questions. The only other person who remembers her was a neighbour. Says a guy was askin' about her. Coincidence or what?'

Mark Hamilton? Or me?

I said, 'Thanks Patrick.'

'You mean that's it? Not like you, Charlie.'

'There's a sister but I'll speak to her.'

He wasn't happy. I said, 'How many driving schools do you think there are south of the river?'

'No idea.'

'Find out. Make a list and start going round them.'

'What am I looking for?'

'One that taught Donna Morton to drive. Got to be a couple of days in that.'

'And in the meantime?'

'Keep the money. Have one on me.'

'One is right. We haven't broken sweat. I've blocked off time.'

I almost laughed out loud. 'Really, I didn't realise. How much?'

'Three days. Minimum.'

'Send me an invoice. The sooner it's in the system the sooner you'll get paid.'

He jumped to his feet. 'For fuck sake, Charlie. Play the game. I don't do invoices. If I started that... where would it end? Before

I know it I'd be payin' tax.' He faltered. 'I'm under pressure, our usual arrangement.'

I didn't ask what pressure – with Pat Logue it was better not to know. Patrick had done a lot of good work for me over the years, and when he had it he was the most generous guy in the world. An advance wasn't a problem. He left with my money in his pocket; that was our usual arrangement. On his way to the door he said, 'See Paul Finnegan died.'

'Saw that.'

'His platinum albums didn't save him. In his teens he was a better than okay goalkeeper. Got an offer from Celtic. The Irish connection. Turned it down and went with the music.'

'Really?' Football didn't interest me.

'Yeah. If he'd stuck at it he could've had his own pub by now.'

I ate in the diner and waited until after six. During the week I rarely went to the club during the day. Without people, without the noise, it was a strange place. Curiosity got the better of me. Alan Sneddon stood in the middle of the floor talking the band through a song. He saw me and came over. We shook hands. I said, 'Too bad about Robbie.'

'Robbie who? Never heard of him.' Alan was wearing jeans, a green and black checked shirt and a dark green corduroy cap, and looked neither young nor old. Artistic types seemed able to keep age at bay better than the rest of us. Of course the hat helped, underneath it he was bald. 'There's someone I want you to meet,' he said and walked me to the stage. 'Charlie, this is Kate. She's joining the band.'

The new Robbie was a woman.

I guessed she was twenty three or four, her hair falling in red tangles, past blue eyes and pale skin, to a white shirt under a black waistcoat and on down to tight jeans tucked inside snakeskin boots. I reckoned she was about five four. Even in heels I towered over her, yet she had the presence of a rock star; everything about her fascinated me. Alan said, 'She's better than Robbie.'

'Better looking too.'

'Well there's always that.'

'What's the idea?'

'With Kate we'll have more attack. I'd like to use it, become harder. She plays really good slide. We'll get an authentic rock and blues sound going. Got one tune down already. You need to listen to this.'

He jumped on stage, enthusiastic as any teenager, picked up his sticks and began a slow count. Need Your Love So Bad is one of my favourite love songs. Nobody ever did it like Kate Calder in NYB that night. When we were introduced her voice had been soft with an accent I didn't recognise; now it changed to a throaty rasp. Intimate and seductive. Shadows closed round her, the club melted away and she sang. Just for me.

At the end Alan Sneddon came over. 'What do you think?'

I pretended a cool I didn't feel. 'Yeah, it's working out.'

'We'll re-launch as Kate Calder and Big River.'

I glanced at his smiling face. 'Robbie Ward will be pissed.'

He grinned. 'You reckon? Shame.'

I'd gone to bed tired, looking forward to a restful night. Needing it. It didn't happen: hour after hour I tossed and turned and kicked at the sheets. Eventually I must have fallen over and for the first time in a long time I had the dream, more vivid than ever; waves crashing against the shore, gulls swooping, crying a warning I heard too late to save me. I couldn't breathe, I was choking. Suffocating. And all the while the voice in my head, urging me on.

Run, Charlie, run!

I wakened with a start, bathed in sweat, heart hammering in my chest, and the taste of salt on my tongue. After that, sleep was impossible.

4

In the morning, out of sorts and irritable, I dragged myself into the day and drove across the river, past the Central Mosque and the Citizen's Theatre. I hadn't been to the Citz since an arty woman called Ziggy persuaded me, against my better judgement, to go to a performance of some heavy Scandinavian classic where the director had the bad guys dressed in Nazi uniforms in case we didn't get it. In the bar I saw several black polo necks and more than one goatee. A bad sign. The first act went on for weeks. Ziggy whispered explanations to help me follow the plot but, even with swastikas and jackboots, it wasn't enough to keep me interested. Nor was she. I assumed the characters all lived unhappily ever after, left at the interval and never saw her again. Relationships don't always work out. Ask Ibsen.

Mark Hamilton's story wasn't uncommon: the marriage breaks down, the husband or wife begins an affair, the affair ends and someone gets hurt. A predictable script. I didn't envy him. Or her. Hamilton had used Donna Morton. He knew too little about her to have been in love. But his certainty she had taken the child seemed far-fetched: nothing he'd told me suggested Donna was implicated. Unless there was more.

On the South Side traffic was light and grey clouds gave a permanent end-of-day look to the city. The abduction had already grown old. That morning it shared page three in one of the red-tops with a bare breasted medical student called Kimberley who hoped to be a doctor one day. Apparently her ambition was to help people. I was sure she already had. A sidebar rewrite of Sunday's shocking events headed Lily: Day Four, kept Kimberley's D cups from falling off the page. When Day Four became Day Twenty

Four she could have the space to herself; the baby wouldn't feature. Newspapers fed on news and there wasn't any. If progress had been made the police were keeping it to themselves.

The ground floor flat showed no sign of life; the curtains were drawn. I knocked on the door. It opened, not much, just enough to let me see a dark haired woman nearer forty than thirty. Donna Morton's sister. Hamilton mentioned alcohol. That battle had been won: the eyes peering at me were alert.

'Whatever it is you're selling, I don't want any.'

'I'm not selling anything. I'm trying to find Donna. She isn't at her old address. I thought you'd know where she's gone.'

'Why? What do you want with her?'

Days earlier Hamilton had stood where I stood. The connection wasn't difficult to make.

Her tone was hostile. 'Who are you?'

'I need to speak to her.'

The door narrowed against me.

'He sent you, didn't he?'

Honesty was as useful as deception.

'Yes, Donna threatened Mark Hamilton. His daughter's been abducted...'

She didn't let me finish. Lucy Morton might've been acting but, if she was, she'd missed her vocation.

'Bastard. That Bastard. After the way he treated her. I pity his poor wife.' She turned her anger on me. 'Get away. Get away!'

I put my foot in the door before it closed. 'It's me or the police.'

'Fuck off!'

A call to Mark Hamilton brought him to the office again. He'd been vaguer than vague during our initial conversation and I needed more. The change, even in a day, was shocking; he'd lost weight, his eyes were shot with blood and I smelled whisky on him. No doubt he'd been using it as a food substitute. The man was living on his nerves.

'Apologies for hauling you here. I know you'd rather be with your wife. How is she?'

He shook his head.

'Destroyed. Jen's asleep. She expects to see me when she wakes. I have to be there. What do you want?'

'It's as you said. Donna moved. Lucy slammed the door in my face.'

'She hates me. I told you.'

About all he had told me.

'I need to get into Donna's head. Right now I haven't enough to do that. I know you met at work. Which agency does Templeton Warwick use?'

My question irritated him. In his emotional state it wouldn't take much. He snapped at me.

'No idea. What the hell has that to do with it?'

'Find out will you?'

Mark Hamilton stared into space.

'Did you and Donna have a bar, a restaurant, somewhere you went regularly? Where did she go when she wasn't with you?'

He inspected his nails, suddenly aloof, a strange reaction from a man in his position.

'Is this really necessary? I mean, how relevant is it?'

'Your daughter's safety may depend on it.'

A low blow.

'Most of us are creatures of habit. Wherever Donna Morton is, she's taken part of her old life with her.'

'It was an affair. A secret. People having affairs don't do much socialising. Now and then we'd have a meal. Never in the centre of town. Christ knows who you might bump into.'

'So where?'

'Can't recall being in the same place twice. We were careful.'

'And Donna was all right with that?'

He glared at me. 'I didn't ask her.'

'How often did you meet?'

'Couple of times a week. At her flat.' He defended himself. 'Look, it was sex. Then she started going on about having kids, the future and how it would be. The future? I was married.'

'So really you can't add anything.'

'The police interviewed me again last night. They're no nearer finding Lily. Jennifer's aged ten years; it's killing her.'

From what I saw it was killing them both.

'Call me on the agency. I'll try the sister again but it isn't much to go on.'

The profile wasn't quite as blurred as I made out: a picture had begun to form; of a needy gullible woman without friends or interests, planning a future with her married lover whose indifference beyond sex must have been obvious; a lady who had deceived herself as much as she'd been deceived. Easy to see how rejection might become revenge. Donna Morton remained a stranger. Her sister could put flesh on the bones, if I could get her to talk to me.

A scrubby rectangle of grass and weeds blocked natural light; an estate agent would describe the property as a garden flat. Lucy Morton was standing by the window surrounded by darkness. The curtain moved and the door opened. Our previous encounter hadn't been a success for either of us – perhaps this meeting would be better. I smiled to help it happen. It wasn't returned. Her opinion of Hamilton was set in stone. She'd lost none of her bluntness and her eyes bored into me in the gloom.

'Me first,' she said. 'You're due an apology from yesterday.'

'None necessary. What I was insinuating wasn't very nice.'

'True, except telling someone to fuck off isn't how I usually behave.'

'Isn't it? I do it all the time.'

'What did you mean "you or the police"?'

'Maybe we should both sit down. I appreciate how you feel about Mark Hamilton. Not many would disagree. You've read about his daughter?'

'Yes, it's awful. Is there any news?'

'No. When they broke up Donna threatened him. He's afraid this is her revenge.'

Lucy Morton reacted.

'That's outrageous. How could he say that? He led Donna on and dumped her. Now he's accusing her of abduction.'

Anger lit her cheeks; her hands gripped the chair. Hamilton better not come face to face with this woman. And I didn't escape.

'How can you work for a man like that?'

'His wife doesn't know about them. He hasn't told the police.'

'Coward.'

'They wouldn't go as softly as I'm going. As it is, Jennifer Hamilton is emotionally and mentally fragile... discovering her husband's betrayal... you can imagine.'

'She'd be better off without him.'

I didn't disagree.

'So you're doing it for his wife?'

'I'm doing it because I took it on. My interest is in finding Donna. Anything you can tell me would be appreciated. The investigation isn't my business.'

'He's saying my sister stole his daughter. He makes me sick. His wife should know what she's married to.'

'I think he's trying to protect her.'

She laughed a bitter laugh. 'Protect himself more like. He wanted his cake and eat it. Donna wouldn't hurt a fly.'

'Where is she?'

'I haven't seen her, not since she told me she was leaving Glasgow.'

'When was that?'

'A year, a bit more.'

'She hasn't contacted you?'

'We don't get on. When Donna was younger she looked up to me until booze took over. I've been sober ten years, one day at a time. I thought she'd forgive me. She hasn't. My sister thinks I've no right to disapprove of her choices.'

'Mark Hamilton?'

Lucy nodded. 'I didn't want her hurt. Once in a while she'd drop in, Friday or Saturday usually. All she spoke about was Mark this, Mark that. I was pleased. Then I met him.'

'Did you know he was married?'

She sneered.

'An idiot could see he wasn't serious about her.'

'That's what you told Donna?'

'It didn't go down well. I lost her again.'

'Did she come to you when the affair ended?'

'No. We'd been out of touch for months. One day a letter arrived – a rant – mostly against me. I went to her flat. She'd gone.'

'Any idea where?'

'None.'

'Mobile number?'

She shook her head. Her reply was terse. 'Look, my sister cut me out of her life. I haven't seen or heard from her since.'

'And you blame Hamilton?'

'Blame? That's a luxury someone like me can't afford.'

'But you do.'

'No. Donna deserved better than Mark Hamilton. She didn't get it.'

'Did she mention friends, people from work?'

'Never.'

'What about a car?'

'My sister doesn't drive.'

'What about you?'

'Lost my licence, didn't I?' She mimed drinking.

'Got a recent photograph of Donna by any chance?'

'No I don't.'

I gave her my card as she walked me to the door. Something about it amused her. She said, 'Do you enjoy your work? Do you get up in the morning raring to go?'

'Not exactly. It's interesting.'

'Of course it is, other people's problems always are.'

Lucy Morton was a person who didn't shrink from taking responsibility for the damage she had caused. Her dislike of my client was undisguised and all the more valid because of her frankness about her own failings. Then again perhaps she knew I'd find out anyway and decided to keep Donna's whereabouts to herself a little longer. It could well be: Twelve Step Programme or not she had no reason to be sympathetic to the case. As for being complicit in the abduction of a baby, I didn't see it. That theory died with no driving licence.

Mark Hamilton called me on my mobile. His voice was thick and flat, he'd been drinking and it hadn't helped. 'Top Temp.' He slurred. 'Donna came to us through them.'

'Thanks.'

'Don't use my name,' he said, and hung up. All of a sudden I'd become the enemy. I put his behaviour down to pressure. And the booze.

Directory Enquiries gave me a number in Manchester.

When I rang a female voice sing-songed down the line.

'Top Temp.'

I started to speak and didn't get far before she cut in and put me on hold with a piano playing in my ear. Jazz did nothing for me at the best of times: today that view was reinforced. A heavy Mancunian accent broke in and saved me.

'Top Temp. How can I help you?'

I told him. Give him his due – he listened longer than his gushy colleague. Marginally.

'You want recruitment North. Please hold.'

Back to the piano. Somehow I'd assumed a business supplying personnel to other businesses would be more efficient. Eventually I spoke to someone whose immediate ambition wasn't to pass me along.

It was reasonable to think they would run some sort of background check to avoid sending people, usually women, to meet a complete stranger in another city. NYB was a convenient cover. I said, 'We're setting up an office and need someone to help organise our systems. At my last place we got an excellent girl from you. I'd like her again, if that's possible?'

'And where was that, sir?'

'Templeton Warwick in Glasgow, a couple of years ago. Donna Morton, is she still on your books?'

'One moment, please.' The line went dead. At least there was no jazz. Two minutes later he was back. 'We can certainly send someone with systems experience. Can't give you the one you had before though. Sorry.'

I hesitated. 'Mmmm, that's disappointing. Is she working for another agency?'

'No idea. She isn't with us. I could arrange for you to interview a couple of potentials if it's going to run for a while.'

'Thanks but no thanks. We'll sort something at this end.'

No address, no friends or family ties and no link through employment. Donna Morton had disappeared. Apart from her failed relationship with Hamilton there wasn't a single connection. She'd probably quit Glasgow, so that just left the rest of the country. Well done, Charlie. My involvement made me uneasy. The life of a child could depend on finding Mark Hamilton's former lover. My original instincts kicked in: this wasn't a case I ought to have taken. This was a job for the police.

The brief introduction to Kate Calder stayed with me. I wanted to see her again. Jackie was waiting for me and grabbed my arm as soon as I came through the door.

'There's a drunk in your office. When he throws up I'd rather it wasn't in here. Customers are funny about stuff like that.'

Hamilton didn't hear me come in. He didn't hear anything. He was in worse shape than the last time we'd spoken, when he hung up on me. His eyes were closed and his head lolled. The suit and the shirt had a familiar look. Well they might. He was wearing them two days earlier, and they hadn't been fresh even then. I shook him awake.

'Come on, Mark. This isn't helping.'

He grunted, sprawled across the desk and went to sleep again. What I had to say would have to wait.

Down in the club Big River were rocking their way through a song I didn't recognise. Alan Sneddon smiled, enjoying himself. The new recruit looked mean and sounded meaner. Even in the empty space Kate Calder had presence, dominating the stage, projecting a fierce energy. No smiles from her. Until the end, then the band grinned at each other and I knew what they knew: it was going to be great.

Later I said to him, 'Sounds like you'll be ready.'

'Sounds like it to me too.'

Kate stayed with the band. I heard their laughter and envied it. I wanted to speak to her. This wasn't the time. A missing child weighed on my mind. A mother lay sedated in the Royal Infirmary not far from where we were; a father was in my office, dying from guilt and, while the police were in the dark about Mark Hamilton's secret, I was all Lily had. It didn't feel good.

Jackie was waiting in the restaurant, not amused. Her mouth was set tight, fingers drumming her irritation.

'He left. Fell against a table. Knocked a soup spoon out of a woman's hand.'

'You sorted it?'

'As always. But it's not on.'

What could I say?

'You're right. I should've kept an eye on him. Sorry, Jackie.'

Andrew Geddes was standing at the bar. No question, he'd overheard. I retaliated first.

'I know what you're thinking. Don't start.'

'Wouldn't dream of it.' He drained his glass and brushed past me. At the door he turned. 'And you don't know what I'm thinking, Charlie. You haven't the faintest idea.'

Pat Logue appeared with a progress report or rather, a no progress report.

'Eleven driving schools south of the river. Been to five. None of them gave lessons to a Donna Morton.'

'Okay, keep trying.'

'Anythin' else in the pipe, Charlie? This won't amount to much.'

'Three days pay for two days work?'

He wasn't convinced. 'One way of lookin' at it.'

'Is there another way?'

'Yeah. I'm at a point in my life where I need regular income. A lift here a tickle there, those days are gone. I have to be able to plan ahead. As and when required, it's too uncertain.' This wasn't Patrick talking, it was his wife.

He said, 'Cut the crap, I'm askin' for a job, Charlie.'

'Let me sleep on it. Work something out. I'll get back to you.'

'Thanks, I'll tell Gail. And never mind, Tojo.'

He meant Andrew Geddes.

'When it comes to findin' people you're a top guy, Charlie. Don't forget it.'

Patrick the Motivator.

As I was leaving, the band drifted past. Kate Calder didn't look at me. I'd missed my chance.

Saturday was overcast, so different from the previous weekend. I stayed home and called Mark Hamilton. Nobody answered. Given the state he'd been in it wasn't difficult to picture the scene at the other end of the line. Around noon I tried again. Nothing. I didn't envy him his hangover although I hadn't had a good night myself. Sleep wouldn't come. When it did it was filled with bad dreams, confused and confusing, leaving me washed out, lethargic and still tired in the morning. A child featured in most of them.

At three Hamilton rang. 'I want to apologise,' he said. 'For yesterday.'

'How are you?'

'Not so good. Overslept. Was meant to be at the hospital. Jen will be frantic.'

'Then you better get going. But we have to talk, sooner rather than later.'

Hope edged his voice. 'You've found something?'

'No, that's what we need to talk about.'

The silence went on forever. Doubt became panic. 'You're quitting, aren't you? You're leaving me? Us?'

'I'm not leaving anybody. When can we meet, there's something we have to discuss?'

He exhaled. 'I'm not sure. Tonight?'

'All right, let's say eight. And lay off the booze, it isn't the answer.'

Jackie's jaw dropped when I walked in at ten to eight. She said, 'Charlie, what an unexpected bummer. It's Saturday This is no place for you. People work here.'

'Very funny. I'm meeting someone.'

'If it's the drunk he's your responsibility.'

Without meaning to she had identified my problem. Mark Hamilton wasn't drunk and, somewhere along the way, he'd managed to find a clean shirt. It wasn't enough: his eyes were haunted by a secret he had no right to anymore. He followed me upstairs and slumped into the chair across my desk. I gave him a drink from the bottle I kept in the bottom drawer and took one myself. Whisky. Not my family's brand. He sipped, close to gagging, fingers trembling, then the alcohol did its work, healing what it had destroyed. I hit him again and he began to relax. The burn in his throat was welcome, more welcome than what I had to say.

He gently traced the tension in his temple. 'I'm not much of a drinker. Not usually. Yesterday was the most, ever. The first couple helped. After that it's a blank. This morning nothing's changed. Same fucking bullshit.'

'You came here last night.'

'Here? Was I all right?'

'No.'

'What did I do?'

'Doesn't matter.'

'Christ!'

'Is your wife any better?'

'Not really, she doesn't speak, stares at the ceiling. Blames herself for going back in the water. Jen can't forget I wanted to leave.'

'What about the police? Any progress?'

'None. There's no sign of the baby. They think she's dead. Jen thinks so too.'

The Hamiltons were living a nightmare and I had allowed myself to become part of it. The mistake was mine. 'Listen, Mark, I've given this a lot of thought. We don't have enough. There's nowhere to go.'

His eyes strayed to the empty glass, guessing what was coming. I didn't offer more whisky. Nothing could soften the reality for either of us.

'You can't keep the affair quiet any longer. You have to tell the police. If I'd found anything, anything at all that led to Donna, there might've been a chance. I haven't. The police need every scrap of information they can get. We can't pick and choose what we tell them. Your daughter's life is at stake. They'll find her, believe me.'

His reaction was unexpected.

'I know. I know. It was madness. I'll talk to them now.' He stood. 'I was wrong to drag you in. Thanks for trying.'

'We were both wrong. Time to do the right thing.'

In the office by myself I turned out the light and took stock; the darkness helped me think straight: I'd had a lucky escape and knew it. The rules of the game hadn't changed. I'd put a spin on them I might easily have regretted. Archie wasn't the only bloody minded Cameron. I had an agreement with myself. No kids' cases. No children stuff.

And if I forgot why, the photograph in my pocket was there to remind me.

5

Fenwick Moor, 4 miles from Glasgow

The men had been friends since school, now Derrick was married – though not for much longer – Gordon was engaged; Billy and John had girlfriends. They shared the same interests: women, drinking and Heart of Midlothian. Saturday was their day. A few pints and off to the match. It was a tradition.

Derrick's new wife didn't get it. In the beginning Sharon found her boyfriend's obsession amusing. She tolerated it to keep the peace but it had no place in her plans. Saturdays would be spent shopping, meeting other couples for lunch and browsing for soft furnishings to complete their home. The football would have to go. Early attempts to change his weekend routine came to nothing: the game was always crucial, a six-pointer, a grudge match or a derby.

Their differences erupted over a caravan Sharon's cousin had at Burntisland and the suggestion that they get away for a couple of days. Derrick bombed the idea. Aberdeen at Tynecastle couldn't be missed. The guys would think his wife had cut his balls off; he'd never live it down. Over the course of a week what began as a suggestion became a power struggle with the future of the marriage at stake. For days Sharon refused to speak to her husband. When she did, she accused him of not loving her. She cried and threatened to go back to her parents. 'I'm your wife, I should come first. Not bloody Hearts.'

Derrick answered with his own logic.

'But Sharon, it's what I do.'

The divorce was rich material for the journey to Kilmarnock, and a cautionary tale: women were all right as far as they went, but some things were beyond their understanding. Derrick's experience made Gordon edgy. His fiancée was pressing him to set a date for the wedding. He'd been keen enough. Suddenly he was having doubts. Maybe she'd expect him to knock Saturday on the head. Give him an ultimatum. Married life or the Jam Tarts? No contest.

Derrick stopped the car at a pub in East Kilbride. An hour later they passed through Eaglesham village and drove across Fenwick Moor. The bleak landscape had no effect on their mood; the beer kept the jokes coming.

'What do the donkeys at Blackpool get for lunch?'

No takers.

'Half an hour.'

The others groaned. Gordon was quiet – he was coming to a decision – the engagement was off. He'd tell Julie tomorrow. She'd be unhappy. Never mind, he couldn't give this up. Like Derrick, it was what he did. One of the guys in the back leaned forward. 'Pull over, need to shake hands with an old friend.'

On the moor a cold wind added bite to a crisp October day. They stood behind the car, too busy swapping the usual comments to feel it.

'Size doesn't matter so they say.'

'Lucky for Gordon.'

'Poor Julie.'

Derrick heard the laugher. He hadn't told them the truth: he missed his wife. Splitting had been a mistake. Saturdays were great but it wasn't a tradition, it was a habit, and he'd been doing it too long. Time to move on. Grow up. The guys would be gutted. Even if there was no way back with Sharon this was his last. She was probably out with her mum, as unhappy as he was at how it had ended. And she was still his wife.

A flash of white caught his eye, incongruent against the rough grass at the side of the road. He got out and picked it up;

a toddler's shoe, not much bigger than his thumb. A child must have thrown it from a car. He stepped on to the moor and walked to a patch of earth, dark brown, still wet from yesterday's rain. His friends were calling. He ignored them. Something lay half in half out of the soil, shapeless, covered in dirt. Paw prints marked the ground: an animal had got there before him. He stared. The shoe dropped from his hand and he wanted to be sick.

There would be no football today.

6

Sunday morning. Mark Hamilton and his family were still in my head. Seven days since the abduction – it seemed longer.

I got up, stiff and sore and made coffee, forcing myself to eat although food was the last thing I wanted. When the Sunday papers fell through the letterbox it wasn't yet light. I collected them and laid them on the kitchen table, determined to lose myself in the supplements; beautiful women and successful men confessing their lives were every bit as wonderful as we all imagined. People you could dislike and not feel bad about it. Mindless drivel in full colour.

I didn't get that far.

The front page headline screamed above a photograph taken under a darkening sky, a white tent with a policeman outside: BODY ON THE MOOR. The police hadn't issued a statement, which meant the report wasn't underpinned by fact. Nevertheless it was written with enough confidence to suggest someone had talked. On Saturday afternoon four football supporters, on their way to watch Hearts play Killie, by-passed the city and drove through Eaglesham. One of them saw a child's shoe on the road. What they discovered ruined their day. Not far from the narrow tarmac strip a body lay in a shallow grave.

Short on detail, the article leaned heavily on the bleak image of the tent and the solitary figure of the uniformed constable. It didn't mention Lily. It didn't need to. Eaglesham connected with the main Glasgow – Kilmarnock road, the road to Ayrshire and the coast.

To the seaside.

Easy to let Lily's father take the blame. With my experience, keeping what Hamilton had told me to myself was inexcusable, an error that may have cost a child's life. Over the years I'd found many missing people and bent the rules now and then to do it; this was different, in more ways than one. There was a code, a line that shouldn't be crossed. Andrew Geddes had warned me off. If he knew the facts, friend or not, he'd be within his rights to arrest me for obstructing an investigation. The Hamilton's marriage would be finished along with my career and, more important, a baby could be dead. Good reasons to admit, even this early, I'd made a mistake.

Three calls to Andrew produced nothing: his mobile was turned off. He could end my misery. Or confirm it. I had to speak to him. It was after twelve thirty when he called me, the detective rather than my pal. I launched right in. 'Do they know who it is?'

His reply was formal, more than formal; chilly. 'Too soon.'

'But it's a child?'

'The victim appears to have been young, yes.'

Policespeak. Then I got it. For once Hamilton had been as good as his word and told what he suspected about Donna Morton. Andrew had put two and two together and realised I'd been in on his secret. My sin had found me out.

'No identification so far?'

His tone was terse. 'Too soon,' he said again.

'Something wrong, Andrew?'

He didn't hold back. 'Fucking right.' His anger boiled down the line. 'You knew! What the fuck were you playing at?'

I hit back. 'Hamilton wasn't going to the police, I persuaded him.'

'And lost nearly a week. Six days after the baby was abducted he turns up with information that might have got her back if he'd told us at the start.'

'He came to me on Wednesday.'

'It took the best part of four days to convince him, did it? Don't believe you, mate.' When he was angry Andrew called people mate. 'If it's true you'd do better asking Alex Gilby if he could use another waiter. Thought you'd be Superman, dive in and sort it. All on your own. All by yourself. Except it didn't work out, you failed.'

I said, 'It wasn't like that' although it had been exactly like that.

He wasn't listening; his voice was cold. 'I could charge you, do you know that? Maybe time in the cells would do you good. There's an excuse for Hamilton, his life's falling apart. What's your excuse, Charlie?'

'There isn't one. I should've turned him down.'

Andrew's breathing was a storm in my ear, a storm that wasn't close to blowing itself out.

'I wonder if I haven't been wrong about you. The rules don't apply to Charlie Cameron, that it? Smarter than the rest of us, are you? History's full of your type. Privileged thick heads. From those wankers in Whitehall your father hangs around with to the charge of the Light Brigade. Reckless bastards who do what they want and fuck everybody else. Confident idiots. Somebody always gets landed with the mess.'

What he said hurt; it was meant to. And he hadn't finished.

'Up here in the frozen north we don't go it, mate. Thought you understood that.'

His final rebuke shamed me.

'A baby could be dead because you can't let go of...'

He stopped short of saying it.

'I made a mistake, Andrew. I know I made a mistake.'

He didn't offer absolution, instead he returned to the distant stranger he'd been at the beginning of the conversation. 'Press conference. One o'clock. STV lunchtime news. I'd watch.'

He hung up.

It was 12.45. The next fifteen minutes were the longest of my life. At a minute to the hour I switched on the TV and waited. Was Andrew right? Had I caused this? The bulletin opened with pictures of a wasteland, tundra washed by drizzling rain, and the wind tugging the walls of a tent, thin walls, barely adequate to the task of masking what lay behind them. Words were unnecessary.

The director let the images tell their own story, the correct decision, just not for me, when the scene moved to the press conference my hands were shaking. A stone-faced senior police officer read phrases from a sheet of paper, a reprieve that could only be temporary.

As yet unidentified… witnessed anything… treated in confidence... come forward.

I poured a whisky and drank, only vaguely aware of the fire in my throat. The rest of the day was a blur. At some point I slept because I woke up on the couch with the room in darkness. A moment of peace then memory flooded my brain, exactly as the day had begun, only worse. I had to get out.

The comfort of strangers. NYB.

Music drifted to the street. I moved past couples chatting on the stairs, their heads close together, eyes locked on each other in a preamble to what would come later. I wasn't the only one in need tonight.

The room was packed; the bar was busy. No sign of Jackie and I was glad. I wasn't in the mood for wisecracks. When the number finished, Big River left the stage to a smooth-voiced DJ, self obsessed and insincere as the lovers on the stairs. Alcohol couldn't fix what was wrong with me. I didn't order. A tap on my shoulder made me turn. The face was familiar. There were stars in her hair. 'Charlie,' she said, 'what're you doing here?'

'I work upstairs.'

'That's not what I mean. I haven't seen you in ages. You didn't call.'

'Did I say I would?'

'Doesn't matter, you're here now.'

She took my hand and dragged me into a corner. Her name escaped me. She put her arms round me and smiled. 'Want a drink?'

'No thanks.'

'Want to dance?'

'What do you think?'

'Want to leave?'

Not the comfort of strangers but near enough.

It was close to noon when I arrived at NYB next day. Jackie was waiting, all set to wind me up. 'Guest appearance last night. You didn't stay long.'

I let it roll over me.

'And the old charisma's still working I hear.'

'I'd leave it if I were you, Jackie. Coffee, please.'

'Not hungry? Can't be a hangover, you weren't drinking.'

She wasn't reading the signs.

'I'll take it by the piano.'

A customer was browsing one of the red tops not famous for sensitivity. This morning it had gone beyond bad taste and the headline was full-on. They say a picture paints a thousand words. Not in this case. The image of the tent was dwarfed by four letters and a question mark, crystallising the horror in black capitals. LILY?

Jackie was bringing the coffee and saw my face.

'You all right, Charlie? You okay?'

Andrew Geddes picked that moment to arrive. He glanced at the front page and came over carrying a whisky. Early in the day for him.

'Irresponsible bastards,' he said. 'Anything to make money.'

Our last exchange was fresh in my mind. I braced myself for another tirade. It didn't come.

'The autopsy was done last night. We got the initial findings an hour ago.'

He waited for me to ask, part of my penance.

'And?'

'A child. Female. Cause of death suffocation.' Andrew leaned on the table. 'When we catch this guy his lawyer will find a medical expert to bamboozle the jury. Say he's insane. But some people are just evil.'

I was stunned. Please god not again.

'The full report will be later today.'

'Has Hamilton been told?'

'Nothing to tell.' He flashed his bad-news grin. 'It isn't Lily.'

Too much. I exploded. My arm cut like a scythe across the table and knocked the drink out of his hand. It hit the floor and smashed, spraying customers with whisky and glass. The coffee went with it. People were looking, I didn't care.

'Fuck off with the games, Andrew, just fuck off with the games!'

'Charlie...'

'No, do better than that, just fuck off!'

7

Aberdeen, 149 miles from Glasgow.

The pages fell from her hands. She let them, they disgusted her. Newspapers really were trash. They'd print any rubbish to sell their filthy rags. Tits and sport and speculation. Pretending to know, pretending to care. And people believed them. The truth wasn't important. Nobody was bothered about the truth. Everybody lied. Men especially.

She dragged her eyes from the headline on the floor and walked to the window. The tide was out. Golden sand, wet and glistening in the morning light, ran in a long curve from the harbour to the mouth of the river Don. Fishing had been the mainstay of the city; now it was oil. In Union Street you could hear every accent under the sun. The boom had peaked but property was still expensive. Renting the upper conversion cost more than a mortgage in other parts of the country. She wasn't complaining. They were safe. For now.

The first days had been the worst. Terrifying. Running like a fugitive, expecting to feel a hand on her shoulder and hear a voice ask what exactly she thought she was doing. They drove south in the early morning and turned off the motorway at Kendal. The Lake District was a good choice; always crowded, an easy place to go unnoticed.

She purchased a cot and clothes after she made the decision. There was no knowing when the chance would come; she had to be ready. Month after month she'd waited. The first lot of clothes got thrown away unworn. And the second: too small. Babies grew so fast. The new clothes were packed away in the boot. Surely they would fit?

Organising the flat by telephone had been a concern but she needn't have worried – it had been easy – and so they went back north. Mother and child. To Aberdeen, far from Glasgow. It would do until she put a proper plan together.

She remembered him blurting out the awful truth, acknowledging the wrong he'd done and the pain he'd caused. He hadn't meant to hurt her. That was a big consolation. Perhaps someday she'd forgive him? Like hell. Pathetic. She was angry at herself for forgetting what every female knew. Men couldn't be trusted. The pregnancy was the last straw; another woman carrying the child that should've been hers. She felt cheated. Desperate. At night, alone in bed, thoughts of suicide tortured her.

But she didn't kill herself. Instead she followed them, hating their happiness. Watching and waiting, and when the chance came she took it. No regrets.

How could a cheap tabloid possibly understand? Tomorrow it would be obsessed by some politician caught with his hand in the till, or a film star showing off her new doe-eyed toy from an orphanage in Africa. The baby would be forgotten.

The police had appealed for witnesses; would anyone who saw anything suspicious please come forward. Blah blah blah. The usual. They didn't have a clue. They could dig up the whole moor if they liked, they wouldn't find her.

She wasn't there.

8

I lay awake with my eyes closed. Opening them would hurt and I was hurting enough. Daylight washed my skin. I sensed the brightness of the room and felt the uneven surface of the couch beneath me. I hadn't made it to bed. The pounding in my head and a dry mouth were bad but they weren't the worst of it. That honour belonged to the postcards from hell, flashes from the night before; NYB and the LILY? headline, Andrew Geddes' grinning face and my reaction.

On the way to the flat I'd taken a giant step towards making a bad thing worse and stopped at an off license on Great Western Road. The Pakistani behind the counter flashing a mouthful of gold fillings and putting up a bottle of Johnnie Walker was the last clear memory I had. What came after was obscured by alcohol and anger; kneeling on the floor holding scissors, surrounded by scraps of newspaper, arguing with people who weren't there. Drunk as a skunk.

Eventually I dragged myself to the kitchen and put the kettle on for coffee. While I waited for it to boil I drank three glasses of water and ceremoniously emptied the little that was left of the whisky away. I didn't say never again but I thought it. The water helped. In the lounge the caffeine brought me closer to recovery. I sipped my way through one cup then another and tried to get a handle on what was happening to me. Drinking had never been a big part of my life, I could take it or leave it. So why were my hands shaking?

I'd once asked Andrew how he coped with what he saw. He didn't hesitate. 'Don't get involved. Only way to survive.'

Easier said.

Hamilton's suspicions were known to the police. No more secrets. I should've been relieved. Not so simple. A child was still out there. With Donna Morton. Or buried in a hole.

I showered, put on fresh clothes and checked the result in the mirror. Not bad if you didn't know better, but not the truth. At NYB I did an impression of the Invisible Man, kept my head down and went straight to the office. Nobody spoke. I didn't see Jackie and wasn't looking forward to meeting her.

I had already strayed over the line. What I did next should have scared me off. Sticking the newspaper reports to the wall was new; the image of the parents consoling each other dominated the centre and drew me to it. I added the photographs from Mark Hamilton and a couple of yellow post-it notes with scribbled questions that didn't include the only one worth asking: why was I behaving like this? Not something I was ready to discuss, even with myself.

Two phone calls later in the morning made things worse, if that was possible. The first was the woman from the previous night – never did get her name – wanting to know when we could meet. I told her a case was taking me south and I wasn't sure when I'd be back. She didn't believe me and rang off feeling foolish and rejected. The second was the last person I expected: Andrew Geddes.

'Yesterday, what I did was out of order, Charlie. It was wrong and I'm sorry. Wasn't trying to...'

I cut him off. 'Forget it.'

'Of all people I should've understood...'

'I said forget it, Andrew. And while you're on the line, lose that fucking awful smiley thing, will you?'

'Don't know what you mean.'

'Yeah you do. The jolly undertaker act. It's offensive.'

Silence.

Broken by him.

'Gave your name to an Alec Downey. Nice guy. If he hasn't been in touch he will. Your line of country. Teenage daughter missing.'

I chose my words. 'The police aren't involved?'

His reply told me that, apology or no, Andrew hadn't forgotten. 'Would it make a difference? Pleased to hear it. No evidence of a criminal act, as far as we know. I'll let Downey tell you.'

In his abrupt angry way Andrew was being a friend, involving me in something that wasn't personal. A distraction. The calendar was clear but the timing wasn't right. My head was all over the place. I wasn't ready. My commitment was to finding Donna Morton and getting Lily back. Anything else was unwelcome.

Of course life wasn't ordered to suit Charlie Cameron. Jackie buzzed me. A Mr Downey was on his way up. I switched to auto pilot. He knocked and came in, a man who had never been young: late fifties, tall and balding – married, according to the ring on his left hand – and unsure about being there. So was I.

'Thanks for seeing me. Should I have made an appointment?'

If Alec Downey had had an appointment I would've cancelled.

'No need,' I said. 'Take a seat. How can I help?'

'DS Geddes advised me to speak to you. About Alison, our daughter. She went to college one day and we never saw her again.'

'When was this?'

'The twelfth of September.'

No police interest made my next question obvious. 'What age is Alison?'

'Eighteen.'

Not a minor.

'She's a student.'

'College or university?'

'College.'

'Which one?'

'Cathedral.'

'How long has she been there?'

'She's in her second year.'

Downey stared at me, waiting for my next question. I didn't have one. I'd stopped listening.

'Sorry,' I said when I realized, 'What did you do when she didn't come home?'

'Reported it to the police.'

He shook his head.

'They weren't interested.'

He corrected himself.

'They took some details and that was it. I thought they'd interview her friends. They didn't. Didn't do anything really. Just asked if we'd had a row. My wife felt so guilty. Still does.'

'She'd fallen out with Alison?'

He rubbed tiredness from his eyes; talking about it was painful.

'They didn't get on. At it every other day.'

'What did they argue about?'

'Everything.'

Teenage boys I understood –I'd been one. The *enemy within* my father called me when I was going through that stage. Teenage girls were a mystery. Then and now. Most families survived, it looked as if this one hadn't.

'How was she with you?'

'All right. Moira's the disciplinarian in our house. Her and Alison were at odds with each other. I was the peacekeeper. Piggy in the middle. Moira sobbing in the kitchen, Alison crying in her room. Half the time I didn't know what was going on.'

'So what happened?'

'The night she left was bad. Not the worst ever, but bad. Alison was upstairs getting ready. She was always going somewhere. We'd stopped asking where. Found out later it was a class do. Moira took her a cup of tea and that was when she noticed her breasts.'

He'd lost me.

'They'd grown. The pill, apparently it causes that.'

'And Moira disapproved?'

'It was a bit of a shock. She never discussed it, at least not with her mother. Moira came right out with it and all hell broke loose. Alison screamed and locked herself in the bathroom. Twenty minutes later we heard the front door slam.'

'Was that the last time you saw her?'

'Yes. Moira ran after her but it was no use. We'd bought her a Blackberry for her birthday. She threw it at her mother. Smashed it on the pavement.'

'She didn't come back for clothes?'

'No. That's why we waited until the next day to report her missing, we thought she'd be with a friend. I mean, what young girl leaves home without her stuff?'

'The police must've thought that was suspicious.'

'Not enough to merit an investigation. Weeks went by and nobody cared. I requested a meeting with a senior officer. DS Geddes suggested I come here. Spoke highly of you. Said you were good.'

'You met DS Geddes when?'

'Friday.'

On Friday Mark Hamilton's double life, his terrible suspicion about Donna Morton and his baby were still secret and Andrew's trust in me was solid. My stock had tumbled since then.

'You contacted her friends I suppose?'

He didn't answer. I tried again. 'Who was she close to?'

The conversation stalled. 'This is difficult, Mr Downey, but you have to tell me.'

He played with his fingers. I said, 'Somebody must know where she's gone.'

'A teacher disappeared at the same time. The police think they ran away together. The college doesn't want to admit it. The publicity wouldn't be good; too soon after the restructure. God knows that wasn't popular. Plenty of disgruntled people up there. And they've just lost an unfair dismissal case. You probably read about it. The tribunal found "an atmosphere of bullying". Senior management got blamed for their dictatorial style. Not a nice place to earn your corn.'

We were losing our way. Cathedral College hadn't led Alison Downey off the straight and narrow.

'Your daughter isn't underage. She can go where she wants. Leaving isn't against the law.'

His daughter was missing and he needed someone to blame.

'But it's wrong. Alison acts grown up. She's not. In many ways she's still a child. She needs to be protected. That's the college's responsibility, surely?'

His expectation was naive. It assumed too much. Downey's understanding of teenage girls, his daughter in particular, was stunning in its lack of balance. In his eyes an older man had led a young girl on. The alternative hadn't been considered.

'So a teacher seduced your daughter and she ran away with him; that's what you believe. What do you expect from me?'

'We just want to talk to her.'

'If she's with this man, even if I find them, she may not want to meet you. Are you ready for that?'

'We just want to talk. We don't want her to make a mistake that might ruin the rest of her life.'

'What's his name?'

'Lennon. Frank Lennon.'

'Was Alison one of his students?'

'Yes. Marketing. She talked about him a lot. Obviously he impressed her. We put it down to teenage infatuation. I went to the college. They checked Alison's attendance records; the day after the row she didn't go to her classes. Nobody's seen her since. They put me in touch with two girls, supposed to be her pals. Never heard of them.'

'What are their names?'

'Valerie Cummings and Rose Devlin. They weren't keen to speak. They saw Alison at the class night out and she was fine.'

'Where was this?'

'The Drum and Monkey, corner of Renfield Street.'

'Did you think they knew something and weren't saying?'

'I got the impression they were closing ranks. Sticking together. Didn't like them.'

'Do you have a photograph of Alison?'

He handed me two. The first showed a dark-haired girl wearing a red and white hat unwrapping presents beside a

Christmas tree. Her complexion glowed and her brown eyes sparkled with youth.

'How recent is this?'

'December before last. I took it. Moira came across the other one in Alison's bedside table. We hadn't seen it.'

The second was a group picture, a line of six teenagers at a club; the three boys were the worse for wear. Alison Downey was on the end, away from the rest. I didn't recognise her – the change was remarkable – and she wasn't brunette anymore. She gazed at the lens, blonde head back, lips parted, giving the camera her complete attention. Moira and Alec Downey had already lost their little girl. They just hadn't noticed.

The young woman I was looking at didn't believe in Santa.

Left to myself I would've stared at the walls for a couple of weeks and replayed the Hamilton case over and over. Andrew had put me back on the horse and, on the surface, the Downey case was uncomplicated: a teacher and a female student had run off together. A shock to her parents and his wife perhaps, though others wouldn't be so surprised. I could imagine the lovers: their intensity, the excitement, the passion. The almost inevitable hurt.

Moira and Alec Downey needed to square what had happened with themselves and know they weren't to blame. Finding Alison would give them that chance. Before I went downstairs I called a guy I knew at Glasgow Airport and asked him to check if a Donna Morton had taken a flight in the past few weeks. A big ask. And a long shot. Mark Hamilton's rejected lover could have left by train without any questions.

He heard me out. 'The police covered this already, Charlie.'

'Take another look, will you?'

Pat Logue was at the bar, in position, newspaper and pint in front of him, ready for a session. In many ways I admired him. He was one of life's optimists. Patrick seemed fresh, probably because of his own golden rule which he stuck to like a religion: no booze on Sunday night. Proof positive he didn't have a problem. I said, 'Anything on the rest of those driving schools?'

'Understood we were off that.'

'We are. Officially, but...'

He held up his hands. 'All right, I get it.'

'Might have something else for you.'

'Good stuff, Charlie. Now?'

'Not yet. Soon.'

He signalled for another drink on the strength of his future earnings. In an emergency Jackie allowed him to drink on the slate. Everybody else paid cash. Once in a while he'd appear with a fistful of money. How he came by it was anybody's guess. He'd clear his debt and be flush for as long as it lasted, then the merry-go-round started again.

'Hear Robbie Ward's gone. Hard act to follow they tell me.'

'Alan Sneddon has it covered. Break your Sunday habit. Bring Gail.'

He sucked air through his teeth, the way car mechanics do when they lift the bonnet and see problems none of the rest of us can see.

'That's two habits, Charlie. Radical.'

'You'll be missing something special.'

'Did Alex tell you to say that?'

'No but I do say it. Alan discovered Robbie Ward. This is even better.'

'I'll think about it.'

He drank the top off his pint, picked up the paper and tapped the front page with his finger.

'Sad, sad, sad. Some people...'

...are just evil

His regret was real. He pushed it away.

'Couldn't sub us could you?'

'You must be psychic.'

Pat took it on the chin.

'Okay,' he said, 'driving schools it is.'

Jackie was in her cubbyhole underneath the stairs: a tiny space crammed with samples, delivery notes and yellow post-its where she couldn't miss them. I wanted to avoid her, at least until the hangover calmed down. No luck, she ambushed me, cheeks flushed with anger, and gave me both barrels.

'What was that scene about yesterday? Anybody else would be barred.'

'Jackie, I've a lot on my mind. Don't push it.'

'Don't push it! We've got customers to think about. How can I run this place with you acting like that?'

'I've said I'm sorry.'

'Actually you haven't, Charlie. You haven't said anything.'

She stormed away. Back in my office I called Cathedral College and asked to be put through to the Principal's office. A female voice, polite and dry, came on the line.

'Principal's.'

'Good morning. My name is Cameron. I'd like to speak to the Principal, please.'

'Do you have an appointment?'

'No.'

'Do you want to make one? The earliest is Tuesday the twenty third.'

'Today would be good.'

I wasn't in the mood for another uppity female.

'Today?' She sniffed and recaptured the high ground. 'Out of the question I'm afraid. Mr Galbraith is a very busy man. His diary's full for the next two weeks. What's the nature of your business?'

My turn: 'It's confidential. But I assure you he will want to see me.'

'Well he has a window on the nineteenth. Four thirty.'

Eleven days. Too long.

'It's about a student and a member of staff. I'm acting on behalf of the parents. I'd like to hear the college's side before I take it further.'

To be fair she did a decent job of staying in control. 'Mr Galbraith is in Edinburgh. He won't be in college until tomorrow.'

'Tomorrow's fine,' I said. 'What time?'

'I could fit you in at two.'

'Two it is.'

Jackie saw me coming and headed in the opposite direction. Noise from the club told me Big River had started early. I went down and stood at the back. Kate Calder was wearing a flying jacket and a blue scarf, rocking her way through a Bonnie Raitt song, breaking off to play slide guitar riffs. If she noticed me she kept it to herself.

At the end of the number Alan shouted to me.

'Ask Jackie to turn the heating on, will you Charlie? Bloody freezing in here.'

Jackie was in the kitchen talking to the chef when I caught up with her. 'Can the band have the heating on in the club?'

She snapped a reply. 'It's turned off during the week.'

Nippy sweetie was back in town.

I held my hands up in surrender.

'Don't shoot me I'm only the piano player. I couldn't give a damn one way or the other.'

Her hard expression dissolved, her lip trembled and she ran out of the kitchen. First Andrew now Jackie. I was on a roll. Two minutes later Pat Logue was in my office.

'Just heading out, Charlie.'

He pointed to the wall and the clipping.

'A bit much for a case we're not on. Officially.'

I kept my head down.

'Sad stuff, definitely is. Aren't gettin' sentimental, are you?'

I stopped rearranging my desk and spoke through clenched teeth.

'Mind your own fucking business.'

'I'm only sayin'. Can't save the world. The best we can...'

'Don't. Don't say anything. Christ Almighty! Advice from Patrick Logue!' I blew up. 'Since when are you an expert? The way you're knocking it back what would you know? What would you know about anything?'

The moment the words were out of my mouth I regretted them. And I saw something I'd missed, the reason he was drinking too much so early in the day. Patrick was struggling.

He stood. 'Et tu, Charlie,' he said and left.

I could add him to the list. Three out of three.

9

Cathedral College overlooked the city centre, a stone's throw from Queen Street station. At the end of the street the forbidding granite of the Royal Infirmary jostled with the cathedral and the Necropolis, reminders of how fragile and temporary life is.

So far I'd succeeded in falling out with three people – I was the common factor. The walk up the hill calmed me and helped me focus on the Downey case. I didn't want it, though even I could see I needed the distraction.

From reception I was directed to the Principal's office. The woman behind the desk stared over horn-rimmed spectacles. Dimples marked the sides of her mouth. Dimples make cute women cuter; with her they didn't stand a chance. She sniffed hostility. She hadn't forgotten. I took a seat without being asked and waited. We didn't speak. At a minute to two she broke the silence in the same clipped voice I'd heard before.

'Mr Galbraith will see you now.'

The Principal didn't offer to shake hands. He was everything I expected. A man with a good conceit of himself; conservative tie, tweed jacket and a smile that lasted less than a second, a reflex from an old hand at faking it.

He glanced at his watch. 'Can we make this brief?'

I pretended I hadn't heard and sat down.

'Thank you for meeting me.'

'Didn't leave us much choice.'

He sniffed. Sniffing seemed to be the in thing round these parts.

'Nothing short of threatening I'm told. Now you're here let's not waste time.'

He meant his time, because it was more valuable than mine.

'I'd like to ask about a student. Alison Downey...'

He held up a hand like a referee stopping play.

'Can I establish exactly who you are? We prefer to know who we're dealing with.' The smile flashed on and off.

'Charlie Cameron.'

'And what exactly is your interest, Mr Cameron?'

I handed him my card. He didn't read it.

'Alison Downey's parents have hired me to look into her disappearance.'

He seemed perplexed.

'Disappearance? Has she disappeared? I know she left us but is that the same thing?'

'So you're aware Alison's not in college? When did she leave?'

Galbraith had done his homework. He opened a folder in front of him and ran a finger down the page. 'Alison Downey. HND in Management. Attendance records show her present the first nine days. Second year begins in September. She was in class from the third to the thirteenth. We haven't seen her since.'

'She started the semester then quit. Isn't that unusual?'

'Not at all. Further education is full of challenges. Student retention is a major problem. Aspiring to standards of excellence is all very well but, to put it crudely, these days we're in the bums on seats business. Attracting people is one thing, keeping them is something else. Every student lost costs the college money. Unfortunately too many are in out of the rain, as soon as an opportunity to earn comes along we never see or hear from them again. Alison Downey was just another one.'

'Don't you follow up?'

'Of course but it's not a concentration camp. We can't make them stay.'

So far Galbraith had been reading from a script he knew by heart, in control, well rehearsed and convincing. My next statement put him on the back foot. 'Alison's parents believe she's with a member of your staff.'

'I can't discuss...'

'A teacher called Lennon.'

'We don't have teachers, Mr Cameron, we have lecturers. This is a college.'

The Principal would have to do better than that.

'Frank Lennon. Is he teaching... lecturing... today?'

He took a moment and finally found the right question, in his position the only one worth asking. He leaned towards me.

'Do the police suspect a crime has been committed?'

I didn't answer. He pressed a button on the desk. 'Then I really have nothing to say.'

As if by magic the door opened behind me. Galbraith spoke without looking at me.

'Miss Shaw will show you out.'

Miss Shaw couldn't hide her delight. Her boss had put me in my place and revenge was sweet. Her face shone with superior malice; those dimples deserved a better home. On Cathedral Street a lazy river of students drifted by, whispering into mobiles, listening to Ipods; in groups all talking at once. Perhaps some of them would talk to Patrick if Patrick was talking to me.

If anybody was talking to me.

It was the middle of the afternoon. There were more than a dozen people in NYB. Most of them I recognised; customers not friends. My friends were Andrew and Jackie and Pat Logue. Without them New York Blue was just another glorified coffee shop in the Italian Centre. A newspaper and a half finished pint sat on the bar. Symbols. It had to be serious for Patrick to leave anything in the glass.

I stopped a waitress. 'Where's Jackie?'

'No idea. Alex was looking for you.'

I tried the kitchen, under the stairs and the stock room. No sign of Jackie Mallon or Alex. I met them coming out of my office. Jackie's face flushed: she'd been caught, hadn't she? Her recovery impressed me.

She said, 'We've been wondering where you'd got to.'

I pretended not to know what was going on.

'Seen Pat Logue?'

'Left.'

'Is he coming back?'

She walked on. 'Didn't say.'

Alex held back; he seemed uncomfortable, not like him. Very little fazed a man who'd spent his life in hospitality, at one time or another, owning some of the best known places in the city. Now, in his early sixties, he took a back seat and let Jackie run the show. With expensive clothes worn casually – moccasin, rolled up sleeves, shirt undone down the front – and white hair that never saw a comb, he looked like a financial advisor who had survived a shipwreck. I wanted to ask how he'd managed to get so far inland. Although money didn't change hands, technically Alex was my landlord. I seldom saw him. Usually he limited his appearances to a couple of times a month. Today, whatever Jackie had been saying had him spooked. He pulled me aside. 'We need to talk, Charlie.'

'So talk.'

'Be better in the office.'

I led the way; he followed and closed the door. I guessed what was coming.

'Look,' he said, 'Jackie's not in a great place right now.'

'I'd noticed.'

'Yeah well, try not to rub her the wrong way, eh?'

He ran a stressed hand through his white hair.

'She's got issues.'

Who hadn't?

'And this room is one of them?'

He didn't deny it.

'Keep her sweet, that's all I'm asking. She's wound up.'

'Yeah, that's no excuse for being a pain in the neck.'

'She's got a point. Can't have people stumbling around drunk in the diner.'

'That was a one off. He's baby Lily's father. He's cracking up.'

'None the less Jackie's trying to run a restaurant. Look, this office is yours. Nothing will change that, but, when it comes to NYB, she's worth her weight in gold. I don't want her to throw a strop and leave, okay?'

'She's hard work right now, Alex.'

He smiled and shook his head.

'I've noticed. Women. Can't live with them...'

'... can't kill them, I get it. Fair enough, I'll do my best.'

He put a hand on my shoulder.

'You're a bit wired yourself, everything all right?'

'Fine, everything's fine.'

The lie came so easily, perhaps my father had been right all along about me becoming a lawyer and a politician; the talent was there. Less than a minute after Alex left the phone rang – my contact at Glasgow Airport.

'Nothing, Charlie. Went back a month. Donna Morton doesn't appear on any flight schedule.'

'From Glasgow?'

'Glasgow, Edinburgh, Prestwick, Aberdeen. She hasn't left the country by air.'

'Did you include domestic? I'm thinking London.'

'Covered that too, as did the police by the way. Same result.'

I thanked him and replaced the receiver.

The day was over bar the shouting. I felt flat. Andrew had helped me back on the horse; staying there was something else. I put my head in my hands and slept but found no peace. My head was out to get me.

Crazy dreams. Bad dreams. Andrew and Alan Sneddon. Patrick and Alex Gilby. Galbraith and his tame witch. And a child on a beach.

I woke in the fading light, with shadows on the wall and the colour sucked from the room.

My joints were stiff and I was cold. The best thing would've been to go home, pour some wine and lie in a hot bath. Instead I went for a drive, telling myself lies about needing to clear my head. Half an hour later I was parked just as I'd known I would be, outside Donna Morton's old flat, empty and in darkness. By all accounts Donna had been a bright girl and not bad looking so how come no one had any contact details for her? Apart from a loser boyfriend she seemed to have been a spectre moving through the world without leaving a trace. Even her troubled sister, Lucy, was on the outside. That couldn't be true. She had to have interacted with other people. The challenge was finding them.

I pulled away from the kerb. Apparently the "do the right thing" speech I'd given Mark Hamilton didn't include me.

Daytime television gets a bad rep. What the critics fail to understand is the up-side. I managed six hundred minutes without thinking even once. Whenever reality tried to break in with news from the world I went to the kitchen and made coffee until the danger passed. Another day of my life I'd never get back; that was fine with me.

On Friday morning the sky was cloudy but the sun was shining. Some people are born with a forgiving nature. Fortunately for me Pat Logue was one of them. Or maybe he just needed the money. He was already in NYB when I arrived, counting the minutes to opening time. He waved. I gestured upstairs. 'Whenever you're ready, Patrick.'

'I'm ready now.'

'Okay. Let me speak to Jackie first.'

Jackie was on the phone. She ended the call abruptly when I appeared. Unlike Pat Logue nothing had altered. Her tone was terse, on the edge of impatience, reminding me of Miss Shaw.

'Whatever you've got to say I don't want to hear it.'

Her lips formed a tight line, daring me to respond. Instead I turned away and left her with her resentment still smouldering. I had my own.

Patrick was due an apology and his wouldn't wait.

I said, 'About the other day, I was out of order. No excuses, I'm sorry.'

He was generous. 'Should've kept my nose out, Charlie. Simple as that.'

'Yeah, you didn't deserve it.'

'Worse things happen at sea. So long as you're okay. Drew a blank with the rest of the driving schools. What else you got for me?'

I told him about Alec Downey and his daughter, Frank Lennon and Galbraith. He understood where he fitted.

'You want me to talk to Alison's friends. Find out what I can about this Lennon guy.'

I gave him the photograph Downey had given me. The party shot. He studied it.

'Nice lookin' girl. Who are the others?'

'Don't know the boys. The girls are Valerie Cummings and Rose Devlin. Downey spoke to them. Told him nothing.'

'Wouldn't expect anything else. I'll go around lunchtime and see if I can catch up with them.'

'If the college get to hear you're asking questions you'll be out on the street.'

He swatted the air. 'No danger. Mature students all over the place. I'll just be another one. What're they afraid of?'

'Publicity. Student runs away with teacher isn't the best advert.'

Patrick picked the photograph up for a second look. 'Nice lookin' girl,' he said again. 'How recent is this?'

'The father isn't sure.'

'Do we know anythin' about Lennon?'

'Only that he worked at Cathedral College and now he doesn't.'

'Married?'

I shrugged. 'Galbraith wants them kept out of it.'

'And there's no law against humpin' the customers.'

'Not unless they're under age. Alison Downey isn't.'

Patrick put the photograph in his jacket pocket and pulled himself out of the chair. 'We'll see what we see,' he said. 'Who knows? Might be lucky.'

In the bar Andrew Geddes was drinking coffee and dunking a bagel in the muddy liquid. He would've ignored me if I'd let him except the road back had to begin somewhere. Only right it started with me this time. I stopped at his table. He turned slowly and gave me his policeman face. I said, 'Alec Downey came to see me. Thanks for the reference.'

'No problem.'

'Not sure I can do anything.'

He just nodded. Unlike Pat Logue, Andrew wasn't close to forgetting. I wanted to ask about the Hamilton case but instead I let him be.

10

Aberdeen, 149 miles from Glasgow.

She'd been right about the newspapers. Fake concern for a couple of days, then nothing. One printed a grainy photograph. A reminder that there was always a chance someone would recognise the baby. She worried about it for days. When the answer came it was so obvious she wanted to laugh out loud.

The police were con artists too. Liked to appear as if they knew something but couldn't say in case they gave the game away. A joke. People went on with their lives and the world turned. In the end nobody cared about what happened in Glasgow. It might have been a thousand miles away; a foreign country. That was an idea.

They fell into a routine. Children needed a routine. During the day they stayed home. At night the city was quieter. She did the shopping when the supermarkets were empty and it felt calm. The fresh air put the baby to sleep. Aberdeen was all right.

A pity daddy wasn't with them.

Daddy had had his chance and blown it.

But she mustn't fool herself. There were problems ahead. Big problems. Accessing the system. Something else to think about. Bridges to cross one at a time.

Schools were already on her mind. Important to choose the right one. And the dreaded first day. It was different now, parents were included, encouraged to be a part of it. None of that awful stuff at the gates with kids crying their eyes out and their mothers doing the same. How traumatic that had been. God knows how many had been scarred by the experience. No child of hers would suffer.

She peeped next door The baby sighed and rolled in the cot. Beautiful. Innocent.

In the lounge she laid out the new clothes and studied them. This was just the beginning: a padded coat and a hat with ear muffs, perfect for keeping the cold at bay; tiny jeans, fawn dungarees and t-shirts; a footballer on the first, a boat on the second, and Thomas the Tank Engine puffing his way across the third one; then her favourite. The cutest thing she'd ever seen. A blue and white sailor suit. Blue for a boy. They were looking for a girl. Adele would be Andrew until they were free and clear.

The old clothes went in a black bin bag. Tomorrow she'd get rid of them and buy more. And toys. Lots of toys. What was the point of having kids if you didn't spoil them?

Childhood should be fun. A mother's job was to make it perfect.

11

Donna didn't have the baby, I was sure of it, but I couldn't let it rest. Patience, they say, is a virtue. So is persistence. I found an online map of Ayr, printed it out and stuck a pin where the abduction had taken place. From that point I marked the routes Donna might have taken and stood back. Added to the newspaper clipping and the photographs on the wall it made quite a collection, though how any of it helped was a question I couldn't answer.

Pat Logue came through the door and fell into the chair opposite.

'Teemin' with kids that place.'

'Did you find the ones we're after?'

'Course.' Spoken with confidence. Patrick of old.

'Teenagers are the most predictable people on the planet, Charlie.'

'Ungrateful. Irresponsible. Self-obsessed.'

'Absolutely. Gail comes close to murderin' our two every week. It's a front. Young people are insecure. They cling to each other. Find one find them all.'

'So you talked to Valarie Cummings and Rose Devlin?'

He wouldn't be rushed. It was his story. He'd tell it in his own time.

'Supposed to be friends. Some friends.'

'They told you where Alison is?'

He ignored the prompt. 'Devlin's the leader. The biggest mouth. She dominates the rest. Remember the boys in the photograph? They were there too.'

'Lucky.'

'No luck involved. They're smokers. Social pariahs. Huddled together outside the door puffin' away. I pretended I didn't recognise them and asked if they knew Alison.'

'And?'

'Instant attitude. "Who wants to know?" That shit. Told them the Downeys were worried sick. No interest. Until I mentioned the teacher. Then it was sly smiles. Devlin laughed, said the whole college knew about them. Valerie Cummings didn't agree. Accordin' to her Lennon wasn't up for it. That got them started. Devlin didn't like bein' contradicted, especially in front of me. Should've seen her face. The boys stayed out of it.'

'Good decision.'

'They know the form.'

'They're mates, surely Alison would've told them? I mean, running away with an older man isn't an everyday thing.'

Patrick said, 'Can't see anybody confidin' in Devlin. Too mean. I was with them for five minutes and nobody got missed – Alison was a slag, Cummings was an idiot. Called the teacher a walking hard-on. The blonde guy, Brian, tried to say somethin' and she turned on him as well. Told him Alison thinks he's a nobhead. Accused him of fancyin' her.'

'How did he react?'

'Closed down. These wee groups have their own dynamics. Rosie's the boss and she's a bitch.'

'So why did Alison hang around with them?'

'Christ knows.'

'What did they have to say about the Drum and Monkey?'

'Only that Alison was there.'

'Was she with anyone?'

'No. But get this. Frank Lennon turned up.'

'Did he?'

'Apparently he goes to a lot of student stuff. Valerie reckons he's okay. If you listen to Devlin he had his tongue hangin' out. A real letch. Manky hanky-panky?'

'Possible. Did Alison leave with him?'

'Nobody noticed.'

'What about the other boys?'

'Didn't get their names. Low men on the totem pole.'

'And they've no idea where the love birds might be?'

'Need to catch them on their own. Devlin's influence is too strong. Won't let anybody else speak.'

'Lennon's colleagues are the people to talk to. Impossible to work with a guy every day and not have an opinion about him. We have to find out what theirs is. But we won't be welcome; you can be sure about that.'

Patrick smiled. 'If I only went where I was welcome I wouldn't be home much.'

The Argyle Arcade has the biggest collection of jewellers in Glasgow. Engagement ring paradise. Tray after tray of a girl's best friends. Stare too long and you could go blind. My eyesight had never been in danger. Alec Downey had mentioned a case of unfair dismissal; the internet did the rest. When I called, Michael Corrigan seemed pleased and suggested we meet in the Arcade's only pub. An interesting choice, Sloans was one of those 'institutions' Glasgow seemed to have so many of; A-Listed, ornate interiors, sculpted plaster cornices, heavy dark wood doors and a ballroom on the second floor. It was like entering a time machine and being taken to some unidentified period in the past. The current owners were making a big attempt to breathe new life into the business. A full programme of events was advertised on a poster at the door – a swing band upstairs, a ceilidh on Friday nights; Mrs Sloans' Cake Salon and the Bad Boy Pub Quiz. Very entrepreneurial although I was unconvinced about Musical Bingo.

A guy sitting at the back against the wall waved to us. I would've guessed Corrigan had something to do with education even if I hadn't already known. He had a scruffy-intellectual-man-of-the-people thing going on – t-shirt, too long hair, a sprinkling of dandruff round the collar of his jacket; a pen between nicotine stained fingers and a folded copy of the Herald across his knees. The sublime to the ridiculous; the Sun lay on the table in front of him next to a paperback biography: the Life of Voltaire. I was certain the book went everywhere he did. Corrigan could read and wanted everybody to know. His image was honed and finessed to persuade anyone interested he was a jaded big-brain. A world weary thinker. Or maybe I was too harsh. 'Spot the teacher,' I said. My aside earned me a rebuke.

'"Judge not that ye be not judged", Charlie.'

Patrick the Righteous.

We'd agreed on one o'clock. Corrigan had started earlier. Thirty five years earlier. Give him his due, he was making progress on the crossword as well as his Guinness. He filled a few more boxes, lifted his glass and swirled the black and white liquid inside.

'I like this boozer. Got atmosphere.'

His eyes were bloodshot but alert.

'You said you needed my help.'

Corrigan wasn't drunk though he was getting there. I gave Pat Logue a twenty, he headed for the bar. 'How long did you work at Cathedral College?'

'Eighteen years, man and boy. Changed the name a few times to protect the guilty.'

'Until you ran into trouble. Sexual harassment wasn't it?'

The act got dropped and replaced by something real.

'Matter of fact it wasn't. Galbraith wanted rid. Jumped the gun and got his fingers burned.' Corrigan grinned. 'They thought I'd go quietly in exchange for a reference. Shit a brick when I took them to a tribunal.'

'Did they catch you or did they set you up?'

'Don't be fucking cheeky. I didn't fit, simple as that.'

'Sacking's a bit extreme. Must be plenty of ways to marginalise somebody without going that far.'

'They'd already done that. Dumped the thickest punters on me, changed the timetable at the last minute. Put my class in the crummiest rooms, miles from anywhere. One semester I was in the basement, beside the boiler. I'm not joking.'

'Why you?'

He smirked. 'Too much to say. "*Not a team player*". Once Galbraith had his shiny new college structure he intended to populate it with clones and drones. Couldn't oblige.'

I believed him. Corrigan's ego shouted across the table, he'd have a problem with authority. Pat Logue came back carrying three pints. As usual, change from the twenty failed to find its way to me. I brought him into the conversation.

'The college gave Mr Corrigan here a hard time, Patrick. Face didn't fit. Couldn't get shot of him fast enough.'

Corrigan made his own case. 'Twice they offered me a package. Not a bad offer either.'

Pat said, 'You weren't tempted to take it?'

'And bring the curtain down on a great comedy?'

He started on the new Guinness. It drew some of the bitterness from him.

'Yeah I thought about it. Fresh start somewhere else. But then they'd have won. Galbraith's a smug bastard, would've loved to send me down the road. So I let it go.'

'Any regrets?'

He stared over my shoulder. 'Only that I didn't see it coming.'

'You're saying it was a set-up?'

He smiled a half-smile and added another word to the puzzle. 'The tribunal didn't put it like that. Galbraith got a bloody nose. He deserved a lot more.'

'You make it sound personal.'

Corrigan reacted. 'They tried to destroy me. As it is I'll be lucky to teach again. It is personal.' He glared at the newspaper and altered something he'd written.

'I'd like to hear your side.'

'Why? What's it to you?'

'They won't speak to me at Cathedral. I need somebody who will.'

He took his time, deciding whether we were worth the effort. I exaggerated. 'Galbraith almost had me thrown out.' That swung it.

'Long version or short version?'

'Any version you like.'

'All right. Two words. Senga Beverage. Forty-four, unmarried, frigid. And, as the kids say, pure dead up herself. Lives for the college. The illiterate hordes are meat and drink to her. In the new structure she was my section leader and we didn't get on.'

I could guess. Senga got the job the older more experienced Corrigan thought should've been his.

'A female boss was a problem for you.'

'Other way round. I was a problem for her. Started finding fault with my work. Demanded to see lesson plans. Lesson plans are typical of the bullshit that gets handed down. Nobody has time for that kind of junk. For the classes she gave me, a chair and a whip would've been more use. Don't like to blow my own horn but I could teach that stuff in my sleep. Have done.'

The smirk returned.

'Once upon a time further education was about standards of learning and qualifications. Now it's crowd control. Least it is down among the dead men where they sent me to live.'

'Your line manager discriminated against you?'

Corrigan pulled a nothing-to-do-with-me face. 'That's what the tribunal found.'

'Where did the sexual harassment come from?'

'From an argument, or rather a series of arguments.'

'With Senga?'

'Yeah with Senga.' He wiped white froth from his lips. 'What kind of name is that?'

Pat Logue said, 'It's Agnes backwards.'

Corrigan scribbled the letters in the margin. 'So it is.'

He was being facetious.

'Never trust a woman called Senga. Jan's another one. Wide berth.'

His performance was getting out of hand.

I said, 'Stick to the story. You argued with your boss.'

'I called her an arse. Because she is an arse.'

'That's verbal abuse not sexual harassment.'

'And it's true. Beverage alleged I made suggestive comments and touched her.'

'Did you?'

He snorted stout. 'Do me a favour. She's a dog. Wouldn't poke her with yours.'

'Were there witnesses.'

'That's just it, the stupid fuckers hadn't any proof. Too keen to do me in.'

'Beverage's word against yours. Good enough for the college to sack you. Not good enough to convince an independent panel.'

'Result,' Patrick said.

'Yeah, they got their knuckles rapped all right. Galbraith had to explain himself to the Board. Victimisation – whisper it – in his squeaky clean college.'

'Did any of your colleagues support you?'

'Can't prove a negative.'

'So no?'

The humour suddenly went out of the lecturer. 'You've had your two-bob's worth,' he said, 'now piss off and let me get on with the crossword.'

'Frank Lennon for instance?'

'This why you're here? Lennon?' Corrigan laughed. 'Funky Frankie.'

'Not a mate then?'

'Another arsehole. Place's full of them. What's he done?'

Even if I'd known I wouldn't have told him. 'Far as I know nothing.'

'Must've done something. Why else would you be here?'

'Lennon went drinking with his students. You ever do that?'

'You're not serious? Drink with the Acne Army, would you?'

I took that as another no. 'Any idea where Frank Lennon lived?'

'No. Heard him tell somebody he rented in Finnieston. On the water across from the old Record building. Caught him with a hard drive loaded with porn have they?'

'What makes you say that?'

'Never know with his type.'

Alcohol distorted his features and made him ugly. He started to push his luck, he said, 'That accent. Buy it on Ebay?'

I ignored him. His glass was empty. He'd be getting no more from me.

'Are you saying Lennon was into porn?'

'Wouldn't surprise me. Spent every minute between classes on the pc in the corner. Saw what he was looking at a couple of times. Big Gal wouldn't approve.'

'What was on the screen?'

He winked. 'Loose lips sink ships. Give you a clue. Every summer he went to Thailand for his holidays. Loved it out there. Ring any bells?'

Mudslinging. He was wasting our time. Senga Beverage and anyone else who'd had to work with Corrigan deserved sympathy. He was a difficult individual. Charmless, toxic even. He lifted his pint. 'Not staying for another?'

Patrick pointed to the newspaper. 'Five across isn't right. "Obstreperous vehicle out for hire". Truculent. Truck you lent. Once you understand how the guy thinks it's easy. Usually takes me six or seven minutes.'

On Argyle Street I shook my head. 'Couldn't resist it could you?'

'Didn't even try.'

'Smart arse.'

'Tut tut. Careful. That sort of remark might be misconstrued.'

'What did you make of him?'

'A loser. Voltaire? Yeah right. Never met Senga. She's probably all he says, but I'm on her side.'

I agreed. 'Corrigan's at odds with the world. He's unreliable. And he's drunk.'

'Doesn't mean he isn't telling the truth. The Thailand remark, he was hinting sex. We never mentioned Alison Downey.'

'He was at it, that's who he is.'

'Rose Devlin said much the same.'

'She's like Corrigan, goes through the day dripping poison. I think he did harass his boss. Sex as a last resort. An attempt at control. The college saw a chance and moved too soon, the tribunal weren't given enough evidence to get it right.'

'Which leaves us with nothin'.'

'Not exactly, Patrick. It leaves us with a flat in Finnieston. Better than we had. We can take another run at the young team. See if we get anything out of the boys. Worst case scenario we get roped in to registering for intermediate car mechanics every Wednesday night.'

'A little education's a dangerous thing, Charlie.'

12

Thursday: the day my mother wanted behind her, so life with my father could return to whatever passed for normal in their world.

I spent the morning in the office reading the paper, making the odd phone call and sending out invoices; killing time. Eventually I needed caffeine and went downstairs. Andrew Geddes was at a table in the corner, as usual, dipping a bagel in his coffee and slurping up the floating bits, making a noise like a deranged truffle hound. We hadn't spoken since he'd blanked my attempt at bridge building. No surprise. Andrew wasn't a man to forgive or forget easily and our friendship was at a low point. Nevertheless he knew the date and was waiting for me, checking I was okay. He looked over the rim of his cup.

'All right Charlie?'

'Fine, Andrew. Yourself?'

He shrugged. For now it was enough. I appreciated his concern.

Later, when I drove away from NYB, weak sunshine followed me to the Clyde Valley, through Lanark, to the outskirts of Biggar and the retirement home where Ronnie Simpson lived. A nurse standing at reception recognised me. I asked her about him. She hesitated then produced a smile. 'He's cheerful. Not in pain or anything like that. Lives in the past a lot, you know how it is.'

Indeed I did.

'Does he get many visitors?'

'Since his wife died you're the only one. You're not a relative, are you?'

'No, a friend.'

I'd met Joan Simpson on a couple of occasions: a nice woman. The Simpsons hadn't had children; with her gone there was no-one to come and see Ronnie. Except me. Once every twelve months. Some friend.

The nurse's pager beeped. She turned her attention to it.

'You can find your own way, can't you?'

She pointed. 'End of the corridor. Same room as before.'

At the door I stopped. It was close to lunchtime and Ronnie was still in his pyjamas under a faded wine coloured dressing gown that hung off him. In his prime he'd been a big-boned man, tall and robust. There was nothing robust about him now. I knocked. He didn't hear. His grey head was bowed, engrossed in what he was reading. Maybe he sensed me there because at that moment he glanced over his shoulder and let the sheets of paper fall from his hands to the bed.

'Charlie!' He laughed a wheezy laugh that broke apart somewhere deep inside him. 'Been expecting you. Saw you in the newspapers a while back. Somebody missing for six months but you found them.'

I fought to keep my voice steady, my reply light. And I understood the nurse's remark. "Not in pain". She had assumed I knew how ill he was. 'Don't believe anything they say, Ronnie, most of it's rubbish.'

'Tenacious they called you. Made you out to be a hero.'

'Sensationalised. Exaggerated. Bollocks.'

Ronnie wasn't listening; he preferred the Daily Record's version to mine.

'Thought, that's my boy, that's Charlie. Doesn't know when to give up. If only I'd had a Charlie Cameron on my team... Pull over a chair and let me have a look at you.'

We hugged and shook hands. In mine his fingers felt dry and brittle, like holding a bundle of clothes pegs. Watery eyes searched my face and imagined it no different. His had the familiarity of a stranger. 'You don't get any older,' he said. 'What's your secret?'

'Can't tell you though the picture in the attic's a helluva mess.'

This time the laugh became a coughing spasm that wracked his frail body, leaving him drained. He wiped his mouth on the sleeve of the dressing gown and put on a front. 'Got yourself a wife yet?' He gave me a sly nudge. 'Must be a few take a shine to a fine young guy like you?'

'You sound like my mother.'

I pulled a bottle of Johnnie Walker Black Label from my coat pocket and saw him light up.

'Here. Don't let the nurses see this or you won't get a sniff of it.'

'Thanks, Charlie. Pour me one, will you? Tumbler on the sink. And don't be mean.'

It was the least I could do for a man who'd been kind to me when I needed someone to be kind and, on more occasions than I could recall, given me the benefit of his experience as a detective, sharing failure and hope with me in equal measure.

On this day and other days.

Now, cradling the glass of whisky between skeletal hands, grinning at me, I wouldn't have recognised him if we'd passed on the pavement, so little did he resemble the Ronnie Simpson I'd known. DI Simpson the first time we'd met, well on the road to becoming a DCI. In a long and distinguished career as a police officer, Ronnie had had more than his share of successes; unfortunately for both of us, Pamela wasn't one of them.

I was a student at Glasgow University when I took a train through to Edinburgh and walked into the first police station I came to. The desk sergeant knew him – I quickly realised every policeman in the capital knew him – and told me where I could catch a bus to the Corstorphine office that served the Cramond area. I was lucky, he was there. That was the beginning of a score of conversations. Always the same. Now he lived alone in this place, his glories faded, just another old geezer waiting for the hammer to fall. Over the years I'd taken to visiting him until we both came to expect it – at the station, at his home in Penicuik after he left the job, and for the past five in his room at the end of the corridor. My parents had their coping mechanisms, maybe even a ritual they kept to themselves. Visiting Ronnie Simpson was mine.

I gestured to the sheets of paper and the manila folders on the bed; three or four of them, one open.

'What're you up to?'

As if I didn't know. I'd seen them as often as I'd seen their owner. Ronnie ran a hand through hair chemotherapy had thinned. He'd be bald soon. The least of his worries.

'Used to dig them out regularly. Don't bother much anymore, no point. Except when you're coming.'

The folders held the cases that got away from him. Not all of them, the ones he hadn't accepted. Pamela's lay on top. He lifted a Herald from the bedside cabinet and held the image of Mark and Jennifer Hamilton welded together in pain on the front page in the air.

'Never ends does it, Charlie?'

'No Ronnie it doesn't.'

'Are they any closer to finding the wee girl?'

For a second I considered lying to him then thought better of it. 'Remember my mate the DS? He keeps me in the loop. Says so far there's no sign of her.'

A story every policeman had heard all too often with an ending that was easy to guess. Time was the enemy. Every hour that passed made it less likely the little Hamilton girl was still alive. Ronnie nodded. 'Be sure to tell him good luck from me, will you?' I said I would.

We talked for a while. Ronnie listened. To his credit he didn't mention his health; he left it for me to raise the elephant in the room.

He was pragmatic. 'They've got me on chemo. At my age? Who're they kidding? I'm on the way out, Charlie.' He smiled. 'If you've gotta go you've gotta go.'

'How many sessions have you had?'

'Three.'

'I could come with you next time?'

'What, and watch my hair fall out? No thanks.'

'Call me if you change your mind.'

I gave him a card; he read it out loud.

'Missing? Always thought it was a good name. Does what it says on the tin, eh?'

Unlike my father Ronnie was proud of what I did.

'If you change your mind...'

'I won't. After this next one I'm telling them to stop the therapy. Knocking hell out of me. Living's over-rated. Joan made it worthwhile. Without her nothing really matters. Except these.'

A withered finger stabbed the bed and the collection of unsolveds he'd taken with him when he left the Force.

'Probably would've snuffed it a while ago without them. Gave me a purpose. Everybody needs a purpose. Couldn't just give up, couldn't do it. Had to keep trying. Stay with it. But as I said, if you've gotta go...'

He pulled on the whisky, coughed into his hand, and came back for more.

'Here,' he waved the empty tumbler at me, 'do something decent. Fill that up. I'm talking up, d'you understand?'

The ex-policeman sounded like Patrick Logue. I did as I was told and when I brought it back, almost over-flowing he pushed a folder into my hands.

'Been meaning to give this to you for a while. Don't know why I left it this late. We've talked through it often enough.'

I hesitated, the cold cases, this one included, had helped the old copper keep breathing. I didn't want to do anything to alter that. And he was telling the truth: we had discussed what was inside more times than I could recall, going over the details such as they were until, inevitably, we ended back where we'd started.

His outstretched arm trembled. 'Take it, take the blasted thing. It belongs to you anyway.'

Suddenly I realised what he was doing and felt a lump in my throat; the circular conversations and the anniversary visits were over. This was the last. Close on twenty years of them, coming to an end. And he wasn't just giving me Pamela's case history. Ronnie was saying goodbye.

On the drive back to Glasgow my thoughts were in the past. I glanced occasionally at the buff folder on the empty passenger seat, a reminder of things better forgotten. I felt low, defeated, and selfishly sorry for myself. Company was the furthest thing from my mind. But at NYB there she was, standing at the 1959 Rock-Ola with her hands in her pockets, running a finger down the playlist; no guitar, although she'd brought her charisma. I stood by the door, watching her read the titles, wondering what her selection would be.

I'd spoken to Kate Calder when Alan introduced us, and remembered the high-heeled snakeskin boots, enough reason to want to know her better; she was the most attractive woman I'd ever seen. Her choice of music surprised me. At Last, Etta James, an electric vocal on a schmaltzy love song. I gave her a moment to enjoy it. She gripped the Rock-Ola with both hands, eyes closed, swaying with the strings. When the record ended she saw me and waved, all the encouragement I needed.

I said, 'Sneddon hasn't fired you already, has he?'

She smiled. 'They're trying a couple of new amps. I've got my sound.'

'So how's it going? Enjoying yourself?'

'Have to ask Alan, he's the boss. I'm loving it. Great band.'

'He told me the launch is Sunday, are you nervous?'

Her hand tightened against the juke box.

'Nervous doesn't cover it. Is there life for Big River after Robbie Ward? He had a lot of supporters. They might not give me a chance.'

'Tell the truth I'm tired of hearing about him. He jumped, nobody pushed him.'

Despite her ability her confidence was low. She needed to believe in herself.

Kate said, 'The Evening Times is doing an article on Alan. Glasgow's Mr Music's latest reincarnation. Hope he gets that in.'

'Robbie was good. People liked him. Now he's gone. That's it.'

She sighed. 'Can't say that makes me feel better.'

'Maybe a coffee will help.'

We sat at a table and ordered cappuccinos. I itched to ask if there was someone, instead I settled for small talk and the chance to be near her. The timing wasn't right. I'd brought back more than the case file. Ronnie was with me. And the moment passed. I covered the name on the front of the file with my hand, hoping she wouldn't ask about it, but she did. 'Is that somebody you're looking for? Alan told me that's what you do.'

Good old Alan.

'Why missing people?'

Kate's brown eyes stared, completely innocent, not understanding. For her it was a simple question and she expected an answer. I pretended to consider it, then said, 'Long story.'

'Think you'll find them?'

'You never know.'

'I hope you do.'

This was a woman with a big heart. She sensed my reluctance and turned the conversation back to Big River. 'So you reckon they'll accept me?'

'Listen, anybody else would have a right to be worried. Not you. You've got the stuff, otherwise Alan wouldn't be going with it. That's the truth. Down the line nobody will remember Robbie Ward, they'll be too busy raving about Kate Calder.'

'You think?'

'Absolutely. You're at the beginning of a glittering career.'

'Yeah?' The doubts were still there. I took a final stab at calming them. 'Imagine how a brain surgeon feels before his first operation.'

'Mmmm,' she said, 'but he doesn't have to sing.'

It was a fair point.

In the office I opened the filing cabinet and slid Ronnie's folder in beside my Pamela file. I wasn't tempted to look inside, I knew what was in there. On other days and nights I wouldn't be able to stop myself. But not today. Not today.

13

No mention of baby Lily in Friday's paper. That pissed me off. It hadn't taken them long to forget. Then what was there to report? Hamilton had told the police about his relationship with Donna Morton and his hunch his rejected lover abducted his daughter in a twisted attempt at revenge. No arrest meant Donna was ruled out or the police hadn't located her. Without Andrew's inside knowledge it was impossible to say. I wondered how Jennifer Hamilton was holding up. Two weeks of not knowing whether her child was dead or alive. Then her husband's betrayal. Could anyone survive that?

Pat Logue acknowledged me with a wave, slid onto the barstool and hunched over the racing section. Usually he'd be scribbling in the margin, making notes, studying the form but today he was subdued. Jackie was giving instructions to a waitress restocking the bar.

I said, 'Patrick seem all right to you?'

'He's hung over. Just not hiding it as well as normal. And for the record, he looks better than you. Sleep deprivation, it'll get you every time, Charlie.'

Closer to the truth than she imagined. Since I'd taken the Donna Morton case I hadn't slept more than a couple of hours a night, and seeing Ronnie Simpson hadn't helped. My eyes were red-rimmed and gritty.

Almost home. Almost safe.

'How can he be hung over?'

A stupid question.

'He drinks. More than any three other people in here. Been doing it for years.'

'Once he straightens up remind him we're supposed to be going out.'

Jackie mumbled something about not being my secretary and kept an eye on the girl filling the cooler with bottles.

He appeared in my office at twenty past twelve and clapped his hands like he was raring to go. Pat the Lad. Whatever he'd swallowed had worked. If I hadn't known better he'd have fooled me. I put the photograph of Pamela back in my pocket and watched him go into his act.

'All set, Charlie? Ready to face the day?'

My eyes stayed on the computer screen. So far Google had produced thirty-seven Donna Mortons – twenty-five on Twitter, twenty one on Facebook, seventeen on both – none of them the Donna I wanted. Everything with this woman was a long shot. Nevertheless my hope was that a lonely girl with almost no friends in the real world perhaps lived on line. Apparently not.

'You're back with us then? Bit quiet earlier, weren't you?'

'Slow starter. Always have been. Not a mornin' person.'

He smiled and almost pulled it off. It was his business. I let him think I believed him.

Patrick edged round the desk and saw what I was looking at.

'Linkedin?'

The expression on my face said Don't Go There. For once he read it right and backed off. On our way out the door he stopped at the bar. 'Minute. Let me finish this,' he said, and downed the best part of a pint in one. What I was witnessing wasn't good. I took a closer look at him; if he was affected by booze he was no use to me. He repeated his hand clapping routine. 'Right, what's the programme?'

'Find the flat. See if Alison Downey's there. Speak to her. Ask her to contact her parents. After that it's up to them.'

'Simple.'

'Simple and easy aren't the same.'

We walked to High Street and my car, past people as grey as the sky. Nobody spoke. Nobody smiled. The city had the

Monday blues. Finnieston wasn't far. By the time we reached Charing Cross traffic lights the smell of beer was overpowering. I opened my window to let in some air and glanced at Patrick. He stared straight ahead, I doubted he was seeing much. He was faking it. I asked if he was okay and got the usual fly-man reply.

'Sound as a pound.'

He lied effortlessly, but then he'd had plenty of practice.

I said, 'Big River next Sunday. Rock and blues. Gail would enjoy it.'

'No can do, Charlie. Never change a winnin' team. Besides, not my kind of music.'

'What is?'

'Classical.'

'Really? Didn't take you for a Beethoven and Stravinsky fan.'

'I mean the Beatles and the Stones.'

Pat Logue was incorrigible. I turned right, under the Kingston Bridge, towards the SECC and the flats Corrigan mentioned; by the riverside, red brick above the residents' car park. Lancefield Quay. In the distance the Finnieston Crane, one of the last reminders of Glasgow's industrial past, jutted over the Clyde.

'You take the top. I'll take the bottom.'

He seemed relieved. Glad to escape. 'What's the story?'

'We're colleagues. Lennon hasn't been at work. We're concerned in case he's ill. Play it by ear. See how far you get.'

People are careless. They make a big deal about having security systems in place then misuse them. I buzzed every button on the entry pad until someone let me in. It never failed. The building was well looked after and neat. "Suitable for the busy professional." Character or charm didn't matter in a place like this. It would sell on the location. You could live here twenty years and still not know your neighbours. Bad news given what I was trying to do.

No answer from the first four; probably out being busy and professional. The fifth door opened. A man in his sixties peered at me. His surprise was genuine; security systems made unexpected visitors rare. That was the idea. I went into my spiel. He listened.

'Don't know a Lennon. Got a few teachers, haven't heard of that one. Ask Walter.'

'Who's Walter?'

'The caretaker.'

'Where do I find him?'

'Good question. Wish I had the answer. Walter has the cushiest job on the planet. Does nothing. Spends most of his time hiding and the rest complaining. But he's a nosy bastard. I'll call and tell him somebody wants to talk to him. He'll try to fob you off. Don't let him. Not much goes on he doesn't know about.'

I heard Walter before I saw him. He appeared at the end of the hallway, shuffling down the corridor in an old pair of fawn house shoes. And he wasn't pleased. I apologised. 'Sorry to bother you. I'm trying to find a colleague of mine. I'm worried he may be ill.'

He cut through my baloney. 'How did you get in? Some lazy bugger buzz you through? When will they learn?'

He eyed me like I was the problem. We were off to a bad start. Pat Logue was a genius with people; he would have had Walter eating out of his hand. I wished I had his talent.

The caretaker shook his head. 'They leave the place open. No wonder flats get tanned.'

'Lennon. Frank Lennon.'

He muttered to himself. 'Supposed to be secure. Keep the door shut.'

I tried again. 'Lennon?'

'Fourteen B. But he's not there.'

'You're certain?' It was an insult that didn't merit a reply. 'When did you last see him?'

Dirty fingers stroked a grizzled chin. 'More than a month.'

'Was he all right?'

Walter blinked indifference. 'All right then.'

'Can we make sure?'

He scratched his cardigan, took a deep breath so I'd understand how inconvenient it all was, and scuffed his way along the block. I followed him to a red door.

'This is him. Want me to knock?'

'Please.'

No one answered. He tried again. 'Told you, he's not here.'

'Maybe he's had a heart attack in there.'

'It's his house.'

Comedy gold from Walter.

I upped the ante. 'Frank might be lying dead.'

'When I saw him he was fine. Need a lot more before I call the cops. The residents wouldn't like it.'

'So you'll wait until you get a complaint about the smell?'

'Smells don't bother me. I'll leave it until somebody orders me to open it.'

'I'm not ordering I'm asking.'

The caretaker had the stripes. He gave his chin another stroke while he considered the options. I pushed harder. 'Just you and me. In and out.'

A big photograph of the queen greased the wheels. He slipped it into his pocket.

'Have to be with you.'

'Goes without saying.'

'Don't touch nothin'.'

'Wouldn't dream of it.'

'If he's in there leave it to me, understand?'

I expected him to produce a ring with dozens of keys, instead he held up one. It came with a lecture. 'Most important key there is,' he said. 'Not a door in the building this doesn't fit. Take it everywhere, no matter what I'm doin'.'

He leered. I faked a grin to keep him sweet.

'Remember,' he said, 'in and out.'

The flat was dark and stifling hot; stale air and fresh paint caught in my throat. In his hurry to get his hands on Alison Downey's young flesh, Frank Lennon had left the central heating on. I'd sold the caretaker a picture of a man forgotten by the world, dying alone and undiscovered. When he flicked the light switch and Lennon wasn't on the floor he couldn't conceal his disappointment. 'Nobody. Okay, show's over. I'm lockin' up.'

'Hold it. He might be in another room.'

He growled. 'Make it quick. You shouldn't be here.'

The kitchen was small, modern and functional and hadn't been used recently. Alison's lover was a tidy man; no cups or plates on the draining board. Everything squared away except for fruit rotting in a glass bowl on the work surface, and something in the fridge covered in grey fur. An unopened pint of semi skimmed milk, well beyond its sell by date and blown, was the final proof Finnieston hadn't seen the runaways.

Frank Lennon's room was similar to the kitchen, neat and empty. The curtains were open. Light poured onto a double bed that took too much space. The bed was new, parts of it wrapped in polythene, and it hadn't been slept in. A PC sat on a pine table under the window. If Michael Corrigan's allegations were true it might be worth a look. Walter must have read my mind. His voice haunted me from the lounge.

'Don't touch nothin'.'

I didn't get the chance. He was at my shoulder.

'No more bullshit. I'm closin' this place.'

His slippers scraped every step to the exit. I gave him my card and asked him to call if Lennon came back. 'Make it worth your while.' He grunted and shut the door.

Patrick was waiting by the car. He seemed better.

'Nada,' he said before I asked. 'No answer from most of them. Workies. Wrong time of the day. Any luck?'

His efforts with Donna Morton's landlord crossed my mind. Maybe he'd been in the pub across the road. I was beginning to mistrust everybody, then again, just because you're paranoid...

'Tell you back at NYB. We need to talk.'

Jackie was behind the bar. Patrick spoke to her in sign language and joined me in the office. Ten minutes later she arrived with two pints, both of them for him. I looked at my watch. Even by his standards he was heading for a session. At this rate he'd be well away and soon.

He lifted a glass. 'First today.' Said with a straight face. 'So, you found Lennon?'

'Where he lives, yes.'

'But not him? And not Alison Downey?'

'The flat's empty. Been empty for a while. Over a month since the caretaker saw him.'

'Could be anywhere. Gretna Green even. Easy to check. Public record.'

'The place has been painted recently. Can still smell it. And how often does anybody buy a bed? Not something you do if you intend to leave. Lennon's a tidy freak yet there's stuff in the fridge that's gone off. Fruit growing penicillin. Doesn't make sense.'

'Teenage girls are emotional. Falling out with her mother might've forced Lennon to move the agenda forward. I think they're in Mexico or somewhere. They'll come back as Mr and Mrs and the parents won't be able to do a thing except invite their son-in-law round for dinner.'

'It was like an oven in there. You're asking me to believe he was in too big a rush to kill the central heating.'

Patrick finished his drink; he was losing interest. 'And all this proves what?'

'That second guessing a stranger isn't easy. I'd like a word with Andrew Geddes. He hasn't been around.'

'Can't say I've noticed.' Not the truth. Pat Logue made it his business to notice. 'Got the case through him, didn't you?'

'Yeah. In spite of what the girl's mother and father think, Lennon hasn't done anything illegal.'

'So how will talkin' to Geddes help?'

'Maybe it won't. I'd still like to speak to him.'

'Rather you than me.'

The other pint disappeared. He stood, twice the man he'd been at the start of the day.

I said, 'I'd like you to go to the Drum and Monkey, find out who was working the night Alison's class went there and talk to them. See if they remember anything.'

'Can it keep? Somethin's come up. Won't be around for a day or two if that's all right.'

'It'll have to. Sure you won't change your mind about Sunday? Going to be a good one.'

'Not my scene, Charlie. Creature of habit. And Gail can't be bothered with the palaver.'

The invitation wouldn't reach his wife. Patrick was at it.

The whole fucking world was at it.

14

St Andrews, 81 miles from Glasgow.

Joe Moffat was never going to be a lawyer or a doctor. He didn't have it. His father was a builder, self-employed. As a last resort Joe went with him but, over the years, margins had been cut to the bone; the business was pushed to cover one wage let alone two.

Three words changed all that; the anthem of the nineties: buy to let.

He was seventeen when his father bought the two bedroom terrace house. From outside it seemed substantial. Inside it was tiny. The Tardis in reverse. The view was the best part. The bridges across the Firth of Forth were even more spectacular the nearer you got. And North Queensferry was very near, almost underneath. Minutes from the motorway. Edinburgh just across the water; the Kingdom of Fife, Dundee and beyond all within driving distance. Location location location. A cliché, and the single great truth that governed property values.

Joe learned the rudiments of half a dozen trades working on that house. Transforming it took longer than his father estimated – it always did. Brian Moffat said properties were like people. No matter how well you thought you knew them they were always capable of surprising you. Dry rot was a problem, subsidence a disaster. He sold North Queensferry and took on another challenge, and another. Twenty-odd years later it was Joe running the business helped by his father. Instead of builders they'd become developers. Not the multi-millionaire kind, steady progress and a decent living.

It hadn't all been plain sailing. The market was more volatile than ever, and the banks were bastards. Real bastards. Success was down to shrewd buying, tight budgets and not allowing their ambition to exceed their reach. What started as a family operation remained just that.

It had taken all Helen's powers of persuasion to get Joe to bring her. 'You'll be bored,' he said. She wasn't. She was thrilled by the atmosphere in the sale room, the signals and signs and the auctioneer rattling away nineteen to the dozen. Her husband was less impressed. Joe spent a large part of his life in places like this. Today they were after a property his father had spotted. An opportunity no doubt, but Joe felt uneasy. It was too expensive, too far away and too much work. If it went tits up he would be left to sort it out. Buying at auction took a cool head, knowing when to push and when to step aside. No place for sightseers. He wasn't happy with Helen tagging along.

The bidding was brisk for Lot 81. An early flurry of interest pushed up the price then faded. People dropped out leaving the serious bidders to fight for the prize. In the end it came down to Joe and a guy at the front in a soft hat and camel coat. Joe passed the limit he and his father had agreed - a balance of the purchase price and the estimated renovation spend against the eventual worth of the property and how much rent it would generate. He raised a finger and the price shot up two grand. If that wasn't enough the other guy could have it and good luck to him.

The auctioneer peered over his spectacles. A shake of the head from the third row.

'The bidding is with the back of the room'.

The hammer fell. 'Lot 81. Sold to number 415!'

Brian Moffat nudged his daughter-in-law in the ribs and pencilled an unnecessary tick in the catalogue against their latest acquisition. He still found bidding exciting. Joe warded off a hug from his wife and shook hands with his father.

Brian and Helen waited outside while he signed a cashier's cheque, collected the keys and calculated the auction house commission. Now that was the business to be in. No calluses, dirty hands or sore backs there. No risk either.

In the car his father congratulated him again.

'Got it. And at the right price. Pay too much and we're no better than busy fools.'

He said the same thing every time they left an auction. In truth they'd shelled out more than they would've liked.

Helen was still buzzing. 'Let's take a proper look.'

Her husband wasn't keen. 'Bit of a drive, isn't it? St Andrews.'

His father weighed in on her side. 'If we go home your mother will only find something for me to do. I'm with Helen. Let's see what we've got.'

Joe pointed the car towards the Forth Road Bridge. On the way across the firth he tried to see the house that started it all. That had been a good business decision. He wasn't sure he could say the same about this one. And it was turning into a day out.

St Andrews had the oldest university in Scotland and claimed to be "the home of golf". Its prosperity was assured. It had the feel of a modern market town with a good conceit of its importance. Well-modulated English accents were common and groups of Japanese tourists roamed the streets, photographing everything.

Property prices were above the national average. Development opportunities were rare. As soon as something came on the market it was snapped up, done up and sold on. The father and son's initial inspection on a rainy day hadn't revealed anything untoward. Behind the near derelict facade was a redevelopment goldmine. Lot 81 could have gone for more. The university meant a constant stream of young people searching for affordable short term accommodation. The plan was a no-brainer: convert the four bedroom house into flats. If they'd got their sums right they could look forward to a steady income until they decided to sell. Money for old rope once the work was done.

But you could never be certain. Like his father said: a building was always capable of surprising you.

From the back seat Helen said, 'Take the coast route, Joe.'

Her husband sighed. The coast road was the long road. They should've brought sandwiches and a flask of coffee and had a singsong on the way. Women were always completely for something or completely against it. Joe emptied his mind and let the car drive itself. Near Pittenweem the sun almost broke through; dark clouds hanging low over the sea defeated it. Brian Moffat pointed to a shape in the distance.

'The Bass Rock. Always wanted to go there. No idea why.'

Nor had Joe. To him the Bass Rock meant tons and tons of bird shit.

The house stood on its own at the end of a road. Paint peeled, plaster cracked and hung in folds from the walls. A depressing sight. They got out of the car. Joe remembered the zeros on the cheque. He was the better businessman but his father had vision; he could strip away the ugliness, the rust and decay, to the potential underneath. Before an architect had even been on site Brian Moffat was able to tell him what he wanted the finished drawings to look like.

Joe spoke to Helen. 'So what do you think?'

'Mmmm.' Her enthusiasm was fading. It would take more than TLC to make something out of this wreck, and she understood why Joe had been on edge.

'Got possibilities, I suppose.'

'Absolutely right. What you're seeing won't exist when we're finished. We'll bring this place back to life and fill it with people. Paying people. Open the door, Joe. Careful where you step, Helen, the wood's rotted. Should be wearing hard hats and safety boots.'

Inside her father-in-law prattled away. 'Need to replace most of it of course. Electrics. Plumbing. The floor will have to come up. Roof will be the most expensive bit.'

He laughed at her anxious expression 'It's doable. And costed. Isn't it, Joe?'

Joe didn't reply. All of a sudden he wasn't so sure.

Enough of the lounge remained for Helen to imagine a home. The ceiling was high and when the boards were off there would be plenty of light. She began to buy into the idea.

Brian Moffat stabbed a finger at a 1930s fireplace. 'That's going.' The sash windows got it next. 'So are they. It's all going.'

Helen wrinkled her nose. 'Damp,' Joe said. 'Hasn't been lived in for years.'

'No. Worse than damp. Bad.'

Brian shouted a warning from the kitchen.

'Don't go upstairs! Not safe! Come and look at this!'

Helen wanted to leave. She whispered to her husband.

'Can you really fix this? I mean, I was prepared for run down but this... Amazed the roof wasn't blown off when the bomb fell.'

Joe made a face. 'Dad thinks we can.'

'But the smell, Joe?'

'Could be the drains.'

'How do you sort something like that? It's awful.'

'We start by securing the structure, then deal with the problems one at a time. Outsource anything too specialised. Not pretty. That's why there's money in it.'

'But why didn't you notice it when you were here?'

Her husband didn't have an answer for her. Helen followed him to the kitchen. Brian Moffat was staring at a line of bells above the door. He said, 'A hundred years ago these told the servants they were required and where. A different world.'

His daughter-in-law couldn't have cared less. 'Can't you smell that? It's like gas.'

'Old properties always smell to begin with. Soon goes.'

Helen covered her nose with her hand.

'Not as strong as this, surely? I can't stand it. I'll wait outside.'

When his wife had gone Joe said, 'Helen's got a point, dad. Never been as strong as this. Can't believe we missed it. Seems to be coming from across the hall.'

'Got tools?'

'In the car. I'll get them.'

The room across the hall had been the parlour, a restful place removed from the noise of the street. The merchant who built it spent winter evenings there with his family in front of a roaring fire, reading the Bible and thanking God for giving them such a fine townhouse.

Joe Moffat took a deep breath and went in. He slid the chisel between the thick straps and tapped it with a hammer. The wood groaned and complained and rose enough to let him force the shaft underneath. Toxic fumes rushed to meet him. He gagged but kept at it until he freed two more boards. Brian Moffat stayed by the door watching his son peer into the hole in the floor, seeing the horror on his face. If only the guy in the camel coat had beaten them.

Joe staggered past his father, through the front door and fell on the grass, retching.

A building was always capable of surprising you.

15

One week after Alec Downey had come to my office and five since the bust-up that ended with Alison leaving, Moira Downey was keen to convince me that Frank Lennon had seduced her daughter. Her brown eyes never left mine while she made her case. Patrick had commented on Alison's looks; she got them from her mother. Mrs Downey was born with high cheek bones and smooth skin and hadn't rested on her laurels. She was confident and opinionated, one of a new breed of women, more sensual at forty than they'd been at twenty. Her dark hair was short at the back, one side longer than the other at the front. An expensive cut. Slender manicured fingers lay in her lap.

She said, 'It isn't difficult for an older man to impress a girl. They've been nowhere and done nothing. Don't get me wrong, young girls aren't saints. But surely it isn't naive to expect people in authority to behave responsibly? I mean, he has to be twice her age. There's no future. He'll get tired of her.'

'Maybe that won't happen.'

She dismissed my optimism. 'Oh please. This man has lived life. What could a teenager possibly have to tell him he doesn't already know?'

How about what was in the charts? I kept the thought to myself.

'He's weak. A grown woman is too much of a challenge for him. So he targets students. It may not be illegal but it's immoral.'

Her reaction was understandable: she was angry. And she was being naive. Pupils took off with their teachers every other day. If you believed the gutter press the older man wasn't always to blame. Condemning Frank Lennon was the easy way out. The evidence was circumstantial. I'd come up against Galbraith, a pompous individual unused to answering questions, anxious to avoid unwelcome publicity for his new college, heard insinuation from an obnoxious former colleague and had malicious tittle tattle reported to me. None of it proved anything except how strange people could be. I knew that already.

Alec Downey's description of the family dynamics put him in the role of junior partner. Having met his better half he hadn't lied. Moira was the disciplinarian he'd said. It was the two strong willed women who didn't get on. His insistence that the college had a responsibility was his wife's voice. If Patrick was right, the runaways were shagging their brains out in Mexico or Thailand. Any day now they'd show up in Glasgow as Mr and Mrs Lennon. Until then there was work to do.

Alison's bedroom might have been the scene of a burglary. Everything was everywhere. Clothes, magazines, make up scattered on top of more clothes and more magazines. It was a mess. Mrs Downey was embarrassed. 'The number of arguments we've had over this...' She was near to tears. 'If I clean it she'll be mad. And what does it matter... I just want her to come home.'

I said, 'I'm sorry.'

She pulled herself together and started on Lennon again.

'He was at the class night out. What possible interest could an adult have in that?'

This wasn't going anywhere, we had to move on.

'Could I see Alison's Blackberry and the most recent phone bill?'

'The Blackberry's in bits. I picked it off the pavement.'

'I'd still like to see it. Girls text all the time; there may be something.'

She opened a drawer and handed me the pieces.

'I'll dig out the last statement. I don't imagine it'll be any different from the rest.'

The Blackberry wasn't broken; it had come apart, and the battery still had power. I switched it on and scrolled through the daughter's contacts. Rose Devlin's number was there among scores of others. Frank Lennon's wasn't. Texts ran into the hundreds, most of them along the lines of "Hi, how are you? I'm fine." I sat on the bed and went through them. As an insight into a young mind it was revealing but unrewarding. Teenage drivel. Moira Downey came back with the bill. I held up the Blackberry. 'Can I take this with me?'

She seemed surprised. 'You've fixed it. Is it any use?'

'Without reading every message I can't be sure. Was anybody at the college close to Alison? Any lecturer she talked about apart from Lennon?'

'In her first year Alison struggled. She was shy. Going straight from school to college was a problem for her. She wanted to leave. I coaxed her into staying. One of the staff caught her crying and took her to the canteen for a cup of tea and a chat. Mrs Armstrong. Alison called her Angela.'

'Was that the only time they talked?'

'Oh no. Alison was in her class for economics.'

'So why didn't you get a hold of her when your daughter disappeared?'

'Mrs Armstrong left to have a baby and decided not to go back.'

Another dead end.

'Does Alison have a password?'

'Now you're asking. No idea.'

It didn't. The emails were even sillier than the texts. But buried under all the nonsense there could be some reference to the lecturer and their plans. I pointed to the laptop. 'Need this too.'

She said, 'Whatever you think.'

I left with the phone bill and the Blackberry in my pocket and the computer under my arm. It took hours to read the emails. Teenagers get a lot of criticism for being self absorbed, all of it deserved, believe me. By the end my brain was mush. Long misspelt conversations about absolutely nothing made me afraid for the future of the species. And not a single line about Frank Lennon. The texts were no better. Lennon must have warned the girl against even hinting at their intentions yet it was impossible to imagine a teenager hadn't confided in a friend. She would be bursting to tell. The secret was just too juicy to keep.

The Blackberry's casing was chipped where it had stuck the ground. In the directory was someone who knew where the runaways had gone. I pressed call and connected with the first person who didn't mind talking about Alison Downey.

Angela Armstrong was very different from Michael Corrigan. For a start she was sober.

We met on Sauchiehall Street outside the Willow Tearooms. She smiled, shook my hand and said 'What a lovely day.'

I hadn't noticed.

On the phone her instructions were specific.

'Book a table in the Room De Luxe. Near the window if possible.'

I'd been happy to oblige.

I had expected to meet an earth mother to a generation of confused students. The reality was very different: a slim redhead who gave me her complete attention and made me believe I was the only other person there. First Kate Calder, now Angela Armstrong. I seemed to be attracting redheads. Her eyes travelled round the room.

'Wonderful isn't it? Are you a fan of Mackintosh?'

'Not a fan exactly. The chairs are better to look at than sit on.'

'Miss Cranston, the original owner, gave Mackintosh responsibility for everything you see, right down to the cutlery. I come here all the time. Shall we order? What do you fancy?'

I could have told her. Instead I followed her lead and ordered carrot and orange soup and crusty bread. 'Do you miss teaching?'

'I miss the students not the college.'

'Too much bureaucracy?'

'One way of describing it.'

'On the phone I said I'd like to talk to you about Alison Downey.'

'Is she all right?'

'She's run away. Nobody knows where she is. Her parents have asked me to find her.'

She put a hand over her mouth. 'Oh no. Poor girl.'

'Your reaction tells me you haven't heard from her.'

'I haven't spoken to Alison since before I left. Must be seven months.'

'But she did talk to you at one time?'

The former lecturer was starting to see me in a new light. 'When you say the parents asked you, what do you mean?'

'I'm a private investigator. I find people who've gone missing.' I tried again. 'Alison Downey confided in you, didn't she?'

'In the beginning yes, when she started first year. Some of the kids don't cope. It's common. Attendance at school is a legal requirement to fifteen years of age. No choice. Colleges and universities aren't like that. If a student doesn't show, nobody sends out a search party. It's a crash course in the big wide world. Not everybody can handle the freedom.'

'Was Alison one of the ones who couldn't?'

She thought about her reply. 'At first, that was how I got to know her. Alison was a quiet girl. Emotional. Easily upset. I came along at the right moment for her.'

'And you became friends.'

'Well, I wouldn't say friends. She needed someone and I was there. When she made the transition she didn't need me anymore. Standard stuff.'

'She stopped speaking to you.'

'Right. It wasn't necessary. She had friends.'

'Rose Devlin's crowd?'

The waitress arrived before Mrs Armstrong could answer. I pressed for a response.

'Not the ideal pals?'

Her eyes flashed. 'You've met them I take it.'

'Not personally. I know about them.'

She changed the subject. 'That accent isn't from around here. English?'

'As a matter of fact no. The accent's English. I'm not. My family moved south when I was ten. They're still there. I came back.'

'"The blood leaps in your veins when you hear the bagpipe's strains," that the idea?'

'Wouldn't go that far. I like Glasgow so I live here.'

'How long have you been an investigator?'

'Too long.'

'So runaways are meat and drink? Have the Downeys contacted the police?'

'Alison's almost eighteen. She can leave home if she wants and nobody can stop her.'

'College wasn't her best choice. And you're spot on. Alison changed after she met Rose Devlin. Went from a shrinking violet to something quite different.'

'To what exactly?'

Angela refused to give it a name. 'It's the freedom thing again. One extreme to the other.'

'But you're not surprised?'

She didn't respond.

'Do you know Frank Lennon?'

'Frank. We shared the same staff room for four years. What about him?'

'He disappeared the same time Alison did.'

'And you think...' She put her spoon down, eating had lost its appeal.

I filled in the blanks. 'It looks as if they've gone together. From your experience of him do you think it's possible? Somebody suggested he might have a preference for young girls.'

She lifted her napkin and threw it on the table. 'Ridiculous. Frank's one of the good guys. Who would say such a thing?'

'Michael Corrigan.'

'Him?' She sneered her contempt. 'He's a reptile. Tried it on with every woman in the department. Don't listen to a word that comes out of his mouth. Frank Lennon is twice the man he'll ever be. Twice the lecturer too.'

'I was told he spent a lot of time on the Net.'

'Frank's a dreamer, always checking flights. Always planning a trip.'

'And always to Thailand. Ever wonder what the fascination was?'

Mrs Armstrong was a loyal friend.

'He loved it out there. Travelled all over the Far East. What you're insinuating isn't fair.'

'I'm sorry. Tell me about him.'

'Frank was one of the first people I met when I started at the college. He was sweet. And he's committed to the students. He really cares. More than most of them do.'

'All right, he's a great teacher, what else? I'm asking what you really know about Frank Lennon so I can make Alison's mother and father understand why he ran away with their teenage daughter.'

'I don't believe that's what's happened. Frank went his own way, sure, but him and Alison? It's crazy.'

The smiling woman I'd met on Sauchiehall Street wasn't in the room. Angela didn't approve of the turn our chat had taken. Redheads were supposed to have a temper: her eyes said the rumours were true. Conversation came to a halt in The Salon De Luxe. Charles Rennie Mackintosh had designed an elegant space where civilised people could have genteel discussions about the weather. This wasn't in the vision.

'I agreed to talk about a student and I resent what you're implying about a good man.'

I held up my hands. 'Please. Please. I'm not trying to blacken anybody's reputation but the facts are: a student and a lecturer have gone missing at the same time. Sources who know them say the man was hot for the girl. When you met Alison Downey she was timid and unhappy. Not how she stayed.'

I put the picture of the pouting blonde on the table and saw the shock on Angela Armstrong's face. What she was looking at was way beyond her memory.

'A colleague, admittedly one with an axe to grind against his former employer, claims he saw Lennon viewing inappropriate material and hints there was more to his obsession with Thailand than culture. According to you, Frank Lennon's a gentleman, a saint even. Alison went missing after a class night out. He was there. Isn't that unusual, Mrs Armstrong, a guy in his thirties hanging out with kids?'

She stared at the image of the young girl, morphed into Lolita.

'No. Not if you'd met Frank. Members of staff often have a drink with students.'

'Not Michael Corrigan.'

I thought she was going to hit me.

'Of course not. He's a lazy waste of space with a vicious tongue. The students hate his classes. T he people who have to work with him despise him. Don't quote him as an example. Frank's a lovely person. He's lonely. That's the worst anybody can say about him.'

She pushed the high-backed chair away and stood. 'And you should be ashamed. Poking around in people's lives. You're no better than Corrigan.'

That hurt.

Andrew Geddes hadn't been in NYB since the day we'd taken the first faltering steps to repair our friendship: Pamela's day. Messages left on his phone went unanswered. Of course his hands would be full with the Fenwick Moor case; not the reason he wasn't returning my calls. And there was no improvement in relations between me and Jackie. As far as she was concerned, speaking to Charlie Cameron was a last resort.

She was itching to push it. She didn't. Wise girl. The conversation with Alex ran in my head. I backed off too. Not the end of hostilities exactly, more an unspoken truce. Late in the afternoon Alison Downey's father called to ask how my enquiries were going. I told him progress was slow but I would keep trying. He rang off. The truth was I had nothing to report. I couldn't get started. My head just wasn't in this. I kept thinking about the Hamilton baby. The result, as Pat Logue would say, was nada. I hadn't seen Patrick in days. I missed him; life was quieter and less fun.

In Patworld "somethin's turned up" could mean anything from winning the lottery to intercepting knitwear on its way to Marks and Spencer. At ten to six I went downstairs. Jackie was at the bar. Her features hardened when she saw me. She moved towards me then changed her mind. I pretended not to notice; it didn't feel right. I liked her. On a good day we were friends. She was sharp and she made me laugh. At the moment none of that applied. Being between losers meant her mood was almost as unpredictable as my own. Except she had chocolate to fall back on.

We were far apart. But that was the way of it. Her eyes followed me until I was out of sight. I guessed we were both in for a difficult weekend.

The Evening Times presented Alan Sneddon as the granddaddy of Scottish rock – not entirely inaccurate – and urged anyone interested in hearing a local legend to get along to NYB on Sunday night. The quarter page advert helped grease the wheels. In Pop Gossip, Lloyd Kennedy announced that the North Wind tour of Australia and the Far East, scheduled for the following spring and finalised days before Paul Finnegan's demise, would go ahead.

And closer to home, Robbie Ward was in the middle of auditions for his own band, as yet un-named.

Fifty hours to the launch. I expected Alan to be upbeat. Not so. Downstairs I gatecrashed a wake. He was sitting on the edge of the stage with the rest of Big River. His expression didn't change when he saw me. I got an anxious smile from Kate Calder and that was it. Patrick had given a master class in faking it. I copied him, clapped my hands and forced lightness into my question. 'All set?'

Alan replied for the group. 'Too soon to know; too late to care, Charlie.'

'That a yes or a no?'

'It's a too soon to know, too late to care. We'll be here tomorrow and during the day on Sunday. If that isn't enough...'

This wasn't how it was supposed to be. Alan was the leader, the old hand. He was meant to inspire confidence. Kate was a beginner, talented sure, but a beginner nevertheless. She drew her faith from the been-there-done-that guy. Then I remembered. Nobody would be stealing Alan Sneddon away from Big River; that ship had sailed. He caught hold of himself.

'The guys have worked their socks off. We know the tunes. It needs a performance on the night.'

'It'll be there.'

He looked away. 'My phone hasn't stopped ringing. Everybody and their granny's promised to come. If half of them show up the place'll be rammed.'

'Even better. The crowd love Big River. Kate's your secret weapon. The icing on the cake.'

In the half-light I saw a man who had given his life to music, who defined himself by his ability, afraid in case he didn't have it any more. For all his swagger, behind the philosophical bullshit, it hadn't panned out for Alan Sneddon. And nobody knew it better than he did. Kate Calder and Big River was probably his last chance to shine.

'We've done the best we could in the time.'

I tried to be positive. 'It's only rock 'n' roll, right?'

He wasn't buying into that idea. He said, 'Not to me it isn't.'

When I left no one missed me.

It would've been easier to go home. That option never stood a chance. Before I reached the top of the stairs I knew where I was headed and, given my mood, not great to start with, lower still after the conversation with Alan, there really was only one place: the office, and the filing cabinet.

The case file Ronnie Simpson claimed belonged to me was beside the stuff on Pamela, collected over the years. Maybe he was right. I wished he wasn't.

I placed the folder on the desk, reluctant to confront what it held. Eventually I opened it and discovered the past waiting for me as I knew it would be. The photocopy of the original police report, discoloured and curled at the edges, lay on top. Reading its brisk impersonal prose reminded me of the frightened child I'd been that day. Pamela's picture, fixed to the inside page, stared at me, her face framed by blue sky. I was standing next to her when my father took the shot on a sunny street in the Algarve.

Our first trip abroad. Our only trip abroad.

She was holding my hand, squeezing it, whispering from the corner of her mouth, telling me to say cheese. The image had been cropped of course. I wasn't in it.

Underneath, the heading Forensic Examination of the Crime Scene promised but didn't deliver. Plenty about what had been tried, nothing about what had been found. Because nothing had been found. Next, a folded A4 with Witness Statements typed on the front and three single sheets inside. In terms of helping solve the crime it managed to be even less useful than the scant forensic evidence. My eyes ran over the statements not worthy of the name. The few people interviewed could attest to noticing a couple of kids playing on the sand and little else.

Half a dozen black and white 10 x 8s taken by a police photographer and a torn pencil sketch of the crime scene with distances listed at the bottom were last.

That was it. No wonder Ronnie's investigation had come up dry. The talking we'd done over the years, the re-tracing, the re-living. All in vain. This sorry excuse for a case file had gone with the DCI into retirement, like a stray dog that refused to be turned away, following him wherever he went.

I understood. Now and then someone would ask me why I did what I did. Looking for missing people and all the shit that came with it. Usually I gave some flippant answer and moved on. But here was the reason, faded and forgotten, tatty and tattered. As real as yesterday.

And it wasn't just about the girl in the photograph. She was gone. It was about me.

16

It started raining on Friday. Two days later it was still coming down. Cold rain, thin rain. Glasgow in October rain: relentless.

Bad nights had become the norm. After yet another one I drove to Ayr again and stood on the Esplanade, staring at the same deserted beach, trying to imagine Mark and Jennifer Hamilton playing happy families for the last time. From the beginning I'd struggled to believe Donna Morton had snatched their daughter; now I was even less convinced. The island of Arran was out there behind a wall of mist and, beyond it, Ireland. Of course there was nothing to see; not Arran, not Ireland, and certainly not anything that pointed to who had taken Lily. I hadn't expected there would be but that didn't save me from the blues and I returned to the city, depressed and irritable.

At night the queue outside NYB pressed against the building, under a dark canopy of umbrellas, round the corner into Cochrane Street as far as the traffic lights. The doorman recognised me and grinned. 'Full house on a filthy night. They better be worth it.'

He was trying to impress the girls at the front. I ignored him and glanced at the eager faces, waiting patiently for the doors to open.

'Can't see it without Robbie,' he said. 'Robbie Ward was Big River.'

If Alex or Jackie heard him this would be his last shift.

The freezing cave of the previous week was deserted apart from the DJ, headphones on, in his own universe. Whatever was coming through the cans had to be good. He didn't even know I was there. Des K was mid-twenties and stocky. His t-shirt asked Does My Head Look Bald In This? It did.

At a minute to eight there was still no sign of Alan or Kate Calder. The bar grill lifted, the music volume went through the ceiling, and space became a rare thing. Alex Gilby stood beside the girls serving drinks. He seemed unconcerned though he had to be worried about the threat to Sunday night business. I left. Nobody missed me. When I returned it was like descending into one of Dante's hellish circles. My eyes got used to the darkness. A crowd twenty deep gathered round the stage. For once the bar was empty. An occasional note, a tap on a drum; tiny sounds that told me the band was almost ready to start. I had a feeling in the pit of my stomach I could neither name nor explain. The atmosphere crackled and Des K milked it dry.

'Tomorrow Glasgow will be talking about tonight! Let's hear it for Kate Calder and Big River!'

The stage lights came on, Alan Sneddon counted them in, and the world exploded in front of me. Kate Calder shook her hair and danced with her white Telecaster. Over the sea of bobbing heads the leader aimed a tight smile at a crash cymbal. A long intro ended when Kate picked up the melody. Her voice snarled and seduced, teased and spat. She was doing what she was born to do. I didn't recognise the song, it wasn't important, but from the first note I realised this was the birth of a great group and a great star. I'd told Alan Sneddon it would be all right. That was talk. This was real.

One tune ended and another began, leaving the crowd exhausted and wanting more. The wooden floor carried the vibrations from the stage to my fingertips in wave after wave. At the end Alan Sneddon pushed through to where I was standing. Not the doomed Alan of Friday, this one smiled and shook my hand. 'You were right,' he said.

'Was I? About what?'

'About everything.'

'So you're satisfied?'

'Yeah. Yeah I am.'

'How long will it last, do you think?'

'Who can say, Charlie, who can say? Ask me another.'

'All right. How's Kate doing?'

'Too easy. Anybody here can answer that.'

'Is she around?'

He leaned closer. 'Is it my imagination or am I detecting an interest that has nothing to do with music?'

He didn't expect a reply and wasn't disappointed. I said, 'So is she?'

'She's in shock. The good kind. Trying to take it in. Her first gig, remember. At her age what isn't possible?'

He clapped me on the shoulder and went to the bar. A pint appeared in his hand by prior arrangement with the management. He sucked the top off, turned and waved. I was watching a happy man, surrounded by people anxious to talk to him. He made a what-can-you-do face and lapped it up.

Alan Sneddon hadn't been kidding. The next I saw Kate Calder was when Big River came out for the second set to a reception that was, if anything, bigger than the first. I stayed where I was. It felt good not to have my head bursting with crazy thoughts and ugly pictures. The band began where they'd left off and the energy coming from the stage never faltered. Need Your Love So Bad blew the roof away and me with it. I took a look at the crowd. I wasn't alone.

And that's when I saw him. Over in a corner, arms folded across his chest and an expression that gave nothing. The fact he was there said it for him. Robbie Ward. What was going through his mind? Kate Calder and Big River? If he was hearing what I was hearing he had to be sick. I felt a hand on my shoulder; it was Jackie.

'Got a visitor. Somebody needs to speak to you.'

'Is this a joke?' I'd forgotten we didn't do jokes anymore. 'Who is it?'

'In my office.' I followed her to the restaurant and the shoebox under the stairs. Jackie stopped. 'This could be trouble, Charlie. Got a bad feeling about it.' The nicest she'd been to me in ages.

The door swung open. Gail Logue sat in the only chair, staring at the walls. I'd known Gail for years and liked her. She was a strong woman. Had to be to cope with the man she married. Tonight the dam had burst. She'd been crying.

'Charlie. Sorry to drag you into this.'

Drag me into what?

'Don't worry about me. What's happened? Is Patrick all right?'

'I haven't seen him in three days.'

'He hasn't been home?'

Gail said, 'Not since Friday.'

'He told me he had things to do.'

'Patrick's always got things do, somewhere he has to be, somebody he has to see.'

I took her hand and led her to my office. Jackie shot a look in my direction. The last time I'd seen Gail and Pat everything in the garden had been rosy.

Gail turned down my offer of a drink and said, 'Patrick looks up to you. A million acquaintances and no friends, that's him. He was in a funny mood. I hoped he might've said somethin'.'

'I got the impression he wasn't doing well, assumed you'd had a row and he was taking it badly. He was hung over on Monday. What happened to his golden rule?'

'The golden rule got left behind last weekend. He fell in the door at two o'clock in the mornin'. And he was rough the next day. Couldn't hide it. No point in askin'.'

'But he came home?'

'Might as well not have bothered. He didn't eat, just sat in the chair starin' at the television sayin' nothin'.'

'Did he go out on Tuesday?'

'Tuesday and Wednesday and Thursday. Friday I heard the door slam and that was it. Not even cheerio.'

'And he hasn't called? Who else have you spoken to?'

She laughed a sad laugh. 'You really don't get it, Charlie. The people Patrick does business with are only interested in what he can do for them. They're not pals. Patrick doesn't do pals. He's a loner. Other couples go out for a meal and a drink. Not the Logues. We aren't close to anybody. You're it for Patrick.'

Hard to believe. 'I thought he was Mr Popular.'

'It's an act. Patrick doesn't share. Apart from me and you there isn't anybody.'

'Have you tried the hospitals?'

'He hasn't had an accident.'

'And you've no idea where he might've gone?'

'Patrick gets involved in some dodgy stuff. I keep tellin' him. You know what he's like.'

Indeed I did. "Dodgy stuff" could mean anything. I remembered the desperation when he asked for a job. The drinking had escalated around then. Now I was hearing the Golden Rule was history. Either the alcohol had spun out of control or he was in serious trouble. Patrick would have the world believe his problems were domestic. But maybe not all of them. Gail was ahead of me.

'I've known him twenty seven years. He was scared. So am I.'

Her hand tightened on my arm. 'Find him, Charlie. Please find him.'

'I will.'

I walked her to a taxi; she'd come for a promise and was leaving with one. A roar of applause followed us from the club. 'Somebody's enjoyin' themselves. Wish it was me.'

If her pig-headed husband had accepted my invitation it would've been. I said, 'New band. Going down well. When things are back to normal come and hear them.'

She smiled. 'That would be nice, Charlie.'

I phoned Pat Logue and got no reply. In the club, Big River had left the stage. The crowd clapped and stamped until Alan Sneddon led them back out. He waved and settled himself behind his kit. Kate didn't look at the audience. Her face shone; she was living a dream and didn't want to wake up. They played Chuck Berry, Sweet Little Sixteen, busked from beginning to end, sounding like they'd been together forever.

I scanned the room for Robbie Ward and saw a woman standing by the wall. Our eyes met. She drew hers away. The comfort of strangers. And I still couldn't remember her name.

It had to end eventually. The guys in Big River linked together and took a bow. Alan held Kate's arm in the air to more cheers. Glasgow had a new star. One final salute and it was over. Jackie was a step in front as usual. She kept the kitchen open so the group could get something to eat. She asked if I was staying. I said yes and squeezed between Kate and Alan at a table next to the Rock-Ola. The mood was high, unrecognisable from Friday. Everybody ordered pizza and red wine.

Alan said, 'Thanks, Charlie, I mean it. Thanks.'

'For what?'

'For listening to me moan. Encouraging me. Nobody believed it would fly without You Know Who.'

'You Know Who was here tonight.'

He grinned. 'Wonder what he made of Kate Calder and Big River.'

'Think he'll be asking for his old job back?'

'That guy can have a job anytime he wants. The gear gets heavier every year; an extra pair of hands would be appreciated. The money's shite though. Nearly as bad as what the band gets paid.'

'Don't think that would suit him.'

'Then he can piss right off. Seriously, was he in?'

'Yeah. Didn't stay though.'

He leaned across and included Kate in the conversation. 'Charlie's telling me about a guy who needs a break. Robbie somebody. Like to help the kid out but...'

Kate said, 'You make a bad enemy. Remind me never to fall out with you.'

He feigned injury. 'Me? I'm a pussycat, honest. Garlic bread, anybody?'

Alex put glasses and two bottles of Champagne in the middle of the table and opened one of them. This was a celebration.

'Don't expect this every gig,' he said. 'After tonight you buy your own.'

Later a question from Kate gave me the opportunity I was looking for. 'I suppose working above a restaurant means you never have to cook.'

'No. I cook. Not very often but sometimes.'

'Any good?'

'Have dinner with me and find out.'

My timing was perfect, everybody was on a high.

'All right. Call me.'

'I don't have your number.'

'Then I better call you.'

Liberated women. You had to love their style.

17

I shaded my eyes against the sun and studied the girl on the shore; laughing, kicking sea water as she danced in the ocean with a guitar slung round her neck. The tide lapped her ankles, she blew me a kiss and I ran towards her. I was close enough to see the smile in her eyes when a banging noise shattered the moment. Someone at the door. My brain began the slow climb through fragments of conversation and jumbled scenes. The hammering continued. My eyes opened. I was awake with the ceiling spinning miles above my head.

We finally quit NYB in the small hours and stumbled into the street. An image of Jackie shooshing us to keep the noise down and getting jeered for her trouble stayed with me. It hadn't taken much to push the guys in the band over the edge into party time. They had something to celebrate. So had I. My reason wore snakeskin boots. I had no recollection of getting home. Alcohol had erased my memory. Clothes lay in a trail from the lounge to the bedroom. I found my trousers, dragged them on and opened the door.

Pat Logue looked the way I felt; he might have spent the night in a field. His jacket was crushed and stained and his hair had gone punk. Thick stubble covered his jaw. The rest of his face was an unhealthy colour somewhere between grey and greyer. He looked like a wild man. He looked ill.

'Sorry, Charlie,' he said and lurched into the room.

'Patrick! What the hell...'

He collapsed on the couch. 'Don't ask. Just don't ask.'

I brought him a glass of water. He eyed it with contempt.

'Haven't got a beer, have you?'

'Where have you been? I tried to call you. Gail's worried sick. She came to see me last night.'

'Mouth's like the inside of a chauffeur's glove. Could murder a pint.'

'You said you needed a couple of days off. That was a week ago. What's going on, Patrick?'

He put his head in his hands. 'Long story, Charlie.'

Compared with the state he was in I wasn't doing too badly.

'I'll make coffee. We've got all day.'

'Rather have beer.'

'You'll take coffee and like it. Then you'll call your wife.'

In the end he got his beer. I settled for Alka Seltzer and a couple of Paracetamol.

'Right. I'm listening. And before this goes any further, tell me the truth or I'm throwing you out.'

He rolled the bottle on his palms. 'Christ I'm bad this mornin'. Head's splittin'. Feel sick.'

Sympathy wasn't on offer. 'The truth, Patrick. Don't mess me about.'

'I'm dyin', Charlie. Got cancer.'

Whatever I expected it wasn't that. I was stunned.

'When did you find out?'

'Eight days back. Found a lump.'

'Pat, I'm sorry.'

He tried a smile. 'Couldn't concentrate. Why I took time out. Propped up a few bars. Mostly I just walked about the city. Wanted to be by myself. Gail knew I wasn't right. I booked into the Lorne hotel on Friday and drank the mini-bar dry, then phoned room service and got them to top it up again. Guess how much for a miniature of vodka. Bloody extortion. Stuck it on the credit card. Debts die with you. It's in my name. Gail won't get landed with it.'

'You shouldn't have kept her in the dark. She showed up at NYB asking where you were.'

He looked contrite. 'What did you say?'

'Nothing. What happened?'

'The Lorne didn't pan. I complained about the prices and got turfed.'

'When was this?'

'Yesterday sometime.'

'And since then?'

'Been in the cells. A copper wakened me, gave me a lecture and kicked me out. Not even a fine. Another beer would be appreciated. Consider it an act of charity for a guy who won't be around much longer.'

I studied him. With Patrick you could never be certain. He was serious.

He said, 'If you gotta go...'

Patrick the philosopher.

'Let me get this straight. You discover you've got cancer, check into a hotel without a word to anybody, drink the place dry, cause a scene and get lifted for being drunk and incapable. And now you're here.'

'Nowhere else.'

I took two cold bottles from the fridge and handed them to him. Why not? He would get them eventually. 'What did the doctor say?'

'Didn't say anythin'. Haven't seen a doctor.'

'No doctor? So this is your own diagnosis?'

He tipped the beer to his lips and pulled on it. 'I know what I know, Charlie.'

Patrick might have something wrong with him or he might not. Without a proper medical examination and a shed full of tests it was morbid speculation. His disappearing act was fear driven. Pat Logue was scared. I changed the subject.

'Surprised the police didn't fine you on the spot.'

'First offence.' He caught my surprise. 'Never been charged.'

A proud record in Patworld.

'Really? Thought you got invited to the Pitt Street Christmas dance.'

'Questioned, never charged,' he said in his defence. 'One reason your pal Andrew is hot for me. He'll need to be quick.'

'Here's what we're doing. You have a shower. Spare razors in the cabinet. I'll rustle up breakfast. Something light; scrambled eggs and toast. You'll call Gail. She'll organise an appointment with your doctor. I'll even come with you. We'll find out one way or the other. If we have to go private we will. And no more drinking. That's all you're getting, okay?'

Patrick had been adrift for seven days. Now I was taking charge. Definite action, positive thought and, with the four bottles of beer inside him, he began to come round. I gave him space to speak to his wife – he wouldn't get a hard time there – then put him in a taxi.

I drank half a litre of water and went back to bed. Pat Logue had distracted me. Dealing with him made me forget about myself. I pulled the covers over my head and went in search of the beach.

When I got there it was deserted. The woman dancing with the guitar had gone. In her place was a boy, wide-eyed and breathless, running for his life.

The door opened and Patrick came through. He nodded to the receptionist. It had to be good news. I said, 'What did the doctor say?'

'Asked what was wrong with me. Stupid question. If I could answer that I'd be doin' his job, wouldn't I?'

'And?'

'It's nothin'. Wants me to go for a biopsy just to be sure, but he's confident. Lumps are common apparently, and most of them aren't malignant.'

'So you're all right.'

'I'm all right. Drop me at NYB for a quick one.'

It was ten minutes to five on a Monday afternoon. Anybody able to make a fast getaway from work was taking the opportunity.

Pat Logue watched the traffic, probably thanking whatever God he believed in. We were passing a newspaper seller on the corner of Glassford Street when he broke his silence.

'Let me get a paper, will you?' He was in and out in seconds, a man reborn. The Evening Times went into his pocket.

I parked in a space near George Square. 'By the way,' he said, 'appreciate what you did for me today, Charlie.'

'You're welcome. You'd spooked yourself. You were fine all along.'

'Thanks just the same.'

In NYB he slid on to his usual barstool. I went to find Jackie. She was in her cubbyhole under the stairs.

'Hi. Last night was great.'

'All part of the service. Everybody enjoyed themselves. Alan Sneddon asked me to marry him.'

'Tempted?'

'If he wasn't bald I might be. Wonder if he keeps his hat on in bed.'

'Only one way to find out.'

For a moment we were friends again, then she dropped the bomb.

'I've been offered a job.'

I hid my disappointment. 'Really? Who with?'

'The Meridian Group. Area Manager Glasgow North.'

'Are you taking it?'

'Said I'd let them know. Obviously it's a big decision.'

'Obviously.'

Jackie kept her eyes on the computer screen unwilling to meet mine.

'Does Alex know?'

'When I make a decision he'll be the first, Charlie.'

On my way out Pat Logue waved me over. The Evening Times was open on the bar. The story was captured in the headline SCHOOL'S OUT and a picture of Cathedral College. Patrick got it in one. 'Michael Corrigan.'

I scanned the text looking for a detail we didn't already have. The article lacked any sense of authority and I understood what had happened. Corrigan put my questions about Alison Downey and Frank Lennon together and uncovered a scandal. Even if it wasn't true it would damage Galbraith's new college. That was the point. How the people at the centre of the rumour – and it was still only a rumour – went on with their lives wasn't important. Corrigan had seen a chance to get revenge and taken it. He was quoted as a former colleague, claiming to have noticed the attraction and shocked at where it had led. The Principal refused to comment, which seemed to substantiate the piece.

Pat said it for both of us. 'Guy's a snake, Charlie. Can't do business with a reptile.'

'Except he didn't know about Alison and Lennon. I handed it to him on a plate. Corrigan's a malcontent on the lookout for dirt to throw and I gave him a bucketful. Client confidentiality went in the bin. The Downeys had a right to expect their daughter's reputation wouldn't be trashed. I fucked up, Patrick. Big time.'

He didn't disagree. A child could have guessed how it would play out. I was reckoned to be good at this game. Not on recent form.

My mobile rang. Alec Downey. He'd seen the newspaper and was calling to share his thoughts on how a private investigation should be conducted, no doubt with the emphasis on private. Clearly my methods weren't working. I'd found zero about where his daughter had gone and got her name in the papers for good measure. Sorry wouldn't cut it.

18

I couldn't escape them and didn't want to. This was the first time I'd seen the Downeys together; chalk and cheese with a common point of reference: they both wanted to string me up.

I thanked them for coming and gave them the apology they deserved. And I was right, it didn't cut it. Wasn't even close. Alison's father listened stone-faced then took his best shot.

'You're a disgrace, Cameron. You let us down. More important, you let Alison down. I hear what you say about Corrigan. That doesn't excuse you.'

His wife waited to unload. Her lip trembled.

'It's impossible to describe how I feel. Words don't seem adequate, but I want you to know you've ruined our daughter's life. What you've done has made it harder for Alison to put this mistake behind her and move on. When she comes home... if she comes home...'

'Mrs Downey...'

Her eyes flashed to the newspaper clipping and the post-its on the wall.

'And where's my Alison's picture? Doesn't she merit your attention? Isn't she good enough?'

'Mrs Downey I realise nothing I say...'

'Then say nothing. I agree with my husband. You're a disgrace. It's as much as I can do to stop from slapping your face. Someone should.'

Downey said, 'Your services are no longer required.'

The emphasis on services made it sound dirty.

'And I'm not expecting a bill.'

'Of course not. Again I apologise.'

And that was that. Case closed, at least as far as my involvement went. I'd been fired.

Jackie poked her head in.

'Another satisfied customer, am I right?'

'Never have anything else. Seen Pat Logue?'

'Not since Monday. Big River are rehearsing tomorrow. Thought you might want to know'

'Come to a decision yet?'

'Not yet. Got a few weeks to think about it.'

'I meant about taking on a bald drummer who'll insist on going out at night by himself.'

'Still pondering my options.'

'Tough call. Don't envy you.'

An invisible force reminded us we weren't pals. Jackie said, 'Gotta scoot.'

'Me too.'

That was a lie. I was officially unemployed. Mark Hamilton was out of my life, I was in the dark about progress in the Lily investigation, and Mr and Mrs Downey would be taking their business across the street.

Not exactly glory days for Charlie Cameron.

To top it all, no contact from Kate Calder. Sixty-eight hours. In my father's world when a politician got dismissed he was described as "spending more time with his family." What was left of my family lived in England. Being unable to join them was a comfort in itself. There are things worse than disgrace and humiliation. Five minutes with George Archibald Cameron and his band of sycophants, for example.

Jackie was considering her options; maybe I should do the same. Time to let it all go? The phone rang. I picked up expecting to hear Kate Calder invite me to dinner. The voice at the other end was short on patience, as if he was calling against his will. Andrew Geddes didn't waste words. He said, 'We need to talk.'

'When?'

'Not today, I'm out of town. Tomorrow. Noon. Your office.'

The line went dead. My guess was he'd spoken to Alec Downey and fancied kicking a man when he was down. Definitely time for a rethink. Big River were rehearsing downstairs this afternoon. I decided to play it cool and stay away. She was supposed to call me. Or was that emancipated female malarkey just for show?

Cool works better in the movies. When music started to filter from the club I couldn't help myself. Big River were working on a harmony, singing the same line over and over. It sounded all right to me. They kept at it. After fourteen attempts even I could hear the difference. Kate saw me and waved. They took a break and she came over.

'Sorry I haven't called. Didn't realise how much the last couple of weeks had taken out of me. Been in bed most of the time.'

I leered on cue.

'Alone,' she said. 'I'm fine now. What about tomorrow night?'

'Where do you want to go?'

'You decide.'

'Meet here at eight and we'll take it from there.'

Sometimes changing your life is just the easiest thing.

DS Geddes fell into the chair on the other side of the desk and ran a hand through his hair. Heavy eyes and puffy skin told me he was exhausted; the Fenwick Moor murder was taking its toll. I got my shot in first.

'Corrigan's a twisted guy who took advantage of the situation to get his own back.'

He gave me a strange look. 'If you say so, Charlie. Who're we talking about?'

'Michael Corrigan. Cathedral College. Hasn't Alec Downey been in touch?'

'Not since I sent him to you.'

'So what's going on?'

'Tell me about this Corrigan character.'

When I finished the story and the scene with Alison's parents he held up a hand.

'All right. I've got it. Some misfit blabbed a half-baked rumour to the press. Happens. Don't beat yourself to death over it. The mother and father have their own idea who their daughter is. A long way different from what you found. They sacked you and it hurts. My advice. Forget it.'

'That isn't why you're here?'

'You're losing it, Charlie.'

He pinched the corners of his eyes.

'Double shifts all week.'

I got the impression he'd planned what to say.

'I was rough on you with Hamilton. Didn't take a big brain to figure you were getting involved.'

'I wasn't. Not with the police case.'

'Yeah you were. I warned you to steer clear, remember? Thought I'd gone all CID, didn't you? There was more than one reason.'

'You believed I'd crossed the line.'

Andrew shook his head. 'You're always crossing the line, Charlie. Christ knows I've helped you over it more often than I'd like to admit. No, I was worried. You were playing with fire and couldn't see it. More, you had a lead in a serious crime and kept it quiet.'

'So what's changed?'

'What do the names Amanda Kelly, Rebecca Patterson, Eva Reynolds, Adele Knowles and Charlene Walker mean to you?'

'Nothing.'

'Kids abducted in the past five years. In every case the adult with them was yards away.'

He watched for my reaction.

'Why haven't I heard of them?'

'You have but because of the time between each one, the distances involved and the complete lack of evidence, nobody put them together. Usually the press are mustard but they missed it too. Fenwick changed that. The police realised the possible connection and formed a task force. Operation Damocles has been going a week. Police Scotland officers from Strathclyde, Lothian and Borders. Our colleagues in England have a number of unsolveds that fit the MO. Christ knows where it'll end.'

'So you're with the task force.'

'Seconded. Been in St Andrews since Tuesday. A developer lifted the floorboards of a derelict property and discovered a body. We think it's Charlene Walker. She was snatched in Dundee Tesco three years back. Mother was on her mobile with the baby in the trolley.'

Andrew let what he saying sink was in.

'Fenwick's been identified as Eva Reynolds, taken from a mother and toddler group in Clarkston.'

'Sexual motive?'

'We don't think so.'

'Is Lily a victim?' He heard the edge in my voice.

'Your guess is as good as mine. The MO fits. Ayr beach was daring. Lily's parents want to believe their child is still alive.'

'But you don't?'

His silence answered for him.

'I thought you suspected Mark Hamilton?'

'Right and wrong. The abduction was days old. Everybody was under the microscope. When I found you'd kept Hamilton's hunch about his girlfriend quiet I realised you were in danger of compromising the police investigation. I lost it. Can't say I feel much different, but if we find Lily's body don't blame yourself. We're dealing with a psycho. Donna Morton's been ruled out. What you held back wasn't relevant.'

'Did you trace her?'

'Disappeared off the face of the earth.'

So I hadn't failed.

'Where do you fit?'

'I was already on the Moor case so I'll be in the Glasgow office. We're starting again on the Hamilton abduction.'

'You'll be re-interviewing the parents and witnesses.'

'Not looking forward to it. I'm told Jennifer Hamilton isn't doing well. Still in hospital.'

'Sad.'

He got up to go. 'Very. They've separated. She's divorcing him.'

'He was afraid of that.'

'Serves him right.'

Compassion wasn't DS Geddes' strong suit. It annoyed me.

'Nobody's perfect, Andrew.'

My sarcasm bounced off.

'Not asking for perfect. Just don't cheat on your wife, dump your girlfriend and expect to come up smelling of roses. Crime and punishment. Cause and effect.'

He drew a righteous breath. 'Not all the rules are written down but they're there nevertheless.'

Andrew was off on one.

I said, 'Sorry we didn't get a better result for the Downeys. Something about it doesn't feel right. They won't be back to you for a recommendation in a hurry.'

'Can't win them all, Charlie. Don't let it get to you.' He narrowed his eyes and inspected me. 'You aren't, are you?'

I lied. 'No.'

'Only that wall tells a different story.'

He let me off the hook. 'Heard the new band's worth a listen.'

'Yeah, they're good.'

At the door he stopped and nodded at the wall. 'Seriously, Charlie, back off. We'll get this maniac. However long it takes, we'll get him.'

Andrew sounded confident. I didn't believe what he was saying. Neither did he.

I wasn't meeting Kate until eight o'clock. Somebody in Donna Morton's old building knew something. Had to. I walked up to the second floor with my footsteps echoing in the deserted stairwell, hearing nothing, meeting nobody. The flat was as empty as it had been the last time I was here and for a moment, my belief faltered. Stupidly, I knocked and peered through the letterbox – not exactly a high-tech strategy. After that I tried the flat opposite and the two on the third floor. No luck. That left the landlord on the first and the one opposite; if neither of them was home my optimistic chat would turn out to be just that.

On my way down I finally got the break every case needs; in Donna's old place a telephone rang. Someone was calling. Calling her? Why was the line connected in an unoccupied house? And closer to home: the memory of Pat Logue coming back to NYB at the double claiming the landlord was reluctant to answer questions. At the very least he should have persuaded the owner to let him inside. Except the usually reliable Mr Logue hadn't pushed it.

Because it had been all about the money that day. An earner. To him, just another case.

I pressed the landlord's buzzer and waited. Noises from inside told me someone was coming. Good, I had my story ready. Donna was my sister, wasn't she? The family hadn't heard from her in months. Our mother was ill, worried sick. The stuff Pat Logue should've tried. I wouldn't be leaving until I'd satisfied myself, once and for all, that Mark Hamilton's former lover had covered her tracks.

As for my oppo, Patrick had dropped the ball.

19

The moment my eyes opened in the morning I thought of Kate. I needed to relax; dinner with a beautiful woman was the perfect opportunity and I was determined to enjoy it.

In the bathroom, the guy in the mirror reminded me of somebody I used to bump into now and then, although he looked better than I felt; brown hair, blue eyes and no obvious flaws.

To the untrained eye.

Once I'd showered and shaved I did some forward planning on what to wear, deciding eventually on an understated, this-is-the-real-me look; black Paul Smith suit and white open-necked shirt. Lately life had become unpredictable. Running around at the last minute wasn't in the plan. A bath, a drink and a leisurely hour spent pulling my image together and getting in the mood, was.

It didn't happen. Any of it.

Donna Morton's landlord had believed my sob story and let me into the flat on the second floor where Mark Hamilton made a promise to his lover he never intended to keep.

'Doing the place up,' the landlord said, and turned the key in the door. 'Needed it. Getting run down.'

I saw what he meant. Houses don't benefit from being empty. This one was as empty as it was possible to be. Every stick of furniture removed and replaced by dust sheets and a ten litre tin of Dulux Orchid White, side by side on faded newspapers stuck in patches to bare floorboards. A wall with a fireplace in the centre was already painted and a start had been made on another. A pair of stepladders hid behind a door. The landlord offered an explanation.

'A while since it was decorated. Doing it myself. The original features are a selling point. Keeping them.'

He studied my face, having second thoughts about opening the flat to me, perhaps.

'Your sister you say? Can't see much of a family resemblance.'

'Half-sister. Our mother re-married.'

I moved the conversation away from my charade. 'Did Donna mention why she was leaving?'

He shrugged. 'She was a quiet girl, a good tenant. Wish there were more like her. I asked about a new address in case there were letters. Told me she'd taken care of everything. Got the impression she wasn't very happy.'

He had that right.

'Bit of a shock when the police came round. They haven't found her then?'

I left his question unanswered. 'Mind if I look around?'

'Suit yourself.'

Apart from the room we were in there wasn't much else to see. What there was had been cleared – a small kitchen, a smaller bathroom, and a single bedroom pretending to be a double. Donna hadn't taken up much space on the planet. I poked around, with the owner hovering in the background.

'Haven't had anybody else in here, have you?'

'Could've had. Didn't like the look of them. I won't have students, not at any price, more trouble than they're worth.'

'So why is the phone still connected?'

He shrugged again. I guessed shrugging was his thing.

'Expected to have a tenant months ago. Been kicking myself. No point now. Work'll be finished in a couple of weeks, then I'll advertise the place. A wee gem like this will go fast.'

I admired his vision and checked the ansaphone. Mystery solved, the only message was from the call ten minutes ago; Donna's dentist reminding her her annual check-up was due. So he knew even less than me.

The landlord glanced at his watch and coughed to get my attention. 'Look,' he said, 'how long are you going to be? I've somewhere I need to go.'

He wasn't the only one.

'A couple of minutes. In a rush myself.'

It was under the sink, next to the rubbish bin. A cardboard box filled with sheets of paper; bank and credit card statements; the kind of stuff everybody means to go through, holds on to, then shreds and throws away without checking. The police who searched here had been as thorough as Patrick. On Donna Morton's final day in the flat she must have been low; disappointed, leaving with nothing. Maybe she just couldn't find the energy to get rid of them.

The landlord showed me to the door. 'She was a nice woman, your sister. Was sorry to lose her. Tell her that.'

'Thanks, I will.'

I arrived at NYB at a quarter to eight, went straight upstairs to the office and tipped the contents of the box onto the desk. The odds against discovering anything were high but false hope was better than no hope. Buried in the pile was the last telephone bill Donna received. Ten calls to three numbers, all local. Small world indeed. One number appeared eight times, I tried it and connected to a high-pitched oriental male. 'Great Wall. How can I help you?' Like me, Hamilton's girlfriend had discovered that cooking for one wasn't much fun; it was a Chinese take-away.

There was no answer from the second number; a recorded message informed me I was through to a city centre hairdressers. The third was different. A woman's voice, thick with alcohol, slurred down the line. 'Yeah? Hello. Who is it? Who is this?'

Lucy Morton. Drunk as a skunk.

Kate was at the bar, talking to Jackie, and smiled when she saw me. I got my apology in early. 'Sorry, one of those days. Haven't even been home to change.'

'You look fine.'

Fine wasn't what I'd been aiming for. Paul Smith would have to keep for another day.

Our booking was for nine o'clock. Still plenty of time to get to know each other. We walked along St Vincent Street to All Bar One and sat by the window, across the road from the Drum and Monkey, where Alison Downey was last seen at the class night out. Unresolved cases gnawed at my brain, demanding attention. Tonight I refused to let them in. We ordered white wine. I pictured Kate when we met at NYB. The contrast to the girl in the band was startling; unrecognisable from the rock chick. In her place a sophisticated lady in a dark blue dress, tiny earrings and high heels. Her hair up.

I said, 'You look wonderful.'

'Think I'd still be wearing the boots?'

That would've been fine by me. I loved the boots.

We went through the Wonder of Me stage, prepared to confess to anything, no matter how attractive it made us seem. She asked how I came to live in Glasgow and I told her, sounding like a rebel who had shunned a comfortable life in the Home Counties. Of course it was bullshit. Then as now I'd suited myself. Thanks to my grandmother, digging ditches was never going to be an option. How I became a private investigator was harder to explain. Maybe there would be a time but this wasn't it.

Kate's background was very different; originally from Islay, two brothers and two sisters older than her. The way she spoke about them said they were close. We swapped funny accent stories and ordered another round. She said, 'You haven't told me much about your family. Any brothers or sisters?'

'No. None.'

My turn: 'So where did the music come in?'

'My mother played piano in church. Any talent is from her. We moved to the mainland when I was a teenager and later to Glasgow. An aunt gave me a guitar as a birthday present. I messed around and managed to find a tune. One night I heard a group at the Arches. The guitar player was amazing. Suddenly I knew what I wanted.'

'You were very comfortable on Sunday considering it was your first real gig.'

'I was petrified. Alan's a perfectionist. Won't let anything go. Those rehearsals were really hard. In the end it paid off. We got through it.'

'More than that, it was a triumph. For Alan especially.'

'Now I know him he isn't as laid-back as he appears. Can't have been easy seeing other people succeed while you stayed behind.'

'He better get used to it. It's going to happen again.'

'You reckon? I'm not ready yet. Not nearly ready.'

'Maybe, but it isn't far away.'

She wasn't at ease with that. She said, 'Let's talk about something else. You must get a lot of women running after you.'

'Is that a statement?'

'So you do?'

I didn't answer.

Kate said, 'I'll take that as a yes then.'

'And I suppose with your guitar...'

Kate laughed. I liked the sound of it. 'What would I do with so much attention?'

'Suck it up through a big straw.'

'Jackie doesn't like me. Caught her glaring at me when we were leaving.'

'You're wrong, it's me she doesn't like.'

'How come?'

I shook my head. 'Life's too short.'

The Ubiquitous Chip in Ashton Lane had been around for as long as I could remember. Bars and curry houses opened and closed, the Chip kept going strong. The food was good although the next day I couldn't remember what we had eaten. Near the end of the meal Kate said a strange thing.

'I feel sorry for Robbie Ward.'

'Why?'

'Couldn't have been nice on Sunday night listening to the band you left tearing it up.'

'No, it probably wasn't. Robbie got carried away with himself. He forgot it was a two-way street. Big River needed him and he needed Big River. He was the guy who called time, not Alan Sneddon. Serves him right.'

It might have been Andrew Geddes speaking.

'Still.'

I dropped her at her door. She didn't invite me in.

She said, 'That was great, Charlie. Thanks.'

'Shall we do it again?'

'When?'

'I was thinking about Friday.'

'That's tomorrow, or rather today.'

'Is it? Doesn't time fly.'

Friday night was, if anything, even better than Thursday. Candleriggs was buzzing. Drinks in Blackfriars, take-away suppers from Gandolfi Fish and a walk along the Clyde. Heading out of October it was probably cold; we didn't notice. On her doorstep we kissed but no invitation to come in. Kate was taking it slowly.

The sun was shining when I arrived at New York Blue next morning. For years I'd had breakfast on Saturday with Andrew Geddes, a habit that began when he was a fresh-faced constable, one of NYB's first customers. I'd noticed him dunking his bagel, ignoring the flaky bits floating on the surface that put everybody else off. We became friends.

It was him who got me my first case, a runaway daughter not unlike Alison Downey. I found the girl. From then on, whenever something came his way that wasn't official police business he gave my name. Today he wasn't around. Operation Damocles? Pat Logue was, he seemed subdued. We didn't discuss his recent brush with death but it seemed to have affected him. The pint of soda and lime in front of him told the story.

'Anything cooking, Charlie?'

I shook my head. 'Sorry, Pat.'

A phone call was all it took to make a liar out of me. The voice at the other end of the line was gruff and unfamiliar. I'd only met him once, a man of few words, most of them negative.

'He's got a visitor. She's here now. Can't understand her.'

'Thanks for letting me know.'

His response was the Walter I remembered. 'Thanks doesn't rattle in my pocket,' he said and hung up. I forgot the Downeys and their low opinion of my abilities and went to tell Patrick the good news. Something was cooking after all.

Walter was on the pavement at Lancefield Quay, still wearing the cardigan and house shoes. He could smell money and was determined not to let it slip through his tobacco stained mits. I parked and we got out. Pat Logue and Walter hadn't met. Patrick said, 'What's the story with granddad?' I told him. 'And he reckons he's on an earner?'

'He is.'

The caretaker watched us cross the road. When we got to him he wasted no time.

'Showed up this morning out of the blue. Put her in the flat. She can't stay. Residents wouldn't like it'

'Any idea where she's been?'

Walter stayed in character. 'Nope.'

'Did she say where Lennon is?'

'Keeps askin' for him.'

He dragged his feet on the floor; we followed. At the door he stopped. It was payday. I stuck another twenty in his hand. He looked at it, unimpressed.

'That it?'

Patrick jumped in. 'You're doin' all right for a phone call. Don't kick the arse out of it.'

Walter wasn't used to blunt, unless it came from him. He gave a dissatisfied snort and let us in. A girl sat on the couch, coat buttoned to the chin, her feet barely touching the floor. It wasn't Alison Downey. I guessed she wasn't more than five feet tall.

Sallow skin, heart shaped face, a button nose, miniature ears and mouth, and almond eyes wild with confusion. She stood. Five feet was way off. She was tiny; a frightened child-woman, looking up at me close to tears. A stranger in a strange land.

'Where Frank? He told me come. Where Frank?'

Frank with an l.

Corrigan had said Lennon was always on the Net, put two and two together and came up with five. Porn. No surprise with a mind like his. Angela Armstrong was a good woman. She had defended her colleague and described him as a dreamer. They were both wrong. Not porn or dreams. Loneliness.

The girl pointed to a suitcase. A Thai Air tag hung on the handle.

'Mai Ling here,' she said. 'Where Frank?'

I got there first. 'Patrick, say hello to the future Mrs Lennon.'

20

Aberdeen, 149 miles from Glasgow.

Of course they would argue. That thought brought a smile. She didn't expect to win any popularity contests during the terrible teens. Adults were the enemy while teenagers were testing their wings. It made her cringe to remember the rows she'd had with her own mother. Every weekend when she was fourteen or fifteen. Most families survived and so would they. Her mother was in a home now. Alzheimer's. No point taking the baby to visit; she was a stranger, sitting in a chair staring into space. At first it hurt to lose someone more each day but now she accepted she didn't have a mother. People came to terms with things. Eventually.

There was one thing she'd insist on. Education. Homework first, television second. Good qualifications opened doors; the circles you mixed in and the salary you made depended on it. Her only real regret was she hadn't understood the value of learning. "Your daughter is a bright girl but refuses to pay attention in class" her school reports said. All true and unfortunately that never changed. She stayed the girl who didn't pay attention and missed the signs.

The signs were there with him. As usual she didn't recognise them. He wasn't in love with her, never had been. The look on his face when she threatened to kill him. Priceless. She didn't mean it. Anger made her say it. Whatever they'd had was broken and couldn't be mended.

But it was fun now, just the two of them. Making plans. Dreaming dreams. Except it wasn't a life and never would be.

They couldn't hide forever. At some point they needed to re-join the world. Stop running. She pored over possibilities, created all sorts of elaborate fantasies – her sister and her husband died in a car crash and she was looking after their child; for a while that was her favourite. Only it wouldn't stand up.

Kids got sick.

The last week had been difficult. It started with a cough and a temperature; nothing really. Then, in the middle of the night, Adele vomited over the cot covers. She cried of course. Young children can't tell you what's wrong with them so they howl the place down. Her mother had told her never to take a chance with children; if they were unwell, don't hesitate, call a doctor. She couldn't do that. There was too much to explain. For a couple of days it hadn't looked good. The coughing got worse. It became a rasp and her little face was on fire. A nightmare dilemma. She dosed her with junior aspirin and rubbed her chest. Then, as quickly as it started, the fever broke. Everything was all right.

Except it wasn't. What about the future? No child goes through life without some brush with illness. Measles, whooping cough, cuts and colds. The answer was obvious: register with another practice and lie. Use the story about taking care of her dead sister's child. Then there would be birth certificates and who knew what else needed. This wasn't the time. Doctors would have been alerted to look for a new registration. Christ, it was complicated. What made life worth living had to be protected. She'd risked so much. She couldn't let it slip away.

Adele was sleeping. She should sleep too. Being a mother was exhausting. Men didn't realise just how exhausting. Yet she wouldn't have it any other way. And of course there were problems. It was her responsibility to sort them. To make them disappear.

That's what mothers did.

21

Walter followed the three of us off the premises. Patrick carried the suitcase. The caretaker had met his match and knew it. He kept his disapproval to himself. Our departure and my cash in his pocket made him bold and brought out the jobsworth in him. With the door closing behind us he went for a final stab at mean. 'Don't bring her back.'

'Let me guess,' I said, 'the residents wouldn't like it.'

Jackie was at the bar in NYB. I waved her over. She gave my oriental companion a long look and was about to make one of her pithy comments. A quote Pat Logue had used on me stopped her in her tracks. I said, '"Judge not that ye be not judged," Jackie. And organise something to eat for this girl, would you?'

She did better. She took Mai Ling with her. Patrick watched them go.

'Well well,' he said. 'Lennon can't get enough, can he? Who would've guessed?'

I didn't reply. 'Give Jackie time to sort Mai Ling and meet me in the office.'

Pat Logue and Walter were cast from the same mould except one was a good guy, the other an awkward old bastard. Both had an eye on the money.

Patrick said, 'So we're on the clock?'

'When are you not on the clock, Patrick? See you in fifteen minutes.'

Pat Logue was street wise. He didn't miss much but this time he had. Mai Ling's china doll perfectness had distracted him. The wider implications hadn't occurred. I wasn't so fortunate. Miss Saigon put a bomb under every theory I'd had. What was left wasn't pretty.

Jackie worked her magic. The Thai girl was calm. I tried to imagine how difficult it must be for her, alone, thousands of miles from home. I smiled to show I was on her side. 'Feeling better?' She nodded. Jackie sat beside her and held her hand.

She said, 'Mai Ling is very sad, Charlie. She doesn't understand what's happened.'

Mai Ling spoke, words tumbling out, fractured and twisted.

'Frank sent ticket, say to come. Meet at airport. No Frank there.'

'How did you know where Frank lived?'

She opened a purse and handed me a sheet of stationary from the Shangri-La hotel, Bangkok. Under the logo printed in blue ink was the Lancefield Quay address.

'When did you meet him?'

She held up four tiny digits.

'And when did you last see him?'

Two fingers, smaller than my pinkie.

'Are you and Frank going to be married?'

A smile creased her flawless face. 'Frank ask me. I say yes.'

'Email?'

'Email yes.'

I reassured Mai Ling everything would be fine and let Jackie take her downstairs so Patrick and I could talk. When they'd gone I said, 'What do you think?'

Pat had no doubts. 'Straightforward, Charlie. Corrigan deserves more credit than we gave him. All those trips to the Far East. Couldn't be about anythin' else, could it?'

He sighed. 'The wee head doin' the thinkin' for the big head. Classic case.'

'How come she has his address?'

'Maybe he was drunk and got carried away when he was mailing her.'

'Sends her a ticket when he's out of his face? Doesn't work for me. Lennon invited her. That's why she's here. He'd had the flat painted and bought a new bed. He was expecting her.'

'Then what was he doing messin' about? Not just messin'.'

'We don't know he was. That came from Rose Devlin and Michael Corrigan. Angela Armstrong was offended by the idea.'

Patrick stuck to his guns. 'They took off at the same time. How old do you reckon Thai Mai is? Sixteen? Seventeen? He likes them young. We've never met him. Guy could be a sex addict.'

'What if he didn't run away with Alison Downey? Where's the evidence? Evidence, not rumour and gossip.'

'He packed his job in.'

'No, he stopped going to work. Not the same thing.'

Pat Logue wasn't persuaded. 'Lust is an awesome force, Charlie. Believe me. Makes men do strange things.'

'Get involved with a teenage student when you're expecting a princess to show up any day? That's not lust, that's insanity. The worst we've heard about Lennon is he had the hots for a female student. Half the male lecturers – some of the female ones as well – must be in the same boat.'

'So you're saying what?'

'It isn't how it looks. We're missing something. Something obvious.'

'I'll go back to the college?'

I remembered Mark Hamilton. 'No. Not before I speak to Andrew, hear what he has to say. My gut tells me this is a police job.'

Patrick saw his gig slipping away, he couldn't hide his disappointment.

'And in the meantime?'

'Check out the gyms near Donna Morton's old flat.'

'Christ, do you ever let go, Charlie?'

'Not unless I'm forced too. Cover the take-away and the hairdressers as well. When women find somebody to cut their hair the way they want they keep going back. The call was a year ago so you're looking for appointments since then. New address, new phone number. Anything will be a result. And Patrick, do a good job.'

'Never do anything else.'

'Not true. Your eye's been off the ball recently.'

'What you on about?'

'Donna's flat. Didn't get inside, did you?'

'The landlord wasn't having it.'

'Since when did that stop you?'

To his credit he agreed.

'Fair play, maybe I could've tried harder, it won't happen again.'

'Just pay attention, will you? This is important. Oh and tell Gail I need a favour. Somewhere for Mai Ling to stay. Just for a few days.'

'I'll ask. Not sure about the answer. Be prepared for a knock back. Gail's got a heart of gold but...'

'No sweat. If she can't help I'll think of something else.'

He got up. 'Not getting very far these days, are we, Charlie? Cases last five minutes then hit a wall.'

'Just the way it is. Taking on Hamilton was a mistake. Andrew should know about Miss Saigon.'

Patrick called in an hour.

'Tried two gyms. Membership records go back three years. Nada on Donna Morton. On the other thing, Gail's up for it. She'll look after Mai Ling. Put her in a taxi and she'll be waiting at the other end. Says she owes you one.'

Thanks Gail.

DS Geddes was a hard man to track down. He didn't answer his mobile and he wasn't in NYB. When I finally reached him he was irritable and distracted. Working with the task force must be a grind. There was no preamble, no small talk. His voice was hoarse; late nights, cigarettes and interviews that went nowhere. He didn't intend to take it out on me. I was just there.

'Only got a minute. What do you want, Charlie?'

'Development with the Downey girl.'

'Yeah, what?' I told him about Frank Lennon's visitor. I'd caught him at a bad time; he wasn't interested.

'And why do I care about this?'

I tried to explain. 'Alec Downey hired me to find his missing daughter.'

Andrew interrupted. 'And fired you, I remember.'

'Looked like she'd run away with one of her lecturers and they were screwing themselves silly somewhere. Half expected them to turn up as Mr and Mrs. This Thai girl blows that idea out of the water. Lennon redecorated his flat, bought a new bed...'

'What are you telling me?'

'Mai Ling says he asked her to marry him and sent her the plane ticket. Can't believe he forgot and pissed off with his student, which means something happened.'

Frustration bubbled to the surface.

'I'm not getting this. Who the fuck is Mai Ling?'

'The girl who arrived this morning.'

Silence at the other end of the phone. I could hear Andrew breathing. Counting to ten maybe. 'Listen, Charlie, the country's overrun with foreign women. Poland, Latvia, from everywhere. Point her in the direction of her embassy and go on with your life.'

'It's suspicious, Andrew.'

'Is there evidence to support that?'

'Not evidence exactly.'

He sighed and fought down exasperation.

'Evidence, Charlie, it's all about evidence. A decomposing body would help. Haven't got one handy have you?'

'Decomposing no. Got a live one from the other side of the world. Almond eyes and tiny feet.'

'No use.'

'I believe her. Lennon must've thought he'd hit the jackpot. She's very beautiful.'

DS Geddes exploded. 'Then you fucking marry her!'

The phone went dead.

Andrew's angry voice rang in my ears. Apart from that the office was quiet. I let the silence wash over me and tried to think. I hadn't had much success with that recently. Geddes' reaction was understandable; his head was full of missing kids and an ex-wife.

Pat Logue said the cases lasted five minutes then hit a wall. He was right and at least some of it was down to me. Tomorrow it would be four weeks since Lily was taken from Ayr beach. Andrew hadn't come right out with it but, reading between the lines, the police were treating Lily as the killer's latest victim. The information I'd kept back wasn't considered important anymore and, with all their resources, they hadn't located Donna Morton. I was off the hook. That's not how it felt.

The Downeys were different. They spent their days casting around for someone to blame. My handling of Michael Corrigan in Sloans made that easy. Moira, the mother, was keen to attack the college, but her daughter changed from a girl to a sexually aware young woman in front of her and she didn't see it. Even when Alison admitted using contraception her parents clung to the image of a sweet girl.

From the start the student/lecturer scenario bothered me. Too many people selling it and not just Rose Devlin and Michael Corrigan. The obstructive attitude of the college fed the rumours. Galbraith's ivory tower took a knock with the Evening Times front page headline. Couldn't happen to a better guy. Not my problem.

It was harder to convince myself Mai Ling fell into that category. Her husband-to-be had disappeared. Nobody was looking for him. Lennon was a forgotten man and Mai Ling was the only one who cared. Thanks to Walter she had landed in my lap. Gail would take care of her. The question was what was I going to do? It didn't take a big brain to put it together.

Whenever a stranger short on hope came to me I told them to begin at the beginning. Good advice. The beginning in this case meant Cathedral College. If you believed the ad in Yellow Pages I was a private investigator. Usually I got paid for my efforts though not always. Once in a while I worked because somebody was lost and somebody wanted them found. Like Frank Lennon and Mai Ling. I'd said it to Mark Hamilton; now I was telling myself: Time to do the right thing. I had a new client.

22

Kate didn't tell me her plans for Saturday and I didn't ask. Early days to be giving up your independence. Was another man in the picture? If not, Glasgow guys must be losing it. I saw her on Sunday, rocking the roof off with the band. She smiled and I smiled back. One of those across-a-crowded-room things that happen in musicals At the end she left without a word. We'd had exactly two dates and one kiss. I lay awake most of the night. Not the best preparation for what I had to do. In the morning I was exhausted and depressed, though not as depressed as Patrick Logue. His timing was usually spot on. He'd have a coffee, pick his horsey selection, go to a bookmaker in Glassford Street and be back minutes before Jackie rang the bell that meant the bar was open. Not today. He ordered a cappuccino and let it go cold in front of him. The newspapers lay unopened. I walked over and sat down.

'Any luck at the hairdressers?'

He handed me a piece of paper no bigger than a cigarette packet with receipts stapled to it.

'What's this?'

'Expenses claim. You said to get it into the system.'

'Expenses for what?'

'The hairdresser and the chinky. Five different people work at the Great Wall. Had to go back three times to see everybody.'

'I asked you to speak to them not become their best customer.'

'Greasing the wheels, Charlie. Had to be done. Gail went to the salon for us.'

'And does she like her new hair-do?'

'Loves it. Says Anton's a genius.'

'So what did you get on Donna Morton?'

'She only made one hair appointment and that was a cancellation. Nothing since. The guys in the Chinese remembered her address and what she usually ordered. Donna was a sweet and sour king prawn with special fried rice. Showed them her picture.'

He shook his head.

'Faces are meaningless to them. We all look the same, apparently. And they haven't seen her. Good call on the prawns by the way; had it twice. The lemon chicken's not bad either.'

'That's it?'

''Fraid so. Always was a long shot.'

'Mmmm. Mai Ling settling in all right?'

He drew me a look. 'Could say, Charlie, could say.'

'Gail and her not get along?'

He faced me. 'No, they get along. Get along just fine. Like a house on fire as a matter of fact.'

'So what?'

'When she arrived, Gail moved the boys in together and gave Liam's room to Thai Mai. They made noises but they were okay. A female next door is a novelty. They're young. Haven't sussed women out yet. They think what you see is what you get. No point in tryin' to explain. They'll learn.'

Patrick caressed the stubble on his cheek, searching for the words.

'Yesterday Gail and her went to the supermarket. She eats different from us. Tons of vegetables. Noodles. Other stuff. I ran them to Asda and stayed in the car. Christ knows how much money that woman spent. Couldn't get all the bags in the boot.

'I'll cover it, don't worry.'

'Forget it. No problem. Last night we had Thai red chicken curry and sticky rice. Then they went to the bingo.'

'You like Thai food, don't you?'

'Love it. Curry was magic. Everythin' was fine. Gail and her doin' the dishes and chatterin' away. No argument about the telly.

I got left alone. This mornin' it went sour. "Mai Ling is unhappy," Gail says, and puts herself in charge of cheerin' her up.'

'You married a good woman, Pat.'

He swatted the air. 'A good woman who'll be on the tiles every night this week. They're goin' out. I'm left with the boys. Tells me she won't have time to make the dinner so sort somethin' for ourselves. It's a disaster, Charlie.'

'You're exaggerating.'

'No I'm not. You haven't seen Gail on a mission. Heard them talking about an Abba Tribute at the King's...'

I cut him off. 'You'll live. Ten minutes.'

We walked across a deserted George Square, bent against a cold wind. Winter was whispering. I told Patrick what I intended. His quarrel with Gail had left him in the mood for confrontation.

'We've been pissin' around the edges,' he said. 'Taken shit from all sides. No more Mr Nice Guys.'

He was winding himself up and trying to drag me along. I stopped under the statue of Sir Walter Scott and restored some sanity. 'Listen, Pat, a bull in a china shop isn't the way to go. We need people to talk to us.'

He wasn't listening. 'Very good, Charlie, in theory at least. What you don't appreciate is some bastards need a good slap. They do. Only thing they respect.'

'Don't see the head of the biggest college in Scotland responding to that approach, although in his case a good slap shouldn't be ruled out.'

At last Patrick had an enemy he could fight. 'Same with the students,' he said. 'Threaten them with the police if they start messin' us about.'

'And what about Miss Shaw, throw her out of the window if she looks at me? The police aren't interested, remember? Me, you and Mai Ling are the only ones who are. I'll go in by myself. You wait outside.'

It wasn't what he wanted to hear. 'So why bring me?'

'Don't worry. You'll get your chance.'

I left him on Cathedral Street and climbed the hill. The college was busier than on my last visit. There was a buzz about the place but no sign of Rose Devlin's gang. Miss Shaw's expression froze in mid-sniff when she saw me; her dimples had the day off.

I smiled as if we were old friends.

'Is he in? Good.'

Shock kept her from answering. I breezed past, knocked the Principal's door and entered. Galbraith sat behind his desk, writing. He didn't raise his head. 'What is it, Emily?'

I said, 'Guess who?' and savoured the look it produced. He scowled and put the pen down. 'What do you want? How dare you...'

'Take it easy. Change of plan.'

'What are you doing here? Miss Shaw!'

Miss Shaw appeared beside me. 'I'm sorry, Mr Galbraith, he just barged in. Shall I call the police?'

I stared at his overfed face; purple could be such an unattractive colour.

'And maybe the Evening Times? Or would you rather hear what I have to say? Your choice.'

His eyes locked on mine, considering his options. He would've loved to have me removed from his office but Galbraith wasn't stupid. He hadn't risen to where he was without knowing how to play the game.

Eventually he said, 'Close the door, Miss Shaw. I'm not expecting this to take too long. I'll call if I need assistance.'

I pulled a chair up to his impressive desk and sat down.

He said, 'Why are you here Mr..?'

The old I-forget-your-name-because you're-unimportant ploy.

I helped him out. 'Cameron. Same as the whisky people.'

He sneered. 'Any relation?'

I gave my standard reply. 'Wish I had their money.'

'Tell me the reason for this outrageous behaviour and go. The college won't give information about students or members of staff. It's a question of confidentiality.'

'How about former members? What's the policy there?'

'I don't know what you're talking about.'

'Frank Lennon hasn't been in the building for the best part of two months. If I were you I'd be asking myself why. Last time we met you wanted to know if it was a police matter. It isn't. Yet. And for the record I'm not representing the Downey family. My client is Lennon's fiancée. Naturally she wants to know where he is. The media have already given the college a good kicking. Believe me, if what I suspect turns out to be true it'll be a massacre. The best thing you can do is drop the attitude and work with me. Cards on the table.'

He kept me waiting then said, 'I'm listening. You've got five minutes.'

It took a lot longer than that; he didn't complain. I told him the story; from the photograph of an innocent girl under the Christmas tree to the rumours about her and Frank Lennon; Michael Corrigan's vile opinions of everyone and everything connected with the college and Angela Armstrong's kinder assessment of Alison as a quiet girl who fell in with the wrong crowd and Lennon, a lonely dreamer; finally the class night out at the Drum and Monkey that so far had escaped serious investigation. Cards on the table I'd said and meant it. Galbraith didn't interrupt. Always the pompous self-seeker, he was humouring me to get me out of his office and out of his life.

Until I arrived at Saturday and the phone call from Walter. He sat forward and gripped the desk. His voice lost its superior edge. No prompting from me; he got there by himself.

'You think they've been murdered?'

'It doesn't look good.'

He asked about the police. I said, 'At this stage they're not involved.'

'So how can I help?'

'I want to interview Rose Devlin and her friends. Everybody who was at the night out. It has to be voluntary, there's no authority.'

'When?'

'Lunchtime if possible. Put me in front of the class then give me a room where I can speak to them one to one. The official line is relations trying to discover where they are. No other possibilities get mentioned.'

'Will any staff be required?'

'Not unless they have something to add.'

'Okay, call me in half an hour. I'll find out where Alison's class is and set it up.'

On my way out Miss Shaw kept her attention on her computer screen. Before I closed the door I heard her sniff. A cold or a cocaine habit? These days anything was possible.

Pat Logue was waiting for me in reception with news from the home front. He didn't ask how it had gone with Galbraith. His mind was on his wife's new freedom and how it affected him.

'Gail called. Liam dropped a bottle of fish sauce. Wants me to buy another one. Thinks I've nothin' else to do?' He remembered where we were. 'What did Galbraith say?'

I told him.

'So we'll get to talk to Alison's classmates.'

'Any that show up. We can't force them.'

'Rose Devlin?'

'If we're lucky. My guess is she'll be there. She likes to go up against authority. Did it with Alec Downey and with you. The opportunity is too good to miss. It tells her gang she's not intimidated.'

Pat said, 'You haven't met her yet. Reckons she's a hard case.'

'Hard enough to keep the others in line? Even the boys?'

'They aren't tough guys. Tough guys don't hang around with girls. I saw a couple of them five minutes ago.'

'Did they see you?'

'Definitely. And they weren't happy. Ruined their day.' He looked at his watch. 'No point in goin' back to NYB. There's a

Sainsbury in Buchanan Street. Better get the bloody fish sauce before I forget.'

I watched him cross the bridge above Queen Street station, shoulders hunched, walking slowly. A man in pain. In the college cafeteria I got coffee from a machine and took a seat at the far end of the room. No one gave me a second glance. The hum of conversation sounded like swarming bees. One girl, white face and black lipstick, looked through me as if I wasn't there. I had entered a world of strange hairstyles and stranger attitudes. An alien world. Corrigan's Acne Army. A boy at the next table was speed writing, copying an assessment no doubt. In terms of his education the road to nowhere. Groups of females swapped gossip. Rose Devlin wasn't one of them.

Galbraith seemed almost pleased to hear from me. He said, 'Come to my office. I'll take you to the class and introduce you. They're doing accounts so a break will be welcome. From there we'll give you an empty room. Not sure who you'll get. Don't let how they dress fool you, they're fantastically conservative. The days of student marches and protesting in the streets, are gone. Wouldn't recognise a cause if they fell over it. Can't connect with the big issues. Politics are a bore, the environment is just some scientists talking. It has to be happening to them.'

'Alison Downey was their classmate and she's missing. How much more personal does it need to be?'

'Don't expect too much.'

The Principal had been helpful, pleasant even, now he reverted to type.

'One final thing. Once you've spoken to them, that's it. Cathedral College is out of it. I don't expect you here again. Do I make myself plain, Mr Cameron?'

23

We followed Galbraith to the second floor, room 211.

'212 is empty. You can use it.'

He knocked on the door and went in. A dozen or so faces stared at us, unimpressed. Rose Devlin was at the back. I'd only seen her in a photograph but I could've picked her out by her expression, somewhere between amusement and contempt. Her default position. Valerie Cummings sat beside her. We stood behind Galbraith while he apologised for the interruption and laid it out and, if I hadn't known better, I would've sworn he was sincere.

'As you know, a member of this class left shortly after the term began. I refer of course to Alison Downey. However it seemed that Alison didn't just leave college. She never made it home. Her parents haven't seen her in almost eight weeks.'

He paused for effect.

'When something like that happens it gives rise to all kinds of rumour and speculation. I expect you read the newspapers. Naturally Alison's mother and father are very upset. They love their daughter and want to know where she is. The college wants to know as well.'

No mention of Frank Lennon, the man who never was.

Galbraith said, 'Mr Cameron is here to ask some questions.'

Eyes dulled by technology assessed me. He held up his hands. 'Let's be clear. No one is being accused of anything.'

He motioned to me. I stepped forward and scanned the rows, searching for a connection.

'I'd like to speak with everybody who was at the Drum and Monkey the night Alison went missing, or any of you who have information about where she might have gone. Nothing you say will be repeated. The police aren't involved at this point. You knew Alison. You can help us find her.'

Galbraith left without a word. He'd made his contribution. We let the kids go who hadn't been to the night out. That brought the numbers down. Patrick stayed in 211. I crossed the corridor to 212.

As I was leaving he whispered. 'Knew Alison? Past tense. Careful, Charlie.'

'Freudian slip. When I finish with one, send in whoever's next. Keep Valerie Cummings 'til last.'

Frank Lennon promised to marry Mai Ling then stood her up. She wanted to understand why. Alison Downey had the answer. Her classmates wouldn't have much to say about the lecturer but they might know something about her. It was the long way home, the only road open. I had to take it. I settled myself behind a desk and pulled a chair opposite. This job had taken me to strange places. None stranger than a Monday morning at Cathedral College room 212.

The first student was Betty Clarke. We shook hands; hers was like Singapore in a heatwave. Betty was nervous. My questions weren't meant to be clever and succeeded. She'd seen Alison in the pub early on and thought she was all right. She remembered Lennon but not the two of them together. I thanked her and she left. The next, Paul Wilson, admitted he was drunk from the beginning and still wasn't sure how he got home. His folks cancelled his birthday party. Paul had hardly spoken to Alison since the start of the semester.

The parade continued and a picture emerged. These kids were a collection of cliques with less in common than I imagined. Nobody had information worth a damn. Most admitted to being wasted and what happened later in the evening was a blur. Alison was there, and at the start she was okay; that much was agreed. A girl recalled her talking to Brian Lawrence and said she seemed upset. Lawrence wasn't in college so I couldn't ask him. I guessed he had ducked out with his pals when he saw Patrick. Strange.

Everybody was telling the truth and nobody was. Drugs never got a mention. Sex was a non event. What kind of party was this?

Rose Devlin closed the door, walked to the chair across from me and sat down. She crossed her legs. The denim skirt rose on her thigh as intended. Dark eyes searched my face for reaction and found none. It didn't faze her. She made a grab at control with a question none of the others dared ask. 'Is Ally dead?

'What makes you say that?'

'She is, isn't she?'

'I've no idea. I hope not.'

She allowed her attention to wander. All part of the performance.

'When was the last time you saw Alison? What was she doing?'

'Running away from him.'

'Him?'

'Lennon.'

No Mr.

'Did you try to stop her?'

'Ally's a big girl. She can look after herself. She's a drama queen. Has to be the centre of attention.'

'Did you see her arguing with Frank Lennon?'

'No.'

'So why was she running away?'

Rose Devlin examined her nails. 'If you knew him you'd understand.'

'I don't. Tell me.'

Nothing.

'What about Brian Lawrence?'

'What about him?'

'Did they fall out?'

'Wouldn't be surprised. He was always trying to get into her knickers.'

'But she wasn't interested?'

'Not in boys her own age. She fancied older men.'

'Like Frank Lennon? He went to a few nights out. Was that because of Alison?'

She smirked.

'Was Alison drunk?'

'She couldn't drink. A couple was all it took.'

'You're saying she was. Were you?'

'It doesn't bother me.'

'That a yes?'

She tried to boss the conversation again.

'Is this what you do? Funny kind of job. Good money?'

I didn't take the bait. 'Has Alison been in contact? After all you're her friend.'

The sarcasm didn't escape Rosie; she lost patience with me.

'Look. She ran out of the pub. He ran after her. That's what I saw and that's what I'm telling you. I haven't heard from her since. Now I want to go, okay?'

It had been short and not very sweet. Devlin's version put Alison Downey and Frank Lennon together. I wasn't sure I believed her. The lack of concern for a missing friend told me Patrick was right. Pat Logue was a shrewd judge. He said Rosie was a bitch. Now I'd met her it was hard to disagree.

No Lolita act from Valerie Cummings although she would have preferred to be somewhere else instead of talking about the missing girl. Questions were answered in a quiet voice I struggled to hear. She lacked the vulgar confidence and overt sexuality of Devlin. A follower rather than a leader. Her teeth and skin were perfect but she probably believed Rose was better looking. I used a sympathetic approach because I thought she cared.

'You must be worried about Alison. You liked her, didn't you?' She nodded. 'Imagine how her parents feel.'

'They must be out of their minds.'

'Has Alison contacted you?'

'No. No she hasn't.'

'Tell me about the Drum and Monkey.'

Valerie took a deep breath. 'I don't remember much. Rose and Alison arrived together. Ally had fallen out with her mum. She went to Rose's house to change.'

A detail Rose had left out.

'Did she borrow her things?'

No she had a bag with her.'

'Did she talk about anybody from the college? Frank Lennon?'

'I didn't hear her. Is that what Rose says?'

'Was she upset about the fall out?'

'Not really.'

'Where was she going to stay?'

'I assumed she'd go home. They'd had an argument. It wasn't the end of the world.'

'What then?'

'She lost it with Brian. He spiked her drink. Put X in it.'

'Why would he do that?'

'Because he's stupid.'

'Or because he fancied her?'

She looked away.

'Where does Brian live?'

'I don't know.' Her first lie and I could see it made her uncomfortable. 'Ally went to the toilet to make herself sick. Brian told me him and Davie were leaving.'

'Who is Davie?'

'David Wilson. Brian was pissed off and embarrassed. Said the Drum was crap and they were going somewhere else, asked if I wanted to go with them. I told him he was a dickhead.'

'Where were they going?'

'Where they always went. The Ark. Tommy had his dad's car.'

'Tommy?'

'Boyd.'

'Is he in college today?'

'Tommy works. When they need him he misses classes.'

'Where does he work?'

'Hilton Gardens Hotel.'

I rolled the conversation back to the Drum and Monkey. 'You didn't go with the boys?'

'I was mad and Alison might need me.'

'Did she?'

'No. She was okay. I saw her speaking to Mr Lennon. Next thing she was shouting and ran out.'

'What did he do?'

'Nothing. Just stood, then he went after her.'

'How long did he wait?'

She thought about it. 'Minutes. Two at the most.'

'So Alison was drinking before she arrived. Brian Lawrence gave her ecstasy. She fell out with him and went to the toilet to be sick. When she came back she made a scene with Frank Lennon and ran outside. He followed her.'

'Yes.'

'Who else saw this?'

'No idea.'

'Where was Rose?'

Valerie shrugged.

'You must've talked about it. What did Brian say?'

'He hasn't been in college much.'

'And none of you discussed it? A juicy piece of scandal like this? I don't believe you. Let's go back to before the night out. Rose said Lennon had the hots for Alison. You disagreed, remember?'

'Rose makes stuff up. It's like a game. Invents something and starts it rolling. Before long everybody believes it.'

'Is that what happened with Alison and Frank Lennon?'

'Not exactly. Ally could be a pain. Always on about older men and how they were attracted to her. Rose got fed up listening to her.'

'And started the rumour about her and a lecturer.'

'Yes.'

'Did Alison know?'

'Of course not.'

'But it wasn't true?'

'That's how Rose works.'

'Did Brian fancy Alison or was that Rose at it again?'

'I told him to forget it. He just laughed.'

A bell rang. The corridor filled with voices. Valerie Cummings had no more to say. She ended the way Rose Devlin had begun, with a question.

'Where is she?'

She. Not where are they. Poor old Frank Lennon; Mai Ling was all he had. Whatever I told her would go the rounds. It was how it worked at her age. I gave the only answer I had.

'I wish I knew, Valerie, I really wish I knew.'

24

The barman at the Drum and Monkey didn't remember Alison Downey or the class night but the bag was there. He was reluctant to open it. When eventually he did it told us nothing and we left more certain than ever that something wasn't right.

Out of the blue, Patrick answered Rose Devlin's question.

'I think she's dead. I think Lennon killed her.'

'Yeah?'

'Yeah. This guy's a loner, hangin' round kids. Somebody his age, what's in it for him?'

'Okay, he's an oddball but why murder the girl?'

'Tried it on, got a knock back and reacted.'

'So where did he hide the body? And where is he?'

'No idea. I don't believe they ran away.'

The lunchtime crowd at NYB had gone back to the snake pits. A few more hours and Monday would be over. Pat Logue's brief rehabilitation after his health scare was behind him. He settled at the bar, drinking a pint and nursed resentment about his wife.

An old rock classic was playing on the Rock-Ola. I ordered a latte and tried to make sense of the interviews at Cathedral College and what we'd found at the pub. The bag was just the latest piece of the puzzle. It was possible Alison hadn't bothered to collect her stuff. Possible but not likely. It didn't sit well with me. No matter what Andrew Geddes said, this was a case for the police. I was on the point of calling him when he walked through the door. He saw me and came over. 'Never get married, Charlie, it's a mug's game. Did I tell you that?'

'Every time we meet, Andrew. Problems?'

He shook his head. 'Nothing but. Elspeth's lawyer thinks my arse is gold lined. I mean what more does the bitch want? She's got the flat and half the money in the bank. Now she's going after the pension. I'll end up in the poor house. Thank Christ we don't have kids.'

'What does your lawyer say?'

'Wonder whose side he's on. Women are like hurricanes. They arrive wet and wild, and when they leave they take the house and the car. So if you're considering going legal forget it. It's...'

'...a mug's game, you said.'

'But you don't believe me. Who is she?'

'It's not like that.'

'Just friends, eh? That's how it starts. Another good man gone.'

'I spoke to you about Alec Downey's daughter, remember?'

'No.'

'Well I did.'

'Oh yeah. You were unhappy because they fired you.'

'Since then.'

'Remind me.'

'You sent a guy to me. Daughter's a student. Disappeared after a family row. Looked like she'd run away with one of her lecturers. The girl isn't under age. No suspicion of foul play.'

'Shagging their brains out somewhere.'

'Seemed likely until a Thai girl arrived at his door. Mai Ling. Claims the lecturer invited her here to get married.'

'That's right. You fancied her. Went on and on about how beautiful she was.'

'No I didn't. Everybody assumed they'd headed for the hills but when Miss Thailand appeared that crumbled. I was at Cathedral College today trying to piece it together. And guess what?'

'What?'

DS Geddes wasn't in the mood for games.

'It doesn't work. No history between them. There's rumour – I even know who started it – it's a lie.'

'So?'

'It's something the police should be on. It stinks.'

'When you talked to me what did I ask?'

'Was there evidence.'

'And you told me, what?'

'I admitted there wasn't as such.'

'As such? Is that the same as no? No evidence. As such.'

He emphasised the last two words.

'Because if it is I'll say it again. The only thing that counts is material evidence. Let it go. You're a talented man, Charlie. I'd back your judgement any day.'

Just not today.

'You may well be right. At this stage it isn't enough. We're throwing everything we have at Damocles. Any idea what that's costing? Like to take a stab at how much progress we've made? I'll tell you anyway. Marginally more than fuck all.'

'No help from forensics?'

'Nothing. These murders aren't recent so that doesn't help.'

'What about the Hotline?'

'A timewasters convention. Usually is. Makes me wish I'd decided to be a postman. I interviewed Hamilton on Saturday. He's a shell. Still convinced his ex-girlfriend is behind it.'

'Donna Morton. No luck with her?'

'Not a bloody whisper. Wonder if he isn't right. Nobody just disappears.'

He was forgetting Frank Lennon and Alison Downey.

'And that's not the worst of it. Spoke to the wife. What a mess she's in. Doped to the eyeballs.'

'What're you going to do?'

'Play the last card in the pack. TV appeal. There's a doubt over whether she's well enough. She insists he isn't included. Can't be in the same room as him.'

'How successful are appeals?'

Andrew paused. 'The truth? Not very. It's a device to keep the case in the public mind. Occasionally someone will remember some detail or other and we'll follow it up. In my opinion it does more harm than good. Huge emotional trauma for the relatives. Don't want to think what it might do to her.'

'When will this happen?'

'Depends on Jennifer Hamilton. She has bad days and terrible days. The best we can hope for is a bad day. I envy you, Charlie. I've been a copper most of my life. Lately I'm thinking enough is enough. And with Elspeth and her lawyer determined to get their pound of flesh, maybe it's time to do a disappearing act of my own.'

'You're not serious?'

'I am. If Lord Lucan can pull it off so can I. Why not?'

'And Sandra? Is she in the plan?' I'd met Sandra when he brought her to NYB for lunch. 'Deserves better, surely?'

He agreed. 'Sandra's all that's stopping me. If it wasn't for her I'd be off.'

Andrew was in a bad place. The rant about his ex-wife was standard stuff. That wasn't it. 'Damocles getting you down?'

'Yeah. The men, the time. Over and over the same ground. Finding nothing. Needle in a haystack. You realise it doesn't matter how much money gets thrown at it, we can't stop the pervs and the psychos. Freaks without a conscience. They don't give a damn.'

'But you do, Andrew, and that's the difference. In the end you always catch them. As for Elspeth, cheer up you could still be married to her.'

'True. How's laughing boy doing?' He meant Patrick. 'Still one jump ahead of the sheriff?'

'He's got woman trouble. Like the rest of us.'

'I've met his wife. Can't understand what she ever saw in him.'

'This from the man who said "I do" to Elspeth.'

'Can't argue against that. I was young. Immature.'

'Thirty two?'

'The best man should've talked me out of it.'

'I tried, you wouldn't listen. No change there. I keep saying this college case isn't right. I don't believe they ran away.'

'Then convince me. Give me some facts. The father reported her missing; we took a look. It's sex. They'll be back when the novelty wears off. That's what happens. The first three months with Elspeth I could've eaten it. After that I wished I had. Lucky there's no kids.'

I agreed with him on that. Andrew was fighting back.

I said, 'One of the students told us Alison arrived at the pub with a bag. The barman doesn't remember her but the bag's still there. Why didn't she pick it up the next day?'

DS Geddes teased a beer mat into bits.

'You're not wrong, Charlie. You're not wrong. Except it's all circumstantial.'

'Well when does it start being real?'

'When we have evidence – that word again – of a crime. Student leaves a bag in a pub. Who cares?'

'And the Thai girl at the lecturer's flat?'

'Same again.'

I gave him Patrick's thinking.

'What about this: Lennon killed Alison Downey and he's on the run?'

That made up Andrew's mind. I was boring him. He decided he had places to go.

'As a theory it's as good as any. Best of luck with it. And by the way, good to see the old Charlie again.'

Was he having a laugh? Or was I getting better at faking it?

Andrew Geddes' visit unsettled me. These days it didn't take much. I pulled Pam's file four or five times and put it back without opening it. In between, I thought about my mother, almost called her and changed my mind. I was in a bad place.

The afternoon dragged on. I remembered the schism with Jackie. Truth was I should've made peace with her before now. I found her in her cubbyhole under the stairs. Her eyes stayed on the pc screen. 'Look, I said, 'about the other day. It got out of hand.'

She glared at the computer. 'You mean, you got out of hand.'

It wouldn't be over 'til Jackie decided it was over.

A pang of irritation rose in me. I was offering an olive branch. Patrick had likened the relationship to a marriage. Not the description I would use though close enough if the Logues and the Geddes were examples.

The call from Kate chased the blues away. Was I hungry? Yes I was. Did I fancy an Indian? Yes I did.

The Moti Mahal was full of good memories. As a student at Strathclyde I practically lived there. Mr Rani Das was a friend. He was old now; Videk, and Geeta, his son and daughter, ran the restaurant. There wasn't a soul on Gibson Street. Glasgow stayed home on Tuesday nights. I waited on the pavement, more nervous than I wanted to admit. Kate sounded fine on the phone but there had been no contact since the previous week, and she had kept her distance at the gig. The thing could be finished before it even got started.

I saw her on Woodlands Road walking towards me. She waved and I knew it was going to be all right. Inside, Videk shook my hand. He told me it was his father's night off; he'd be sorry to have missed me. Geeta arrived with spiced onions and poppodoms and a smile that never changed. This family lived and breathed their business. It was who they were. Jackie Mallon did the same at NYB.

Kate said, 'They like you in here. What's the story?

I told her: about weekends drinking lager and eating vindaloo, leaving out the affair with Fiona Ramsay and my broken heart. Kate wasn't a fool; she realised there was more. We sat at a table in the corner. Apart from us the Moti was empty.

Kate said, 'I owe you an apology.'

'What for?'

'Sunday. I avoided you.'

I considered lying and decided against it. 'I noticed.'

'Sorry.'

'But why?'

'Because I'm not sure, Charlie.'

'About me?'

She searched for the words.

'I won't compete with other women. You have to know that.'

the comfort of strangers

'Who's asking you to?'

'Don't let the rock chick fool you. I'm a one man woman. Corny but there you go.'

'Pleased to hear it.'

She laughed. 'Yeah right. Seriously, you're deep. We haven't known each other long yet sometimes I look at you and you're not there.'

'Cases can suck you in, some more than others, I'm here, don't worry about that.'

'For me it won't work any other way. No secrets.'

'No secrets.'

She seemed relieved. 'That's why I've been holding back.'

'Really? You can't imagine those guys at the front with their tongues hanging out want guitar lessons, do you?' I took her hand. 'I'm kind of old fashioned myself. I want you, Kate. Only you.'

Videk opened his notebook ready for our order. I said, 'Two curries, rice and Nan bread.'

'What kind of curry?'

'Any kind.'

'Boiled rice?'

'Doesn't matter. And make it take away. Better still, we'll come back later.'

We headed for the door. Videk called after us. 'Later tonight?'

'Not tonight. Definitely not tonight.'

25

We were on the sofa in my flat and Kate had her arms round me. STV News was giving the appeal plenty of coverage. A fresh-faced reporter talking to camera supplied the background for anyone who had been on Mars and wasn't aware of the case. Jennifer Hamilton, flanked by senior officers, was led to a table and a bank of microphones. I remembered the shot of Mark comforting her – the photographer had been nominated for an award – distraught, crying, clinging to her husband. A mother who had lost her child.

I hadn't met the woman whose insistence on a final swim had given someone the opportunity to steal her daughter. Clearly that knowledge was too hard to bear. Then her husband's confession; the affair with Donna Morton and the certainty his former lover had taken Lily. Emotionally bent, Jennifer Hamilton broke and retreated inside herself. Four and a half weeks after they walked on the sand swinging their child between them, the family was damaged beyond repair; destroyed by guilt and betrayal.

The medical people had done their best but the result was still shocking. She was stick-thin and frail. Her hands shook. She read in a tiny voice, devoid of feeling; the woman was spent. I wondered if she even understood where she was or what she was doing. The policemen on either side of her stared ahead, willing the painful show to end. At one point she faltered and missed her place. Off screen someone offered a gentle prompt and guided her back to the script. Kate squeezed my hand so tight my fingers were numb. A senior officer closed the appeal with a reminder that any information would be welcome, no matter how insignificant it might seem. When it was over I turned the TV off and tried to pretend I was all right.

Kate said, 'Has this anything to do with the case you're working on?'

'Yeah, sort of.'

'Sort of?'

I gave her a version that skirted the truth and avoided the messy bits, which was most of it: Mark Hamilton had come to me desperate to exhaust every avenue in the search to find his missing daughter. His story was heartbreaking, moving, and of course I'd been anxious to help. However, abduction was a crime, police business, my hands were tied, I couldn't get involved. No mention of Donna Morton, sleepless nights wrestling with an old terror, or the reason I'd been ratty with everybody since Lily's father washed up at my door.

Kate listened; the sad part was she believed me. For two days we had laughed and loved and planned. With good reason I felt unworthy of her. She took my hands in hers. 'Do you want me to stay, Charlie? I will.'

In the end she didn't. I drove her home. As she was getting out of the car Kate said, 'When will I see you?'

I had nothing planned. Hadn't given it a thought. Off the top of my head I said, 'Saturday. Eight o'clock. In the morning.'

'Where are we going?'

'Surprise. You'll see.'

The flat was strange without Kate. I made coffee and stared at the dead television screen, still seeing Jennifer Hamilton and her tenuous grip on sanity. Andrew's call took me by surprise.

He said, 'Did you watch it?'

'Yes.'

'Awful wasn't it? And she's back in hospital. It was too much for her; she collapsed. Lily isn't the only victim. There's an inquiry. Whose bright idea was it to put a woman in her condition on TV? The doctor's covering his arse, claiming he warned us this might happen.'

I didn't respond.

'Told you, Charlie, I told you to steer clear. Sooner or later a high profile case becomes a blame game. Wish I'd taken my own advice.'

'The appeal wasn't your idea. You were against it.'

He laughed a tart laugh. 'Wasn't anybody's idea, apparently. DCI Baillie's being hauled across the coals. Poor sod. Today makes us look clueless, which we are. And heartless. The press will have a field day. Why did we wait so long? One look at Jennifer Hamilton should tell them. Won't be buying a newspaper tomorrow, that's for sure.'

'Mark Hamilton must be in hell.'

Lily's father had been reduced to a bit player, a bystander to the drama of his own life.

'Saw him in Cowcaddens outside the studio. We had instructions to stop him if he tried to get in. Thank Christ he didn't. It's a big enough mess without that.'

'So what now?'

'Man the phones and hope. Keep going. We're in a trough.'

'Can't get much worse.'

'Don't you believe it, Charlie.'

For the first time in two months Lily was back on the front page. Or rather her mother was. A close up captured the emptiness and the pain medication could dull but not cure.

The headline said it all. SHATTERED.

I didn't read the story. It wouldn't enrich my life. Avoiding it wasn't so easy. The appeal meant the paper could rehash all the previous articles on the abduction. Pages of it. At NYB I said good morning to Jackie and got daggers for my trouble. I ducked. They flew over my head and stuck in the wall. Pat Logue took a break from toying with an espresso to give me the benefit of his experience. His opening sentence told what was on his mind.

He said, 'They won't let it go, will they?'

'Sorry, Patrick?'

'Women. Don't cross them, it's not worth it.'

'You're talking about Gail I take it?'

I wasn't in the mood to listen to this but I didn't have the energy for another fight.

'Talkin' about all of them, Charlie, every last one.'

'What's the problem this time? Mai Ling?'

'Mai Thai's a symptom. Gail's reason to abandon her kids and her husband.'

'Where were they this time?'

'Salsa lessons at Arta. Me and the boys are eatin' toasted cheese instead of a proper dinner. I've told her it's not on.'

'Is she listening?'

'Can't say she is.'

'How about Mai Ling? She all right?'

'Only see her on her way out the door with Gail.'

'And tonight?'

'King Tut's Wah Wah Hut. The woman's gone berserk. Stark starin' female.'

I got between him and a monologue.

'Got to make a decision about Lennon. Nobody's interested but us.'

'Put Mai Thai on a plane and let it go.'

'Not until we've dug deeper.'

Patrick was in his head. He couldn't stay away from Gail. He said, 'I heard them talkin'. Jackie's name got mentioned.' He lifted a newspaper off the bar. 'Seen this?'

'Yeah. Even worse on TV.'

'What was your pal thinkin'?'

'Not his decision.'

'Well whoever it was deserves a red card.'

'Andrew agrees, and he doesn't expect it to lead to anything.'

'So why go through with it?'

'Because the police are clutching at straws. Somebody knows what happened to that child. Jennifer Hamilton is all they have.'

'Husband missin' I notice.'

'She didn't want him there. They've split. The marriage is over.'

Patrick went quiet. 'Ours is goin' the same way. I'm up to here with it. If Gail keeps on I'm offski. Honest, Charlie, you wouldn't believe it. Me and the boys don't matter. Enough's enough, know what I'm talkin'?'

'Sorry, Patrick, it's my fault. I shouldn't have asked Gail to let Mai Ling stay.'

'No, Mai Thai's the excuse. If it hadn't been her it would've been somethin' else.'

'A few more days, a week at most. I'll do what Andrew says and send her home. You can get your lives back. I saw how worried Gail was when you did your disappearing act. She loves you, no doubt about it.'

'Nice try. It'll take more than that to convince me. Should see her. Done up to the nines. The boys don't say but they aren't happy either. They're beginnin' to catch on to females. Probably the one good thing to come out of it. Not as keen as they were to share their space. Mai Thai wasn't travellin' light after all. Had the kitchen sink in that wee case. Like the fuckin' Tardis. Now we've got clothes everywhere. Lotions and potions in the bathroom. Our stuff's been moved. Can't find it for jars of cream. Assumin' you can get in the toilet. Liam asked what women do in there.'

'Give me a week.'

'If I can hold out that long. No room at your drum I suppose?'

'Bad timing, and that isn't the answer. Either we get something concrete on Lennon or we let it go.'

'Cops aren't interested so why should it bother us?'

'They're wrong, Patrick. Andrew is off the mark with this one. He's preoccupied, otherwise he'd see it.'

'And our job is righting wrongs, that it? Batman and Robin. Lennon did the girl in and he's runnin'. Hasn't been back to the flat or the college because he's scared the police will be there. Face it, Charlie, it's a bust. But have your week. Then bye bye Mai Thai. She's gone or I am. No more kidology.'

He muttered to himself. 'Stark starin' female.'

26

Aberdeen, 149 miles from Glasgow.

Yesterday she found someone. A man who knew a man. A birth certificate wasn't a problem he said. Give him a few days. Just like the movies, all it took was money. Once she had it she would apply for a passport for the two of them. Then they could go wherever they liked. Maybe America. Looking over her shoulder would be a thing of the past.

That called for a celebration, and a celebration meant new clothes. Kids grew so fast they needed a whole new wardrobe every couple of months. In a shop window she'd seen the most beautiful pink and white dress, so gorgeous it was a struggle to stop herself from buying it. But no, frilly dresses would have to wait; there would be plenty of those in the future. She settled for jeans, a jumper and shoes in a bigger size.

They'd started going out in the morning. She'd been terrified until she realised nobody was paying any attention to them. And why would they? Women with children were a common sight. A shop assistant remarked she'd never seen a more beautiful little boy. Boy. How easy it would be to slip up and use her proper name.

Since then they'd been into town on the bus, walked along the shore, and fed the ducks in the park.

Her baby was sleeping. She wouldn't let her out of her sight. Impossible to imagine hurting a little thing like that. She would kill anyone who tried to take her. Kill. Not the angry threats she'd made when he told her what had been going on. For real. Without question. Life was precious, especially a young life with so much to look forward to; taking away the opportunity to experience the richness of it was a sin that demanded death. No she'd do it all right. Do it and not think twice.

On the television in the corner, Jennifer Hamilton sat between two policemen, reading a prepared statement. Her face was gaunt, her voice a whisper. Millions would pity her. But millions didn't know what she knew.

She switched the TV off and went to check on the baby. Adele was lying in the cot with the covers kicked to the bottom. The sweetest thing. Nobody would harm her.

Her mother wouldn't let them.

27

The overnight temperature had dropped close to freezing. I waited in the car, watching the last icy cobwebs of frost melt on the windscreen. Kate appeared in a long grey coat, black boots and gloves and a beret. We kissed. 'Roll up for the mystery tour,' I said.

She smiled. 'Where are we going?'

'Wait and see.'

I pulled into the road and headed for the motorway. The sky hung low, heavy with snow. Christmas was still a long way off. It didn't feel like it. That was wrong. I had found a beautiful woman and, despite the video in my head that kept me awake at night, being with Kate Calder made it easier. I was falling for her. Correction. I was already there.

When we passed Livingston she said, 'I'm guessing Edinburgh.'

I toyed with her. 'Maybe. Maybe not. We could be taking the Forth Road Bridge. Or the airport. I did say bring your passport, didn't I?'

'Yeah, I'm right. Edinburgh. Why so early?'

'Don't be impatient. All will be revealed.'

The capital was busy. I parked off Fountainbridge Road. We got out and walked arm in arm down Lothian Road and turned right into Castle Terrace. Kate said, 'I still don't understand.'

'You do eat breakfast?'

'Of course. Just not used to travelling the best part of fifty miles to get it.'

'Ah, it's not any old breakfast.'

A line of blue and white striped awnings gave her the clue. She clapped her hands. 'The Farmers' Market. I've been meaning to come here for years. Fantastic.'

'First stop, coffee.'

As markets go Edinburgh is small, less than sixty stalls, but the quality is there. Most of the stallholders are producers, passionate about what they do. Kate bought pork chops from Oink, venison from Well Hung and Tender, and sun-dried tomato and buffalo sausages from a herd reared on a farm in West Fife. Because of me Patrick Logue had been abandoned. Four of their buffalo sausage rolls and a couple of bottles of organic beer would be welcome.

Kate said, 'So what about this breakfast?'

'What do you fancy?'

'I'm thinking porridge.'

'Then porridge it is.'

The Castle rose above us, stark and imposing against the clouds. Kate spooned oats into her mouth. 'Porridge alfresco. Thanks for bringing me, Charlie.'

'Where will we go next?'

'Once more round the stalls then wherever you like.'

We strolled along Princes Street, just us and half the population of Japan. There was already a queue at the Scott Monument. Kate pointed to the Gothic rocket ship opposite Jenners.

'Two hundred and eighty seven steps. Up for it?'

'Is this a test?'

'Hadn't thought about it but now you mention it...'

'Then what choice do I have?'

The first hundred steps weren't a problem. The next hundred were a challenge. On the last eighty seven my calf muscles screamed. Male pride kept me going. The stone-carved characters from Scott's writing were the excuse I needed to take a break. Sixty four of them, thank God. With their help I made it. And the view across Edinburgh was spectacular. Kate held on to me. 'What a city and what a great day.'

I accepted the compliment and returned it. 'My thoughts exactly. We'll do it again.'

'Soon?'

'Soon as you like, except let's give the zoo a visit, easier on the legs.'

On the drive west, Kate closed her eyes and sang softly. I glanced across, imagining the curve of her body beneath the coat. She said, 'Those sausages sound good. Could cook them if you like.'

'Is this how it's going to be? Food and sex, sex and food?'

She opened one eye. 'Got a better idea?'

The sausages were first class.

Kate made coffee and I checked my mobile. I'd missed a call from Andrew. The last time I saw him he'd been struggling. I apologised. 'Mind if I take this? Friend of mine not doing too well.'

'Sure.'

He answered on the first ring. 'Charlie. Tried to get you earlier.'

'What's wrong?'

He drew a breath that started in his boots.

'Can't talk now. Phone you later. Problems, the newspapers know about Damocles.'

'When did this happen?'

'Some smart arse put two and two together.'

'How?'

'Somebody on our end. Always the way.'

'So what do they know?'

'All of it. Everything. And I said it couldn't get worse. Jesus Fucking Christ! Any edge we might've had is down the Clyde. While he thought he was getting away with it there was a chance he would get careless. That's gone. You wouldn't credit the flack that's flying.'

'Keep your head down.'

'I'm trying. And listen, sorry to break into your weekend.'

'Forget it, Andrew.'

'Honestly, Charlie, that postman job's looking better and better. To put the tin lid on it Elspeth's Rottweiler wants to meet. Good job it isn't today. I'd tell her to go chase herself.'

I waited for him to repeat his mantra that marriage was a mug's game. He didn't, he was beyond it. A fine policeman was losing heart; good news for the killer.

I drove Kate home on Sunday once we'd given the sausages another try.

In the evening when I arrived at NYB there was a problem: the best kind for Jackie and Alex; a queue. They'd be lucky to get everybody in. Tonight Big River would play to a full house. Jackie wasn't around. Unusual to say the least. Was that a sign? I hoped not.

I went to the club a few minutes before Big River came on and squeezed in at the back near the bar. Word was out; the new band was hot. Already they had a following, and I was right, the crowd of guys at the front were interested in more than the music. A roar went up when Big River appeared. For Alan Sneddon it must've felt good. To come back so strong after losing Robbie Ward was a trick not many could have pulled off. All because he'd heard a girl in McCormack's trying a Fender Strat.

They blasted through the first half. Kate was unrecognisable from the woman singing in the car coming from Edinburgh; raw and throaty, every inch a rocker. I couldn't see though I was willing to bet she was wearing those snakeskin boots.

When the DJ began his second set I noticed someone I recognised. Gail Logue. A very different Gail from the last time. Ten years younger, strutting her funky stuff. Two other women danced beside her. Mai Ling and Jackie Mallon. No wonder

Patrick wasn't happy. His wife had rediscovered herself and was loving it. Mai Ling was making a heroic attempt to forget about Frank Lennon. Succeeding by the looks of it. The Jackie I met every day was business Jackie. This lady's mind was on having a good time. And she looked great.

Towards the end I lost sight of Gail and Mai Ling – they must have left. I wouldn't tell Patrick. Jackie was deep in conversation with Alan Sneddon, heads close together. I could guess where that was going. A vision of her spooning low fat yogurt into her mouth rose before my eyes. I wasn't wrong.

In the morning she smiled at me, the first in weeks. Pat Logue stayed at the bar all day and drank even more than normal. He took the organic beer and sausage rolls and gave me a nod and a reminder.

'One week, Charlie. Can't say fairer.'

Things with Kate were moving fast, perhaps faster than was wise for either of us; an indication my emotions were getting away from me. As if I needed one. I had suggested Kate bring clothes to the flat and make space for herself in the wardrobe. Not moving in exactly, moving closer. Thank god. Kate Calder was exactly the distraction I needed. She arrived at my door with three suitcases and a taxi downstairs filled with more. Not what I had in mind. Space in the wardrobe rolled into space in the bathroom and additions to the kitchen I hadn't spotted but sensed. I hid my dismay while a deeper appreciation of Pat Logue's difficulty settled in me.

Women organise things. Get used to it. It's what they do.

By the time she finished I had two drawers and no hanging room to speak of. Shaving foam, razor and hair gel huddled in the corner of a shelf, displaced by white jars and sprays with flowers on them. Patrick's sons wanted to know why women took so long in the bathroom. I could tell them.

Kate said, 'It's an awful lot of clothes. Hope I haven't forced you out.'

'Not at all. Move anything in the way.'

Empty words. From both of us.

'By the way, this fell out of your jacket when I was hanging it up.' She handed me the photograph. 'Nice kid, who is she?'

I tensed. 'Just something I'm dealing with.'

'Is she missing?'

Her eyes stay on my face a moment longer than they needed to before her attention moved back to finding room for her caravan. Later we discussed Alan and Jackie and the subject didn't come up again. Kate was delighted for them.

She said, 'Haven't known Alan long. All he has in his life is music. You should've seen him at the rehearsal, like a dog with two tails.'

'See. Told you she wasn't interested in me, but yeah, Jackie's a workaholic. Can't be good for her. There has to be balance otherwise one day you'll wake up and it'll be too late.'

I heard myself and wondered how I'd survived before Kate Calder came along with her calming influence.

We stayed up late, drinking too much wine, talking about how it had been before we met. The next morning I woke with rain on the bedroom window and Kate Calder beside me. Behind my eyes hurt. Caffeine was the answer. I slipped out of bed, pulled on jeans and went downstairs to the kitchen. A cup of Columbian Extra Dark cleared my head enough to remember things I'd said and promises made in the wee small hours. I intended to keep those promises. No difficult decision. At last I'd found someone to spend life with. If Kate still had doubts she kept them hidden. We fell asleep in each other's arms with dawn breaking over the city.

In the bathroom, I ran water until steam clouded the mirror, squeezed shaving foam into my palm and lathered my face. Andrew was picking me up in an hour. Plenty of time.

I didn't know she was there until a kiss brushed my left shoulder. I smiled and started to turn. She wouldn't let me. Hot breath seared my neck and roared in my ear, fingers following an invisible line from my chest to inside my jeans. The top button was already undone. She took hold of me. I shivered and grew in her hand. The denims edged down my thighs to the floor and I was naked. A noise I didn't recognise broke the silence; it came from me. Kisses changed to bites. Gentle massage quickened to urgent strokes.

I broke free and crushed her breasts against me. Our bodies pressed skin against skin, but Kate wasn't ready to relinquish control. She dropped to her knees and took me, licking, sucking, swallowing me whole. I threw back my head and tried not to lose it. At the last moment I pulled away and fell to the floor. She joined me, found me, and the excruciating pleasure started again. I spread her legs and buried my tongue between her undulating buttocks. She called out, raked my back and climaxed.

We rose to our feet and crashed against the wall, locked at the mouth. My hands cradled her cheeks and I pounded her, thrust after thrust with Kate matching me, bucking and fucking, giving as good as she got.

The end was a tsunami that lifted us high above the earth and washed us up on a distant shore, spent and exhausted. When we recovered Kate said, 'So you're sure you don't mind about the clothes?'

'Absolutely fine,' I said, and meant it.

28

Jackie picked Monday morning to break the news. I'd ordered a macchiato. She brought it over with two tiny biscuits.

'I've come to a decision, Charlie.'

'Oh yeah, about what?'

'The offer I got weeks ago. The job with the Meridian Group? I'm taking it. I'm leaving.'

A hundred thoughts charged though my brain, most of them selfish, none of them positive. 'When?'

'They wanted me to start right away. I told them it was too near Christmas. It wouldn't be fair to quit New York Blue with the bookings we already have.'

'So when?'

'January. I've told Alex I'll work December. That gives him time to find somebody else.'

Somebody else? She had to be joking; there wasn't anybody else. Jackie Mallon was one of a kind. That wasn't what I said.

'Sorry you're going but perhaps it's for the best.'

My reaction took her by surprise.

She swept to the bar leaving me with a problem. The current arrangement allowed me to have city centre office space free. With Jackie gone and in spite of what I'd done for Alex in the past, that could change. A new manager keen to make an impression might want to turn the office into a private dining room. For all the wrong reasons I suddenly wished I had mended some fences earlier.

I headed upstairs to find I had mail. One letter; a reminder from Yellow Pages hidden in a chatty paragraph and signed by A M Norman, whoever he was. Because I was valued customer – is there any other kind? – Norrie was pegging the fee for another six months. The empty space and the silent telephone made me wonder if it was the deal he thought it was. My only client was Mai Ling. She wouldn't be paying me anything and, unless I found Frank Lennon, it was going to cost the price of a ticket to Bangkok. Not a great business model.

I assessed what I'd learned. Michael Corrigan said Lennon was a sleaze. Angela Armstrong called him sweet. "One of the good guys". Rose Devlin insinuated that if I'd known the missing lecturer I'd understand why Alison Downey ran from him. But then Rose "made stuff up" according to Valerie Cummings, who didn't share her friend's opinion and came across as reliable. A nice girl in the wrong company.

The most compelling evidence was at Lennon's flat; the smell of recent redecoration and the new bed.

Old ground.

The only people I hadn't managed to speak to were the boys. Valerie gave them an alibi of sorts saying they'd quit the Drum and Monkey and suggested she went with them. When the student and the lecturer fell out they had already left.

I buzzed Jackie and told her to ask Pat Logue to join me. He brought his pint. By the look on his face it wasn't bringing him much joy. Patrick was in the doldrums, ready to launch into another moan about his wife. I got in first. I said, 'Loose ends. Can't call it a day until we've explored every possibility.'

'Thought we had.'

'No. Brian Lawrence keeps coming up. Him and his pals, Davie Wilson and Tommy Boyd.'

'Back to the college, is it?'

'Not much point. Galbraith won't help. Told me not to expect anything else from them.'

'He's a balloon.'

'Sticks and stones.'

'So what?'

'The boys left the Drum and Monkey and went to the Ark.'

'Don't know it.'

'It's a student bar in North Frederick Street. Call me when they show.'

'Sorry, Charlie, no can do. No karaoke clubs and student bars. Have to protect my sanity.'

'Don't go in.'

'Stay outside? In this weather? For how long?'

'For as long as it takes.'

He downed a third of his drink in one and wiped white froth from his top lip. 'Startin' when?'

'Tonight.'

He sighed. The world was against him. 'Nothin' doin' at home anyway. Which one am I looking for?'

'Whoever shows up.'

'Think they've done somethin'? I mean, they asked Valerie Cummings to leave with them. As alibis go it's not bad.'

'They're all that's left, Patrick. You keep telling me the case is a bust. This is the last throw. If their story pans then you and Andrew are right and it's over.'

'Fair play to you, Charlie, a mongrel with a bone couldn't have held on tighter.'

Pat Logue called later, just checking in. No sign of Brian Lawrence or his pals. It could be a long wait. That night I had the flat to myself. I'd spoken to Kate on the phone. She seemed distracted. I asked if she was all right and she said she was fine. Something in her voice told me she was holding back. Moving in had been exciting; the sex was wonderful. Perhaps we had progressed too quickly for her. She could be having second thoughts. I'd tried to keep what was on my mind away from Kate – God knows I hadn't been easy to work with – maybe she'd sensed some of it and decided to pass after all. A couple of times during the day I spotted Alex and Jackie deep in conversation and wondered if my office wasn't part of an attractive new package to keep her at NYB. On the way home I stopped at the Moti Mahal, got dinner and fell asleep on the sofa before I ate it. The insistent ringing brought me back to the world. It was Patrick: the boys had arrived at the Ark. What should he do? I told him to stay in the background, grabbed my car keys and left, pleased to have something to do.

It was cold. Snowflakes fluttered from the darkness. Glaswegians didn't do Tuesday night, especially in November; restaurants were empty, the pubs were deserted. Apart from the occasional straggler there was no one on the streets. And it was only nine thirty. I drove fast through Charing Cross and along Sauchiehall Street until the one way system forced me on to West Regent Street. The lights at George Square halted my progress.

A homeless man in a heavy coat, several sizes too big, crossed in front of the car and gave me a baleful glance. My life was a breeze compared with his. I tried to imagine how anybody living rough got through the winter.

Patrick was on the pavement in North Frederick Street.

'They're playing pool,' he said.

'All of them?'

'No. Just Brian Lawrence and Davie Wilson. Lawrence is the leader. Can tell by the body language. Not the type to let a girl bully him. I'm surprised Devlin gets away with it.'

'They haven't seen you?'

'Only went in as far as the door. Told you, Charlie, student boozers aren't for me. Too many young upstarts. The two at home are enough, thanks very much.'

The Ark was busier than most places in the city. A couple of dozen guys spinning out their loans. This was the place to do it. A yellow card pub, which meant deals on food and drink.

Patrick pointed to the blonde haired boy chalking a cue and his mate stretching across the green baize. Unturned stones. They didn't notice us until we reached them. Their expressions hardened. The jungle drums had carried the message. No questions about who we were; they already knew. Andrew would have used his warrant card as his introduction. I lacked that authority. These guys didn't have to give me the time of day.

I said, 'Who's winning?'

Brian Lawrence's eyes met mine. 'Davie. Fancy a game?'

Pat said, 'I'll play the winner.'

Davie Wilson potted three in a row. The next ball rattled the jaws of the pocket and stayed out. On another day it would've gone in.

Patrick said, 'No luck.'

Brian stepped forward, eyes narrowed, studying the table. Our being there seemed to bring out the best in him. In minutes only one ball was left. I waited until he had the shot lined up before I spoke.

'Seen Alison Downey on your travels?'

The ball hit the pocket dead centre and disappeared. Davie tapped the edge of the table.

'Shot.'

Pat Logue racked, tossed a coin and caught it on the back of his hand. When it was in the air Brian called heads.

'Heads it is.'

'You break.'

Patrick positioned himself, feet apart, head steady, eyes following the length of the cue.

'Loser buys the beer, okay?'

The pack split with a crack; nothing went down. Brian Lawrence lined up a loose ball and put it away. Another followed, and another.

I nodded at Davie. 'Is he better than you?'

He allowed a slow smile to play on his lips.

'No chance. Beginners luck.'

'So Alison, when did you last see her?'

Brian didn't allow me to interfere with his game.

'Haven't, she must've dropped out.'

'Your conclusion or Rose's?'

'What's that supposed to mean?'

'She makes the decisions in your group, doesn't she?'

Brian screwed up his face. 'Get real.'

'And she's Alison's friend, right?'

The boys looked at each other.

Davie said, 'The Drum a couple of months ago.'

'Anything about her strike you as odd?'

'No she was fine.'

'Was she drunk?'

Brian potted another ball. 'Yeah, she'd had a few.'

'Frank Lennon hasn't been in college either. Were they together?'

'Saw him. Saw her. Not together.'

Patrick still wasn't off the mark. The student was beating him easily. If he was concerned it didn't show.

'Was it a good night?'

A fortunate ricochet helped one ball go down, left a second one hanging over the pocket and set up an easy third. Brian shrugged, indifference rolled off him.

'It was all right.'

'Why leave early?'

'Same old faces. Wasn't in the mood.'

He had two shots left: a risky double and his final ball. He took the first and sank it. His beginner's luck was holding.

'Nothing to do with the row you had with Alison?'

'Ally fell out with everybody.'

'Did she fall out with you?'

'Only every day. She wasn't keen on me.'

Davie laughed. 'Maybe it was your aftershave.'

'But you were keen on her. You gave her Ecstasy.'

For the first time his confidence faltered.

'That's a lie. I had it but I didn't give it to her.'

'Not what I heard.'

'Somebody's talking out their arse. Never happened.'

'Sure?'

'Ally was pissed. Not my fault.'

'And Lennon?'

'Hardly spoke to the guy. He was in the pub when we left.'

His ball lay against the cushion. Brian had lost his composure; he rushed it and missed. Patrick walked round the table chalking his cue, whistling silently, assessing the spread. He bent to take on the first shot and didn't rise until he'd cleared the table. The boys watched in silence. When the final ball disappeared he put the cue down.

'I'll get that drink next time.'

In the car I said, 'For a while I thought he had you.'

'For a while so did I, Charlie. Now let's put Mai Thai on that plane.'

29

Hawick, 99 miles from Glasgow

Seven women to every man. He'd read that fascinating statistic somewhere.

He gazed up and down the High Street. Certainly plenty of females. He should have come here before.

In the beginning the adventures were restricted to one a year and far from where he lived. Once he'd driven to Blackpool. Instinct told him to forget it that day. Instinct was never wrong. The right opportunity came in Carlisle on the way home – a mother of three, harassed out of her mind, waiting inside the station. Whoever was meeting her was late and the children were howling. The eldest, a boy no older than five, ran back to see the trains. The woman chased after him leaving her eighteen month old daughter. He was parked on a double yellow line less than ten yards away. It couldn't have been simpler. Yet it didn't satisfy him. No risk worth talking about. When his hands trembled and his heart raced in his chest, those were the best, the ones he lived for. Knowing at any moment it might be over; the distracted adult suddenly turns, or happens to look up; the chase and the inevitable capture. Thinking about it made the hairs on the back of his neck stand on end and brought the empty feeling to his stomach. There was nothing like it.

No plan. All off the cuff. Circumstances presented themselves and he made the decision. Usually he drove somewhere, parked, and walked around window shopping, keeping himself to himself. Sometimes he'd have a bite to eat. It amused him to sit in a crowded tearoom with mothers and their obstreperous children. Obstreperous. An old fashioned word his grandfather had used; it summed them up. Noisy whinging brats. Disruptive yahoos. He shouldn't be too hard on them. Their behaviour distracted their keepers. Carlisle was an example.

The more he studied people the more he realised most of them were thick. Not fit to be in charge of kids. They couldn't keep their minds on the job, and, when it went wrong they'd scream the place down. What did they expect? He wasn't complaining. Those same fools made it possible. If they were paying attention the way they were supposed to the drive back would be unbearable. He had travelled all over and found excitement beyond anything he could've imagined. A good run. Remarkable considering. Today it was Hawick. Border country. And seven women to every man.

He had lunch in the Golden Wok; chicken fried rice without the chicken. These foreigners shouldn't be allowed to come here. When he'd eaten most of it he called the waiter over and pointed to the plate. 'Where's the chicken? There's no chicken in it. Haven't you heard of the Trades Description Act?'

The man peered at the last couple of forkfuls and wagged a finger.

'You should tell me no chicken. Now too late.'

On the street he was angry. He had drawn attention to himself. That told him he wasn't focussed. Chicken fried rice! Sharpen up or forget it. Get in the car and go home. He was beginning to dislike Hawick.

Later in the afternoon he noticed a steady stream of women parking prams and buggies at the door of the town hall. The board outside told him the attraction. Weight Watchers. 3pm-4pm every Wednesday. Some brought a friend for support; the friend was the slim confident one who smiled. He pictured the scene inside: a line of chairs against the wall, females hoping against hope their sacrifice wasn't in vain, or that their weakness wouldn't be punished. In the middle of the floor the dreaded scales that never lied and a trim lady with a clip board recording the results, congratulating, encouraging and consoling. He didn't understand obsessions like food and alcohol; the only advice he gave his patients was if it made you feel bad, don't do it.

It was turning into a wasted trip. A lost argument over a greasy Chinky and nothing else. He stood in a doorway and timed a beefy thirtysomething in and out in twelve minutes. Going by her expression, not good news. No, if this was all there was he'd pass. Where was the thrill? Unless he finessed the game and gave them a chance. Say eleven minutes. Make it interesting, ten and a half.

Nobody could accuse him of taking advantage like the Chinaman and his breed.

The woman was obviously stressed. Perhaps her day hadn't gone any better than his. Or maybe she was haunted by the memory of those chocolate biscuits and a truth she couldn't escape. "Oh dear, Sheila, that is disappointing, isn't it?" A moment on the lips...

The buggy went beside a cream pram that must have cost the proud grand-parents plenty. The mother spoke to the child.

Goo-goo. Ga-ga. Take a long last look, mum.

He checked his watch and started the countdown. Three females came out, glum faces comparing notes, making promises none of them intended to keep. He laughed a nervous laugh. First stop the cake shop, eh ladies? Blow away the blues. Not for them of course. A treat for their husbands. Not for them. They were on a diet.

After eight minutes his palms started to sweat. At nine his breathing came in shallow gulps. On ten minutes he crossed the road. His heart thudded against his chest, pins and needles sparked in his fingertips and he felt lightheaded. The child was asleep. He released the brake, pulled the buggy out and headed down the street, so excited he could barely see, but he didn't run, he walked. This would be one of the great ones. He was elated.

The cry broke the spell. A shrill sound that rallied the women in the hall. He heard them coming after him and quickened his step. Something struck his shoulder. He let go of the buggy. It trundled in front of a car, almost under the wheels. He ran. A passer-by stuck out a foot and tripped him and he fell full length. Before he could recover they were kicking and punching, tearing at him. A false nail ripped his cheek. Shoes became weapons. His jaw cracked. Blood blinded him and he lost consciousness. His last memory was cursing snarling females, hissing and spitting and wounding him.

Seven women for every man.

The call came at midnight. DS Geddes drove through Peebles and Innerleithen, ghostly and deserted, to Hawick and the Borders. There was nothing on the road. Just as well. DCI Baillie put a hand against the dashboard.

'Christ's sake slow up, Andrew, he's not going anywhere. No need to kill us.'

The detective inspector had spent most of his career in Manchester and was used to the city. Racing through the sticks in the dark wasn't an experience he welcomed.

The DS kept his eyes on the road. 'Can't believe we might have him. Hasn't sunk in.'

'We don't have him, not yet.'

'How bad is he?'

'Broken arm, broken femur, broken jaw, cracked ribs, concussion. Lucky they didn't do for him. Ever had a fight with a woman? Well don't. It's a lose lose situation. If you hit back you're a bastard. If you don't they murder you. He got attacked by a gang of them. Wouldn't wish it on anybody, except knowing what he's done it couldn't happen to a better guy.'

'And they're holding him at the hospital?'

'Under guard. For his own protection in case they come after him. Feelings are running high in the town. He won't be going far.'

They discussed their approach. DS Geddes said, 'Can I have first go at him? I saw what he did to Eva Reynolds.'

'If you like, just don't expect him to cave in. No conscience, sick bastards never have.'

A crowd gathered at the hospital main door. Four uniformed officers barred the way. Geddes pulled into the car park. He said, 'Looks like the final scene from a Frankenstein movie. The villagers out to destroy the monster.'

'Apt. Our job is to make sure a jury gets to meet the monster in person.'

They pushed through the crowd to angry shouts. The OIC introduced himself and filled them in.

'DI Lawler. Just as I said on the telephone, a woman leaving Weight Watchers spotted a man taking a buggy with her son in it. She ran inside screaming. That brought the whole class out. They caught him further along the street and laid into him. Bastard nearly had the kid under a car.'

'Where is he?'

'First floor. Two of our men are with him.'

'Got a name?'

'Yes. Credit cards say he's Richard Hill.'

The name flashed in Geddes' brain.

'We're doing background. Should know more in the morning. But he's not local.'

'Has he said anything?'

The policeman smiled. 'With his jaw wired, not much. Maybe he'll be in a more chatty mood with you. And good luck. I'm guessing this isn't his first. Hope you nail him.'

DCI Baillie flashed his warrant card and one of the uniforms opened the door. Richard Hill was bandaged from head to foot, his leg suspended in a sling, a match for the one cradling his arm. It was clear the man was in pain. His eyes darted between the visitors. DS Geddes pulled two chairs over to the bed and sat down. He studied the face hidden behind the dressings and felt a stab of recognition. A nod from the senior officer gave him permission to begin.

'They say people like you really want to get caught, is that true?'

No answer.

'Not responsible for their actions. Find that hard to believe.'

The eyes stared hatred.

'You made a name for yourself down here today, Richard. Not every man gets a hammering from a bunch of farmer's daughters. You're a VIP. A very important pervert.'

Hill whispered through swollen lips. 'I'm going to sue them.'

Geddes leaned forward. 'Listen' he said, 'there's a mob outside who want us to look the other way. They think you should be strung up by the balls. Personally I don't agree, but I can see where they're coming from. Now let's start at the beginning and cut the fucking crap.'

30

The telephone rang for what seemed like two minutes after I finally managed to fall over. Outside it was still dark. I brushed sleep from my eyes and looked at my watch: ten past six. Who the hell was calling at ten past six in the morning? At the other end of the line Andrew sounded out of breath.

'Heads up, Charlie. Got somebody in custody. A doctor would you believe? Name of Richard Hill. Be on the news in an hour or two. Wanted you to know before it breaks.'

'The Hamilton case?'

I heard him inhale. 'It's a possibility.'

'Thanks, Andrew. Thanks for telling me.'

I lay on the bed with my heart drumming. Irrational. Kicking every ball, Pat Logue would say. Not healthy. Not good. I couldn't allow myself to be thrown off every time the Ayr abduction was mentioned. Up and down like the grand old Duke of York.

Get a grip, Cameron!

At the end of a wasted day I went back to the flat. It was empty. Kate was at her place. Our last conversation still rankled. I got the impression she was holding back and heard relief in her voice when the call ended; a far cry from the woman who ambushed me in the bathroom.

Patrick's haste was understandable; he wanted shot of Frank Lennon's Thai girlfriend as soon as possible. Unfortunately he was too quick to draw the final line under the missing student and the lecturer and had forgotten the third boy. Tommy Boyd was the last piece in a puzzle that had never come together. Talking to him might be going through the motions but there was nothing else.

I switched the TV on and tried to find something interesting. On one channel a guy with a Geordie accent said, 'Day Seventeen. Jason makes toast.'

Judge not that ye be not judged.

Except life really was too short. I zapped the big button and watched the screen go black. The door knocked. Andrew Geddes looked dead beat. Operation Damocles had added years to him. He fell into an armchair.

'Sorry to intrude, Charlie. Just needed to talk to somebody. Tossed a coin. You lost.'

I got a beer from the fridge and handed it to him.

He said, 'Rather have a whisky if it's all the same to you.'

'Sorry. Out.'

He pulled the top off the can and gulped half of it down.

'Why did I have to marry the most unreasonable woman on the planet?'

'Elspeth's still at it?'

'Can't deal with it right now.'

'Thought you'd be cock a hoop. You caught your man.'

Andrew rubbed his eyes. 'Not that simple, Charlie. He's been charged with attempted abduction. He'll go down, no question, but he hasn't admitted to anything else.'

'Then maybe it isn't him.'

The suggestion irritated the detective. 'It's him all right. Absolutely it's him. You have to understand, this is the next stage. In his twisted mind he still has control. The families need a body to bury. They need closure. This guy could give it to them. By staying silent he hurts them even more. Ever wondered why Ian Brady won't tell the police where all his victims are buried? Think he can't remember?'

He answered his own questions and didn't register my reaction to his words.

'Because knowledge is power. It's a game.'

'So what do you do?'

'Keep at him. Play to his vanity and hope his God complex gets the better of him.'

'Did you interview him?'

He nodded. 'This guy took a child from outside a Weight Watchers class, got chased down the street and almost sent the baby under a car. Broad daylight. Two dozen witnesses, and you know what? All he talked about was how he was going to sue the women who caught him. Classic psychopath. Face to face with that kind of madness, it's frightening.'

slapping the sand, crunching shingle, beating against rock

Andrew was taking it hard, harder than I'd ever seen him. This wasn't the moment to pressure him with questions.

'And when I come off duty, Elspeth and her Rottweiler are waiting for me.'

'Have another beer.'

'Thanks, I will. What's going on with you?'

I gave him a can and told him again about Galbraith, Rose Devlin's gang and the night at the Drum and Monkey. He smiled when I described Mai Ling and Pat Logue's marital disharmony. Anything that upset Patrick was good news.

'Pleased to hear somebody has him on the run.'

'One student I haven't been able to talk to. A boy called Tommy Boyd, part of the gang. Works at a hotel near the SECC. Looks as if he's packed in college, too. I'm going to see him tomorrow, assuming he's still there.'

Andrew finished his drink and pulled himself out of the chair.

'Got to hand it to you, Charlie, you're a trier. Should've joined the Force instead of this PI shit.'

'Too much like my father. Can't be an Indian. Have to be a chief.'

'You said it.'

'So I'm wasting my time.'

'It's your time. Told you what I think.'

'I know. They're shagging their brains out at a B & B in Paisley. Maybe they are. But for two months?'

'Your pal won't put up with his house guest much longer. Can't say I blame him.'

'She'll be on her way to Thailand in a couple of days. Lennon let her down. That's all she understands.'

'If she's as good looking as you say, she won't have to wait for another one to come along.'

DS Geddes could be an unfeeling bastard.

'Hope you break Hill.'

'The ball's in his court. Problem is he knows it.'

Pat Logue and the detective didn't see eye to eye. For once Patrick and Andrew were in agreement; I was barking up the wrong tree with Downey and Lennon, yet I wouldn't back off. Staying focussed brought results but it could also become obsession. Once I'd spoken to Tommy Boyd that would be it for me. There were more important issues to resolve, like where the hell Kate had put the razor blades.

Patrick was in a good mood. For him the end was in sight. The week he'd given me was almost up.

He beamed. 'What's the plan?'

'Go to the Hilton Garden Inn and talk to Tommy Boyd.'

Pat said, 'Then straight to Trailfinders and get Mai Ling booked up?'

'Probably. Her and Gail still out on the town?'

'No. Worse. They stay at home watching the E Entertainment channel and giving each other manicures. Mai Ling's getting above herself. Told me to turn the TV volume down the other night. Not asked. Told. Straight red, no question. Was all I could do to keep from wringing her delicate neck. Gail heard her and didn't say anything. If she doesn't watch it she'll be out on her arse along with her pal.'

Patrick felt better for getting that off his chest. 'So you see, Charlie, nothing personal and all that, but you're into time added. This kid is the last kick of the ball.'

In the car he gave his attention to where we were going and why.

'Something occurs to me about Tommy. He's part of the Devlin gang and one of the musketeers, except he never gets a mention. The quiet man. When Lennon and Alison fell out he was on his way to get the car. Don't expect him to have anything new to say. Everybody agrees he wasn't there.'

The Hilton Garden was on the river, by a weird irony, not far from Frank Lennon's flat. This part of the city was different from the rest of Glasgow; regenerated, redeveloped. When tourism was the Great White Hope the old docks were in-filled and the Scottish Exhibition and Conference Centre was built. Millions were poured into the Destination Glasgow dream. Delegates meant bed nights, restaurant bookings; increased spending in the shops and hotels like this one.

I pulled into the car park, got out and shivered. A cold wind was coming off the river; a storm was on its way. Patrick pointed past the Finnieston Crane to the Clyde Auditorium next to the SECC, known as the Armadillo because of its shape. Pat said, 'Fantastic, isn't it? Keep the parliament, that's what I call vision.'

I couldn't share his enthusiasm. My mind was on the final unturned stone. We went to reception and asked if Tommy Boyd was working. A bright eyed blonde told us he was in the restaurant. I checked my watch: ten minutes to twelve. Lunch service wouldn't start until half past. We pushed the glass door open and bumped into two young men wearing white shirts and black waistcoats, standing by the till. I knew Tommy was one of them.

I said, 'Tommy Boyd? Can I have a word?'

He took a step away, instantly wary.

'What about?'

'Alison Down...'

The sentence stayed unfinished, he pushed past me, knocked Patrick to the floor and ran. I went after him. Outside was empty space, a couple of acres of parking for the SECC. Nowhere to hide.

The boy raced along the embankment towards the Armadillo. In my heart of hearts I had accepted Andrew Geddes and Pat Logue were right and I'd been chasing shadows. It didn't seem like it now. Tommy could give me twenty years. I could kill myself trying to stay with him. If he dived into the Clyde I would need to go in. Not the most attractive choices. What happened next surprised me.

He threw himself at the fence around the Crane, gripped the links and began to climb. It wasn't high, nine or ten feet, enough to deter most people from trying to get over it. At the top his shirt caught on the barbed wire and ripped. He didn't notice. He didn't stop. He didn't look back.

We only wanted to speak to him. Why had he run? And why here? I watched him pound up the first flight of steel stairs and heard Patrick behind me.

'Where does he think he's going?'

The boy stopped on the third tier and stared at us. His body shuddered; he was crying uncontrollably. I shouted to him to come down. The wind tore the words from my mouth. He looked at me. I saw his face and knew the crane was no accident. I dragged off my coat.

Pat said, 'You can't be serious, Charlie. Call the police, let them deal with it.'

'No time.'

Patrick wasn't getting it. 'Where can he go? The cops will talk him down.'

'He's not coming down. He's going to jump.'

'Why would he?'

'Look at him, he's desperate. Call Andrew. Now!'

It took a lot of effort but I managed the fence. The next bit was harder. Six metal ladders leading to the revolving platform and another to get to the top. The Finnieston Crane stretched 175 feet to the sky – three times the height of the Scott Monument.

Tommy Boyd was above me and out of sight. I could hear his footsteps echoing. The first flights were no problem. Edinburgh had been good practice. By the fifth I was breathless, my calves hurt and a dull ache in my chest warned me I was pushing it. The sixth staircase was a bridge too far but I couldn't stop. One last effort brought me into the cabin with CLYDEPORT written on the side. I collapsed with the steel floor cold and hard under me.

Tommy was at the end of the jib 200 feet away. I got to my feet and walked towards him. He saw me and straddled the railing that went all the way round, half on half off, one leg dangling in space.

The sky darkened; the storm was closing in. On the ground a crowd gathered to watch the excitement. At this height, with no protection, the wind was strong. It blew the boy's hair and played with the torn shirt sleeve.

'Easy, Tommy. Take it easy.'

I edged forward.

'We can talk about it. It'll be all right. I promise.'

He gazed across the city to the Hilton Garden. He should be serving soup to businessmen, instead he was inches from death. He lifted his other leg over. Through the spars I saw the people below pointing up at us. At any moment Tommy Boyd could be gone. If he jumped there was nothing I could do. I wouldn't get to him in time. A gust rocked him; his body swayed. The clouds opened. Rain started to fall. Big rain. Fat rain, tiny bombs exploding in sheets on the jib. The storm had arrived. One slip would be enough to send him down. He spoke through sobs and rubbed his eyes with his knuckles like a tired child.

'It wasn't me. It was them. They did it.'

Lying was all that was left. 'I know. Davie told me. Nobody's blaming you.'

I had his attention.

'Nobody blames you, Tommy.'

He repeated his mantra. 'They did it.'

I held out my hand, willing him to take it. 'Come out of the rain and we'll talk about it. Tell me what they did.'

31

The Drum and Monkey, Glasgow.

September 12.

Brian Lawrence put three tablets on the table and pushed them towards his friends. 'One for you, one for you, and one for me.' He swallowed. Davie did the same. Tommy Boyd hesitated. 'Not tonight, Bri.'

Brian shook his head. 'You're such a loser sometimes, Tommy, do you know that?'

'Got the car.'

'Chill out. And get the drinks in.'

His eyes travelled round the pub taking in the faces, strangers most of them, even after a year in the same class. Davie and Tommy were his friends, Valerie was all right too. The rest were numpties. He wondered where Alison and Rose were. Rose wasn't a numpty. She was a bitch.

Brian said, 'You're sure you don't want this?'

Tommy held his ground. 'Can't. Sorry.'

Brian put the X in his shirt pocket.

The DJ was playing Beady Eye. Rose Devlin waltzed in with Alison Downey behind her and came over to the boys. Alison was carrying a duffle bag; she looked stunning, then she always did. She went to the bar, leaned over the counter and gave the bag to the barman. Brian watched the short skirt ride up at the back. Rose saw him and smiled. She was in a good mood; the girls had split a bottle of wine before they left her house.

Rose said, 'I'd forget it if I were you. It isn't going to happen.'

Brian pretended he didn't understand. 'Don't know what you're on about.'

'Then you're even thicker than I thought.'

Alison came back with two glasses and the girls moved on. Davie said. 'Why do we hang out with that cheeky cow?'

Tommy said, 'You know why.'

Brian said nothing.

The Drum was busy when Frank Lennon arrived. He made the rounds. Lennon was unusual. He actually liked the kids he taught, socialising with them was a way of breaking barriers. Valerie Cummings was with Rose and Alison. Alison said something the lecturer didn't catch and giggled behind her hand. He pulled Valerie aside. 'What's she been drinking?'

'They started early. Rose is okay, Ally can't handle it.'

'For god's sake keep an eye on her. Don't let her have any more.'

When he'd gone Valerie spoke to Rose. 'He's worried about Ally.'

'Hope you told him to mind his own business.' She took money from her purse and gave it to Alison. 'You go. I can't be bothered. Same again.'

'Not for me,' Valerie said. 'And she doesn't need another drink.'

Nobody told Rose what to do. 'Why don't you mind your own business as well?'

Davie and Tommy were playing against each other on the machines. Brian was alone at the bar. Alison slipped her arm round his waist. Her eyes were glazed. She said, 'Rose likes to wind you up.'

'I ignore her.'

'Good.'

Their eyes met. The girl went into a tease. She ran her hand over his chest and stopped at the pocket.

'What's this?' Her fingers dipped inside. 'Look what I've found!'

Brian grabbed her wrist. 'Give it back, Ally.'

'Why? Is it for me?' She laughed. 'Tell the truth, you brought it for me, didn't you?' Her face was inches from his. He wanted to hit her. She spat the words and let the tablet fall from her palm.

The boy dropped to the floor and felt for it in the darkness. The girl taunted him.

'In your dreams.'

He picked the tablet up and stormed away, cursing.

Valerie came over. 'You all right, Ally?'

Alison said, 'I don't want Brian hanging about with us.'

'What's he done?'

'I'll talk to Rose.'

Valerie persisted. 'What?'

'Ecstasy.'

She got the drinks and paid. Brian rejoined his friends. Davie said, 'What was all that about?'

'Don't ask.' Ten minutes later he said, 'This is crap. Let's get out of here.'

'And go where?'

'Anywhere. Tommy's got the car.'

Davie spoke to Tommy. 'Brian wants to leave.'

'It's only half past ten.'

'Yeah, but Alison knocked him back. We'll meet you outside.'

Alison Downey had already forgotten Brian Lawrence. Her attention was on Frank Lennon talking to a group of students. She joined in, dominating the conversation with questions and interruptions until, one by one, the others drifted away and she had the lecturer to herself. Alcohol made her reckless.

Rose watched her squeeze into his seat, put her arms round him and bury her face in his neck. Rose smiled; in the morning Ally would be sorry, she'd make sure of it.

Brian stopped on his way to the door. 'We're off, Val, want to come?'

Valerie turned on him. 'What did you do to Ally?'

'Nothing.'

'Don't lie, you gave her an X.'

'She tell you that?'

'Rose is right, you're stupid. A big wee boy.'

Brian didn't care anymore. 'Think what you want.'

Frank Lennon had an intoxicated female student nuzzling his ear and didn't like it. He eased the girl off him as gently as he could. She seemed to come awake and realised she was being rejected. Her fists beat him. She swore, struggled out of the armchair and ran.

Davie and Brian were walking down Renfield Street when Alison Downey staggered past. She said something Davie couldn't hear and crossed to the other side. Whatever it was sent Brian into a rage; he'd taken all he was going to take from this bitch. He chased after her with Davie behind him. He grabbed her by the hair, dragged her into Renfield Lane and hurled her against an empty rubbish bin.

His hands clawed at her blouse. The buttons popped; one of her shoes came off. Brian pulled her bra with so much force the fixing sheared and her breasts fell out. He slapped her and bit her nipple. She screamed in pain.

There were people at the corner of Gibson Street near Central Station. Further down a crowd waited for a bus. Where they were on Renfield was deserted.

A taxi with its For Hire sign lit ran by. In the lane opposite, the Horse Shoe Bar must have had a quiet night. Nobody was around. Brian slapped the girl again. Davie heard her moan.

He said, 'For fuck's sake, Brian, that's enough.'

But it wasn't. Nothing like.

Frank Lennon was sorry he came to the Drum and Monkey. His first reaction when Alison threw a strop and ran was to let her go. If her friends had been around he would have told them and they could handle it. They weren't. That made it his responsibility. He wasn't comfortable with a girl on her own so late at night in the city, especially one who'd had too much to drink. He went outside to the corner just as Brian Lawrence hauled Alison into the lane. Lennon didn't think twice; he raced towards them. Davie saw him coming and put himself between the lecturer and what Brian was doing. Lennon landed a blow on the boy's temple. For a moment he was stunned, then he recovered and snapped: the other side of Ecstasy, the side that never gets talked about, kicked in. The student punched the older man and punched him again. Lennon fell backwards, his head struck the kerb. The moment he heard the crack Davie knew.

Alison was against the wall. Brian's right hand was over her mouth, the left tight round her throat. His trousers were at his ankles but he'd given up trying to rape the girl. He couldn't get an erection. He was trying to shut her up. The screams faded. She didn't fight back or defend herself. Her tongue hung slack from her mouth and her eyes were closed.

Davie stared at Frank Lennon's body. Seconds before he'd been alive. Now he was dead. The boy ran into the street waving frantically. Tommy was the only car at the lights half a block away. He took a chance and went through on red.

'Reverse. Reverse.'

'Reverse? What's going on?'

'Brian appeared from the lane, completely calm. Unnaturally calm. Dark patches stained his white shirt. He said, 'Reverse the car, Tommy. Do it now.'

They lifted the bodies into the boot and drove down Union Street. Brian took the wheel. The bus hadn't come; the crowd was still waiting. Tommy was in shock. He couldn't get his hands to stop shaking. His voice was a terrified whisper.

'You killed them. You killed them.'

Brian's answer chilled him to the bone. 'We're okay. Nobody saw us.'

Nobody had. Glasgow didn't do Tuesday night.

We were soaked to the skin. It didn't matter. The wind tugged Tommy Boyd's hair. Tears dried on his cheeks. Reliving the events had empted him.

'And that's what happened. One minute I was waiting for the lights to change, the next I was lifting dead people into the boot of my dad's car. I didn't want to. I wasn't asked. I was just there.'

It wasn't the end of the story. 'Where did you go?'

'Drove around. How long I can't remember. Every time we passed a police car I freaked.

Brian said, "Get a grip, Tommy, for fuck's sake." Davie knew an old abandoned brick works in Whiteinch. It took ages to find it but we did. That's where they are. We piled bricks on top of them. It was dark. Probably didn't hide them very well. Brian dropped Davie off at his house, then me, and walked home. Said it was safer. I lay awake all night thinking about it, terrified my dad would find bloodstains. At six o'clock I couldn't stand it any longer. I went to the car and checked. There wasn't any blood. There wasn't anything. Brian told us to act normal. Show up at college the same as usual. That was too much for me. I couldn't pretend. Rose would spot it a mile away, so I quit and haven't been back.'

'Have Brian or Davie contacted you?'

'No.'

'What about the college?'

'They sent a letter. I got to it first. My parents think everything's all right.'

'What've you been doing every day?'

'Working my shifts at the hotel. The rest of the time just wandering around.'

'For two months?'

'I needed to be on my own. Brian and Davie joking, laughing like they'd done nothing wrong...'

Tommy stopped speaking. He was the weakest link. The least able to live with the deaths of Alison Downey and Frank Lennon. He wasn't a murderer. None of them were. Nevertheless two people were dead. You didn't have to be a murderer to kill.

On the SECC concourse a police car slewed to a halt. Two officers got out. In the distance the flashing light of an ambulance on its way. The fire brigade wouldn't be far behind.

Ibrox stadium rose above the tenements on the other side of the river. On this side the blackened spires of Glasgow University pointed at the muddy sky. Over Tommy Boyd's shoulder a British Airways jet made its descent to the airport, unaware of the drama below.

And the rain came down.

Frank Lennon had lost his chance of happiness and his life. Somebody had to break it to Mai Ling. I guessed that would be me.

Tommy said, 'So what now?'

There was no short answer, no quick way to tell him his future had changed. I didn't try. I put my hand on his shoulder.

'For a start let's get off this bloody thing.'

32

The justice system is based on the presumption of innocence. In the Scottish Borders it was being tested and found wanting; the chase along Hawick High Street and a dozen witnesses made it difficult to keep an open mind. The public, already angered by the serial killer revelation, were convinced the man now in custody in Glasgow was guilty.

The arrest dominated the news. A crowd of angry women had done what Operation Damocles with all its resources couldn't. Andrew Geddes wasn't around. No need to wonder why. Hundreds of man hours, skill and experience hadn't brought the result. Great detective work played no part. It was luck. In the end, to some degree, it always was.

There was a definite improvement in Jackie's mood since Sunday; the rumour about bald men must be true. All of a sudden I wasn't the enemy. A line had been drawn and the terse little episode was behind us. Even Pat Logue noticed.

'Somebody's happy. Wonder who he is. When a woman smiles, seven times out of ten she's got a new guy or new shoes.'

On my way out my mobile rang; an unfamiliar number. The caller didn't introduce himself. It took fifteen seconds to realise it was Ronnie Simpson, frantic with excitement, his voice high-pitched, breathless, the words tumbling out.

'It's him! Tell your pal it's him!'

'Ronnie? Hold on. Calm down. What do you mean it's him? Who?'

'He's a slippery bastard, Charlie, slippery as they come. Couldn't prove it. Had to let him go.'

'Ronnie. Ronnie. Who're you talking about?'

'Hill. Richard Hill. Hawick. Tell your mate. Was having the chemo and missed it. Didn't have enough energy to read the paper.'

I couldn't believe what I was hearing. Ronnie Simpson knew the suspect Andrew had in custody.

'Wait a minute, Ronnie, you're saying you met this guy?'

'Right.'

'When was this?'

'The last case I worked on. It's in one of the files. Come and get it.'

Wherever I had been going got forgotten. I went back to the office, phoned Andrew and agreed to go and see Ronnie with him next morning. The DS, normally a stickler for protocol, was happy to relax his rigid moral code.

'Thank Christ for somebody ignoring the rules. And slippery is right. We'll need everything we can lay our hands on to nail this guy. What did Ronnie say exactly? Tell me again.'

I did. But Andrew's anticipation pouring down the line had infected me. At the end of our conversation my pulse was racing and Pamela was in my head. Maybe there was a reference to a Richard Hill buried in the notes. I took out the file, started to open it then stopped myself. Ronnie Simpson was talking about somebody else's child, somebody else's son or daughter. Just as loved, just as missed. It couldn't always be about me no matter how much I wanted it.

I closed the folder. Tomorrow would arrive soon enough.

Andrew guided the car crazy fast round the twisting road more suited to sightseers and Sunday traffic. I wasn't ready to die.

I said, 'Slow down will you?' and got ignored.

To our left, the river Clyde rushed by foaming coffee and cream against rocks on its way to the city and the coast thirty miles beyond. Andrew blew the horn at a dawdling Fiat and managed to inject an extra measure of irritation into it. The driver was unimpressed and stayed in the middle of the road. Andrew exploded. 'At this rate we'll be overtaken by some wee girl on roller skates.'

He pounded the top of the steering column. 'Come on, come on! Edge up!'

At a blind bend he accelerated and flew past the slowcoach, glaring at the blonde behind the wheel, reminding me of the alarming statistic that policemen were involved in more accidents than any other section of the population, apart from teenage boys.

'A woman. Might've known. Worst in the world. The mirror's for checking their make up.'

'Take it easy.'

He wouldn't be told. 'It's true. Most of them think the indicators are a soul band.'

The DS was wired, more irascible than usual, hoping against hope Ronnie Simpson had something he could use. The pressure of Damocles was telling. He was lashing out at his favourite target: women. I let him get on with it, gazed out of the window and thought about Kate. Outside Biggar, fear of being disappointed began to make him mistrust. I heard it in his voice.

'What's Ronnie like. You told me he's old, how old?'

'Old and tired, Andrew, but as sharp as you or me.'

He mulled that over in silence for a while. I said, 'He wouldn't bring us up here on a wild goose chase. If he says there's a connection you can bet on it. Remember, in his day this guy was a very good copper. A great copper.'

Suspicion rolled off him; he couldn't help himself.

'I believe you, Charlie. It's the "in his day" bit that worries me.'

The nurse I'd met on my last visit greeted us. I got the impression she was waiting for me.

'He's expecting you,' she said. 'His blood pressure is through the roof. Too much excitement won't be good for him. We've only just got the blood sugar level back under control. Apart from everything else, Mr Simpson is diabetic.'

She shot an accusing look at me. 'Some idiot gave him alcohol. Could've caused a stroke.'

I studied my shoes.

Ronnie was sitting on the bed holding a folder to his chest as if he was afraid to let it go. He seemed to be wearing somebody else's clothes and more hair had gone from his head. His skin was the colour of putty, yellowed and dark beneath the eyes, hanging in pouches. I wondered whether the cure wasn't worse than the illness. He brightened as soon as he saw us.

'Couldn't sleep last night in case I lost this. Had the light on every couple of hours, rereading it.'

'This is the friend I told you about, DS Andrew Geddes.'

Andrew shook Ronnie's emaciated hand. 'Please to meet you, sir.'

Nice one, Andrew.

Ronnie said, 'Been over this file so often I know what it says by heart.'

'Then let's hear it.'

He drew himself straight, turned to the detective sergeant and delivered his report, one copper to another. 'Eighteen years ago, Leela Malik, a nine year old Indian girl disappeared in Tranent one Wednesday on her way home from school. Two pals walked her to the end of her street and left her sixty yards from her front door. The wee girl never got there. At three fifteen in the afternoon she vanished. Broad daylight.'

'The parents were originally from Hyderabad and had been living in the town for eleven years, seven of them running a newsagents. Three weeks earlier they'd reported some local youths making a nuisance of themselves. Hanging around the door intimidating old ladies going in and out. Doing a bit of shoplifting probably. The aggravation got so bad the police were called on two occasions. Of course, by the time the uniforms arrived the boys had moved on. When Leela went missing we hauled them in. Frightened the crap out of them but couldn't find anything to connect them with the girl.'

Andrew said, 'So you thought racial.'

'Right. A team conducted door to door interviews with every resident in the area. Nobody had a bad word to say about the Maliks and didn't know anybody who did.'

It was a curious spectacle: Ronnie with colour in his cheeks, rattling off an old case without referring to the file, an impressive performance from a dying man, and Andrew, listening to every word.

Ronnie Simpson said, 'Of course we got the parents in, separately and together. Poor people couldn't understand what was happening to them, devastated they were, especially the mother. Can still see her face.'

He ran his tongue over his cracked lips.

Andrew said, 'Where does Richard Hill fit?'

'He was the family doctor. If there had been abuse in the past, bruises for example, he might have witnessed it. Interviewed him myself at his surgery.'

'And?'

The old copper shook his head. 'Claimed he hadn't seen the Malik kid in a long time.'

Ronnie broke from the story and added something that wasn't in any report.

'He smiled a lot. A child was missing and Hill sat there smiling. Hated him for it. Still do.'

The policeman returned to the narrative. 'Halfway out the door it occurred to me to ask how recently he'd treated any member of the family. Made a show of getting the receptionist to bring through the appointments diary. Turned out Mrs Malik was at the surgery the previous week.'

'Was her daughter with her?'

'No, she was by herself.' Ronnie stared at Andrew then at me, looking for absolution. 'Thought no more of it 'til I was back at the station.'

Andrew knew where he was going. 'You wondered why he hadn't told you.'

'Struck me as odd. The abduction was in the papers, on the news. Tranent's a small place. Not too many people called Malik in the town.'

'What did you do?'

'I was convinced Hill was hiding something. If he'd seen the mother why had he not mentioned it? He was one of four doctors in the practice, all male. I spoke to the other three.'

For the first time the ex-policeman glanced at the file.

'Murdoch, Louden and Mackenzie. As a colleague they had no complaints. Described him as professional and hard-working. None of them had been to his house. Knew next to nothing about him outside of work. The next day, off his own bat, he showed at the station with an alibi. A strange thing to do because he hadn't been accused of anything, let alone charged.'

I said, 'Why would he do that?'

'He knew he'd slipped up. Wanted to eliminate himself from the investigation he said. Wasn't smiling anymore.'

'What was his story?'

'The surgery was closed on Wednesday afternoons. He was there dealing with paperwork. Told me the receptionist would verify it.'

'Did she?'

A coughing fit delayed his reply; telling this came at a price. Andrew brought a glass of water, Ronnie took a sip and carried on.

'Yes. At that time, Eileen Morrison had been employed at the surgery for five years. She confirmed she was with the doctor.'

'Did you believe her?'

He made a face. 'No choice. Made a statement, didn't she? He fingered the folder on the bed. 'It's all here, every word.'

'Yeah, but did you believe her?'

Ronnie looked Andrew in the eye. 'I'll tell you something I've never told anybody. I went back. Two years later I went back to Tranent to speak to Eileen Morrison. No badge, no authority. I just needed her to tell me the truth about that Wednesday.'

'What did she say?'

'She was dead. Suicide. Sleeping pills. She'd left the practice suffering from depression.'

He let what he was saying hang in the air.

'Eileen Morrison had two children, a boy and a girl. It was the daughter I spoke to. Her brother wasn't around. Overdose like his mother. His body was found in a rubbish skip in Wester Hailes. I managed to get a look at the autopsy. Johnnie Morrison had at least nine substances in his system when he died. Not heroin. Not cocaine. Tranks, barbies, benzos, block-busters. Even anti-histamine. Prescription drugs. Doctor's drugs.'

Ronnie Simpson's face said it for him. He still hadn't forgiven himself for letting Hill get away.

'Hill was supplying him?'

'At the time I considered it. Much later I thought of something else. Mrs Morrison's son was an addict – she could've been writing prescriptions for him and got caught. That would've given Hill a hold on her. The hold he needed to force her to say he was with her the afternoon the Indian girl disappeared.'

It sounded possible.

'A nice theory, unfortunately, no proof. Eighteen years I've spent on this. Nobody closer to it than me. When I said I could still see Mrs Malik's face I wasn't exaggerating. Why I couldn't sleep last night. I'm as certain now as I was then. Richard Hill murdered Leela Malik.'

The effort of telling his story had taken its toll, the light had gone from the old policeman's eyes and his voice cracked with emotion.

He said, 'The man you have in custody is a child killer. Do better than I did. Don't let him get away.'

33

Govan Police Office, 923 Helen Street, Glasgow.

Operation Damocles Headquarters.

Govan was the largest and most modern police station in the city and home to Major Investigation Teams [MITs], the modern version of the Serious Crime Squad, the obvious choice for Operation Damocles headquarters. High profile detainees were held there. And suspected killers like Richard Hill.

The atmosphere in the incident room changed with the arrest. Hope replaced frustration. Half a dozen photographs dominated one wall: beautiful faces, three of them dead, the others missing. Lily Hamilton was number six. The team, one hundred and thirty officers in total, had known dark days but now there was light at the end of the tunnel. They had their man. All that remained was proving it.

Hill arrived in Glasgow with a charge of attempted kidnapping against him. In spite of the overwhelming evidence, hiring Anthony Baresi suggested he intended to mount a defence.

The Baresi family, fourth generation Italians nicknamed the Scotia Nostra, were a legal dynasty. Anthony was the son of Marko Baresi and grandson of Lucca, a legend in the city. In 1959 Lucca was counsel to Thomas Dolan, a thirty five year old bricklayer accused of murdering seven people, including John and Maureen Telfer and their two teenage children in their Paisley bungalow. Late into the trial the defendant chose to represent himself and sacked Baresi. It was the last bad decision he ever made. His insanity plea failed to persuade the jury and, at eight a.m. on a cold March morning, the judgement of the court was carried out on Barlinnie gallows; the second last man to be hanged before capital punishment was abolished.

Lucca recognised his dismissal as a huge stroke of good fortune. Nothing would have changed the outcome of the trial. Dolan was guilty and destined to die. But the sacking shone a spotlight on the tall quietly spoken lawyer. One man's life was over, another's just beginning. Overnight, Baresi was famous.

High profile cases became the firm's speciality, many, not all, successful. Through the years Baresi remained the brief a murderer dismissed to his cost. Marco followed him into law and into the thriving practice. Less talented than his father, lacking Lucca's quick wits and his ability in front of a jury, he compensated with hard work and won some impressive victories. Anthony inherited his grandfather's flair and his father's ethic. He wouldn't need them on this case.

DS Andrew Geddes sat beside DCI Baillie across from Richard Hill and his lawyer. If anything Hill's injuries looked worse than they had in Hawick. Gauze covered his left eye, livid cuts marked his face and his right cheek was yellow and blue and black. Gaps in his teeth confirmed the intensity of the attack on him. The first interview had been a rant with Hill demanding action against the women in Hawick. Apart from that he'd stared into space and refused to speak. Baresi insisted his client's complaint be logged. His request fell on deaf ears. The detectives asked their questions. Hill refused to respond. Hour after hour.

By the end of the second day he still hadn't admitted to the offence in the Borders.

The officers gathering background spoke to colleagues and neighbours. Everyone who knew the doctor was shocked. The usual adjectives, courteous, quiet, unassuming, were pressed into service to describe the man who had stolen a baby and been brought down by a pack of angry females.

There was little for Anthony Baresi to do. Silence was his client's best defence; apart from Hawick the police had nothing. In the corridor frustration got the better of DCI Baillie.

'How much longer can he keep it up?'

Geddes said, 'Almost as long as we can. Patience.'

It was a battle and so far Hill was winning.

Baillie was leading Operation Damocles. Baresi asked for a meeting with him.

'Cards on the table. Charge him or send him back to the Borders. How many chances do you think you get?'

Baillie wasn't intimidated. 'As many as we like until we're satisfied.'

Baresi advised his client his best interests would be served by staying tight-lipped. Hill smiled. The lawyer took it he understood and agreed. By any standards the next session was bizarre. Hill was a different man, arms folded, relaxed; enjoying himself.

And he spoke.

For fifty minutes he presented an eloquent case for Scotland remaining in the Union. No one interrupted. Baresi stared ahead, unable to understand why his client had disregarded his instructions.

When Hill finally shut up DS Geddes said, 'Politics? Amazed you find the time between healing the sick and strangling kids. Tell us something interesting. Tell us about Ayr beach.'

Hill just smiled. The DS addressed his colleague.

'We've got it wrong. This guy hasn't got the nuts. We're looking for somebody with, dare I say it, style. Doctor Dick's a sad old paedo.'

Hill scoffed. 'Dear dear. Amateur psychology. And I'm expected to fall for it. Do me a favour.'

Geddes ignored him. 'Hawick can have him; he's a star down there. This is Glasgow; he's nobody. Send him back.'

The detectives stood. Baillie turned off the tape and ended the session. To Hill the DCI said, 'You'll be taken to the cells until transport can be arranged.'

The doctor mocked the officers. 'That it? That the best you've got? Thought you big city cops would have more.'

Geddes had been waiting for an opening. This was it.

'More? You mean like Leela Malik?'

For a second Hill was off guard. Geddes pressed home the advantage, he said, 'I was speaking to an old friend of yours, Ronnie Simpson. Remember him? He remembers you.'

Hill recovered and let loose the arrogance he'd been barely holding in check. 'Ronnie Simpson. Be old Ronnie now. Ninety five if he's a day.' He laughed his schoolgirl laugh. 'Another one who thought he was clever. Expect he's senile.'

'Not senile enough to forget the mistake you made. Shitting yourself when you realised, so he says.'

Geddes cut Hill out and spoke to Baillie, his voice full of contempt. Exactly as they'd rehearsed it. 'Richard here showed up with an alibi before he'd been accused of anything. Can you believe that, sir? Shaking in his shoes. Blackmailed a woman into saying he was with her. And he thinks he's clever.'

Hill's grin was unconvincing. 'Couldn't prove it though, could he?'

'No, I'll give you that. But Ronnie remembers you because you were jammy. A jammy bastard he called you. He agrees with me you're a sad deluded paedo who's been lucky.'

'Lucky?' Hill sneered. 'Some luck.'

Geddes' face was so close to Hill's he could smell his breath.

'Forget Ayr, or Tranent, you're an incompetent who's managed to get away with it. Only an idiot would have done what you did in Hawick.'

The doctor smirked, back in control.

'Oh I've got away with it all right. More often than you would believe I've got away with it.'

Baresi tried to stop his client speaking.

He said, 'I have to advise you it's in your best interests to say nothing.'

Hill ignored his lawyer. 'Anne Marie Bradley.'

He savoured their surprise 'Have your attention now, have I?

Geddes felt as if he'd been punched. Baillie sounded casual, almost bored. 'Pulling names out of the air won't get us anywhere, Richard.'

'Out of the air? Is that what I'm doing? Coatbridge. Place there called The Lochs.'

Geddes whispered to his superior. 'Can we have a word?' Outside he said, 'Anne Marie Bradley, ring a bell?'

Baillie shook his head. 'He's playing with us, Andrew. Wants his moment in the sun. He'll have us digging up half the country. There's no Anne Marie Bradley listed.'

'Not now there isn't.'

'What do you mean not now?'

'Anne Marie Bradley was outside her house in Airdrie. Her mother could hear her talking to imaginary friends. When the chatter stopped she went to see what her daughter was doing and couldn't find her.'

'How do you know all this?'

'It was big news at the time. You'd be in Manchester. Anne Marie was never seen again. She was eight.'

'And you were in uniform.' The implication dawned on the senior man. 'So when?'

'Twenty years ago. Even further back than Leela Malik.'

'Fuck!

DS Geddes pulled at his collar and gathered his coat around him. On a sunny day this would be a pleasant place to spend an afternoon; boats for hire, swans on the water. Nice, though not enough going on to attract big crowds. Good for a picnic and a great place to hide a body.

The forensics team had been there since early morning. They didn't speak to each other. Andrew Geddes didn't envy them their job. It had taken them until noon to find the burial site. Now it was three o'clock. Still a lot of work to do. The initial opinion, based on the length of the femur, was a child aged between six and nine. Decomposition was well advanced. The pathologist wasn't prepared to hazard a guess as to how long it had been in the ground but the detectives knew: Richard Hill had told the truth. The revelation rocked the investigation. A meeting of senior officers was already scheduled, which the deputy chief constable would attend. The DI wasn't looking forward to it. Too many questions he couldn't answer starting with what the discovery of Anne Marie Bradley meant in terms of victims.

Back at headquarters officers were trawling through two decades of unsolved abductions and missing person reports to cobble a response. Twenty years was a helluva long time.

DCI Baillie sat in the car, on the phone. When the call ended he joined his DS.

'This operation was always big. Now it's mega. The deputy chief's joining the party.'

Geddes sympathised. 'Covering their arses.'

Baillie said, 'Focus on the upside.'

'There's an upside to this?'

'Absolutely. Different if we were chasing our tails but we're not, he's ours. Likely something in it for us once we put him away. Every cloud and all that.'

Andrew Geddes didn't hide his disgust. 'A bunch of women did our job. And with respect, I can't see an upside to dead children.'

The detective inspector was unmoved. 'Don't take it personally. We didn't kill those kids, but we've got the guy who did.'

34

Aberdeen, 149 miles from Glasgow.

She called her mama for the first time. Mama. Just the greatest thrill.

It was getting better. They went out every day now. People nodded to her on the street and smiled. She smiled too for a different reason; the birth certificate was in her bag. A white-haired lady stopped and chatted. Probably just nosey. She made sure the conversation stayed general. Wouldn't it be like the thing to give them away because she couldn't keep her mouth shut?

Aberdeen was an all right place. They could live here, but that wasn't the plan. Away. Far away. That was the plan. Where no one would find them. Somewhere with decent weather. It was November. Aberdeen in November wasn't nice. She wanted her daughter to grow up with the sun on her face. Her duty was to make it happen.

She collected an application form at the post office. It took ages to fill it in, checking and rechecking every detail in case she made a mistake.

Allow four weeks the passport office website said, depending on the time of year. Difficult to imagine them snowed under in winter. Snowed under. Jokes now was it? She was more relaxed with every passing day. It was going to be all right. Every night she poured over flights, imagining their new life. Keep it simple, nothing complicated, that was the key

Recently she found herself thinking about her father. A good man. A kind man. His hard earned savings made it possible. If he were here he'd understand. This wasn't revenge. She had trusted and been betrayed. It was about what was right. What was fair. She'd only taken what was hers. Nothing more.

A laptop was a present to herself so she could look for flights. When the passport arrived they wouldn't have to hide. The masquerade could end.

Life could begin.

35

A line of jets stood idle on the rain-washed tarmac. The storm that began when I was on top of the Finnieston Crane had washed the city and blown on by, in other parts of the world a cue for the sun to shine. Not in Glasgow. At this time of year cloudy skies and showers were the best we could hope for.

The airport was close to deserted on Sunday morning. We sat on stools at Costa Coffee drinking caramel lattes and waited for the departures screen to tell us when Mai Ling's flight to London Heathrow was boarding. From there she'd connect to Thailand. Gail held her hand, whispering reassurance. Patrick read the paper, relaxed. Normal service was about to be resumed in Patworld. When the women went to the toilet he dropped the pretence.

'All over bar the shoutin'. Never thought this day would come. 'Course I'm sorry how it turned out and all that, Gail's gutted for her. Tragic.' He turned to the sports pages. 'Rangers could only manage a draw. It's an ill wind, eh?'

Sun tanned people with duty free bags came through customs. Patrick saw them and confided in me. 'Mai Thai wants us to visit her in Bangkok. Gail's keen. Don't fancy it.'

'Yeah, why not?'

'I reckon Bangkok's like your granny's fanny. Got a fair idea where it is but do you really want to see it? Know what I'm talkin, Charlie?'

I knew all right. I also suspected he was in for a shock. The Logue household wouldn't be returning to how it had been and, if Gail decided she was going to Bangkok or anywhere else, it would be a good idea to get out of her way.

When it was time to say goodbye we walked as far as we were allowed. Gail and Jackie hugged Mai Ling. Brave smiles all round. I shook her hand and wished her luck. Patrick held back, unable or unwilling to fake regret.

Going to the car Gail said, 'She'll be all right, won't she?'

I told her what she wanted to hear.

Strathclyde police had handled everything like it was another day on the farm, which for them it was. There was no family and no will. The flat in Lancefield Quay would be sold and a decision made on where the money should go. Mai Ling had known the lecturer a matter of months yet her shout was as good as anybody's. If the Thai girl had cried when I told her that her husband-to-be was dead, it would've been easier to understand. She didn't, she didn't do anything; she listened in silence, nodded and went to her room. Two days later she thanked me with a bow for her ticket home. Since then she'd been subdued. Inscrutable is a cliché but that's what she was.

The funeral had been an eye opener. Frank Lennon lived for thirty-five years and must have met thousands of people. In death six attended and none of them really knew him. A Humanist minister did the "ashes to ashes" thing. Mai Ling stared straight ahead and Angela Armstrong looked sad. The rest of us – me, Patrick, Gail and Jackie – were there to make up the numbers. Cathedral College was notified about the arrangements. Perhaps Miss Shaw neglected to pass them on because no one represented them.

At NYB Jackie went to work and organised lunch. We picked at it. None of us had an appetite except Patrick who ate enough for everybody. Gail was unhappy with him and left. I went upstairs to the office and he headed for the bar.

The Lennon case had brought me down. Davie Wilson caved in, confirming what Tommy Boyd told me and adding details of what had gone on in Renfield Lane. All three were in custody: Lawrence charged with murder, Wilson with culpable homicide. Tommy Boyd, a guy in the wrong place at the right time, was an accessory. The law would take its course. I was out of it.

Kate moving in with me was supposed to bring us closer but she seemed to be looking for excuses to stay away. In the past week I'd seen her twice, briefly, and we hadn't shared a bed. She was having second thoughts.

Sunday night had become Big River night. The band was established and now when they played, a full house was a given.

Big River got better every week and as Kate's confidence grew it showed in her performance: not the insecure lady I'd bumped into at the Rock-Ola. At the end of the gig I saw her talking to a man I couldn't place. She came over. I said, 'One of your many fans?'

Her reply came a little too fast. 'Just a guy who likes my voice.'

We chatted about nothing. 'Are you planning to come over?'

'Would you like me to come over?'

'No invitation necessary. Wasn't that why you dumped a boutique on me? Use your key. I'll expect you.'

I went to bed at three, alone. Kate didn't come. I expected her to call the next day. That didn't happen either. Moving in with me, even part-time, was too much too soon. It was over and she couldn't bring herself to say it.

Tuesday morning dragged into Wednesday night, then Friday, until a whole week had gone by. And with every passing day my mood sank. We deal with bad stuff that falls into our lives in different ways. Mai Ling quietly accepted, Jennifer Hamilton went to pieces, Pat Logue got drunk and Tommy Boyd almost threw himself off the Finnieston Crane. My reaction was to sit in the dark and stare at the walls.

That was what I was doing when DS Geddes came into the office unannounced. He was in worse shape than me. His opening observation told me all I needed about his state of mind.

'Bloody weather. Doesn't know how to do anything but piss down.'

'Take your coat off.'

'Nah, it's the price of living in Scotland.'

I remembered the passengers at the airport, smiling and brown. 'When did you last have a holiday?'

He snorted. 'Can't afford it, Charlie. Lucky if I'm left with my bus fare home.'

'Seriously, Andrew, a break isn't a luxury. I'd be lying if I said you were looking well.'

'Pot calling the kettle black, isn't it? Looked in the mirror yourself lately?'

'I'm concerned about you.'

'Yeah? Well, thanks for cheering me up. Just what I needed on top of yesterday.'

'What happened yesterday?'

'Only signed my life away.'

Elspeth.

'She got me, Charlie. Kept on going until she got me.'

'How so?'

'Half the pension. Add that to an even split of the cash, plus the house. Claims she gave up a promising career to support me.' He massaged his temple. 'Spent every afternoon at her mother's is how I remember it, drinking tea.'

'What did she do before you married?'

'An assistant librarian. How's that for a promising career? And I didn't ask her to pack it in. Came home one day and told me she'd handed in her notice. Gave some stand by your man guff that boiled down to her being a lazy bitch. You know it wouldn't surprise me if this was the plan. Now she can afford to be with her mother. Fact I wish she would – the old bastard died five years ago.'

I waited.

He said, 'It's a mug's game. Steer clear' and pointed at the wall.

'See you decided to ignore me.'

'Didn't ignore you. Don't have a choice.'

Andrew let it go. 'Appreciate the call on the boy. And congratulations, by the way. Heard about the lecturer. Said there was something off with that one from the start.'

Success has many fathers, failure is an orphan.

'I feel for Tommy Boyd. He got roped in. He wasn't involved in the violence.'

DS Geddes put me in my place. The mood he was in I expected nothing else.

'That's a decision for the jury, Charlie. It's what he did after he was roped in that's landed him in the shit.'

It was going to be a difficult conversation. 'How's Richard Hill?'

'Enjoying his moment in the sun. He's throwing them at us. We're up to seven. Four of them weren't even in the reckoning. Christ knows how long he's been at it.'

I tensed. 'How long do you think?'

He shrugged. 'Twenty years definitely. Probably more.'

This was new. My voice faltered.

'How many more?'

'No telling. He's sixty. Depends when he discovered he could lift a kid and get away with it.'

'So twenty five. Maybe thirty?'

Andrew's attention was back on the wall; he missed the colour draining from my face. My hands started to shake. I thought I was going to be sick.

...footsteps... racing...

'Could be, yeah. Why stop there? Forty's a possibility.'

...slapping the sand...

A voice I didn't recognise said, 'Any names?'

'I asked him, Charlie, there was no reaction to Pamela. I don't believe he did it but if it even smells like him...'

Andrew was speaking from miles away.

...crunching shingle...

'As for the Hamilton baby,' he shook his head, 'bastard denies it. Playing I-know-something-you-don't-know. You should see him. He smirks and smiles two minutes after describing stuff worse than you can imagine. Thirty years. Forty years. Doubt we'll ever get it all.'

...beating against rock... gaining.

Suddenly I wanted him to leave. My head was pounding. Go Andrew, please go.

...the touch of a hand...

He read my mind and moved towards the door. 'The Lily abduction was daring. Crazy daring, Hill's trademark. Mark Hamilton calls umpteen times a day. In the beginning I spoke to him. Not anymore. The man's obsessed. And he's ill. Last I heard, Jennifer Hamilton was out of hospital but the woman will never be right. That's the saddest part. These psychos damage everybody involved.'

Even the police.

...no one there

Even me.

36

Kate came round to the flat unexpectedly. She didn't offer an explanation for Sunday night and I didn't ask. It had been a week. Seven days apart should be a long time for people in love. It felt too soon. An unwelcome intrusion. From the moment she came through the door the atmosphere was off. I was off. The conversation with Andrew had me reeling.

Kate accepted a kiss on the cheek without kissing back, let me take her coat and walked into the lounge. Even then I knew it wasn't going to end well. We spent an uncomfortable half hour waiting for pizza, sitting apart saying nothing, avoiding each other. I opened a bottle of red wine and poured two glasses. The pizza was a waste of money – we hardly touched it. Kate pushed the box away and lifted her glass, still full, but didn't drink.

She said, 'We need to talk.'

I was about to discover what was going on but whatever it was I wasn't ready for it. I tried to sound relaxed

'So talk.'

'About the photograph.'

My reaction took both of us by surprise. 'Don't go there, Kate, not tonight. I can't discuss it.'

Before she could reply I picked up the box and went to the kitchen. She followed me.

'Not good enough. You haven't been honest with me, Charlie.'

'Yes I have.'

'Oh please, don't make it worse than it is.'

'I've been as honest as I can be.'

She laughed. 'What's that supposed to mean?'

'What it sounds like. I haven't lied to you.'

'No? No? We had a deal. No secrets, remember?'

I marched into the lounge and got the plates.

'This isn't a good time. Believe me.'

'Then when is?'

I made a futile attempt to avoid the inevitable.

'Kate... Kate... you don't understand.'

The words, sounded weak, even to me. She stood in the middle of the floor, hands on hips, demanding answers to a barrage of questions.

'Who's the girl? You're married, aren't you? She your daughter?'

The afternoon revelation had left me emotionally spent. Kate's third degree was the tipping point. The plates crashed into the sink; one of them shattered. My finger brushed against a shard and started to bleed. She didn't notice. Even if she had she wouldn't have stopped. Her accusations fell like blows I couldn't escape. Then they were blows as her fists pounded my back.

She screamed. 'You bastard! It's true! You bastard!'

When it was over we faced each other, exhausted and sad. Blood dripped on the floor between us.

She said, 'You've hurt your hand. Did I do that?'

'It's nothing.'

My reply hardly registered; her expression showed her shock.

'I'd better go.'

'It isn't how it looks.'

Her lip trembled. 'Doesn't matter anymore.'

'Kate...'

She shook her head. When she'd gone I got a cloth and cleaned up the mess.

It was ten o'clock and freezing cold when I arrived back at NYB. Big River would be already into their second set. I wasn't here for the show. Jackie assumed I'd been downstairs.

She said, 'Just get better and better, don't they?'

Not the most objective view in town, given how tight she was with the drummer.

'Pat Logue and Gail are in. He asked if you were around. If I hadn't seen it with my own eyes I wouldn't have believed it. Call the Guinness Book of Records.'

When I didn't respond she gave me a funny look and went back to whatever she was doing.

At the bar I ordered a double whisky, changed my mind, made it two doubles and took them up to the office. On the wall behind my desk Jennifer Hamilton's grief stricken face and the picture of their baby given to me by her husband reminded me of the case Andrew had warned me off. DS Geddes had been right. The investigation had ruined everything. Why hadn't I listened?

For what seemed like a long time I argued with people who weren't there and still wound up losing. That defeat, the latest in a long line, lifted my resentment to new heights helped by the alcohol. Finally I marched down to the club, unsure what I was going to say or do. Jackie spoke. I didn't hear her. I was out of control and I didn't care.

The temperature was like the Sahara only hotter. Almost immediately my shirt was soaked in sweat. The Logues were standing at the bar, where else? Patrick waved. I pretended I hadn't noticed and pushed through the crowd; I wasn't in the mood for his football Patspeak or wide boy philosophy bollocks tonight.

I pulled myself in front of a guy in a Scotland rugby jersey a good head taller and four stone heavier than me; in a fight, no contest. He didn't appreciate it and put his hand on my shoulder to haul me back. I snarled and shoved harder, not the reaction somebody his size was used to. Maybe it was the fever in my eyes that changed his mind. He said something that was drowned by the music and decided to let it go. I shrugged him aside and continued.

On stage the set was almost over, Kate had been enjoying herself until she saw me and looked away. At the end I hung around like a petulant teenager waiting for her to appear. She didn't. Alan Sneddon did. Whether Kate asked him or whether he volunteered I had no idea. Either way it wasn't what I wanted. He came towards me with his arms out.

'She won't speak to you, Charlie. I'd leave it if I were you.'

Except he wasn't me.

He said, 'Kate doesn't want a scene.'

The whisky had stolen whatever reason I had left. 'You telling me how to behave, Alan? Don't. Please don't do that.'

He put himself between me and the dressing room.

'Tomorrow's another day, mate. Things will look better in the morning'

I spoke through gritted teeth. 'Don't call me mate. I'm not your mate. I'm not anybody's mate.'

I stormed away, up the stairs and into the street. From somewhere behind me a voice shouted 'Charlie!'

The pavement was covered in frost, white stars twinkling beneath my feet. The moon drifted across a dark sky. I hadn't brought a coat and the night air was bitter. It didn't matter I was already numb. Footsteps echoed in the deserted city. Mine. I turned into Albion Street. Halfway up three youths were drinking cans of Carlsberg. One leaned against the wall. They noticed me and recognised the highlight of the weekend coming towards them.

Whispers. Sniggers. Drunken laughter.

Two of them strolled into the middle of the road. The leader refused to be hurried. He finished his lager and casually pushed himself upright. I kept going. They barred my path, cocky and confident. Three against one does that to some guys. The problem wasn't going away. I stopped and took a look. In Glasgow trouble wears Hugo Boss and drinks imported beer, except when Matalan and Special Brew get the vote.

Two of them had a duelling banjos thing going on; large foreheads and sunken eyes. Brothers. Early twenties, ugly from a diet of Pot Noodle, cheap wine and bad genes. The smaller guy had been really unlucky; when they were giving out heads he must have wandered into the extra-large department, or maybe he was breaking it in for somebody else. The leader was the superior intellect though I doubted it stretched to reading. He gave his hard man chat a try. Arrogance hadn't come from a couple of cans. He was high. They were all high.

He hooked thumbs into the waist band of his jeans and stepped into the light. His smiling face held an impressive collection of second prizes. Some folk never learn.

He slurred. 'Cold isn't it? You should be in bed with a Horlicks.'

Part of me wanted to tell him this was a bad idea. Another part was happy to let him go where he was going. We had something in common. The one on his left was keener than keen, swaying like a boxer, flexing his fingers, grinning a gap-toothed grin; impatient for the fun to start. In an ideal world I'd take the main man first. Then again it pays to be flexible. This guy would do.

They circled like hyenas, not an inappropriate comparison, animal cunning was their strength. My eyes darted from one to another, struggling to keep the three of them in my line of vision. Mr Keen couldn't wait and ran at me. Silly boy. A boot in the balls diminished his enthusiasm. He hit the ground holding his groin.

Down not out.

Whatever else I had to stay on my feet. If I slipped I wouldn't get up. The Runt on the right saw his brother fall and lost his head. He aimed a fake Nike at my legs. I moved. He sailed on by and cracked his skull on the ice.

Down and probably out.

I was enjoying myself and I hadn't had to do much to stay ahead. Moonlight flashing on a blade said that could change. Mac the Knife watched too many movies. He passed the weapon hand to hand, staring hate. But his heart wasn't in it. Unfortunately for him, mine was.

A lunge, not even close, slicing a hole in space. I went the orthodox route and landed two on his chin. He staggered a few steps and swore at Mr Keen. 'Sully! Sully! For fuck's sake get up!'

Sully was still on the floor. A kick in the head discouraged him. The leader panicked and charged, waist high. My knee connected with his jaw. The light flickered in his eyes and he collapsed.

Down and definitely out.

Bad judgement. Tonight they'd picked on the wrong man.

I straddled his chest and pounded his face with my fists, frustration behind every blow. His eyes were closed, he was unconscious. I didn't stop. I hit him. Again and again.

Arms locked round me and wrestled me away. It had to be the brothers back in the fight. A familiar voice whispered in my ear. 'Charlie. Charlie. Easy, Charlie. You'll kill him.'

It was Patrick.

They say history is written by the winners. I'd taken on three thugs and beaten them.

That meant my version of what happened was *the* version. I told the police I'd needed some air and had gone for a walk round the block. Plausible enough. All the best lies are. They congratulated me on taking a stand and recommended I never do it again. Mr Keen and the Runt were in the cells; they'd be having sex with their sisters in no time. When the Royal Infirmary said he could go, Mac the Knife faced a serious charge. As for me, I had been lucky. Thanks to Pat Logue I wouldn't be joining him.

Tonight I didn't feel very lucky.

37

My life was coming apart. I'd become a walking shell barely able to function. Somebody I didn't recognise, somebody I didn't like. My relationships with the people closest to me – Andrew, Jackie, Patrick Logue – showed me they agreed. But how it ended with Kate was hardest of all. The chance had been there. I'd thrown it away. Losing Kate Calder was a bitter blow I doubted I would get over. Behind me the undeniable evidence of a man obsessed mocked me for the fool I was. I ripped the clippings, the map of Ayr and the notes from the wall and tore at them, close to tears as they fell to the floor.

At the door to NYB, rain bounced off the flagstone pavement, so hard that at first I didn't see him peering through the deluge, less than ten yards away. No coat or hat. How long had he been standing there? In the fading light his face was ashen, his hair was plastered against his head and water ran into the dark hollows of the eyes. Grief had made a thin man thinner. He seemed not to notice his sodden clothes.

I called his name; he didn't respond. Seven weeks and two days since Ayr beach, the last time they'd been a family, and still no one was able tell him what had happened to his daughter.

His hand was cold and wet. I took it and led Mark Hamilton out of the rain.

The whisky bottle was in the drawer where I left it. I poured a stiff one and pushed it across the desk, hoping he wouldn't notice the mess on the floor behind me. This was a different Mark

Hamilton: the drink stayed in the glass. Somewhere along the way he'd discovered booze wasn't the answer but not before it had ravaged him. Lily's father had drunk himself sober and paid the price. He dripped water over the carpet while the light etched charcoal lines on his face.

He started as he meant to go on, with an accusation. 'You said they'd find her, they haven't.'

'It isn't over, Mark.'

His ragged voice found enough strength to contradict me. 'Yes it is. They aren't even looking. They've given up.'

'The police never give up.'

'They've given up. Remember what you told me about doing the right thing?'

I closed my eyes against what was coming.

He said, 'You can't walk away.'

'Mark...'

'You can find her.'

'So far the police have failed. Why would I succeed?'

He was deaf to me. 'I want you to try.'

A teenage waitress arrived with soup and crusty bread. Jackie didn't miss much.

I said, 'Have this and we'll talk. You need to take care of yourself.'

The thought amused him. Hamilton smiled and swung his left arm in an arc; a violent reaction from a desperate man. The glass and bowl crashed to the floor, vegetable fragments splashed the wall. His mouth was taut with resentment.

'I told you who'd taken Lily and why. Donna Morton. To get back at me. You persuaded me to tell the police. Well I did. And what've they done?'

He trembled with frustration. 'Nothing! Nobody cares.'

'We all care, Mark. Donna disappeared.'

''Course she did, she had to, she's got Lily.'

In a crazy way it made sense, except a mile from where we were a monster was playing a sick game, spinning out a decades long catalogue of filthy crimes, bit by bit, that probably included this man's daughter, and getting his jollies denying it.

I kept my voice low and even.

'Give the police time, they'll find her, and Lily if she's with her.'

'Not good enough. I want you to do it.'

I held up my hands. 'I'm not the right guy for this, Mark?'

He had no doubts. 'You're exactly the right guy. The sister, start with the sister. She never liked me. She's protecting Donna.'

'I've spoken to Lucy Morton. Twice. She has no idea where Donna went after she left Glasgow. I was in the flat. It was empty. They're not there.'

Nothing made a difference; his conviction was absolute.

'Lucy's in on it. Has to be. Yeah, one of them stays with Lily, the other goes for food. Nobody recognises the baby because they don't take her out.'

Listening to him weave a fantasy he could live with was painful. The Morton sisters were in cahoots. The police couldn't see it. Neither could I. In his dream his daughter was safe and well. All it required was me to go and get her.

I tried one last time to free myself from the nightmare I had stumbled into. I said, 'Mark. Listen. Honest to god. You'd be better with somebody else handling this.'

He poked the air with his finger, and snarled.

'You owe me.'

Like Alec Downey, someone had to be to blame.

'I don't owe anybody.'

He was in a place where I couldn't reach him.

'I trusted you.'

'And I did my best.'

'No, your best would've got Lily back. Be honest, you know I'm right.'

'Mark...'

'Are you saying you aren't willing to even look? That it's nothing to do with you?'

The guy was close to a breakdown, emotionally all over the place, how could I refuse?

'No, I'll look. I'll talk to everybody this time, not just Donna's sister. I'll want to meet Jennifer.'

A tick started at his right eye. The mention of his estranged wife was the trigger. His reply was angry; defensive.

'Leave her out of it. She's been through enough.'

'No can do. You're asking me to find your little girl. All right. But nobody gets a pass.'

Hamilton's collar had suddenly become too tight; he loosened his tie and undid the top button.

'Jennifer won't speak to you. She doesn't speak to anybody.'

'When was the last time you saw her?'

'The day after the police told her about Donna. I went to the hospital. She was asleep. I sat by her bed until she woke up. I can still hear her screaming at me. After that they wouldn't let me in. Then I received a letter telling me she wanted a divorce. A friend says her cousin is taking care of her.' He paused. 'It happened just the way I said. If you had found Donna, if Lily had been okay... it might've been different.'

He was back in the land of make believe. Few relationships could survive what the Hamilton marriage had gone through. I said, 'I'll tell the police I've been hired to locate a missing person. See what they have to say about it.'

'What can they say? They had their chance.'

'Not how they'll view it. Professionals don't appreciate amateurs muddying the water.'

'Then fuck them.'

'Where are you staying?'

'I packed in the job before it packed me in. I'm in a B & B in Renfrew Street 'til what's left of the money runs out. The Adelphi.'

I buzzed the bar and asked for another plate of soup. The same waitress brought it.

'Eat it this time, and give me a contact number?'

He lifted the spoon. 'Forget Jennifer. She won't open the door.'

I said, 'We'll see. Eat.'

Later, I parked in Queen Street and walked through George Square. The weekend was beginning, the atmosphere electric. It fitted my mood, still wired from the fight.

He was standing at the bar with a large whisky in front of him. No hello, no handshake: just a nod, the kind you give a stranger in the street. His mood hadn't improved. He glanced at his watch. 'Haven't really got time, Charlie. Sorry and all that.'

Not the start I'd hoped for, especially with what I had to say. I took the calm option.

'Appreciate you coming. I know you're busy.'

He snorted into his drink and threw it back.

'Busy? Is that what I am?' The bartender refilled his glass, I guessed not for the first time. 'So what do you want?'

'I'm good, thanks, how about you?'

He glared and shook his head. 'Always the smart arse.'

'You've got Richard Hill. Has Donna Morton been ruled out of the Lily Hamilton investigation?'

'Considering we haven't found her.'

'Is that a yes?'

He rolled the firewater round in the tumbler and changed the subject. 'This is great whisky. Your old man knows what he's doing. You should try it.'

'No thanks.'

'Never understood your problem. Cameron's single malt is a peach. Anybody would be proud to claim their family made it. Not to mention...'

He rubbed his thumb and forefinger together.

'Oh I forgot, daddy's cut you out of his will, hasn't he?'

Andrew was in a mean mood.

'I've never tried it. And they don't, a Japanese company makes it.'

'Same difference.' He studied me through an alcohol haze. Geddes could haul it away with the best of them; he must have started early.

'This, never touch your own whisky thing, what's the point? Your old man doesn't even know.'

'It's a long story, Andrew. You haven't got time, said so yourself.'

He lifted the glass in a toast. 'Touché, Charlie. Another day, eh?'

I repeated my question. 'Is Donna Morton still in the picture?'

He considered his reply. 'No idea. And that's official.'

He was telling me the case had hit a wall. Nobody was looking for the woman Mark Hamilton believed had his daughter. 'So what's the thinking?'

He placed a hand on my shoulder. Andrew was drunk. He said, 'This'll make you laugh. Got a phone call yesterday. Guess who from? The Wicked Witch of the North.'

'Elspeth?'

'The very same.'

'Not more demands?'

'No, she apologised. Said she was sorry it ended the way it did. Apparently it was the lawyer's decision to nail me to the cross. Elspeth was against it. She only ever wanted what was fair.'

'Now she tells you.'

'Absolutely. After the hell they've put me through. Started on about the good times, how it hadn't all been crap. We'd been happy once. Maybe if we'd had children things would've been better. Then she cried. Couldn't get her to stop. And she still loves me. I'm the only man she's ever really loved.'

His eyes misted.

'With all that's gone on, the resentment, the bitterness, it was hard to hear.'

'What did you say?'

Cameron's finest burned his throat, he grimaced and slapped the glass on the counter.

'Told her to go fuck herself. What do you think I said? Jesus Christ, Charlie. Catch on will you.'

Black and white.

He returned to the conversation as if we'd never left it.

'Honestly? We're lost. Hill's having the time of his life. Ronnie was right about him being a slippery bastard. Three days ago he had us digging in the Leadhills. Supposed to be where he buried Rebecca Paterson. We trooped down there and drove round until he told us where to stop. Seven hours later we drove back. Fuck all. I was sitting next to him. Swear to god he was smiling. All he ever does. I wanted to kill him. And that's how it's been. Gives enough, just enough, to keep us with it.'

'Like what?'

'Off the record. The Carlisle kid, St Andrews...'

'Fenwick Moor?'

'Yeah. It took a while but yeah.'

'So how many so far?'

'Nine.'

'Why give him the satisfaction? Why not do him with what you have?'

He turned a joyless eye on me. 'Hill's finished. He realises that. What's left is the game.'

Andrew paused. 'Imagine playing cards with the devil. With his deck. We win when he lets us win, when it amuses him. He's toying with us.'

'Is anybody on the Hamilton abduction?'

Another whisky appeared. He let it sit. The session was almost over.

'Everybody's on it. Me. DCI Baillie, the whole fucking task force is on it.'

Anger and alcohol combined. The storm inside him was ready to blow. I knew how that felt.

I said, 'Mark Hamilton came to see me.'

Andrew was ahead of me and saw where the conversation was going. Where it had always been going. And he didn't like it.

'Donna Morton. He's asked me to find her. Again.'

DS Geddes did the talking now. The merits of Cameron's whisky and tales of emotional ex-wives had no place in it. The Detective said, 'I told you before to steer clear, mate. That advice hasn't changed. The Lily Hamilton investigation is very much alive. There are rules. You forgot them last time. Forget them again I can't help.'

Andrew wasn't sober but suddenly he wasn't drunk, and he'd arrest me without a second thought. Friend or no friend.

I stood my ground. 'Mark Hamilton withheld potentially vital information – until I persuaded him to come to you. This is different. Donna Morton's a missing person. The police don't know where she is. Her sister doesn't know. Somebody wants me to look for her. The question's straightforward. Is she a suspect in the abduction of Lily Hamilton?'

We stared at each other like a showdown in an old cowboy film.

'Yes or no, Andrew?'

He lifted the glass and drank what was left.

'You never learn, do you? This whole mess is poison, get away from it. There's nothing good in it for you.'

'Yes or no?'

He brushed hard against me on his way out.

'You'll go your own way, you always do.'

I took that as no. It had taken most of my life but finally I was ready and I knew where I'd be tomorrow.

38

Cramond Shore, Edinburgh, 43 miles from Glasgow

I parked in front of a row of whitewashed houses trimmed with black that stood on one side of the street, turned off the ignition and listened to the engine cool while I waited for my hands to stop trembling before I got out of the car. My chest felt like it was being crushed and my breathing came in shallow hurried gasps, as if I'd been running. And in a way I had. All my life.

On the water the sun was falling. An in-coming tide already covered the causeway, leaving the tips of the WW11 coastal defence placements known as The Dragon's Teeth to break the waves in a mile long line to the island. Come summer, small craft, hulls freshly painted red or yellow or blue, would anchor in the harbour where the Almond River met the firth. Even without them it was nice, beautiful in fact; picture postcard pretty, and the last place on earth I wanted to be.

I turned my collar against the cold and started towards the beach.

Thirty years ago my family lived here. In those days my father belonged to a group of died-in-the-wool Tories who worshipped the Iron Lady and considered themselves the future of the party. Heir to Cameron Distillers and already deputy CEO, he'd married Eleanor Dundas, youngest daughter of the fourteenth Earl of Meldrum, who produced two healthy children. Rich and sophisticated, successful and good looking, they must have seemed a perfect couple, and George Archibald Cameron – Archie to his friends – could have been forgiven for believing the angels smiled on him, that he'd been born lucky.

Until then, maybe he had.

The images in my head ran like an old home movie, disjointed and scratchy and out of sequence. More a dream than a memory. How often growing up had I wakened in the dark with the shadow of Cramond in the room. And after, tossing and turning, weighed down with questions but not the answers, until dawn's early light found me exhausted, withdrawn, and no wiser.

I wondered if my parents ever came to terms with their loss. I know I hadn't. Easy to blame them although that was unfair. Our house was yards from the front. My sister and I spent most of our time on the beach; it was our playground. Us kids had been given the standard warnings about talking to people we didn't know – in one ear and out the other – we endured these lectures with solemn faces, and by ourselves sniggered at the killjoys.

Somewhere near the middle of the beach I stopped and scanned the horizon. To my right a curl of sand and rocks swept towards Platinum Point and Leith, in the other direction the Forth road and rail bridges at Queensferry dominated the horizon. I hadn't been back since we left and wouldn't have come if it wasn't for a man with a secret too terrible to keep and too awful to live with, begging me to find his missing daughter. Mark Hamilton was the catalyst. His tragedy forced me to face my own demons. Here. On Cramond Shore.

This was where they lived.

Time had swallowed most of my childhood memories, but not all.

I was five years old; Pamela was eight. Blonde and big-sister bossy. We were pretending to be fishermen, a game we played often, dangling sticks with string on the end in the pools of water left by the tide. I had my shoes and socks off; Pam was wearing a red dress. She wasn't there when the unfamiliar voice spoke to me. My father was working on a speech he was due to give at some meeting or other. Pamela had coaxed him to come and play with us and he'd said he would. When he didn't she'd gone to look for him.

I can't recall the stranger's words exactly and it hardly matters: something about tiny crabs in a pool further along. Did I want him to show me?

In my mind the light is behind him, blurring his outline and darkening his features. I have to look up and shade my eyes to see, yet I'd recognise him, I've always believed that. He took my hand and we started walking. Then Pam was racing towards us waving, shouting 'Run, Charlie! Run!'

I didn't run, not at first. Not 'till she kicked him on the shin and he let go of me. I heard Pamela scream and wanted to look over my shoulder but was too scared. Instead I did what she'd told me to do and ran. Along the sand, across the shingle that hurt my feet, over the rocks, then the grass. Deaf to everything except the sound of footsteps coming after me.

Slow motion. All of it.

After that is a jumble: fragments of a drama I didn't understand; the old doctor peering over his spectacles and calling my mother lass; adults speaking in whispers, glancing in my direction, and knowing they were talking about me. A blonde policewoman who said her name was Rhona told me not to worry. Rhona smiled a lot and gave me a glass of milk, then spoiled it by asking the same things over and over until my head hurt. At the centre of it, a tall man in a dark suit who seemed, even to my young eyes, to be in charge: DI Ronnie Simpson as he was then. My parents are there of course, in a corner of the room by themselves, my mother weeping, my father holding her. And finally, the big black car that came and took me away.

Just me.

It was almost dark. Everyone had gone. My mother settled me in the back seat and gave me a kiss. The clearest memory is of my father, a step behind her, gaunt and distant, unable to look at me. She put on a brave face; where did she get the strength? Leaning in the window, smiling at the boy but speaking to the man behind the wheel. 'Drive carefully,' she said. 'Precious cargo.'

The search went on for weeks and found nothing. We never saw Pamela again.

I spent the rest of that summer with my aunt in Pitlochry. The next time I met my parents we didn't live in Scotland anymore, and my relationship with my father had changed forever. I'd always been sure he held me responsible for what happened. So did I. Common ground at least. In our house nobody spoke about the tragedy: Pam's name wasn't mentioned.

A wave crashed against the causeway, a big one, loud enough to startle me, and with it came an overdue moment of clarity.

My parents had suffered more than I would ever know – my father especially. He had promised to come with us. Instead he'd stayed home working on his speech for the Tory faithful. If he'd kept his word, Pamela would be alive. No coincidence that after that awful day Archie and Eleanor began spending time apart, one in Norfolk the other in London. Political ambition had nothing to do with it. Their marriage was in trouble. They had lost a child. They were in pain yet they'd protected their boy. A million tears would have been cried for Pam, just not in front of me.

As for the Cameron men, our problems were the problems of fathers and sons the world over. We didn't get along. It happened. Too different or too the same? My mother would know.

The putt-putt of a diesel engine broke into my thoughts. A boat, grey against a grey sea, moved through the water with a flock of seagulls swooping and diving in its wake for whatever was being thrown overboard.

On a sunny afternoon not unlike this, a madman had invaded our golden lives and stolen a daughter, a sister; a lovely little girl, leaving us to deal with the tragedy in our own way, as individuals, not as a family. Cruel and terrible though it was, the abduction hadn't broken us. We had.

I'd always believed my father blamed me. He didn't; he blamed himself because he should have been there, on the beach. And we would have been safe.

For a smart guy I hadn't been very smart. But I was glad I'd come back.

Forty years Andrew had speculated. I punched speed dial on my mobile. He answered right away.

'DS Geddes.'

'I want to see him.'

'Charlie?'

'I want to see Richard Hill.'

Irritation blew down the line. 'Why for Christ sake?'

'Because I might have met him before.'

The catharsis was short lived. During the drive to Glasgow, thinking about my parents and what I was about to do, my palms stained the steering wheel and I wanted to throw up. Revisiting the scene, confronting the fear, had taken courage. I gave myself credit for it. So much about what happened on that fateful day, and the days and years that followed, became clear. Then the past and the present melded and breathed new life into old ghosts. Getting involved in the Hamilton case had been a risk I thought I understood. I hadn't.

Andrew agreed to meet me upstairs in NYB when his shift finished. Recent experience had shown it wasn't the best time for him. The pressure of Operation Damocles and his ongoing tussle with Elspeth had left their mark. I was certain if we were introduced now we wouldn't become friends: he was too crusty, hard line intolerant; always close to losing it. His estranged wife hadn't had it all her own way in the difficult stakes though underneath was a good guy drowning in bad stuff.

Jackie saw my face and kept her distance.

She said, 'Andrew Geddes is in the office.'

I opened the door, braced for what I'd come to expect from him lately; barked questions and brusque ultimatums. "This better be good" threats and jaded dismissals of anything I told him.

That wasn't what he gave.

He was on the floor on his knees, the newspaper clipping in one hand and the photograph of Mark Hamilton's daughter in the other. He laid them on the desk and came towards me.

'Elspeth always complained I left everything at my arse. Nice to prove her wrong.'

'I have to see Hill.'

He nodded. 'Take a seat, let's talk about it.'

Usually it was me encouraging somebody to relax, tell their story any way they liked. Today it was my turn. I took my own advice and started at the beginning, and I didn't hurry. Andrew knew about Pam, but only that she'd gone missing. It was time to tell him everything. For forty minutes he allowed me to speak uninterrupted. When I came to the abduction and broke down he stayed where he was until I got hold of myself.

At the end he said, 'A lot of baggage to be carrying around. Thanks for sharing it with me.'

I wasn't finished. 'It was me he was after. Pamela got in the way. I was the one he wanted.'

Andrew didn't argue. 'That's what makes you so good at this; you've been there, you understand.'

He waved at the room.

'You don't need the aggravation. Christ knows looking for people isn't exactly glamorous. But there are exceptions. Cases like the Hamilton kid should be avoided like the plague. Got to protect yourself.'

I thought he was going to add I told you so. I was wrong.

He said, 'We know Hill's been at it for a helluva long time, so yeah, he might have taken your sister, though that's not how it looks, and Charlie, think a minute. It was thirty years ago, is there really any chance you'd recognise him?'

'I have to try.'

Not much of an answer but enough.

His voice was gentle. I was talking to a friend. He put a hand on my shoulder. 'You were a child, a frightened wee boy. You weren't to blame then and you're not to blame now. It wasn't your fault.'

'But if it is him..?'

He got to his feet and gave me a long look. 'So long as you think you're up to it.'

'Have to be up to it, won't I?'

'All right. Consider yourself helping the police with their enquiries.'

Most people would avoid coming face to face with a monster. I had no choice. My motive wasn't revenge, no biblical eye for an eye closing the circle. None of that interested me. Like the families of so many victims, mine had been denied closure, the chance to draw a line under the awfulness that had visited us, and go on.

Who was I kidding? Closure was a bystander's idea. The truth was it could never be over for Mark and Jennifer Hamilton. And seeing Richard Hill wouldn't be enough to set me free, but it would be nearer than I had ever come.

I entered Govan Police Station with Andrew at my shoulder, sensing his stocky presence rarely more than a yard away. I was grateful but he needn't have worried. I was calm. Unnaturally calm considering I'd lived this moment in a hundred troubled dreams. Now it was here.

If it was Hill, what would my reaction be? Would I want to feel my hands on his throat and watch the light fade in his eyes as his soul, damned to hell, left his body? Could I hold on long enough before they dragged me away? And if it wasn't did that mean I'd go on hoping against hope, believing against everything rational that somehow somewhere Pamela was still alive?

On the other side of a glass panel three men sat at a table. Two listened while the other gave a potted history of famous military disasters.

I said, 'His lawyer doesn't look happy.'

Andrew filled in the background.

'Threatening to quit. Claims defending this bastard is affecting his mental health. Grandfather must be turning in his grave. Although I know how Baresi feels. Baillie's not far behind him. Nor am I.'

Hill said. 'The Alamo. A tiny adobe walled mission in the middle of the prairie. Why not just go round instead of spending days and days shooting at it?'

He laughed in a high pitched girly giggle. His audience was unimpressed. Andrew said, 'See what I mean. Nutty as a fruit cake. And having the time of his life.'

I filtered the crazy monologue and studied the face: was this the man who murdered my sister? It might be. It could be. I felt sand under my feet and heard a stranger ask if I wanted him to show me what he'd found. Pamela was shouting 'Run Charlie! Run!' Then the sand became rock, the rock became grass. And I wasn't calm anymore.

Andrew touched my arm. 'It's all right, Charlie, it's all right.'

My heart raced and sweat coated my forehead. Behind the glass DI Baillie's expression was stone. The figure in my nightmare was slim and dark. When he'd held my hand I remembered bone. Hill was chubby. Jolly even. He sniggered and spoke to Baresi in a voice a world away from the one in my head. Andrew was beside me, closer than ever, his face pale in the harsh strip-light. He whispered 'What do you think?' and repeated the advice he'd given in the car.

'People change, factor that in. Imagine the guy you saw, older, heavier. Feel his energy. Say it's him. Say it's him and I'll nail the bastard.'

DS Geddes' need was almost as great as my own. I turned and caught the disappointment in his eyes; he couldn't hide it and didn't try. Later he organised a driver to run me home. As I was getting in the car I said, 'Andrew. I'm sorry, really I am.'

His reply was soft. 'So am I, Charlie. So am I.'

Somewhere over the Kingston Bridge, with the river Clyde a black smudge and the city twinkling below, my breathing returned to normal, my pulse slowed, and I accepted, finally, I would never know what really happened to my sister that afternoon on Cramond Shore.

But whoever kidnapped Pamela, it wasn't Richard Hill.

39

Donna's sister wasn't answering her phone. Could be she wasn't at home. More likely she was determined to begin the weekend at her own pace. At noon I drove across the river to find out for myself.

Outside the basement flat was more overgrown than I remembered: the scrubby rectangle was a couple of feet high. It wouldn't take much to keep the postage stamp under control. No one had tried. My shoes sounded heavy on the stone steps. At the bottom I knocked on the door and saw the curtains move. I knocked again. Seconds later it opened.

Lucy Morton hadn't changed apart from the fact that she was drunk. She smiled a lazy smile, her eyes had a yellow glaze and her hair hadn't seen a brush. Underneath the garish pink housecoat she was tiny. I followed her into the lounge; the lights were on. A bottle of Gordon's gin, less than half full, told the story better than words.

She turned in the middle of the floor and held out her hands for me to put the cuffs on.

'It's a fair cop, governor, I'll come quietly.'

Lucy started to laugh and cried instead. I got her seated and tried to figure what had happened. She volunteered the information.

'I was lonely. Thinking about Donna, about how I'd let her down. It was too much.'

I picked up the bottle and took it to the battlefield the kitchen had become. A month's worth of unwashed dishes crowded the sink. Judging by the smell the windows hadn't been opened in as long. Two bowls, one with water one with food, took me by surprise; Lucy had remembered to feed the cat but not herself. Plastic bags, tied at the top, waiting for somebody to take them to the bin, tinkled when I lifted them. It wasn't my place to interfere. We all make our own road to hell. Putting the kettle on didn't strike me as intrusive.

I said, 'Let's have coffee.'

'Rather have a gin.'

Her life, her house, her call.

'Well I'm having coffee. Why don't you join me and we can talk?'

Of course there wasn't any milk. How could there be? This woman hadn't been over the door in weeks. At the back of the cupboard an ancient tin of dried milk long past its sell-by date, added colour if nothing else and helped me believe the coffee might be drinkable. It wasn't. Not important. It was a prop, a distraction; an alternative to alcohol, if only until I left. I set it on the table where the Gordon's had been and got my first real look at Donna's sister. Ten years of sobriety hadn't saved her. In the end it counted for little. The feisty lady who'd told me where to go was a memory.

Beginning was the hardest part. Lucy did it for us. She dried her eyes and said, 'I'm not blaming you, don't think I am, but after you'd gone it came crashing in. There's only me and Donna and we're strangers. I couldn't tell you where she was because I didn't know. My sister, my only family. That man was wrong for her. One day she would've seen it. Instead of protecting her I criticised. I drove her away. I do that, I drive people away.'

'"Fuck off!" I remember.'

'Yes. Sorry about that.'

'You already apologised.'

'Did I? When I felt myself wanting to drink I should've called a friend. I went to a pub and stood at the bar gazing at the bottles on the gantry. Some of them were new to me. I chose the one with the nicest colour and worked my way through them. Easy really. Afterwards I was ill though it didn't end there. I was off and running, back to where I'd been a decade ago, except worse. Much worse.'

She flapped an arm at the room.

'Now look at me.'

'Why don't you stop? Today. Right now.'

Her reply was frank and honest and shocking. She said, 'I don't want to. The minute you leave I'm having a gin. A large one.'

For people like her a large one was the only kind.

'Is that wise?'

'That's how it is.'

As conversation killers go, it was first rate. Lucy's fingers trembled; she lifted the coffee and had to put it down. I wasn't so lucky. I got to taste it. Her eyes wandered to the kitchen and the booze. The only reason she didn't finish the bottle was because I was there.

A tattered remnant of self-respect made her speak. 'What must you think of me?'

'My opinion doesn't matter. I'm not here to judge.'

For a second I glimpsed the Lucy Morton I'd known; assertive, defensive, shooting from the hip. 'So why are you here? Still trying to make out Donna stole that child?'

'Trying to find Donna, that's all.'

'Haven't you got better things to do?'

She started to cry again.

'Better things than watch a pathetic woman destroy herself?'

It was obvious she hadn't seen her sister or anybody else.

'Look, is there somebody I can telephone? Anything I can do?'

Her head came up and a light came on.

'Another bottle. You could get me another bottle of gin.'

Not what I had in mind.

'Not a good idea, Lucy.'

She snapped. 'Forget it, I'll go myself. You offered to help.'

Lucy Morton wasn't in a fit state to go anywhere; she was using me.

The games people play.

'I'll give you the money if that's what's bothering you.'

Cheeky.

I couldn't win. I could walk away or bring the last thing she needed. I said, 'I'll get you gin on three conditions. You have a shower and you eat something.'

'That's two, what's the third?'

'Make a call to whoever you should've called in the first place.'

She said, 'You're wasting your time.'

Of course she was right. I ignored her. 'Shower, eat, call. That's the deal.'

'And I get what?'

'What you want. Gin.'

'Two. Two bottles.'

I stood firm. 'One.'

'Litre.'

'One bottle. This offer closes in thirty seconds.'

'All right. If it makes you happy, all right. But Gordon's, none of that cheap crap.'

The way she was going "that cheap crap" would seem mighty attractive soon.

I said, 'I'll start on the kitchen before they condemn it.'

She pulled herself out of the chair.

'You're a good guy. Why are you siding with Hamilton? When his wife got pregnant he dropped Donna without a second thought. He's a snake. I hate him.'

Lucy was in a half world of maintenance drinking. Not dead drunk just never sober; a place logic couldn't reach. Somewhere along the line she'd made a decision about booze and turned her back on ten good years. I didn't understand her and if I explained the Hamilton saga she wouldn't understand me.

'I'm on the side of a thirteen month old girl called Lily. The only side there is.'

She stared at me then climbed the stairs, muttering to herself. I went to the kitchen, emptied the sink and ran the water until it was hot. Washing up liquid sat unopened in a cupboard underneath. I took the plastic bags outside and stacked the crockery in an order that made sense. Some of the plates were so congealed I wondered what the hell had been on them. Gradually the mountain morphed into another mountain on the draining board. At least it was a clean mountain. A dull hiss percolated through the ceiling. The shower; things were moving in the right direction. The nearest shop was on the corner. I walked. Twenty minutes later I was back with milk, a loaf, tins of soup, cat food, cornflakes, boil-in-the-bag junk and a bottle of Gordon's. A deal's a deal.

Lucy had changed into a skirt and top and dragged a comb through her hair. She was in better shape, brighter, the yellow gone from her eyes.

She said, 'Thought you'd left.'

'No luck. Still here. How do you feel?'

'Bloody marvellous. How about you?'

It was important to get her to eat. She wasn't keen. Scrambled eggs were as much as she could face. Even then she only took a couple of forkfuls. Lucy was suffering. The shaking in her hands became more violent. A dark green bottle on her kitchen table could make it go away. I didn't offer. She didn't ask. Drink it or pour it down the sink. But it was her decision.

Milk made the coffee almost fit for human consumption. We sat in armchairs across from each other surrounded by silence, like old friends. I checked my watch. She noticed. 'Don't let me keep you. You've been more than generous. I feel a lot better.'

'You're not keeping me. I have to be somewhere at three. Plenty of time.'

More than generous wasn't enough. Out of the blue Lucy said, 'I don't know where she is and if I did I wouldn't tell you.'

I believed her. On both counts.

'You don't know Donna. She couldn't hurt a child; she loves children.'

'So why hasn't she come forward? The police have been looking for nearly two months. Come on, Lucy, that isn't normal, is it? And you're wrong about me and Hamilton. My only interest is in getting his baby back. Your sister could put herself out of the picture in five minutes. Unless she can't. And if that's the case your loyalty is seriously misplaced. Donna wouldn't hurt a child. Donna loves children. All right, prove it. Tell me where she is. Show her to me.'

She shifted in the chair and balled her fists, not in anger; cramp. Pins and needles. A film of sweat broke on her forehead. Her body was demanding alcohol.

'I haven't seen her since she left Glasgow.'

I took a card from my wallet. 'Give me a ring if you hear anything.'

Lucy didn't respond; she had her gin. I could fuck off anytime I liked. The sooner the better. She wouldn't be unhappy to see me go.

She said, 'Thanks for the scrambled eggs.'

'No problem. One more thing. The third condition. You promised to make a call.'

Her shoulders sagged. She rubbed her arms and shivered. The monsters were coming. The easier option was a few steps and an arm's length. She had to want what I was suggesting, really want it, or it wouldn't work. No one knew that better than her.

'Think I should?'

'Ten years is a long time to hold it together. You might never see Donna again, but if you do... if she comes through the door... she'll expect her big sister to be waiting, so yeah, I do.'

The number was on her speed dial. She waved me goodbye and gave her attention to the most important call of her life. Her voice quivered. 'Tom? It's Lucy. Could you come round? An hour would be great. No I won't. I'll be all right 'til then...'

I let myself out.

40

I made a call to the number Mark Hamilton had given me. His home, or what used to be his home. A firm, confident female voice answered. The cousin. I started to introduce myself.

She interrupted. 'Let me stop you, Mr...'

'Cameron.'

'Jennifer isn't well enough for visitors. That's why I'm here. If you could try again, say in a month, she may be better, but I'm afraid it just isn't possible to see her today.'

A well-rehearsed spiel from someone determined to do their job but not as determined as I was to do mine.

I said, 'I'll be there at three o'clock. Do the best you can with her. It's important' and ended the argument.

According to the Tron clock it was five minutes to two. I drove through Merchant City and parked beside City Chambers. Lucy Morton's system was crying out for alcohol, mine pleaded for a decent cup of coffee. Jackie had spent hours sourcing suppliers, tasting and testing; years of trial and error to arrive at the perfect blend. The best espresso I'd ever had was in Milan. NYB was nearly as good, and I needed it.

A dozen people spread across the room. Saturday shoppers taking a break. I recognised a green corduroy cap hiding behind the Herald at a table against the far wall. The bean wasn't the attraction for Alan Sneddon. Jackie was in the diner. He smiled, laid the paper aside and signalled me to join him. I sat down. 'Hope you aren't keeping the staff from their work.'

'No chance. Jackie goes on auto pilot, blind to everything except business.'

'Any gigs lined up?'

'Yeah. A residency in Edinburgh, Faslane Naval base once a month and a couple down south. It's beginning to build.'

He should have been pleased. He didn't look it.

'We were going into the studio in the new year but that's on hold. See if I still have a band.'

He'd lost me. 'What do you mean?'

'Kate. Hasn't she told you? Sorry, man, I thought you knew. Our girl's been offered an audition with North Wind. Paul Finnegan killed himself – another rock 'n' rock casualty – Lloyd Kennedy decided against cancelling the tour. Finnegan's been on his way down for a long time. Kennedy must've guessed the party was over and made his own plans. Had somebody checking out what's going on in Glasgow. Probably the same routine in every city in the U.K. What's going on here is Kate. 'Course it's a huge leap but she's got the stuff. No question of turning it down. If she gets it I'm buggered. Again. What can you do?'

I understood: she wanted away from me.

He said, 'Nobody's fault. They approached her couple of weeks back. Sod's Law, that's all.'

North Wind was the big time. Kate would have to leave Glasgow. "Sod's Law." I couldn't have put it better.

Jackie saw the long faces and buzzed by.

'You guys all right?'

'Fine.'

'Don't look fine.

'We're fine.'

'Can I get you something?'

I felt as if I'd been punched in the stomach. 'No, we're fine.'

She went back to making Alex money.

Alan said, 'Kate's short on experience. Could go against her.'

'Not a chance. She's sensational. Lloyd Kennedy should snap her up. North Wind could do a Fleetwood Mac.'

'You're being very good about it, Charlie. Considering.'

He meant considering I would lose Kate. Alan Sneddon didn't know that had already happened. The future played out in my head. The drummer couldn't have been more wrong. Whatever it looked like I wasn't good about it.

'First Robbie now Kate. You must be gutted?'

He shrugged. 'I'll find somebody else. The next Eric Clapton might be in Denniston, practicing in his old man's garage. Told you before, Charlie, it's a long game.'

I admired his ability to put on a brave face. Better than me. 'Besides,' he said, 'it might be the moment to join the mainstream.'

'What, get a job?'

'The universe giving me a message, who knows? Standing at the crossroads, all that blues shit.'

'I prefer the new Eric practising in a garage option.'

'So do I but...' He nodded towards Jackie behind the bar checking the till.

I said, 'That serious?'

He turned his face away. 'You've never been married, have you? Neither have I. Can't help thinking I've missed something good.'

The wrong time to share Andrew Geddes' philosophy on the subject. I kept it light.

'Happens to the best of us. If we're lucky.'

I made a show of looking at my watch and got up. Alan caught my wrist. 'Don't blame her, Charlie. Shit happens.'

He was being kind.

'Yeah,' I said 'I've heard.'

In the car the implications of the North Wind audition started to dawn: Kate was trying to hurt me. Finding out by chance was the worst kind of surprise. She should have told me. I was sad and angry at the same time.

The news could hardly have come at a more awkward moment. In minutes I would be asking Jennifer Hamilton to relive a tragedy. Every report said the woman was fragile. One of us needed to be unemotional. I didn't give much for my chances.

I drove slowly, fighting to bring myself under control. A guy in a cream Volkswagen overtook me, blasting the horn because I was holding him back. He swore and shook his fist. I wanted to drag him from behind the wheel and beat his stupid head bloody. Kate was leaving and there wasn't a damned thing I could do.

I pulled over and tried to get a grip. After all it was only an audition. She might not get it. Lack of experience might go against her, Alan Sneddon said so. If Lloyd Kennedy turned Kate down I could still have her. A mean selfish thought. I caught a glimpse of myself in the rear view mirror. Was wishing a beautiful talented woman would fail the best I could do? Unfortunately yes. My better angels had deserted; it was all about me.

Big boys don't cry, that doesn't mean they don't want to.

Not long ago life had been sweet, though Alan was right: shit did happen. The woman I was on my way to meet knew that better than I did. When a break appeared in the traffic I slipped the car into gear and rejoined the flow.

The Hamilton house stood back from the road; a 1950s bungalow with brick facing and bay windows. I parked at the gate and walked up the path. A woman was waiting, sitting in the alcove, looking out. When she saw me she got up and met me at the door. It opened before I reached it and the cousin Mark Hamilton told me about, the voice on the other end of the phone, stepped outside. Her expression said she hadn't appreciated our earlier exchange and intended to square the score. I guessed she was in her mid-thirties, no makeup, black hair cropped short; a strong character used to getting her own way.

Introductions were unnecessary. She launched right in.

'Look, Mr...'

'Cameron.'

'... I don't think you appreciate the situation. Jennifer has had a terrible ordeal. She really isn't well enough. As I said, this isn't the best time. Jennifer spent weeks in hospital. The TV appeal set her back. She wasn't ready. Why couldn't the police just do their job?'

She folded her arms across her chest.

'The doctor has her on medication. Most days she's a zombie. I'm here to make sure she doesn't come to harm, you know, forget she put the chip pan on and burn the house down. So I really am sorry, I don't think you can see her.'

This woman did a lot of thinking. On another day I might have reasoned with her, understood where she was coming from. This wasn't that day.

'Where's Jennifer?'

'Still in bed. And she...'

'Get her up. We need to talk about her daughter.'

She hissed at me. 'It's been eight weeks. The wee girl's dead. That animal they arrested in Hawick killed her. Leave Jennifer alone.'

Unfortunately she couldn't see inside my head, otherwise she would've shut up and did as I asked. I was ready to explode. All I needed was an excuse. She was handing it on a plate. I kept my voice under control.

'Get her up. Get her up now. And don't fuck me about.'

She recoiled. 'I don't think you need to take that tone.'

'Listen...'

'Amanda.'

'... nobody cares what you think. Do it.'

I waited in the lounge. Muffled voices drifted down the hall. The room was ordinary and completely impersonal. No photographs. No reminders. A flat screen television with the volume low showed a presenter gushing happiness because the blue team made ten pounds profit from selling an old vase with a crack in it. Joy for a tenner, the world to live in.

Adding a baby to an already troubled relationship was a high risk strategy. In the Hamilton's case it had saved the marriage. An unguarded moment on Ayr beach allowed someone to steal the focus, the common factor; the glue holding the thing together. And it fell apart. What little remained was destroyed when Mark Hamilton had confessed his suspicions about Donna Morton and the affair came tumbling out.

Amanda led her into the room. My memory was always the newspaper shot; the distraught mother in a bathing costume. This wasn't her. Nor was she the woman who broke down during the TV appeal. She had deteriorated. Seeing her stunned me for the second time. Lucy Morton had been drunk – Jennifer Hamilton was spaced out. Her eyes were glass. Hair fell untended across her forehead and in the flesh she was thinner. She shuffled like an old lady. Slow steps. Baby steps. I had to remind myself I was witnessing emotional collapse not the ravages of some wasting disease.

My own disappointment was small set against the trauma she had endured. Her minder had right on her side; her concern was justified. In her shoes I would've kept the Dalai Lama at the door.

She helped her into an armchair and placed a tartan blanket over her legs. The women exchanged whispers, words not meant for me. Amanda had courage, her duty was to protect; however formidable I seemed it didn't stop her admonishing me.

'Five minutes, no more. Don't upset her.'

I wondered how that would work given the nature of my visit. She spoke to Lily's mother and patted her hand. 'Nothing to worry about, Jen, I'm here.'

Jennifer said, 'Don't go.'

More hand patting and daggers for me.

'I won't. I won't.'

Amanda stood behind the chair, poised to shut down anything that threatened to stress her charge. Jennifer Hamilton shared the same hopelessness I'd seen in Lucy Morton's eyes, except Lucy's problem had a solution.

I didn't rush. 'My name is Charlie Cameron. Thanks for speaking to me. I have some questions about your daughter. Is that all right?'

On the television the blue team scored again. Fourteen quid for a table with shaky legs and a bit missing.

She said, 'Do you know where Lily is?'

'I'm looking for her.'

'I know where she is. Why doesn't somebody get her?'

Amanda's eyes bored into me.'

'We will. Let's start at the beach. Did you notice anyone?' The first thing the police would've asked. She nodded. 'She was watching. She was there.'

'What was she wearing?'

'She was there,' she said again. This wasn't going to be easy.

'How do you know it was her?'

No reply.

'What about before, in the supermarket, walking down the street?'

Jennifer snapped into the present, a mood swing straight from the Exorcist.

'They think Lily's dead. I know she isn't. That bitch has her and it's all his fault.'

'Because of the affair?'

She raised her hands in front of her as if the mention of it was a blow. 'I won't talk about them. I won't talk about what they did. Mark caused this.'

'He knows and he's sorry. I appreciate how difficult this must be, Mrs Hamilton.'

A lie. And a stupid thing to say. I had no idea.

'Don't call me that.'

A flutter of applause from the corner: the red team was making a late comeback. Jennifer gripped the chair, shaking her head from side to side like a child in a tantrum. 'What he did. I won't talk about it. I won't.'

I spoke softly. 'It's okay. You don't have to.'

Amanda signalled my five minutes were up. The TV credits rolled at the end of another pointless half hour. The screen went blank and came to life again, so fast there was no time to react.

A band flashed – BREAKING NEWS: DOCTOR RICHARD HILL CHARGED WITH TWELVE COUNTS OF MURDER.

Three men, grim faced, waited to begin. I recognised the deputy chief constable. He coughed into his hand and started to speak. The words were lost but the message pulsed on and off – DOCTOR RICHARD HILL CHARGED WITH TWELVE COUNTS OF MURDER.

A noise started deep inside Jennifer Hamilton and grew to a wail. She punched her face with her fists. Blood burst from her nose. She screamed, tearing her hair, raking the air.

'No! No! No! Noooo!'

Amanda grabbed her wrists. The beating stopped. She said, 'You should leave.'

'How does she know about Hill?'

She put her arms round the sobbing rag doll and didn't answer. There was nothing for me here. The tartan blanket had fallen to the floor, I put it on the sofa, probably the most useless gesture of my life, and left with Jennifer Hamilton's screams echoing in my head.

Maybe they always would.

41

It would be good to report that up close and personal with Lucy Morton and Jennifer Hamilton's problems mellowed me. It would be good, but it wouldn't be true.

I spent Monday trying not to think about Kate. We hadn't spoken in days. My calls had gone unanswered. I would see her at the gig and wasn't looking forward to it.

The papers were full of Richard Hill. Profiles of the victims ran between two and four pages. Twelve innocent faces smiling for the camera. Lily Hamilton wasn't one of them. Operation Damocles was criticised for keeping quiet about the killer in the early stages. The police response was well considered. No bodies meant no evidence. Until recently they were working on a theory. With Hill's arrest in the Borders, the pieces began to fit, exposing the biggest murder spree in the history of Scottish law enforcement.

And it wasn't over. There was more to come.

One normally well balanced conservative publication fell from grace by speculating in its headline that the Hamiltons had run across the madman on a sunny day in September. The suggestion, gross and unsupported, was emotive enough to boost circulation. Andrew Geddes had said as much. I hoped it wasn't true.

The visit to Jennifer Hamilton had been a disaster. My father was well regarded in the political circles he moved in for being 'strong'. Bull-headed. I seemed to have inherited my share. The pitiful scene the previous day wouldn't have happened had I listened to Amanda and taken no for an answer. Food for thought.

I mooched round the flat replaying the information about the abduction and discovering there was none. Nothing new at any rate. No more than on the day Mark Hamilton stumbled into my office with his guilt and his outlandish conviction that Donna Morton had stolen his child. What had become of his daughter remained a mystery I wasn't close to solving. Neither were the police. Richard Hill hadn't admitted to Ayr beach. DS Geddes talked about the games psychos indulged in, the perverse satisfaction they got causing pain, even after the fact. The Hamilton child was recent; the publicity surrounding her disappearance might add value in a diseased mind. Maybe he was saving the sickening revelation for a special moment. Teasing it out, maximising the hurt. Perhaps Lily was the icing on the cake.

I wandered aimlessly through the rooms wishing things were different. In the bedroom I opened the wardrobe. Kate's perfume lingered like a beautiful dream, her clothes still on their hangers.

Pat Logue was where he always was, at the bar. I expected jokes instead the fight never got a mention.

He said. 'Glad we went last night. Gail loved it. Kate reminds me of me.'

'You were a singer?'

'Yeah. Gave it up when we got married and went into business.'

He meant resetting.

'Speaking of business, Charlie, you owe me some money.'

I owed him more than money. He'd saved me from doing something terrible.

'And excuse me if I'm out of order. You're not exactly up to your armpits. Could be time to revisit the marketing strategy.'

The ad in Yellow Pages.

I said, 'Famine or feast, Patrick, that's how it works' and bought him a drink. Jackie pulled me into her cubbyhole. 'Heard you bumped into some nasty people. Are you all right?'

'No bones broken.'

'Kate must've been frantic.'

Kate didn't know.

Jackie said, 'Alan filled me in on the audition. Good news for her, not so good for you guys.'

'Has Alex found a new manager yet?'

'Not yet.'

'You're not easy to replace, Jackie.'

She agreed. 'No I'm not,' she said. 'Problem is, if Kate joins North Wind it could mean Big River fold. Selfish, but part of me hopes she doesn't get it, and not just because Alan will be gutted.'

Join the club.

A week's worth of drama had begun with Andrew Geddes' bombshell, Mark Hamilton's desolate figure standing in the rain, and agreeing to take his case a second time. Then the inevitable row with Andrew and the scene with Kate sandwiched between Lucy Morton's and Jennifer Hamilton's troubled lives; Alan Sneddon's devastating news about the North Wind audition, not to forget almost beating a moron to death. And topping it all, my return to Cramond and the face to face with a madman. Quite a haul.

Since then it had gone quiet. No visitors. No calls. Not even Mark Hamilton. I almost phoned Kate a dozen times but didn't. The clothes in the wardrobe became a symbol of hope. As long as they were there it wasn't over. Without them I had nothing.

On Wednesday I spoke to Alex.

'Listen, I'm sorry about Jackie. I really tried. She wouldn't meet me halfway.'

'Relax, got it sorted.'

'Pleased to hear it,'

'Case of a woman with PBT. Pre Bonus Tension.'

So NYB didn't need a new manager after all. That night when I checked the wardrobe the clothes were still there.

Friday brought sunshine, blue skies, crisp air and not much else. Late in the afternoon, Jackie buzzed to let me know I had visitors. Only the mildest purr in her voice told me she'd got what she wanted. The women were at the bar, drinking orange juice. I recognised one of them. The other held out her hand.

She said, 'Hello. I hear you've been looking for me. I'm Donna Morton.'

Seven days since I'd seen Lucy Morton and the difference was remarkable. I didn't have to ask if her friend came round. He had, and she was back on track. She told the rest.

'A postcard dropped through the letterbox. From Donna, asking me to meet her at the airport. After all this time I couldn't believe it.'

The women beamed at each other.

Lucy said, 'I promised to let you know if I heard from her. I've done better than that; I've brought her to see you.'

'I'm amazed.'

'You washed my dishes. It was the least I could do.'

Donna didn't resemble her sister; she was taller, blonde where Lucy was dark. Her suntanned chubby face had avoided the aging effects of addiction. Mark Hamilton described her as dull, accused her of going on about children. I disliked how he dismissed her as a person. If you promise to leave your wife, the other woman has a right to think you're serious. Hamilton wasn't serious, but his lover had had her wish.

Donna Morton was pregnant.

And not just a few months. Seven or eight. They talk about pregnant women glowing. It's true. A special kind of light shone from Lucy's sister. We went upstairs to the office. I offered coffee, both wanted tea. Over Earl Grey and ginger snaps the mystery was revealed.

'So where have you been?'

'Lots of places. London at first, Spain for a while.'

She patted her stomach

'I got this in Greece.'

'Is the father with you?'

'It wasn't the father I wanted.'

'Mark Hamilton thought you'd stolen his daughter. Said you threatened him.'

Her answer reminded me of her sister's honesty about past mistakes the second time we met.

'I did. He'd hurt me. I wanted to hurt him. The night he told me his wife was pregnant and he couldn't see me anymore was the worst of my life. It took a long time to get over it. I felt betrayed. All the words, all the promises. And I believed him. What a fool.'

Lucy said, 'He's a snake. He was using you.'

'Yes he was. Except he wasn't alone. I was using him. I was thirty four, my clock was ticking. I told him I was on the pill when I wasn't.'

'But it never happened.'

She laughed. 'Oh, it happened all right, just not with him.'

'When are you due?'

'January the twenty fifth.'

'Boy or a girl?'

'A boy.'

'Got a name?'

'January the twenty fifth? Has to be Robert.'

Robert Burns, Scotland's national poet, born January twenty fifth 1759.

'Although first babies always keep you waiting, he'll probably arrive on the fourteenth of February.'

'Valentine Morton? In Glasgow? Give the kid a chance.'

Lucy said, 'We're going to bring him up together. Do you think two women will be bad for him?'

'Not a bit. He's a lucky lad.'

Donna said, 'There's no news of Mark's baby? His poor wife. And him. When did she go missing?'

'Nine weeks on Sunday.'

'Lucy reckons this serial killer took her. Doesn't bear thinking about.'

'The police can't prove anything. Have you spoken to them?'

'Our next stop. If I'd known I would've contacted them at the beginning.'

Her sister jumped to her defence. 'Donna's done nothing wrong.'

'No one's saying she has. The police just need to be told.'

At the door Lucy shook my hand. 'If I hadn't made that call on Saturday... I can't thank you enough.'

I borrowed from Alan Sneddon. 'It's a long game.'

Not a bad philosophy from a private investigator whose only case just disappeared.

42

Govan Police Office, 923 Helen Street, Glasgow.

The clock on the wall said five minutes to twelve. Saturday ending, Sunday about to begin. Anthony Baresi was tired. He wanted to go home; he wasn't needed. He had become part of the audience, a witness to a macabre performance that had been going on for weeks. As a boy he'd listened to his father and grandfather discussing their cases, not certain what the words meant. As a man he understood. People did terrible things to each other, from spontaneous violence erupting over an ill-chosen word to revenge planned and carried out with cold detachment. Baresi had seen it all. Nothing prepared him for what he'd heard in interview room No 4. His family attended mass. Sophia, his wife, insisted on it. Tomorrow they would go without him. Anthony Baresi wasn't on speaking terms with God.

The lawyer's three children were young, the eldest seven. Better not to think about them. He checked his watch and wondered what old Lucca would've made of it.

The original charge against his client was forgotten. The rant against the injustice done to him now appeared farcical. Baresi recognised it had been a ploy. Hill's refusal to acknowledge his interrogators, the rambling soliloquies unrelated to the crimes, then the admissions, teased out, sometimes true sometimes false, in an elaborate sham. It seemed months since he'd told them about Anne Marie Bradley and began his tale of evil.

When one became three and three became four.

At five Hill was officially a serial killer, describing what he'd done in detail, laughing at the horror on the detectives' faces and admitting his one regret was it had come to an end. On several occasions he returned to silence as a weapon, ignoring everyone in the room, including his lawyer. The next day he would be jovial, happy to recount what he called "an adventure" and finish by giving a name and a location. Emma Small in a field near Shotts. Lauren McLaren down an abandoned mine shaft in Ayrshire.

He suggested they dig fifty yards left of the eighth green at Easter Moffat Golf Course. The police did and found nothing. When they told him he grinned. He'd pulled the same stunt in the Leadhills. He lied for fun. Every other day he revealed a new atrocity. Because he could. And five became seven. Then nine.

Richard Hill was insane.

DS Geddes found it hard not to strangle him with his bare hands. The detective had lost weight and hadn't slept properly since Hawick. Being around this animal, knowing what he'd done, was more than he could stand. They'd met before. The killer didn't remember but Andrew Geddes remembered.

Midnight came and went. In between sessions Anthony Baresi tried to put his revulsion aside and counsel his client. It was clear Hill would do whatever came into his head.

The lawyer said, 'Why hire me if you never intended to use me?'

'But I am using you. You're here. And since you ask it was the name. Baresi. Would've preferred your grandfather. Forty years too late for him. Can't have everything.'

And nine became twelve.

DCI Baillie wanted to call a halt to the interview process. Operation Damocles had succeeded. The senior officer was satisfied. His sergeant wasn't.

Geddes said, 'We don't have him for the Hamilton kid.'

'He's admitted a dozen murders and committed Christ knows how many more. Why deny that one?'

'He can sense we want it. Put it to him again.'

Baillie sighed. 'It's over, Andrew, let's tie it up for the fiscal and go home.'

'Once more. It's him. Absolutely it's him.'

The detectives rejoined Baresi and Hill. Baillie restarted the tape. 'For the record I'm going to recap, starting with Anne Marie Bradley in Coatbridge. You've admitted to abducting and murdering Amanda Kelly, Peter McMillan, Rebecca Patterson, Eva Reynolds, Bobby Cunningham, Adele Knowles and Charlene Walker. You've also confessed to the unlawful slaying of four other children; Lauren McLaren in Ayrshire, Stephanie Nicholson in Carlisle, Billy Elder in Musselburgh and Sheila Powel in Kirkintilloch.'

Baresi didn't confer with Hill. DCI Baillie nodded to his sergeant.

Geddes said, 'Think you're going to be famous, Richard? Nothing of the kind. You'll be forgotten in a couple of months. In Carstairs with the rest of the nutters. Give it a year and nobody will remember your name.' He gestured to Baresi. 'No trial, you won't even have the pleasure of dumping your lawyer. Would've been a nice touch. Keeping up the family tradition. But it's not going to happen, is it?'

Hill turned to the senior officer. 'How did the football go? Did Hearts win?'

Geddes wasn't fazed.

'A Hearts fan? I'm beginning to understand. '

'You don't understand half of it.'

'Give me time, Richard, you'll tell me. Can't help yourself. You're after a big reputation. Forget it. You're like Hearts, second rate. Always will be.'

The policeman stood behind Hill and whispered in his ear. 'Lily Hamilton. Now that was Premier League. Broad daylight. The parents yards away. More daring than running down the street with a push-chair.'

'A dozen not enough for you?'

Geddes kept after him. 'You'll always be the guy who got the shit kicked out of him by the bingo brigade.'

'I doubt it.'

'Sure you will. Tell me what happened on Ayr beach.'

'No idea, I wasn't there.'

'Another one of your games?'

Hill laughed his girly laugh. 'Thought you liked games? Getting plenty of practice at losing them.'

The DS exploded. He grabbed the arms of the chair and spat the words in the killer's face.

'You're a twisted pervert who murders innocent kids. You don't deserve to live.'

Hill was amused. 'Nobody's perfect, Sergeant. And it still wasn't me.'

Baillie said, 'Not tempted to go for number thirteen, Richard?'

Hill smiled. 'Thirteen. Unlucky for some.'

Four a.m. DS Geddes drove along a deserted Paisley Road West. In the passenger seat his senior colleague was silent. During the journey neither man spoke. They were beyond words, even swear words. That took energy and they had none. At three o'clock Hill had announced he wanted to talk. The detectives got the news and dragged themselves reluctantly from their beds less than two hours after they got into them.

The car turned into Edmiston Drive with Ibrox stadium looming in the darkness. DI Baillie tried to break the spell the killer had cast. 'Might go to the game next week. Do something enjoyable for a change.' He paused. 'If watching Rangers could be classed as enjoyable. Heard Celtic have put a referee on the transfer list after a disappointing display against Hibs.'

Another day it would have been worthy of a smile. Not now. Geddes voiced what they were both thinking. 'He's got us at it. Out in the middle of the night to hear his view on some crap nobody's interested in. Laughing at us.'

Baillie said. 'Can't be sure. Can't ever be sure with him. He's admitted to a dozen. How many more is anyone's guess.'

'Except it isn't about more. They're all important. This bastard could give up another dozen and it wouldn't make any difference to him. He knows the Hamilton's are suffering right now. This minute. Hill could help them. He won't because that's all he has left. That's his power.

'Maybe this will be it.'

They turned right into Helen Street. Geddes glanced at Baillie. The DI was faking it for his benefit and he wished he wouldn't. He'd heard enough bullshit to last a lifetime and was certain he was about to hear some more.

Anthony Baresi didn't acknowledge the detectives when they came into the room; he kept his face turned away. Richard Hill grinned. Baillie and Geddes' body language revealed what he'd hoped to see. They were beat. That meant he was winning. Chalk one up for his team. Policemen/beat. The pun amused him. He drew his strength from a different well. He was fresh, relaxed, at peace with himself; ready to play another round of cat and mouse, with him as the cat. The policemen looked the way they felt. Despite having the most prolific killer Scotland had known in custody they were dispirited. The job wasn't done and only Doctor Richard Hill could decide if it ever would be.

The previous twenty four hours were the most difficult, fourteen of them spent listening to Hill confess and retract, admit then deny all he'd said, between long periods of silence and even longer rants on everything from genetically modified crops to the offside rule in football. Whenever he was asked about Ayr beach he refused to answer.

He seemed able to sense when time was about to be called on his performance. Before he was taken back to the cells he'd throw out a name, sometimes familiar sometimes unrecognised, and the whole exhausting charade would begin again. Hard going.

Anthony Baresi was the most affected. From the beginning the relationship between the accused and the lawyer hadn't gone well.

Hill refused to take direction, not just ignoring but flouting his counsel's advice. Twice Baresi threatened to ask to be removed from the defence. While his soon-to-be-famous client raved on, his eyes glazed and his expression set. He said nothing and stared at the floor, wondering perhaps what his grandfather would have done.

Hill said, 'Sorry to haul you back in lads. Thanks for coming.'

The detectives sat down. DCI Baillie led the way.

'I'm assuming this is important, Richard. Tell me I'm right.'

'It's important to me, Inspector. Very important to me.'

Baillie trailed fingers through the stubble on his jaw. 'Mmmm, not convinced that's the same thing. Let me lay it out for you, and before you say anything remember I'm getting paid for this, so whether I'm at Tulliallan giving new recruits the benefit of my experience or attending some boring seminar on how to motivate staff, end of the month the salary hits the bank. Same goes for DS Geddes.'

Hill's grin didn't falter.

Baillie said, 'Considered bringing the Encyclopaedia Britannica and asking you to read it to us. Seeing we're here, might learn something, know what I mean, Richard?'

Hill was apologetic. 'I can go on a bit, can't I? It's the position. Doctor. People hang on your every word. Don't like to interrupt. Holding court becomes a habit.'

'Top tip. Keep your stories short, otherwise you lose your audience.'

'I'll bear it in mind, Inspector.'

Geddes studied Baresi. The lawyer hadn't attempted to engage with the proceedings. He'd given up. Wherever his mind was it wasn't with this nonsense. DCI Baillie leaned on his elbows.

'So, what's the big deal? Why am I missing my beauty sleep?'

Hill looked away, suddenly unsettled. 'Ayr beach. September.'

'The Hamilton kid. Lily?'

'Was that her name? I'd forgotten. So many to remember.'

Baillie and Geddes tensed.

Richard Hill said, 'I want to go on the record.'

43

Aberdeen, 149 miles from Glasgow.

No sign of the passport. It had only been three weeks. Hard not to worry although the baby wasn't news anymore. All the attention was on the serial killer. A dozen victims. Those poor children. Too horrible to think about. She couldn't imagine how a parent got over something like that. Probably they never did.

His name was Richard Hill, a doctor. He was the one who was sick. How do you deal with a mad dog? She had no hesitation. You put it down. Put it out of its misery and be done with it. Of course she realised that wouldn't happen. Society thought itself too civilised for that. People were told to understand. His father abused him, his mother let him. Not good enough. Tell it to the families. Tell them. Her conviction was absolute. There was only one way with a pervert. Give her the lever. Let her pull the switch.

Her heart beat faster; she was upsetting herself. The animal in Glasgow wasn't the problem; an excuse to vent her frustration. No, the problem was the bloody passport. And it didn't matter about it being too early. Logic didn't help. Every day she waited for the postman to come, and every day the same crushing disappointment when there was nothing.

It was December now. Christmas was just round the corner. Their first Christmas together should be special. Any mother would feel the same. If only somebody would process her application she could plan their celebration. They might even have it in their new home. She hadn't decided where that would be. There were lots of good places to raise her daughter.

The previous week she'd bought suitcases. One each. Matching of course. Every night she packed something else in them to help make what they were doing more real. Not the blue outfits, they wouldn't be going with them, they'd served their purpose.

They were all set.

Where was the bloody passport?

44

Andrew Geddes' call brought me into the world. 'He admits it. He admits he killed her.'

I struggled to come awake. 'What are you telling me, Andrew? Who?'

'Hill killed Lily.'

I let what he was saying find me. 'Has Hamilton been told?'

'Not yet. The bastard won't give us the body.'

'But you believe him?'

His gruff voice lacked its usual bite. I heard tiredness. It wasn't the old Andrew speaking.

'He's pulled us all over the place. Every so often something he says turns out to be true. One piece of information at a time, that's how he plays it. Holding out on what he did with Lily after he took her is par for the course, a juicy secret he's saving for later. In his sick brain that makes him superior.'

I asked again. 'So do you believe him?'

He sighed. I was wrong, not just tiredness. Defeat. 'Honestly, Charlie, I've no idea. Thought you'd like to know.'

Andrew needed to talk to somebody. I gave him my news.

'Donna Morton showed up yesterday with her sister.'

For a moment he said nothing, then, 'I hadn't heard. Where was she?'

'Abroad. Getting pregnant. Due in a couple of months. All she's guilty of was falling in love with another woman's husband.'

'So Morton's out of the picture. Hamilton got it wrong. And screwed up his marriage.'

'Well wrong. His affair wasn't tied to the abduction.'

'Which brings us back to Hill. He's in later today. The story might be different by then. He's a psycho, sly as a fox. He'll milk it dry and tell us in his own sweet time. Same with the other twelve. For him it's almost as much fun as murdering the kids.'

The task force had done what it was supposed to do. Operation Damocles was a success. A serial murderer was in the cells yet, instead of celebrating, the detective sounded beaten.

'Does Hamilton know his ex-lover's in town?'

'I spent last night trying to contact him but he wasn't answering his phone.'

'It's the wife I feel sorry for, not him. If you play with fire...'

Andrew's attitude never failed to irritate me.

'He had an affair. It happens. God knows it's cost him.'

He came back at me, almost shouting.

'And people got hurt. He ought to be there for the mother, and would be if he hadn't blown it. He gets no sympathy from me.'

When he had gone I tried Hamilton's number again. No joy. It was nine thirty; chances were he was drunk and sleeping it off. I made coffee and sat by the window, wondering what was wrong with Andrew Geddes.

During the night it started to snow. By morning it covered Glasgow. The sky was dark, heavy with more to come. Winter was here in earnest. The temperature had been dropping for days. I hadn't noticed. Part of me was on a beach with a happy family enjoying the last rays of an Indian summer; the rest was listless and depressed, not interested.

The clothes in the wardrobe were no substitute for Kate. In less than a month it would be Christmas. I didn't feel very festive.

By noon the next day, traffic had ceased. The tire marks of the last vehicles were covered in minutes. My car had become a shapeless mound, indistinguishable from the others parked on the street. Every so often some brave soul bent against the elements and trudged through the white mist, each leaden step taking them closer to their destination. I hoped it was worth it.

I was at a loose end. Unemployed, perhaps unemployable. Over the years I'd built a reputation but lately my mojo wasn't working. Could be time for a change.

Standing at the crossroads, all that blues shit

I called once more. No answer. Hamilton's life had imploded. Being told his infidelity hadn't been responsible for his daughter's abduction wouldn't bring a lot of comfort now. It was all I had.

Around three in the afternoon the light began to fade. The twin beams of a gritter cut through the gloom, strafing the road behind with rough stones, too late to make a difference. The metaphor didn't escape me. Plenty of will, no shortage of resources, but a baby was still missing.

My mobile rang. Mark Hamilton sounded drunk and far away, and he was crying. He slurred. It was impossible to make out what he was saying. I caught snatches. '...me ...Jen wanted... too late...'

'Where are you, Mark? Where are you?'

'...best thing... thanks...'

'Where, Mark? We need to talk.'

'...no use... no...'

He'd refused whisky in my office, I'd heard enough drunks to realise this was something more.

'...off ...'

'Listen to me. Tell me what you've taken.'

'...better ...'

'What have you taken?'

The line died. I pressed redial. No one answered. All of a sudden staying home wasn't an option. He'd told me he was living at the Adelphi in Renfrew Street. Directory Inquiries gave me the number. A male voice with an Asian accent answered. I asked him to check on Hamilton and heard the telephone crack against the reception desk. Nothing happened for a while, then he rasped into the receiver. 'Not there. Must be out again.'

What the hell would anybody be doing out in this?

'Try again.'

He ignored me. 'Call later,' he said and hung up.

Hamilton might not be at the Adelphi but there was nowhere else. I threw on a coat and stepped into Siberia. Cold air burned my throat and wind drove icy darts into my face. Walking fast wasn't an option; my feet slid away from me. Snow clung to my shoes and stuck to the bottom of my trousers. The car was inches deep in virgin snow, the wheels low, frozen in place. I fumbled for the key and forced it into the lock. The door opened, slicing the top off the pavement snow and piling it in a mini drift. I turned the engine over, half expecting to hear a humping drone. The Audi was better than that: it fired and settled to a satisfying purr. Waiting for the de-icer to clear the screen let the insanity of what I was attempting catch up. By then it was too late. I was in business. Now all I had to do was reach a main road and trust someone in the city council had listened to the long-range forecast and got the gritters on the job earlier than the one I'd seen.

Usually the drive from my flat to the main road took two minutes. Today it took twenty. The temperature hadn't risen much above zero since the previous night. Under a zillion beautiful flakes of frozen water the street was glass. I nosed along in second gear. The traffic lights were red. God was having a laugh. I didn't wait. Mud brown tracks cut Great Western Road on either side. I followed them into the city.

Vehicles were parked. Parked or abandoned? Either way I was the only idiot driving. Visibility was poor but good enough to convince me the journey was doable. Instinct told me it was necessary. The tyres crunched over the surface. Every so often I felt the wheel go slack and the Audi glided. I didn't fight it – it righted and I crawled on. Glasgow was a ghost town; in three miles I saw four cars and one pedestrian. Many of the shops hadn't bothered to open and those that had had to be regretting it. The sky seemed close enough to touch and street lights glowed with unnatural intensity. The clock on the dash said three thirty five: easy to believe it meant a.m.

Park Road led to Woodlands Road and a slow steady climb from the West End to the city centre. A Peugeot travelling in the opposite direction came towards me, the driver tense, sitting forward. We waved to each other like survivors of a nuclear holocaust.

Sauchiehall Street was unrecognisable from the day I met Angela Armstrong in the Willow Tearooms. I drove past the Garage and the McLellan Galleries, following the slush marks, left and left again, and slid to a halt. This was as far as the Audi would take me. Renfrew Street hadn't seen a gritter; the road was pristine. Now the fun would really begin. I'd have to walk.

The gradient wasn't steep but in the conditions, it was difficult. Each step required more effort than the one before. By the time I'd gone a hundred yards my lungs were on fire, every breath scoured the inside of my throat and my heart pounded in my chest. Further up, Glasgow Art School, Rennie Mackintosh's greatest work according to some, loomed to my right, its classic lines blunted. The wind tore at my coat and my eyes hurt. I stopped at the brow of the hill, not through choice, and remembered why I was here. If Mark Hamilton was wandering around in this, God help him.

A line of bed and breakfast places materialised on the other side of the street. I crossed without checking to see if anything was coming. Four doors down, an unlit neon sign told me I'd found the Adelphi. I climbed the stairs and went inside. At first all I could make out were vague shapes, blurred and incomplete. I assumed the glare of ice and snow had blinded me. That wasn't it. I couldn't see because it was dark. A bulb, not more than forty watts, hung naked from the ceiling. Behind an ancient desk a sallow skinned man in his fifties huddled over a one bar electric fire. My unexpected entrance provoked no reaction. He didn't move or speak. He was wearing a charcoal car coat with a faux fur collar over a cardigan and shirt. Both maroon. The guy who'd been in such a hurry to hang up.

'Somebody has taken an overdose. I called.'

His reply remained unchanged. 'I told you he's not here.'

'In this weather? He has to be?'

He scratched a goatee clinging to his pointed chin and spoke, his accent a crazy mix of Bangalore and Barlanark.

'He goes out a lot.'

We must have met in a previous life because it took less than ten seconds to dislike him. I said,

'And you are?'

'The owner.'

'I meant your name.'

'Mr Banagova.'

'Which room is his?'

'Fifteen. Third floor.'

I raced up the stairs. Timer switches triggered dull light. The corridor smelled of garlic and cat piss and was barely wide enough to allow people to pass. No emergency exits. This was a death trap. Hamilton had fallen fast, farther than I could've imagined. The burden he carried had driven him down.

Footsteps echoed behind me – Mr Banagova, interested at last. The top of the building was worst; bare boards, foul odours, not even a low watt bulb. A skylight allowed me to see the only room. Pounding the rough panel brought no response. I tried the handle. The door was locked.

'Mark! Mark!' My voice boomed. 'Mark!'

Banagova was at my back.

'Not here. I told you.'

I raised my fist. 'Open it. Fucking open it!'

Banagova's hands fluttered in the air.

'The key's on the desk. I'll get it.'

'Don't bother.'

I stepped back and kicked the door in.

Mark Hamilton was on the bed. I touched his arm; his sleeve was sodden. I barked at the Indian to put the light on.

Hamilton's face was bloodless and his eyes were closed. I raised the lids. He was unconscious. A packet of Diazepam lay on the floor. I picked it up and put it in my pocket. Banagova stood whimpering by the door that had given so easily, dancing a little dance, wringing his hands. Minutes before he couldn't have cared less. Now he was a gibbering wreck, no use to man nor beast. I shouted at him.

'Pull yourself together and call an ambulance! Now!'

I hauled Hamilton to his feet and walked him round the room. It was a short walk. His pulse was shallow, almost gone. Unless he got to hospital he wasn't going to live. A gust of wind rattled the window frame. I'd forgotten the blizzard.

There was nothing to do but wait and hope, and try to understand how it had come to this.

They took him to the Royal, where Lily's father had been a daily visitor when his wife stood at the edge of the abyss, crippled by grief and remorse. Now it was his turn. I didn't see the journey to the Infirmary. I was in the back but it must've been a scary ride.

By a strange quirk I'd become the person closest yet I hardly knew the man. I was all he had. There would be no one else. Not tonight. Not tomorrow. I'd told Andrew Geddes that Mark Hamilton had paid the price. How little I knew. When they wheeled him inside A & E, nobody offered encouraging words. They believed he was dying. I believed it too.

Some young doctor asked if I knew how many pills he had swallowed and when. I gave him the packet I'd lifted off the floor and the time of Hamilton's garbled call.

The doctor said, 'Do you know why he might want to kill himself? Was he depressed?'

'Yes.'

'What about?'

'He'll tell you himself when he comes round.'

'Let's hope we're not too late.'

He noted my name and mobile number and said they'd be in touch. He didn't say when. I didn't ask. If Mark Hamilton didn't make it, he would leave this life convinced he was to blame for his daughter's abduction. Donna Morton's unborn child proved he wasn't.

I left the hospital and walked along Cathedral Street and Sauchiehall as far as Cambridge Circus. It was dark. The storm had blown itself out. The Audi was where I left it. Without the wind and the snow, Renfrew Street wasn't formidable at all – just a bunch of low rent student flats; drab, uncared for, and worth a fortune. I drove home at a snail's pace, so tired all I wanted was sleep. My own troubles seemed insignificant. Solvable. At one point I started to phone Kate and chickened out. Instead I opened a tin of soup and ate it out of the can. On my way to bed I checked the wardrobe.

It was empty.

45

Next day the white world was in retreat, wet patches marked the ground and small waterfalls cascaded from the roofs across the street. Thaw. Snow was great fun when you were a kid. After that it was a hassle.

My legs ached so much I could hardly walk. Every muscle screamed. Jackie would get enough material out of it to last 'til New Year. I decided not to give her the pleasure. I told her she wouldn't be seeing me and got the usual wisecracks about how would they survive. Between winding me up she said, 'Missed a great show last night. Epic. Kate was awesome. The weather affected the crowd but not much. Still plenty busy. Thought you'd be there.'

'Something got in the way. Unavoidable.'

'Mmmm. Kate was disappointed. She left without saying goodbye to anybody.'

Jackie didn't know we'd split. She wouldn't hear it from me.

No word from the hospital meant Mark Hamilton was still in the land of the living. I called. The patient was stable and conscious. In the afternoon I went to see him, hoping my news about Donna Morton would do him some good. A doctor from the High Dependency Unit brought me up to speed.

'He's been lucky. If he'd taken Paracetamol the damage to his liver and kidneys would be irreversible. Diazepam causes sleep, then coma. We pumped his stomach. His temperature's still high. Looks like pneumonia's the danger. We'll keep him in for observation and assess his mental state. Nobody does what he did without a reason.'

Few had better reason.

Hamilton was in a room by himself, just him and a bank of machines, purring reassurance. He was awake, lying on his back. I said, 'Hi, how you doing?'

He stared at the ceiling. His voice was weak. If I expected gratitude for saving his life I was out of luck.

He said, 'You should've let me die.'

'Couldn't do that. You're punishing yourself for something that had nothing to do with you. Donna showed up.' He stirred. 'She doesn't have Lily.'

'You found Donna? Where?'

'She's been abroad. She didn't know what's been going on.'

He ought to have been relieved.

'Do you hear me, Mark? It wasn't your fault.'

His eyes closed and his lip trembled.

'That means the psycho the police arrested killed her. What she went through. My beautiful baby.'

What do you tell somebody who has tried to kill himself? The truth? What was the truth?

Hamilton turned away, distraught. 'You haven't done me a favour.'

I tried to reach him. 'Listen, Donna Morton's out of the picture, Hill admits to a crime one day and denies it the next. You can't believe a guy like that.'

'It's been nine weeks.'

'Yes it has, and so long as there's even a sliver of hope you have to hold on to it. Her mother can't help. That child will need her father. Lily will need you.'

Nice speech.

I didn't expect to see Mark Hamilton again. He'd hired me to find Donna Morton and I had. The abduction, as Andrew Geddes hadn't been slow to point out, was police business. In the push and shove I'd shut Kate out instead of confiding in her. And paid the price. Now it was too late tell her. Well played, Charlie.

With nowhere else to go I went to New York Blue. This late in the day it was empty. The only customers were Pat Logue and Alan Sneddon. It was unusual for Alan to be hanging around. I guessed he was here to keep Jackie off her work. Patrick was at the bar. He greeted me with the self-interest that was his trademark.

'Anythin' on, Charlie, the fans are askin?'

'All quiet on the Western front.'

He made a face. 'Said it before and I'll say it again. You're a top guy at this findin' punters lark. How come they aren't beatin' down the door?' He supplied the answer. ''Cause the message isn't gettin' out there. Your marketin' sucks. Ancillary workers like me are sufferin'.'

Patrick the Disadvantaged.

'Why don't I buy you a pint, Patrick? Restitution for my thoughtless inefficiency.'

'If you insist, Charlie. Wouldn't say no.'

He nodded towards Alan Sneddon sitting near the Rock-Ola.

'Drummer Boy's been here all afternoon. Keen. Wonder how long that'll last?'

He sounded like Andrew. Alan was wearing the green corduroy cap. Maybe he did keep it on in bed. I made a mental note to ask Jackie and joined him.

'Hear I missed a great gig. Meant to be there.'

'Missed more than that. Kate was upset. The North Wind audition is tomorrow. She's leaving tonight. I promised to see her off.'

'You know it's over between us?'

He shook his head. 'She's mad at you – not the same thing.'

He leaned across the table. 'Kate's going to get the job. Lloyd Kennedy will snap her up. He's been around. He'll know the real McCoy when he hears it. That stuff about experience is bullshit. She's a talent. I'm resigned to losing her. No way she'll stay with Big River. Can't happen. Next month, next year. She'll move on. Has to.'

'Alan, why are you telling me this?'

He stood. 'Because it's the truth. And because she doesn't want to go. The Euston train leaves at quarter past eleven. She's meeting me at ten. Coffee and a pep talk.'

'Where?'

'The Shell.'

The Shell at Central station was a favourite meeting place. A First World War 15 inch Howitzer converted into a charity collection box. At ten o'clock most trains had gone. Not many people were around. Outside, taxis sat in a line, their engines running, waiting for passengers who would never arrive. Glasgow didn't do Tuesday night. Monday wasn't a big favourite either.

I stood on the corner of Gibson Street, yards from where Frank Lennon and Alison Downey had died. Kate was expecting Alan Sneddon. God knows what her reaction would be when I showed up instead. At a minute to the hour I saw her, coming down Renfield Street on the other side, shoulders hunched against the cold, hands in her coat pockets, wearing the snakeskin boots.

She looked unhappy. When she crossed at the lights I moved to the ticket office and watched her pass. Before my time the Shell had stood in the middle of the concourse; these days it was relegated to a spot between W H Smiths and a hole in the wall cupboard the cleaners used. Kate stopped and looked around. I ducked out of sight. In the afternoon, surprising her had seemed a good idea. I'd jumped at the chance to apologise and send her off on her big adventure. Now I was having second thoughts. Alan was a musician. He appreciated what Kate was getting into. He'd have the encouraging words, the upbeat chat; a respected player who knew what he was talking about. I couldn't match him. All I had was how I felt. Selfish? Maybe I was the last person she needed.

She checked her watch against the clock suspended from the station roof. I walked towards her still wondering if I was doing the right thing. When she saw me her jaw dropped.

'Charlie? What're you doing here?'

'Alan told me he was meeting you. He won't be coming by the way.'

Her lip trembled. 'I'm sorry, Kate, I should have trusted you. There's so much you don't know. I was wrong. But none of it's what you think.'

I put my hands on her shoulders and looked at her.

'Now isn't the time. We'll talk when you get back. This is your big chance. It's a great opportunity and you deserve it. You'll blow them away.'

'This is the time, Charlie. The girl in the photograph, she's your daughter, isn't she?'

'Her name's Pamela. She was my sister.'

People passed on their way to their destinations as the hands of the black and white clock suspended from the roof counted off the minutes. We didn't notice.

I glanced at the ground. 'Don't you have a suitcase?

'I didn't bring it.'

'Where's your guitar?'

'At home.'

'Wouldn't you be better with your own instrument?'

'I won't need it.'

'I mean, the sound...'

'I'm not going.'

What she was saying failed to register. 'Alan's sure you'll get the gig.'

'I won't...'

'Don't say that.'

'... because I'm not going.'

'What do you mean, not going?'

'I'm not leaving Big River.'

My turn to be shocked. 'So why are you here?'

'I only decided an hour ago. Alan has his phone off. Easier to keep the arrangement. But I'm not getting on the train. Don't try to change my mind.'

No chance of that.

I said, 'So, what about us? You and me?'

Kate kept me waiting. She said, 'Decision time, isn't it?'

I held my breath.

'Fish suppers or sausages?'

46

And we lived happily ever after?

Not quite, but it was good.

Ten days before Christmas the festive spirit finally caught up with me. I invited Alan and Jackie, Patrick and Gail, and Andrew and Sandra, to dinner at NYB on Friday night, then on to the Barrel Vaults, a pub Pat Logue had introduced me to, to listen to some music. The only one who grumbled was Andrew Geddes. Spending an evening in Patrick's company didn't appeal. In the end he agreed, if only to stop Sandra complaining about being neglected. Operation Damocles was winding down. Richard Hill had confessed to two more murders. Fifteen in total. Sentencing had been delayed pending psychiatric reports that would tell us what we already knew: he was a heartless killer and completely insane. There would be no merry Christmas for Mark Hamilton. His daughter had never been found.

Women have some strange ideas. Kate insisted we stand at the door, beside the tree Jackie had spent an afternoon dressing, to greet our guests. She was wearing a simple black dress and looked stunning. I loved the way she could alternate styles: rock 'n' roller one night, girlfriend of the future king the next. The Logues arrived, brushing snow off their coats, with Jackie and Alan right behind them. Holly, coloured balls and tiny gift wrapped boxes surrounded the bar. Patrick glared at a stranger sitting in 'his seat'.

I was beginning to think Andrew and Sandra weren't coming when they appeared. Sandra went into a huddle with the other females. Bonding came easily to them – the sisterhood in action. Guys are more reserved. Especially these guys.

I ordered drinks. Pat Logue inspected his pint with the eye of a serious consumer.

'First today,' he said and glanced at his wife.

The leash was tightening; his days as a wild rover were drawing to a close. Mai Ling's visit had opened doors. The Logue marriage was under new management.

Alan spoke to Andrew. 'Every time I open a paper the number's gone up. Is it still fifteen?' He was talking about the serial murders.

Andrew was guarded and gave a policeman's reply.

'That he'll admit to, yes.'

'There's more?'

Andrew moved off the subject. 'Hear the band's doing well.'

'Kate writes great songs. We're going into the studio in January to put down some tracks.'

Jackie couldn't help organising us. Her leaving had died a death. With Alan she had a life away from New York Blue. All work and no play... and, not that it mattered, I liked him.

I'd asked Jackie to make sure Patrick and Andrew weren't seated beside each other. That would be pushing it. When the meal was over, taxis took us to the river. The Barrel was busy. I thought we were lucky to get a table together until I realised Jackie had organised that, too. On the tiny stage four long haired geezers chugged their way through Howlin' Wolf and Robert Johnson. The all-male audience lapped it up. Conversation was impossible. We saved it for the break. A passable version of Smokestack Lightnin' brought the first half to an end. Gail Logue was next to me.

I said, 'Heard from Mai Ling?'

'Yes, we email. She wants me to go over.'

'Will you?'

'Probably not. Wouldn't want to leave Patrick and the boys.'

'Thanks again for looking after her. How was King Tut's?'

She smiled and leaned closer. 'No idea. We weren't there.'

'Thought the two of you were on the razzle every night. Clubbing it, salsa lessons, falling in the door out of your faces at all hours.'

Gail smiled a slow smile. 'Can you keep a secret? Salsa lessons, yes, but there was no clubbing it. We went to my pal Joan's – her husband works away – and split a couple of bottles of cider.'

'A couple?'

'Well, maybe more than a couple.'

'An Abba Tribute? Come on.'

'Sold out. Couldn't get tickets'

'So where were you?'

'The first night I took Mai Ling to the bingo. She loved it. That's where we were most of the time. Patrick got it into his head we were off and running. I didn't enlighten him. He's used to being the wanderer. Good for him to get a taste of his own medicine.'

'You lied to him.'

'Charlie, we're married. That's what married people do.'

'You're a wicked woman, Gail Logue.'

'Yes,' she said, 'I suppose I am.'

'It worked.'

She shook her head. 'It won't last. My husband's a rolling stone. And know what? I wouldn't want him any other way. But it was fun making him jealous. Mai Ling was like a daughter. Promise you won't tell.'

'Cross my heart.'

Kate tapped my shoulder. 'They've asked me to sing.'

'Don't unless you want to.'

'It's all right. They've asked Pat as well.'

'How do they know about him.'

'The bass player's a friend of his.'

So was half of Glasgow.

I said, 'Are you enjoying yourself?'

She said, 'Absolutely. The girls have hit it off, especially Sandra and Gail.'

Bad news for the men.

Alcohol loosens tongues. Not Andrew Geddes'. Even with a few drinks he seemed tense. I wondered again if Operation

Damocles had been good for him, or had Elspeth's Rottweiler twisted the knife in deeper. The group came back on and Kate joined them. She borrowed a guitar, had a word with the band and sang Dimming of the Day. It was a moment. The pub went quiet to listen to a star. Kate Calder was the centre of my universe, but nothing is forever. I'd learned it was a long game. When it was time for her to do what she had to do I wouldn't try to stop her.

Two songs became four songs. The audience wouldn't let her finish. At the end she came over and kissed me.

I said, 'You're wonderful.'

'What a coincidence, so are you.'

Kate was a hard act to follow. Pat Logue wasn't intimidated. He had a confab with the musicians and sang Sweet Dreams. I stole a glance at Gail; her eyes were shining. Patrick always had a story and most of the time he was telling the truth. He'd mentioned he could sing though I hadn't expected him to be this good. His voice had depth and a richness that surprised me. Different from Kate but great nevertheless.

The crowd cheered for more. Patrick wasn't having any. He spoke into the microphone.

'That's yer lot.'

He sat down next to me.

I said, 'Why didn't you do another one?'

'Unwritten rules of showbiz, Charlie. Always leave them wantin' more.'

He put an arm round his wife.

'I gave it up for this woman.'

Gail said. 'Good decision. What would you do without me?'

'Same as I do now, except oftener.'

She glared. He said, 'Banter, Gail, banter.'

The Logues were fine. Better than fine.

Gail fell into conversation with Sandra. Synchronised head bobbing – the women were becoming friends.

'Gail's happy.'

Patrick agreed, kind of.

'Tonight she is. Mai Thai started somethin'. I'm gettin' talk about another baby. We've got boys. Gail would love a girl.'

'Then why not?'

His reaction was unexpected. 'Why not? We're only beginnin' to get our lives back. In four or five years our two will be out of the house. It's called freedom. A baby would be a disaster. Fortunately it can't happen.'

He used his fingers to mime scissors. 'Firin' blanks, Charlie, firin' blanks.'

'Does Gail know?'

'Know? It was her idea.'

Seven people were having a good time. Everybody except Andrew. I made another attempt to draw him out of his shell, his depression, or whatever was dragging him down. I talked and he listened until I stopped talking. Jackie unwrapped herself from Alan and came over. Her eyes were glazed. She wasn't a drinker, it didn't take much to affect her. She opened with an intriguing admission.

'It worked.'

'Did it.'

I hadn't a clue what she was on about.

'There wasn't a job – that was a lie.'

I played along. 'Well well.'

She didn't pretend remorse. 'I'm not leaving. I'm staying at NYB. I helped build it. I deserve a share.'

Indeed she did.

'Pleased to hear it. And I'm sorry for flying off the handle. You had a right to be angry. Had a lot on my mind.'

Booze and secrets don't mix. Alan saw us talking and came over. He was pissed. He took my hand and wouldn't give it back.

'Thanks for a great night. And thanks for persuading Kate to stay.' He hugged both of us. 'Have you two made up? Some things are meant to be. Like Jackie and me. Did she tell you?'

'Tell me what?'

He seemed surprised. 'The Psychic Hotline predicted she'd meet an interesting stranger.'

He pointed to his chest. 'I am that man.'

'The Psychic Hotline?'

'Spooky or what?'

'Fate.'

'Yeah, fate.'

Jackie said, 'I only called it a couple of times.'

Too many glasses of wine had dulled her to the consequences of her boyfriend's remarks. The Psychic Hotline was dynamite info I could use for years.

She threw a final insult my way.

'You really think I'd leave NYB because of you? Dream on.'

She jeered.

'You're losing it, Charlie. Three months without me and the business would be in the bin. That tight-arse Gilby's got to be up against the wall before you get a fair shake out of him.' She eyed me through an alcohol haze. 'With the odd exception, like yourself. Whatever you did for him it must've been good. What did you do?'

'I forget, Jackie. It was a while ago.'

She got up, swaying. 'But how could I leave? I couldn't.'

Since the storm it had snowed on and off. We waited for a taxi on the pavement with flakes drifting round us and the temperature heading below zero. I overheard Sandra and Gail making arrangements for the four of them to have dinner. Andrew and Patrick would be delighted. Not.

At the flat, Kate fell into bed and was asleep in minutes; I wasn't so lucky. In the dark, with moonlight streaming into the room, I tried to make sense of something Donna Morton and Patrick had said. When I finally nailed it the best part of the night had gone. I stared at the ceiling, hearing the rise and fall of Kate's breathing, cursing myself for being so slow.

I got up, made coffee and stood at the window waiting for the new day to arrive. Stars peppered the black sky. I might be wrong but I knew I wasn't. The answer had been in front of me from the beginning. I'd been blind. I'd seen Mark Hamilton's pain and listened to his unlikely suspicion that Donna Morton, bent on revenge, had taken his daughter. But Lucy's sister wasn't involved, wasn't even in the country.

And Richard Hill was doing what he always did. Lie. He hadn't abducted Lily.

She was still out there.

I showered and dressed and drove across the city to a house I'd visited only once before. The door opened. When the woman saw it was me it started to close. I put my foot in the way. Animosity hissed from behind the frame. 'You've got a nerve. Haven't you done enough damage? She isn't well.'

'I have to speak to her?' I pushed past, into the hall, and made for the bedroom. Jennifer Hamilton was sitting up, eating breakfast. She looked haggard. Wild. Her expression froze when she saw me. 'What are you doing here? Get out. Get out!'

Too much time had been wasted. I wanted the truth. I said, 'Tell me about the affair.'

She turned away. 'No. No. I won't talk about what he did.'

I leaned closer.

'Not Mark's affair, Jennifer. Yours.'

47

Pat Logue was standing at the old post office building in George Square, stamping his feet to keep warm, pleased to see me because the car meant escape from the cold. I pulled over and he got in. One look at him was enough. Patrick was hung over.

He assumed I was in the same state.

'You okay to drive, Charlie?'

'To drive yes. To get stopped, no.'

'Where are we going?'

'To see a man about a baby.'

'Bit early for cryptic, isn't it?

'Thought you were good at crosswords.'

I filled him in about my visit to Jennifer Hamilton. 'Something you said gave me the clue. "Firing blanks". When I asked Hamilton about Donna Morton he knew almost nothing. He lied to her about leaving his wife – he was using her for sex. He couldn't realise she was using him to get pregnant, telling him she was on the pill when she wasn't. But she was out of luck. Same story with his wife. Jennifer wanted a baby for years. Hamilton said the marriage was rocky. I can believe it. He wasn't the only one having an affair.'

'Then Jennifer got pregnant.'

'Her husband assumed it was his and dumped Donna. After that things were better between Mark and Jennifer. Until Ayr beach.'

Patrick said, 'I always thought Hamilton's theory was farfetched.'

'Somebody took Lily.'

'Yeah, Hill. He confessed.'

'Not Richard Hill. I'm guessing Lily's father.'

Pat Logue's incredulity was understandable; he didn't hide it.

'And you expect to find her with him?'

'Three months later? Don't expect to find anybody. Wherever he's taken her they won't be in Glasgow. It's the usual trawl: the neighbours, local shops. Jennifer Hamilton will have to do what her husband did – tell the police there's another possibility.'

Patrick was unimpressed.

Traffic churned the snow into slush. I drove to the address in Pollockshields, a sandstone semi-detached with a well-kept garden and a FOR SALE sign planted in the middle of the lawn. The curtains were drawn. A black Volvo was in the drive. I stopped and we walked up the path to the front door. A gold rectangular name plate said Barrymore. I knocked. No answer. I knocked again and heard footsteps coming downstairs.

A man in his mid-thirties opened the door. He wasn't handsome: short dark hair, waist already thickening – in a dozen years he'd be tubby – and tell-tale eyes; bloodshot and tired. Women didn't always fall for the best looking guys.

'Sorry to break into your Saturday. My name's Cameron. I'd like to talk to you about someone.'

'Who?'

'Mrs Hamilton.'

His reaction was unexpected. No bluster or outrage, just a defeated sigh.

He said, 'You better come in.'

We followed him to the lounge. Stale cigarette smoke mixed with curry hung in the air. He pulled the curtains. The remains of an Indian takeaway and an unfinished glass of lager sat on a coffee table next to an overflowing ashtray and half a dozen empty beer cans. The weekend was off to a poor start. Patrick shot a glance at me that said we were in the wrong place.

I ignored him and spoke to Barrymore.

'Selling up?'

'Divorce settlement. Tried to hold on to it but...'

He shrugged. 'Wife wants her share.'

Andrew Geddes would identify.

I introduced myself properly. He didn't waste time with denials.

'I read the papers. I know what's happened, but I haven't spoken to Jennifer. How can I help?'

'It was her who called a halt to the relationship?'

'Yes.'

'How did you feel?'

'What do you mean?'

'Were you sad, angry, disappointed... what?'

'I was upset, naturally. Her marriage was in trouble. So was mine. I'd hoped we might make a go of it. I'd told Marion.'

'But that's not what happened.'

'Jennifer decided to give hers another chance.'

'But your marriage ended not hers. And you were upset? Just upset?'

Barrymore said, 'I thought we had an agreement. I was hasty. And yes I was angry. Of course I was angry. What's this about?'

I stuck to asking the questions.

'Do you have children?'

Paul Barrymore was frank. 'That was the problem. The affair wouldn't have been the finish. We could've worked it out. We were, until Marion discovered Jennifer was pregnant. She put two and two together. Said she'd never forgive me and there was no way back for us.'

'Why did she leave?'

'You mean instead of me?'

Exactly what I meant.

'I was prepared to go. I was at fault. Marion couldn't stand being here. Too many memories. Most of them unhappy. At first she moved to Paisley, then Bishopton. We were talking about getting back together when she heard about Jennifer.'

'So where is your wife now?'

'Her father died two years ago and left her money. Financially she's well fixed. She's a free spirit.'

Barrymore picked up a piece of paper by the phone. Three addresses were written on it, two of them scored out.

'The only reason I have it is to redirect her mail. There's no contact.'

He read out the last one.

At the door he said, 'More than once I've thought about calling Jennifer. Somehow it doesn't feel right. I envy Marion, able to go where she wants. As soon as this place sells I'm leaving Scotland. A fresh start. Do what Marion's done.'

In the car I held the steering wheel with one hand and used the other to phone DS Geddes. Andrew sounded depressed. I said, 'Have an idea where the Hamilton baby is.'

He cut me off. 'Forget it, Charlie. Hill asked to see DCI Baillie this morning to tell us what he did with her.'

'Out of the blue? Why? Why now?'

'Because he's crazy.'

'And has he told you?'

''Course not. You know how the bastard works. He might never tell. The parents will be informed later today. So whatever you're thinking, leave it.'

The line went dead.

Pat Logue caught the gist. 'So that's that,' he said. 'Drop me at NYB.'

'Too early. The bar doesn't open for another hour.'

'I'll wait.'

I ignored him. 'Call Gail. Tell her we'll pick her up in fifteen minutes.'

'Why? You heard your pal. Hill's admitted it.'

'Patrick, call Gail. We need her.'

48

Aberdeen, 149 miles from Glasgow.

When it fell through the letterbox, excitement overwhelmed her. She tore the envelope open and there it was. Seeing it in black and white made her cry.

Marion Barrymore, mother. Adele Barrymore, daughter.

She went online and booked the flights, earmarked weeks ago. Luckily there were still seats. They'd soon be heading to another continent. And then? Well, that was the adventure, wasn't it?

Tomorrow it would be eleven weeks since the scorching afternoon on the beach, although she'd been following them for months. The stupid bitch should have drowned, and would've, too, if her husband hadn't dived in after her. Then again she ought to be grateful because he left the baby alone. Adele wouldn't remember any of that; she was too young. In time neither of them would remember.

Her fingers traced the gold crest on the front of the passport. It was official.

The taxi office said twenty minutes. Best they could do on the second last Saturday before Christmas. No problem; the flight wasn't until four. Their cases sat in the hall, all packed and ready.

She took a final look at the flat. It was nice but she'd make their home nicer. Days earlier she had bought a tree. Just in case. Not a real tree. One that came already decorated with lights that turned different colours; Adele was playing on the floor beside it. She'd change the baby's clothes at the airport before they checked in. In a few hours they'd be where no one would find them.

Of course they'd say she was evil, a monster who had committed a terrible crime, but she was the one who had been wronged; how could taking something that belonged to you be bad? If things had gone as they should, there would have been no need to do what she'd done. Though she couldn't lie to herself, she'd wanted to hurt them, hurt both of them. That day some instinct – a mother's instinct – told her the opportunity would arrive if she was patient. When she saw them walking along the sand towards the quiet street beyond the Esplanade where her car was parked, she knew it had come. A stroll before heading home, smug bastards. Not so smug now.

Adele gazed up at her and smiled. Such a beautiful little girl. And all hers. In the end it had worked out. Who would have believed it would be so easy. Child's play really.

A car noise drew her to the window. The taxi had arrived.

49

Gail was waiting on the pavement. Apart from when she came to the club distraught about her missing husband I'd only ever seen her smiling. She wasn't smiling now. This was not how she preferred to start her day. Patrick got out and whispered his disapproval of what I was doing in her ear. They got into the back leaving me in the front, very definitely on my own.

At Charing Cross we joined the motorway and headed north. The atmosphere could have been sliced and served on china plates in the Willow Tearooms. A glance in the rear view mirror showed expressions united in resentment. It was going to be a long journey.

On the other side of the Forth Bridge, Patrick voiced his objections again.

'Hate to say it but you're way off on this one, Charlie. Don't mind helpin', no problem with that, but this is over the top.'

'She's alive, Patrick. Hill didn't kill her.'

'Not what he says.'

'He's playing with them. It's who he is.'

So far Gail hadn't spoken, now she did.

'You really believe the baby's alive?'

'I honestly do, Gail, I honestly do.'

'And that's why I'm here?'

'Yes, and thanks for coming.'

Further north, snow piled in drifts at the side of the road and grit crunched under the tyres. The Kingdom of Fife slipped behind us. We by-passed Dundee and pressed on. I didn't allow myself to think about what I was doing, I just drove. A kind of peace settled round us. I took advantage.

'Everybody connected to this case has lied. Until last night I was convinced the exception was Jennifer Hamilton.'

'Took a chance goin' to see her after the last time, didn't you?'

'Only thing left.'

He gazed out of the window, resigned and unhappy. 'Bloody long trek if you're wrong. Even if you're right it's probably too late.'

'We'll see.'

In Aberdeen I stopped to ask directions, lost my way and found it again. When we got to the street Paul Barrymore had given us my heart was racing and I wasn't alone. Pat Logue rose between the seats, scanning the numbers.

'There,' he said, 'number 42.'

A taxi purred at the pavement. Dirty smoke escaped from the exhaust and joined the cold air. A woman disappeared inside; she had something in her arms.

Gail's fingernails bit into my shoulder.

'Hurry, Charlie.'

I gunned the Audi and felt its power.

The taxi's right indicator winked yellow. They were leaving. I cut in front, braked hard and was out of my seat while the car was still rocking. For the driver, a routine run to the airport had suddenly become a scene from the Flying Squad. Strangers surrounded his vehicle and his passenger was screaming at him to drive. He couldn't oblige; he was boxed in.

Marion Barrymore was fastening the seatbelts when we arrived to spoil her day. I opened the door. Her face was white with anger. Spittle flecked her trembling lips. Beside her on the seat was a Marks and Spencer carrier bag. And a child. But something was wrong – the coat and hat were blue, so were the mittens.

Blue for a boy.

For a moment my faith faltered. Doubt rushed in. The woman sensed my confusion and seized her chance to regain control. She spoke to the driver, forcing authority into her voice.

'I don't know who these people are. We've a plane to catch.'

On instinct I picked up the bag. Inside were disposable nappies, a dummy, a bottle of juice and clothes. The clothes were pink. All of them.

'Not today, Marion, you're not going anywhere today. It's over.'

I said, 'Go Gail' and watched her release the seatbelt and lift the baby free. The driver was stunned, mesmerised by the speed of it. Marion Barrymore sobbed and slumped forward, defeated. Stealing another woman's child was a monstrous act but she wasn't a monster, just a sad lady who needed help. In minutes they'd come for her. What happened after that was for others to decide.

Gail held the most famous baby in Scotland in front of me. She kicked her legs; little woollen fingers gripped my thumb.

Precious cargo

Since the Indian summer days of late September I'd read her name in newspaper headlines, talked and thought and worried about her with the rest of the country. We hadn't met. Until now.

Years down the line the big brown eyes studying me would break a few hearts. They already had.

I said, 'Hello, Lily.'

The nurse at the retirement home had used the card I'd given Ronnie to let me know he wasn't there any longer. I drove with Andrew and Kate to where he was now. At three o'clock in the afternoon it was already getting dark; the atmosphere in the car matched it. We didn't speak much. Nobody was in the mood. Visiting a hospice will do that to you.

Ronnie was under the covers, hooked up to a machine that was probably keeping him alive a little longer. His head looked shaved but wasn't. The church ran St Mungo's; apparently Joan and Ronnie had been regular attenders, just one of a thousand things about the former policeman it was too late to discover.

An oxygen mask covered most of his face and his eyes were closed. I asked the nun who had shown us to his room if he could hear. 'Perhaps,' she said, 'it's not easy to tell. He drifts in and out. Talk to him. He'll sense you and be glad you've come.'

I bent over the bed. His breathing was so shallow he seemed already dead. 'Ronnie. Ronnie. Brought somebody to see you.'

Kate stood beside me, smiling an uncertain smile. She took his hand in hers and tried to rub warmth into the pallid skin and the blue veins underneath. Ronnie's eyelids stayed closed, his features expressionless. It wouldn't be long. Andrew had held back. Now he came forward and whispered in the dying man's ear.

'We got him, sir. Richard Hill. We got the bastard.'

"He'll sense you" the sister had said. Of course she was being kind. Ronnie was on his way to a better place, one without killers and cold cases and missing children.

When Andrew spoke I was certain there was a flicker at a corner of Ronnie's mouth. Not much, just enough to let me believe the message had got through.

Seeing what I wanted to see? Maybe. But I'd settle for it.

Patrick sat in my office with the cares of the world on his shoulders. I'd paid him for the work he'd done, but he wasn't happy, still pushing me to employ him full time.

On recent form nobody would call my business lucrative. The Downeys sacked me. Mark and Jennifer Hamilton had their lives to rebuild; perhaps two wrongs could make a right. I was way down their list. That left Frank Lennon. Invoicing a dead man wasn't the brightest idea. Pat Logue had made more out of the cases than I had. Of course he didn't see it like that. His Thailand problem was back. Mai Ling had called Gail.

'Was hopin' she'd stick to her side of the planet,' he said.

'She is.'

'I mean really stick to it. No contact. Gail's agreed to visit her in the next couple of months.'

'Will you be going?'

He answered in football jive.

'If selected, Charlie. Don't fancy it, but, if selected.'

It would depend on what his wife had in mind. I struggled to find a silver lining.

'Could be worse. She might be coming back here.'

'Yeah, how am I goin' to pay for it? Any idea how much flights cost? I'll tell you. A bomb.'

He was forgetting. If anyone knew it was me. I'd paid Mai Ling's fare. Jackie stuck her head round the door.

'Guess who's joined North Wind?'

No takers.

'Robbie Ward.'

Patrick said, 'Get that from your spirit guide? Ask him what's going to win the 3.30 at Kempton Park.'

Jackie was unfazed. 'Somebody heard it on the radio.'

Her announcement was greeted with silence; nobody cared, there were more important things. The day before had been bizarre; the painful conversation with Jennifer Hamilton, Paul Barrymore struggling to come to terms with the damage he had caused, and the drive north.

Patrick's flippant comment in the Barrel Vaults started me down a different road. Before that my focus had been on Mark Hamilton and his affair with Donna Morton. I'd been looking the wrong way from the very beginning. Andrew Geddes' unshakeable conviction that Richard Hill had taken Lily made it easy to believe that option, and I had.

Almost.

Hill or Donna Morton? No other possibility got considered. Yet the clues were there, hidden in a web of secrets and infidelity. I didn't blame myself for not making the connection. None of the players had told the truth. Their lies had cost two marriages, left two women mentally ill, and seen the attempted suicide of the man at the centre of it. Donna and Lucy Morton were the only ones who survived.

And baby Lily.

Everyone else had crashed and burned. Righteous judgement. Andrew Geddes would approve. On cue Andrew appeared. He hesitated when he saw Pat Logue. According to Jackie, Gail and Sandra had organised dinner for later in the week. There would be no escape for the men. Wouldn't mind being a fly on the wall at that one.

Andrew was a lot of things but magnanimous wasn't one of them. He had a talent for rewriting the past. His memory was selective. He was able to summon events from a parallel universe at will and slot them in. Anything that didn't suit got altered or forgotten. He brought me the news. 'Marion Barrymore's on her way to Glasgow as we speak. Not my case, thank Christ. DCI Baillie was in at the beginning, probably land on his desk. Good luck to him. Don't say it too often, Charlie. I was wrong about the baby.'

Alison Downey and Frank Lennon too. This wasn't the moment to remind him.

'Does that mean I was right?'

He let the sarcasm fly over his head.

'I was so certain it was that bastard Hill.'

'You got him. That's all that counts.'

'Yeah, eventually.'

He looked round the room, afraid of being overheard, and whispered.

'I met him, years ago. Got called to a complaint. Some man loitering outside a school in Baillieston. It was Hill. We spoke to him. Had to let him go. Nothing to charge him with. But it was him.'

Now I understood why Andrew had been so wired. 'When did you realise?'

'In Hawick, soon as I saw him. Wanted to tell you before.'

The uninvited visits to my flat, the rambling conversations. And the anger. Andrew blamed himself.

'What else could you do except let him go?'

'To murder kids. How many lives might've been saved?'

I turned his own words on him. 'A killer crossed your path. You didn't let him escape. My advice. Forget it.'

'I can't, I've tried.'

'Try harder.'

He stared at me. I drove the message home.

'You did nothing wrong. Shit happens.'

My mobile rang and broke the tension. It was Kate. We talked for a minute. I couldn't stop smiling. Tomorrow would take care of itself. Today Kate Calder was with me and that was enough. Andrew eyed me suspiciously. The Andrew of old.

'Careful, careful. Don't be in too much of a hurry there.'

'I'm not.'

'Pleased to hear it. Just don't fall into the trap like the rest of us.'

'I won't, 'I said. 'It's a mug's game.'

He seemed relieved. 'You're catching on, Charlie. At last you're catching on.'

When he'd gone, I sat for a while not thinking about anything very much. Out of the blue, Maryanne Mulholland came into my head. I'd told her to call her mother. Good advice. Maybe I should take it myself.

And the files on Pamela, what about them? Should I get rid of them? Move on?

In the end I wasn't ready. Alive or dead Pam was my sister. We'd had little enough time together. I'd come across the photograph in a drawer on a visit from Strathclyde Uni. to my parents. Whenever I got a new wallet, Pamela's picture was the first thing I slipped inside. Thirty years. A lot of wallets. And a long time to be holding on; to the blonde haired girl who saved my life, the awfulness of Cramond Shore, and all the sad sorry rest of it. Andrew had said some people are just evil, it was true.

The faded image went in the folder. Both folders went back in the drawer. Way back. I doubted I'd ever open them again.

But you just never know.

I let a moment pass before lifting the telephone and dialling the number. A woman's voice answered.

I said 'Hi mum, it's Charlie. Listen, I'm planning on coming down. Next week sometime. Will dad be around? There's someone I'd like the two of you to meet.'

Epilogue

Shotts maximum security prison,

16 miles from Glasgow.

A week before final sentencing Richard Hill sat behind the reinforced glass partition. When he saw who his visitor was he grinned.

'Mr Geddes, didn't think we'd be meeting again. What brings you here?'

Hill didn't wait for an answer, he went into his act.

'Missing our little chats, are you?' He chuckled. 'Me too.'

The detective remembered the hours, the days, the weeks this amiable madman had messed with their heads. He hadn't seen Richard Hill in months and had hoped never to be in the same room as him again. Ten years into the future he would read a newspaper report about a hunger strike over some perceived injustice. A minor loss of privileges. That would be this monster. Demanding his rights.

Yet he'd had to come. Couldn't stay away. Charlie Cameron deserved to know.

Geddes studied the face; chubby before, glowing with health when he'd turned their stomachs with his revelations; thinner now, dark patches in the corners of the eyes. Hill wasn't as relaxed as he pretended. Of course that was impossible. The heinous nature of his crimes meant he would always be looking over his shoulder.

Even as a protected prisoner, every second spent out of his cell, every trip to the showers or brush against an inmate on a landing, could end in sudden violent death from a weapon specially made to be used on him, wielded by some righteous rapist. There was a hierarchy of offences in places like this. Richard Hill rated lower than pond life.

He spoke as if he was taking about a mutual acquaintance.

'DCI Baillie not with you?'

The detective chief inspector had put in for early retirement. Hill played a big part in that decision. Geddes set aside his revulsion.

'This isn't a social call, Richard.'

Hill pouted. 'Really? How disappointing.'

'I'm wasting my time but there's something I want to ask.'

'Ask away. Ask away.'

Hill's hand fluttered in the air.

'You know me well enough by now... Andrew. It is all right to call you Andrew, isn't it?'

Geddes didn't answer.

'Anne Marie Bradley wasn't the first, was she? It didn't begin there.'

'First. Fifth. What does it matter?'

'Cut the crap, Hill. Who was the first?'

Hill picked at a ragged nail. 'I honestly don't remember.'

Geddes' fists balled at his side. 'Yes you do, you lying bastard.'

'You're beginning to remind me of old Ronnie. Poor Ronnie. Took it personally. Almost confessed just to cheer him up.' Hill sighed and shook his head. 'But I really couldn't say. There were so many. Let's talk about something interesting.'

'Was it Edinburgh? Was it Cramond Shore?'

Hill smiled an apologetic smile. 'Lost me again I'm afraid.'

'An eight year old girl. Pamela.'

The psychopath folded his arms.

'You've tried this with me before. There wasn't a Pamela.'

'Yeah there was. She was abducted. Your MO. Where did you bury her?'

'Oh I get it. Since I'm going to be in here for the rest of my natural why not tell you something to let you sleep at night.' He laughed his giggly laugh. 'Help you. Did you really think I'd do that?'

'No, I knew you'd do what you always do because you're sick. A depraved excuse for a human being.'

Hill faked insulted. 'Dear dear. Harsh. And we've been so close, you and I.'

Geddes stood, he'd expected nothing and he wasn't wrong, coming here had been a mistake. Hill saw the opportunity and played the policeman like an expert angler.

'Mmmm,' he said. 'Cramond. Cute wee thing. Brunette.'

'Blonde.'

'Blonde, blonde, of course.'

Over anxious, Geddes had broken the cardinal rule of interrogation: never give anything away. He cursed his stupidity. 'It can't make any difference now. Where is she?'

The killer considered the question. Minutes passed. Geddes pushed for an answer and felt anger rise in him. 'Admit it you bastard. Admit it!'

Hill's eyes filled with a familiar light. His features relaxed, at peace. He sat motionless. Silent. Staring at the wall. Seeing what only he could see. Geddes held his breath, sensing a breakthrough. He detested this creature yet, when he spoke, his voice was gentle; coaxing. Near to pleading. 'Where is she, Richard? Where?'

Hill's eyelids fluttered like a sleeper coming awake, gradually returning from wherever he'd been. He seemed perplexed. 'Sorry, Detective,' he said. 'What was the name again?'

THE END

Acknowledgments

The notion that a book is the work of one person is a myth. Most will have had many contributors, known and unknown, before they ever get near a publisher; from the faceless few who patiently trawled the manuscript in search of a misplaced comma, to the guy in the pub one Friday night with a memorable line that stayed in the mind until the opportunity to use it presented itself years later.

So it has been with me.

My gratitude goes to my family in Scotland, especially my mother who devoured every story and came back for more; in Greece, Charmaine Fueggle and Jeni Riley for their support in the early stages, and Brenda Clark, who loaned me her old PC when mine broke down, to keep the process going. Michael Vredegoor believed in me from the beginning and said so.

Thank you.

Also, Hugh Cameron, the first to voice the opinion that I could do it, and Alan Campbell; shouting encouragement from the touchline, while Liz lay by the pool and did the actual reading. Again, thank you.

Special mention is due DS Alasdair McMorrin of Police Scotland for so generously giving me the benefit of his experience and his invaluable insights into how real policemen operate, as well as keeping the football chat going. And Jamie Coleman, a rigorous critic who changed the way I looked at the story and made it better as did Martin Pickering with his eagle-eyed editing.

Mariusz Kozinski at 0141design in Glasgow produced the striking artwork for the cover and guided the Luddite I will always be into the new century. Thanks, mate.

Lastly, my wife Christine, the unsung hero; her unfettered imagination is on every page. On a particularly unproductive day when, despondent and defeated, I told her the book wasn't going to work she said, 'Don't be silly, of course it will. You're making it up, aren't you?'

With that and the unselfish assistance of so many others, all I had to do was write down the words.

Owen Mullen, Crete. October 2015

Lightning Source UK Ltd.
Milton Keynes UK
UKHW04f0633211018
330924UK00001B/98/P